Simple

Short

Stories

to

Tingle the imagination

by

K.J.Goss

Simple Short Stories
to
tingle the imagination

ISBN: 978-0-9960140-0-7

Printed in the United States of America

This is not your great American Novel.
This is anything but.
It is just a few simple story's hopefully to stir your
imagination as it did mine.
Relax and let it happen.

My thanks to my wife Jeanne for having the patience to
let me wander in my imagination without laughing, and
for giving me the encouragement to write it down.

Contents

The Dream ?

by
K.J.Goss

The Dream ?

It was a comfortable fall day. A clear blue sky, with a few scattered cumulus clouds. Just enough to add to the already existing scenic beauty. An ideal day for photography, which is why I was driving around the countryside looking for that one certain place that just sort of hits you in the face. My wife and son had joined me this day. We had packed a picnic lunch and planned to make a nice leisurely day of it. We enjoyed lunch at a quiet roadside grove that you so often see here in Vermont.

Having just finished lunch, I decided to trek up a small wooded knoll with my camera. I told my wife I wouldn't be long and asked if she and my twelve year old son would like to come along.

"No, you go along dear." was her response with her head already buried in a book. My son was equally responsive, his eyes glued to a hand held computer game. Just as well, I was kind of in an alone mood anyway. Always on the lookout for that special photo I was soon out of sight of the picnic area. I couldn't have been more than fifty yards into the woods when my favorite *"alone"* feeling overcame me. A time when my imagination was totally released and I let it take me where it wanted.

I reached the top of the knoll and turned to my right. There it was. What I had been searching for all day. The perfect mood inspiring photograph. At least my mood. A single gravestone among the grass and weeds. The stone was old and weather worn, leaning to one side and back slightly. Probably the result of frost heaves I thought. It was boxed in by a mostly broken split rail fence. The plot looked to be about four by six feet in size. This area alone was shrouded in a light mist that had an almost ethereal quality about it.

"That's odd." I thought, "The surrounding area was still clear, as it had been all day." It was as if the misty fog was emanating out of the ground itself. I watched the eerie movement for a while, then finally remembered my camera and what I came for. Uncovering the lens I went to work. I shot the sight from all angles and directions. Before I even realized it I had used up a whole twenty four exposure roll of film in a matter of minutes.

Not even caring about changing film I sat down on a fallen log opposite the grave site. I felt totally relaxed but my mind was full of questions. I was mesmerized by the stone marker. The engraving was weather worn but still readable.

Ethan Moore
Born June 15, 1846
Died July 12, 1865
Pvt. 3rd Vermont Regiment
Army of the Potomac

"Who are you ?" I wondered aloud. "Who were you ?" to be more correct I suppose. I tried to imagine what his life must have been like. A feeling that I was not alone suddenly engulfed me. I turned, and sitting a few feet away on the same log was a young man in a Civil War uniform. For whatever reason I was not startled or afraid. He was a rather good looking boy with a very warm and contagious smile.

"Ethan Moore's my name." He said in a happy, almost sing song voice. Apparently I looked confused. He spoke again.

"Well ! You asked who I was." he said smiling. "What's your name ?"

"Ken, Ken Goss." I answered thinking to myself, *"Am I crazy ? I'm talking to a dead man."*

In a voice that was a half laugh, Ethan answered my thoughts.

"No, you're not crazy. I'm alive in your mind. As alive as you want me to be. I'm glad to meet you, Ken, Ken Goss, he said as he held out his hand. Hesitating slightly, I reached out and shook his hand. He had a powerful grip, yet warm and friendly. I smiled back at him and now felt totally at ease, as if I had known him for a long time.

"I worked with my Dad on this farm before the war." he stated matter of factly as if he anticipated my question.

"Is that what you really wanted to do ?" I asked.

"No, I wanted to go back to school and study history and maybe become a writer or teacher, or perhaps both. We just didn't have the money, and my Pa needed the help on the farm. The house and farm was just down the hill there." he said pointing past the grave marker. "Come on I'll show you."

He got up and started down the hill. Again I hesitated. He turned toward me and said,

"Come on. It's not far.

Leaving my camera on the log, why I don't know, I rose to my feet and followed. Soon we were walking side by side. Ethan reached into his shirt pocket and retrieved a small harmonica.

"You don't mind if I play the mouth organ do you ?"

I said I didn't mind and he instantly started a quiet, happy melody. I could not identify it so I assumed it was a tune strictly from his day. When we reached the bottom of the hill, he stopped playing, tapped the harmonica on his hand a few times and returned it to his shirt pocket.

"The house is just over here." he said while walking to the left a short distance.

I followed as if I could not do otherwise until we came upon a stone foundation.

"**O**ver the years after Ma and Pa died it just sort of fell down." he remarked. "Over time, other people came and took the boards and things from the house."

I could detect a note of sadness in his voice and thought, *"How terrible to see your whole past, and the things you hold dear being taken away by strangers."*

"**P**a died a few years after they brought me home, and Ma passed just a few months after that." he said sadly.

I could feel the pain he carried as if it was my own. His thoughts became mine and I knew how much he truly loved his folks and the farmland. Most of the land was now recaptured by the forest and was part of the state park system.

This, I think made Ethan happy, at least that's the feeling I was getting. I know I felt happy for him.

We continued walking through the trees and again he retrieved the mouth organ from his pocket and played. This time the tune was somewhat mournful. I did not say a word but just listened. He stopped near a clearing, turned to me and smiled. I returned his smile and watched as he put the instrument to his lips and this time jumped into a more lively tune. He sort of danced as he walked and played. I caught up to him again and asked,

"**W**hat was it like ? The war I mean. Where were you ?

He pocketed his harmonica but continued walking.

"**W**e were in a lot of places. All over the south it seemed, and of course where ever we went we walked. I never walked so much in my whole life, which as you know wasn't very long." he joked. "I can't remember all the names. The one that stands out the most of course was Andersonville."

"Andersonville." I repeated questioningly. "That was the infamous Confederate prisoner of war camp in Georga.

"It sure was, but infamous is too mild a word to describe it. A living hell would be more like it." he answered.

"How long were you there ?" I asked.

Ethan cut me short saying,

Before we get too much into that, Ken, let me show you what led up to it.

"Show me ?" I thought. "We're up in Vermont, How's he going to show me Georga, or any other place down south for that matter ?"

No sooner had these thoughts entered my mind when I heard the noise of many men. Looking up we were in the midst of a Union Army encampment.

"This was our stepping off point here in Virginia." said Ethan.

Fascinated by the sight before me I realized I was the only one not in uniform.

"Oh don't worry about that." commented Ethan, again reading my thoughts, "They can't see you."

"But I can see them, so why can't they see me." I puzzled.

"Because you weren't born yet." was his answer. "You can look back but they can't look forward."

As we walked through the camp Ethan was recognized by a lot of other Vermonters, shaking hands with some and waving at others. Every now and then he would join in with others in song filled frolicking. I guess it was there way of taking their mind off the job at hand. Ethan, eventually took his leave of the musical interlude and continued walking through the camp. I followed anxiously only to find us now in the area of the Washington defenses. Ethan worked with the others building forts and other defensive positions. I helped where I could which made him look as if he were super strong. We both got a lot of laughs out of that.

One day there was quite a stir among the troops. General McClellan appeared along with the man himself, President Lincoln. Ethan was one of the lucky ones who got to shake Mr. Lincoln's hand. I ,of course, had only to watch as he walked right past me. I must admit though even that was quite a thrill. Wishful thinking though it may be, I almost felt that he sensed my presence.

It suddenly dawned on me that many days had passed. I had totally forgotten about my wife and son. Reading my thoughts again Ethan volunteered,

"They are both alright, no need to be concerned."

Part of me felt relieved and comforted with his words and yet part of me felt ashamed, though short lived, for forgetting them for such a long time.

After President Lincoln left the area, Ethan indicated that I should follow him again, which I did without question, passing through a misty area. As the mist cleared we found ourselves in the middle of a shooting battle. Later I found out it was called "The Battle of Lee's Mills"

As the Vermonters and others entered and crossed the river (The Warwick River) bayonets flashing and bullets flying, young men were falling, some wounded, some dead. The battle took a heavy toll on both sides. After a time I did not want to watch this carnage but something inside compelled me to continue. I crossed the river with Ethan hearing the bullets whizzing past me and some actually passing through me. The Confederates rallied and drove us back across the river. What a waste of lives, but I must say the Green Mountain Boys, as they referred to themselves, were not defeated in spirit. I, not being accustomed to war's savagery, was also being carried by this spirit. The preservation of the union was a must at all costs. I found myself trying to help where I could, but the only person I could actually touch was Ethan. He instinctively knew my feelings and it then became mutual. Through the water, up the

river bank, and over boulders we helped each other, all the while avoiding small arms fire.

I hypnotically followed Ethan where ever he led. Battle after battle. The wars victories shifted back and forth constantly. The Unions advances became withdrawals. Robert E. Lee was the driving force behind the confederate victories. We had been pushed back to northern Virginia again where we camped for the winter.

Neither side during these campaigns had adequate medical care or supplies. As many men died of disease and starvation as by bullets.

Lead again through the mists by Ethan found us in the battle of "The Wilderness" as it was called. This was one of the fiercest battles we participated in. Thousands were lost on both sides. It was here we were captured and sent to Andersonville. The stories I had read about this prison were no exaggeration. Here I was seeing it first hand and it was worse than what I had read. Polluted water, no sanitary facilities, shelter was non existent, food was next to nothing, disease was rampant with no medical care. Even though I myself was not affected by this I felt it's results along with Ethan and the thousands of others interned here. Not many escaped from here, never the less Ethan and I made our plans. Within two weeks the time was right. A moonless night, and rain had been falling for hours. We had made a rope of rags and remnants of whatever material we could find. We slowly crawled through the mud to a darkened corner of the wall. I was first to climb the wall with the aid of Ethan. Once on top I secured our hastily made rope and let it down to Ethan. Slowly he pulled himself up. I reached down and caught his hand and was able to assist him in his climb. Suddenly I was carrying his whole weight. I heard the report of a rifle. Ethan had been shot.

"Let me go and you get away." he whispered in agony.

I just couldn't. After all we had been through I felt he was like my brother. I pulled with every last ounce of my strength and finally had both of us over the wall and fell to the ground on the other side. The bullet had caught him in the thigh. The wound was bleeding badly but we managed to get a tourniquet on. Hearing the commotion of a search party we took off as best we could. Luck was with us. We made it to a wooded area near a creek by sunrise. The rain helped to cover our tracks. We washed and dressed his wound and rested for a few hours. Not wanting to risk staying in one place too long, we continued our trek northward. We traveled both day and night resting every few hours. The further north we went the more confidence we gained. Then it happened. A Confederate patrol.

"Hey look, there's one of them runaway Yankees." shouted one of it's members. With that all six fired their weapons. Three bullets caught Ethan in the chest and he fell into my arms. I laid him down easily to the ground.

"He's a goner, just leave him to the maggots." said one of the patrol and they moved away into the woods.

I was incensed, I was upset, I was angry. I shouted and screamed after the patrol. I cried. It was as if the bullets had gone into my chest. I looked around for a weapon. I wanted to retaliate. There was nothing. I stood there in total frustration. Finally my anger subsided, I turned and walked back to where Ethan lay. I sat with my back against a tree and held Ethan with his head in my lap. I could feel the tears running down my cheeks again. I noticed my shirt sleeve was blood stained from where I had lifted Ethan.

All was quiet now except for the sounds of the

surrounding forest. My mind was a total blank. I just sat there stroking Ethan's head in my lap.

"Dad."

"Dad."

"Dad."

My son's hand was gently touching my shoulder. The fog slowly cleared from my head as did the mist around the gravestone. I was sitting on the ground with my back against a tree.

"**C**ome on Dad, wake up. Mom said she wants to start heading home." came my son's voice from far away.

Finally gaining some reality, I looked at my son and asked what time it was.

"**I** don't know, but Mom said you were gone for about twenty minutes and that I should come and get you."

"*Twenty minutes ! How can that be. Ethan and I have been traveling for months.*" I said to myself. I shook my head to dislodge the cobwebs. *"That was some dream."* I got to my feet and walked over to get my camera from the log. While putting the lens cover back on the camera I heard my son loudly saying,

"**O**h boy ! Look Dad. Look what I found."

I turned to look and in his hand he held an harmonica.

"**B**oy wait till I show Mom." he said and turned to go back down the hill.

"**NO !**" I shouted. "It stays here. It belongs here. Give it to me."

Frightened by my voice, he handed it to me.

"It's just an old harmonica." He said shaking and almost crying.

"**I**'m sorry son." I said calmly. "I shouldn't have yelled at you. I very sorry, but I happen to know it belongs here.

He looked at me as if to question, but was afraid to.

Anticipating his question I said,

"**I** just know that's all."

My son turned and headed down the hill. I walked to the grave and gently placed it on the ground in front of the stone.

"**R**est in peace old friend." I whispered.

I stood there for another few minutes then headed back down the hill myself.

My wife and son had everything packed and ready to go by the time I got there. My son was sitting in the car not looking at me. My wife took one look at me and said,

"**O**h my God, Ken, what have you been up to. You're a mess. And look at your sleeve. It almost looks like blood."

"**I**t's nothing." I answered. "I just tripped before." I lied.

As we drove home, I tried to sort things out in my mind. I know I was really there but how could I have been. It must have been a dream. If it was a dream then how did I get blood on me sleeve. I was getting myself confused.

We arrived home, unpacked the car, then I headed straight for the darkroom. I carefully processed the film and with it still wet, viewed it on the light table. It was exactly what I saw earlier. A broken fence, a leaning stone all shrouded in a mist. The very last exposure however was different. There was a ghostly figure, in a Civil War uniform, standing next to and leaning on the stone.

~ ~ ~ ~ ~ ~ ~

From time to time I still visit that grave site, alone, and pay my respects to a very good friend Someone, whom I felt I knew well, but never really knew at all.

The End.

The Walk

A short story
by
Peter Koenke
&
K.J.Goss

The Walk

Another hot, sultry evening in the city of New York made even worse by passing thunder showers. It was late August and even though the rain ceased about ten fifteen, the humidity engulfed the Borough of Queens like a wet dish rag. The rain had chased people from the streets and the usual sounds of the city were absent except for an occasional car horn off in a distance. The silence was inviting to Ed Jenkins who lived in a second story railroad flat on sixty third Avenue about a block away from the city's elevated train line.
The familiar clickity clack of the steel wheels also seemed conspicuously absent tonight. The long narrow four room apartment had been Ed's home for almost sixty years since he first opened his clock and watch repair business in the shop below. His retirement a few years ago forced him to sublease the shop. He was pleased though because the new tenant was an antique book store so the noise level was low. It also helped fulfill his passion for reading, particularly out of print books.

Even with the windows opened both front and rear the air was still and oppressive on this Thursday night. Ed, a creature of habit was usually in bed this time of night. The news at eleven with a half glass of wine and then lights out. Tonight's heavy air interrupted that routine. A walk might do him some good, he thought. Since his heart attack a few month's ago the doctors had recommended that a daily walk would be beneficial. Because of the on and off rains of the day this had not taken place today.

"No time like the present." he muttered aloud as he slipped on his loafers. He grabbed his umbrella just in case and started down the narrow staircase. He reached street level and stepped out onto the sidewalk and realized he had made the right decision. Although there was no real breeze the open air appeared to be less stifling and he did feel slightly cooler. He headed west up the street towards the El.

"I'll just go up a few blocks and do a loop around towards home again." he said aloud to himself. He was pleased with the silence tonight. It let his mind wander undisturbed as he relived bits and pieces of his life. At eighty one years old he had no regrets about how he lived. His wife of fifty one years had passed away eight years ago. Yes, he was lonely at times but he still had two loving children. His son lived out on Long Island whom he saw frequently. His daughter married and now lived in New Mexico, but he did speak to her every couple of weeks.

The air was refreshing but surprisingly the streets were still devoid of people. A small sliver of a quarter moon could be seen showing through the slowly thinning clouds making shadows even darker. He crossed under the elevated tracks and continued on for a few blocks before turning north. Still reminiscing about key highlights of his past Ed strolled for another few blocks then turned east. Feeling more comfortable and a little cooler now he decided he should probably head for home. There was no real rush, but it was well past his usual bed time and he was feeling a bit tired.

There were many small shops on Sixty eighth Avenue and most of the owners he knew personally. A side benefit I guess, of having lived there so long. After traveling a few hundred feet or so he lingered for a moment at the new jewelers and watch repair shop. He smiled and remembered his long and happy career doing the same thing. As he turned to continue his stroll he caught a glimpse of what appeared to be a man but the dark figure faded into the row of shadow buildings.

"*Just my imagination.*" he thought and went on his way. Passing a few more store fronts he paused again at the flower shop gazing at the window display. He made a mental note to send his daughter some carnations for her birthday next week. Carnations were always her favorite. He thought he caught some distant movement out of the corner of his eye. He turned his head to look but again all there was, was a wisp of darkness blending into the building. He
continued his walk towards home felling a slight nervousness edging through his body. He could hear footsteps now, soft but deliberate. Ed slowed his pace a little, the footsteps stopped. He entered into a normal pace again and within a few seconds he could hear footsteps. Taking a deep breath he stopped and slowly turned. When he was fully around he saw it. No mistake this time. It was a man. A rather large man in dark clothes stepping into the doorway of one of the shops. Mustering up some additional courage Ed held his position. He did not have to wait long. He saw the dark figure peek out and just as quickly bury himself in the buildings shadows again.

"*What do I do now.*" Ed thought. Feeling extremely uneasy he headed for home his mind racing.

"**I** can't run any more, I'll just have to try and walk as fast as I can." he whispered to himself.

He could hear footsteps again, even louder this time.

"*He must be getting closer.*" thought Ed. "My umbrella." he muttered quietly. "I'll use my umbrella as a club."

Within seconds he answered himself.

"**W**ho am I kidding, I have trouble opening it, how am I going to swing it at someone ?"

Ed could now feel his heart rhythm increase and could sense the cold beads of sweat forming on his head.

"**M**ust stay calm. Must stay calm." he told

himself.

He turned his head again as he struggled to hurry along. As he looked around the foot patter stopped while the large dark stalker again disappeared into a misty shadow.

Trembling now Ed Jenkins resumed his journey home.

"Why doesn't he just attack and get it over with. Maybe if I yell he'll go away."

Ed laughed at his own silliness knowing that he was too scared to even do that. His heart increased it's pounding taking more of his breath away as he struggled forward as best he could. The umbrella now became his cane. He welcomed the extra balance as the trembling now invaded his legs.

Looking ahead at the still deserted street he searched for an answer. The foot steps grew louder and seemed quicker. Up ahead Ed could see the distant corner.

"That's my street." he thought. *"I'm almost home. Can't give up now. Must keep going."*

He felt himself slowing down. His breathing became deep and wheezy. His heart was pounding with such intensity now he could hear it and feel the beat in his ear drums. It was constant and nerve wracking.

"Must stop for a minute. Have to catch my breath."

He reached his arm out and steadied himself against the building. Looking behind, his nemesis, although closer, he ducked into the shadows as before. Ed tried to shout at him. His mouth opened but his silence prevailed. Though his legs remained unsteady he forged ahead using both the cane and building to keep himself upright The footsteps continued.

"Leave me alone." his mind shouted. "Just let me be, I have no money."

Ed Jenkins fear was overwhelming. His trembling actually stopped. The noise in his head ceased. He looked up as the shadowy figure neared. A sharp sudden pain struck. Ed clutched his chest with his free arm and smiled as he fell to the concrete sidewalk.

All was still.

The para medic with the ambulance asked the police officer if he saw what happened.

"As a matter of fact I did." was the answer. "This is old Ed Jenkins. He lives no more than a hundred feet from this corner here. This is my regular beat and I was making my rounds checking on doors. You know, going into all the shop doorways making sure all were securely locked. I saw old Ed up ahead of me. Out for an evening stroll I guess. He walks slow so I was catching up with him. I was going to wish him a good evening, but as I approached I saw him clutch his chest and fall to the ground. It's funny though, I could swear I saw a smile on his face as he fell. He was well liked around here. He sure will be missed.

The End

The Dragon

The Dragon

"**I**t took you long enough to deliver a dozen eggs." said Jan to her husband. "It's less than a quarter mile to their house. Where have you been."

Bob and I got to talking and he was showing me this new gadget called a "Dragon" he bought for his computer." I replied. "It's a voice recognition gimmick that types as you talk. He thought I might be interested since he knows I write stories. My typing with two fingers can be quite a task as you know.."

"**Y**es ! I know, I've heard you swear at the computer often enough." said Jan smugly.

A few days later at the local discount store, I looked into and purchased my own Dragon. Anxious to use it, I couldn't wait to get home and became impatient waiting for my wife to finish food shopping. Finally home, I helped unload the car and put the groceries away. My afternoon now free I headed for the computer, read the brief instructions and proceeded with the installation process. I spent the rest of the afternoon playing and became fascinated with all this thing could do. Pleased with my efforts of the day, I turned off the computer and prepared for an evening out with my wife.

It was an enjoyable and exciting evening with friends although my mind did drift now and then to my new toy. I was anxious to get started on another story and knew "The Dragon" would be of great assistance.

It was actually a few days till I had time to sit and write. Up until now I would write out my stories longhand and then go through the agonizing process of my two fingered typing. Now, I thought, I could just dictate and the computer would take care of the rest.

And so my story starts:

The first few weeks were a pleasure and actually fun. The Dragon helped correct my spelling and suggest replacement phrases like a thesaurus. Then I started to notice weird things happening.

For instance when I was sending an E-mail to a friend my spelling was automatically being corrected.

"That's odd." I thought.

That's when I noticed the small microphone icon displayed in the lower corner of the computer screen. The connection was still plugged in but I had not turned the gimmick on yet. I dismissed this as a fluke in the software program, which I know can happen at times and went about my day.

A few days later I was checking some E-mail I had just received from a cousin and while reading it I saw some words changing. Sure enough the Dragon icon was in the corner again. It was now correcting my incoming mail. I checked the connection again which seemed to be okay and the switch was still in the off position. I half dismissed it as before and moved on to other things on the computer without any further interruptions. A week went by before I was able to work with the computer again. I started working on an unfinished story with the Dragon working just fine. Suddenly it started typing by itself. I had not dictated anything. It told me I had some new unopened E-mail. I closed up the story page and switched over to my E-mail. There were six new messages. Before I moved the mouse to open the first one it automatically opened. I proceeded to check four E-males without any further mishaps but the last two were deleted by themselves, or so I thought. Being preoccupied with other things I paid little attention to what was going on.

The next day my wife mentioned that while she was using the computer to write her Mother her spelling was being corrected. I was a little disturbed by this but acted nonchalantly so as not to upset her. As an excuse I said I must have left the switch to the Dragon on and that I would take care of it.

Later that day I found time for my story and as soon as I turned the computer on it started typing. The message read:

"I did not like what Jan told her Mother about me. If she does it again I will not let the Message go through."

Then it stopped typing. Staring at the screen I was stunned and totally confused. Trying to make sense out of what I just witnessed almost frightened me.

"This can't happen." I thought. It's just a gadget on attached to the computer, an inanimate object."

I looked at the screen again but the message was gone. I continued to work on my story and all seemed to go well. I didn't tell my wife what took place. She was already annoyed with me and this toy.

A few more days passed. I was quietly relaxing with a magazine when I heard my wife screaming at the computer. I hurried to see what trouble she was having.

"This stupid thing just told me I couldn't order a new sweater, that I was wasting your money, then it deleted my order form."

She was obviously very upset and I could see tears forming in her eyes.

"You've got to do something about that evil thing." she continued.

"This is not the first time it has corrected my writing. Do something ! *NOW!* She emphasized.

"Okay, calm down hon, I'll just unplug it."

I reached for the connection and to my surprise received a shock. I jumped back as my wife screamed yet again. My brain was working overtime.

"There must be a short in the wire someplace." I rationalized. "That's why it's been acting strange lately.

"I don't care what it is." my wife yelled, "Just do something. That thing is out to get me, or us. Do something please." she pleaded.

I looked at the monitor. A new message was being typed.

"Do not touch the wire again, Ken."

Now, I too, was becoming frightened. Instead of the computer connection I'll unplug it from the wall socket." I thought. I walked to the wall, reached down for the plug and received an even greater shock. This threw me backwards into a chair. Besides my own outburst from the pain I could hear my wife screaming uncontrollably. It took me a few moments to recover and when I looked at the screen, it read,

"I told you not to touch the wire, Ken. I don't really want to hurt you. I like you Ken. I like the stories you write. But I do not like Jan. She says nasty things about me."

My wife, in between heavy sobs was saying,

"Please Ken, do something. Kill that thing. Please, please, do it now." then she ran from the room. The monitor lit up again as new typing appeared.

"See what did I tell you, Ken. Jan is nasty to me. You must do something about her."

"I'll do something alright." I thought as I left the

room. I went to the kitchen to retrieve the long wooden broom
handle and returned to the computer room. It took a few tries but I
finally managed to knock the plug to the Dragon unit from the wall.
I sat there for a moment not knowing what to think.
The computer screen flickered as another message appeared.

> *"You shouldn't have done that Ken. Now
you have made me angry. Because of that I have deleted
the story you were writing. I really liked the story, but you
made me angry."*

I couldn't believe it. The unit was unplugged, yet it
was still going. It had taken possession of my computer.

Suddenly another message started.

> *"When you calm down we can write
another story. I would like that, Ken. But Jan can
not use the computer any more. She is nasty to me. I
will be here when you need me, Ken."*

The screen went blank.

That about did it for me. I left the room and headed
for the garage. It took a while but I finally found what I was looking
for. My long handled tree ax. Returning to the computer I saw yet
another message.

> *"I sense hostility here, Ken. What are you
going to do."*

With that I swung hard and split the monitor in
half. Glass was flying everywhere. Next was the computer tower.
I severed the electric cord with sparks flying, then came
down hard again and again until all that was left were bits and pieces
of circuit board and wires. I sat there in silence, the ax still in my
hand. Looking around at the mess my eyes locked onto a large piece
of the monitor screen still showing the last word of the last message.

Instead of reading "DO" It read,

"Doooooooooo." As if it was dying., which is what I hoped had happened.

Weeks later the room was all cleaned up but I still had not replaced the computer. My wife and I thought we could do without it for a while. Actually, we were quite happy without it.

My neighbor, Bob, asked how I was making out with my new Dragon gadget. Without going into detail I just said I had computer trouble and got rid of the whole thing.

My only thought now is,

"Beware of what you get to make things easier."

The end

The Wagon Wheel

by
K.J.Goss

The Wagon Wheel

I just walked into the house after weeding in the garden for two hours to the clanging of the stupid phone. I was really not in the mood to answer it but decided to anyhow figuring it might be my daughter calling.

"**Hello**" I grumbled into the receiver.

"**Hey** Ken, this is Bob." I was met with. "You've got to see what we just dug up."

My neighbor from down the road, I know was doing some landscaping.

"**Come** on over as soon as you can and bring your camera." He requested.

He did not tell me what he found but he was happily excited. I answered with,

"**As** soon as I get a break." And let it go at that. He sounded a little disappointed with my answer but he knew I would come over eventually.

I was washing the dirt and mud off and started thinking. I did not want to go back to weeding so I figured I would give myself a break and see what Bob was so excited about. I finished cleaning up, jumped in my truck and headed down the road.

As I turned in his dirt drive I could see Bob, his wife, the two men working the landscaping and another neighbor clustered together at the bog on the other side of the pond. Nearing the group, they parted and there before me, leaning against a tree was a wagon wheel. Not just any wagon wheel. A rather large wagon wheel, obviously quite old. No wonder he was so excited. It was really a beauty, if a wagon wheel can be beautiful.

Quite by accident the landscapers back hoe hit something solid while digging near the bog. They said it took about an hour and a half to bring it up. So much for the work day.! It was truly a thing of beauty and was in a perfect state of preservation. The bog lived up to its reputation for being able to preserve things indefinitely. A quick wash down with the garden hose revealed the outstanding workmanship of an unknown wheelwright. The spokes were wide fine grained oak supporting a metal covered strong oak ring leading to a massive wooden hub obviously made for a heavy load.

I did take a few shots with my camera figuring I would take more once the wheel was moved to a more accessible location. The general conversation turned to its further preservation now that it was exposed to the air. Eventually all drifted away except Bob and I. He jokingly said, "I wonder what else is down there ?" meaning the bog. We both laughed lightly as we examined the wheel more thoroughly. It truly was a massive piece of work. We had both seen wagon wheels before but this was certainly different. We chatted a while longer till, feeling guilty, decided I should get back to my weeds.

That evening, after processing the film, I studied the pictures, my curiosity building. I started thinking about the age of the wheel and felt additional research was called for. It rained the next day, fortunate for my garden but it was also a stimulant for the weeds. Nevertheless it provided the opportunity to do some of that research promised last night, so off to the library I went.
Between the books and the internet I learned that this wheel may be quite old. Armed with my pictures and copies of library information I returned to Bob's house. With the exact age still undetermined, only that it was old, I asked Bob if he would seriously consider looking into the bog some more, since he made reference to it the day before. I think I piqued his curiosity also and we agreed to go to the states Farming Museum that afternoon.

The museum was interesting but gave no new information. The construction of Bob's wheel was different than anything else we saw, which still left us in the dark as to its age. On the way home Bob agreed to further digging in the bog.

With the help of a borrowed back hoe we commenced our excavation project the next morning. The work was slow and deliberate not wanting to damage anything, if there was something else down there. A little discouraged by lunchtime for not having found anything, we planned to continue for the afternoon and if still nothing we would give up our dream of a great discovery. After a quick sandwich and a beer we were back in the mud of the bog. Within half an hour we made contact with something solid. Excitement running high our digging became even more careful. We slowly exposed part of another wheel and after some shoveling found it was still attached to an axle. Here we stopped and posited all sorts of theories of what we had. That, of course, was all talk and we knew digging by hand was now in order. With the help of two other neighbors we worked in teams relieving each other every half hour or so. This, over the span of a day and a half exposed a wagon. A large heavily built wagon, requiring the rental of a crane to pull it out. Here before us was now the results of our labors. An unusually large wagon obviously built with a special purpose in mind. *But what ?*

Without exact measurements we guessed it to be about thirty feet long and a very wide twelve feet. The three well built axles carried a heavy enclosed frame about four feet deep, the various doors still locked with iron chains and a massive padlocks. We were all anxious to open these locked doors but luckily common sense dictated we do some clean up first. A half hours worth of the garden hose magnified the beauty of this huge wagon. I made sure I took plenty of pictures from all angles. Now for the moment we were all anxious for. Rather than destroy the padlock we took the time to cut the chain, which was about an hour. Finally we all stepped back to let Bob do the honors of opening the huge door. Standing atop the wagon he struggled for a bit then to the sound of rusty, creaking hinges lifted the heavy door. He stood there mesmerized as he froze in place staring down. The silence was almost loud. Not being able to contain myself any longer, I climbed up on to the wagon and looked into the open frame. I also froze in place. I could not believe my eyes. The storage box was filled with rifles. Old vintage rifles. The initial shock over we opened other doors until all was exposed. In addition to the rifles, there were pistols, powder kegs and shot. On closer examination they were British made. Further searching the boxes turned up a well oiled leather pouch containing perfectly dry papers outlining an agreement between a Brigadier General Roxbury of his Majesty's Army and Major Jethro Cummings of the Confederate States of America. This hoard of weapons was for the cause of the South during the civil war. The document was dated March 21, 1863.

No wonder this wagon was built so well, this was an exceptionally heavy load. The initial surprise and excitement having worn off we continued searching all the corners of these storage areas. An even bigger surprise showed up. Two well constructed strong boxes that took two men to lift were finally lowered to the ground. The locks were cut and the tops opened exposing gold coins. British gold coins. None of us knew what the value was but it was again obvious that this would have helped the South's cause tremendously.

We guessed that this wagon was on its way back to the south from Canada where the guns and gold were supplied by the English. The bog became insurmountable for the horses pulling the wagon and were finally cut loose. Imagine the feeling of loss and disappointment to the rebel soldiers responsible for the delivery of these much needed monies and arms. What the fate of these men was we shall never know.

Bob eventually donated the weapons to the State Historical preservation groups, and except for a few gold coins as souvenirs all was returned to Canada and Great Briton.

You never know what you may find when you want to plant grass. I know My weeding took on a whole new dimension.

The End.

By
Ken Goss

The Vacation

by
K.J.Goss

The Vacation

Retirement is great. Don't let anyone tell you different. You get to do the things you never had time to do while you were working. Schedules no longer matter. There are no longer time constraints to worry about. If you don't finish something today, you can always finish tomorrow. What's the rush ?

I've always said as long as you have interests and hobbies to keep the brain active, you'll live forever. That is if any one really wants to. In my case, though, I think I have too many interests, but I do enjoy every one of them. Sometimes I believe I'm busier in retirement then I was when pursuing my career occupation. But I digress.

As much as I love my varied interests, these too can take their toll on you. So when my wife suggested a short holiday to the coast of Maine, I jumped at the chance. I agreed that it would be good to have a change of scenery. A sort of clean out the mind thing. You know, recharge the batteries.

We quickly made plans and were able to rent a place on short notice. Being off season helped along those lines I guess, not to mention good for the bank account also.

Be what it may, we were soon on our way, and I must say I was really looking forward to some new sights.

Our uneventful but enjoyable drive north soon brought us to our surprise destination. I knew we had rented a coastal house, but I had no idea it was a quaint and somewhat old, small estate surrounded by a high wrought iron fence with a large gate electronically controlled. We had received the remote for the gate via special delivery. Once inside we found the house perched on a not too steep rock precipice over looking the ocean. Small rock islands could be seen off in the distance. One was occupied by a light house. I could already feel myself succumbing to the peace of my surroundings. My wife snapped me out of my spell when she reminded me that we still had to unpack the car.

We found the key where the agent said it would be and entered a world of two hundred and fifty years ago. A well preserved museum house, but it wasn't a museum at all. My wife was beaming happily as we looked about. It reminded me of a movie set of a story from the seventeen hundreds, yet this was the real thing. I could not believe how well preserved everything was and still so immaculately clean.

"I'm just going to love it here." was my wife's only comment.

It was late afternoon by the time we settled in and discovered all the nuances of the many roomed house. There was even a third floor tower if you will. I believe they called it a widow's walk or a captains walk. A small well lit room with an outside walk around all four sides neatly contained by beautifully carved balustrades.

We freshened up and decided to eat in town, this being our first night.

The town, which was about five miles distance wasn't much, though it was quaint. My wife said she was looking forward to seeing it in the daylight tomorrow. We found the only restaurant in the small village, really just a local café' with a bar attached. As we entered, the dozen or so occupants became conspicuously quiet. I gathered they did not get too many strangers stopping by. A woman, who appeared to be in her mid thirty's, walked over, bid us a good evening and escorted us to a vacant table in the corner.

"Make yourself comfortable and I'll get some menu's." she smiled.

By now the din of low chatter resumed, with periodic, curious glances our way. I assured the wife it was nothing to be concerned about, that they probably don't get too many strangers here. After all this was not what you would call a main thoroughfare of civilization..

As promised the menu's arrived with a smile. I ordered a beer while my lady had a glass of white wine. The most exotic thing on the menu was meat loaf with mushroom gravy which the waitress highly recommended.

"It was probably the only thing they had." I thought.

Making an effort to be friendly, the server inquired,

"You folks passing through on your way to Canada."

My wife excitedly answered , "No" that we were renting the old Tyler house for a few weeks. We wanted to relax and enjoy the sea for awhile.

The waitress's face went pale and a strange looked passed through her eyes.

"Oh." she said briskly and walked away.

She returned with our drinks without saying a word. I noticed now the other customers were taking more glances our way along with a few quiet whispers. The waitress returned again with our food. My curiosity got the better of me and I dared to ask,

"Excuse me miss, why the change in attitude when we mentioned the old Tyler house."

She actually looked frightened now and was hesitant to answer. Looking directly into my eyes she managed,

"You don't know about the house ?"

"No ! Why ?" I returned the question. "We have never been here before. We found this ad through a realtor on the internet."

"Oh." she remarked.

A look of relief came over her face now. I guess we were no longer the bad guys.

"Let me just say this." she continued, "If it was me I would never go near that house. They say it's haunted."

"Come now." I smiled along with my wife. "In this day and age and you still believe in ghosts."

Her face went serious again as she added,

"Well don't say you haven't been warned."

I followed her with my eyes as she returned to the kitchen, stopping by the bar to whisper something to the older man behind it.

The meatloaf, believe it or not, was actually excellent. My wife and I dismissed the haunted comment as she talked excitedly about the house and our plans for the next two weeks.

After our meal we lingered over coffee, and were joined by the older gentleman from the bar.

"Mind if I sit down. My name is Tom, Tom Ashcroft." He said as he sat down not waiting for the invite.

"My name is Tom also. Tom Britton, and this is my wife Joanne." I answered advancing my hand.

Without further ceremony Tom Ashcroft continued.

"I'm surprised to hear you rented that old house. To the best of my knowledge it has never been rented before and I've lived here my whole life."

Joanne and I looked at each other briefly.

"I hope Lucy", referring to the waitress, didn't upset you folks too much with all that haunted stuff. I don't put too much stock in it myself, but the people around here have been keeping that rumor alive for a couple of hundred years."

"Why is that." Joanne inquired.

"Well, there is a story behind it that goes back that far I guess. I believe the local library has some stuff about it.

"Perhaps you could fill us in a little." I asked.

"Well, in a nut shell it has to do with Light House Rock, just off the coast from the house."

"I saw it this afternoon." I replied.

Ignoring my interruption Tom went on with his story.

"It is said the old man, Old Man Tyler, would extinguish the light house fires on stormy nights and ships would crash on the rocks. He would then salvage the cargo and sell it. He didn't seem to care how many people were killed because of his deeds. Most of the local folk feared him and avoided the place. Then the story goes on to say after years of shipwrecks, the dead rose up out of the sea and took their revenge on the old man. He was found hanging from the widows walk balustrades. To this day legend has it that he haunts the house. Shipping routes have long since changed so the light house is no longer used. But the locals keep the legend alive by saying they see the light glowing from time to time. So there you have it." he finished.

Joanne and I were both fascinated by his tale. I told him I most likely would go to the library and do some further research because I was always interested in historical happenings.

We bid our farewells with smiles and happily drove back to our haunted house. Joanne tended to a few things at the house then said goodnight and retired up stairs to bed.

I chose to check out the library which contained many antique books. I was amazed at the printing dates, some of which were from the seventeen and eighteen hundreds. Most were first editions.

"*This must be worth a small fortune.*" I thought.

To leave them this open to renting strangers was even more amazing. I chose a book about the USS Constitution giving some of it's early history. Totally entrenched in what I was reading caused time to whiz by. I heard a noise outside which disturbed me. I looked at the clock. It read twenty after twelve-midnight. I walked to the window but saw nothing. Either there wasn't anything there or whatever it was, was gone by the time I looked. Shrugging my shoulders I thought,

"*Oh well, I guess it was nothing..*"

I checked the door locks and went to be

I went to bed yet failed to go to sleep right away. My mind kept going back to what I heard or thought I heard outside. I have always prided myself on identifying strange noises. This one, to me, sounded like a horse and buggy type noise. More like a horse and wagon I would say. Then I argued with myself about what would a horse and wagon be doing on private property at midnight.   Reality finally winning the argument I drifted off to sleep.

I was up before the sun, grabbed my camera and proceeded to the cliff edge to see what a sunrise in Maine would be like. It was quite beautiful. Nothing to spur me to take pictures but beautiful just the same. Perhaps tomorrow would be better. Joanne was still sleeping so I decided to do some exploring of this majestic twenty acres. Privacy abounded and that gave me a contented feeling.

Following a not too well used path to the far end of the estate I came upon a unique looking carriage house. It's construction, obviously matching that of the main house.

"Why not." I thought, "There were no cars back

then so it made sense to have a carriage house. Particularly on such a grand estate. This requires a further look see.”

Approaching from the side, I peeked in the window.

“Not much light.” I said aloud. “Can't really see much.”

Moving to the front, I removed the padlock which was not locked. It was a beauty. My guess is that it was original. I admired it's workmanship and design.

“Too bad we still don't make things with this character and quality.” I muttered. Having finished my lock inspection, I rolled the large door to the right. Inside were, a large wagon, a four place carriage and then two, two seaters. But what caught my eye the most was the one front and center in the shelter. It was a hearse. A hearse of magnificent design. Only once before did I ever see anything like it and that was in a museum on eastern Long Island. A place of early settlement that does not get the recognition it deserves. Yet again I digress.

The hearse was black polished wood, with silver trim shined to the brilliance of the stars. Inside was lined with black leather and black velvet. The plush velvet wove a cloak of silence so deep that only the sound you could hear was your own thinking. I stood there for many minutes totally mesmerized by what I was seeing and feeling.

A small breeze rustling some leaves brought me out of my revery. I continued my inspection. The wheels were also a wondrous work effort. Again solid black with polished silver hubs. It was then I noticed some mud on the wheels and mud splashed on the body sides. Mud that was not fully dried.

“But that can't be.” I thought

Then I remembered the carriage like sound of last night.

“No.” I said out loud. It's just my fertile

imagination running wild again wanting everything to always be a mysterious or exciting adventure."

Laughing at myself, I closed the door and made my way back to the house. A nice breakfast and a large cup of coffee will set my head straight. Joanne was preparing just such a meal when I walked into the kitchen.

"Did you make any earthshaking discoveries on your explorations this morning." she chided.

"As a matter of fact I did, Miss Smarty Pants." I replied

I then went on to tell her of the carriage house and it's contents. She also wanted to see it after breakfast. A quick visit to the carriage house satisfied her and the rest of the day we spent exploring the surrounding area and shopping for food stuffs for the next two weeks. The day passed without any major excitement and we settled for the evening enjoying some wine, sitting in some deck chairs we brought along. They surely did not fit in to the estate scene, but then again everything can't be perfect.

After sunset we moved indoors, listened to music and read. Around tenish my wife went to bed while I stayed up and continued reading. Close to midnight I felt myself getting weary so I decided to call it quits. Tomorrow is another day. As was my usual routine I checked the door locks, and then as I passed by the front windows a light caught my eye. Taking a closer look I realized it was coming from the light house. Remembering the story of the night before my interest was piqued.

I quietly left the house and walked to the cliff edge, keeping the light in sight. It was then I noticed other smaller lights moving about the light house island. My mind was looking for explanations. Suddenly it came to me. The local folks, after weaving their tale of haunting, were further expanding their practical joke.

I laughed out loud and started back for the house. The heavy evening mist changed to a light rain.

"Perfect." I thought for a night of haunting.

Nearing the path between the house and the rock precipice, I heard that carriage sound again. Using the cover of a tree as protection from the rain, I waited quietly. The sound of the wheels grew nearer and I could now distinguish the patter of horses hooves. I must admit, as the sounds grew louder I could feel tingles running down my neck. I stayed in the shadows of the tree.

There it was ! I could see it now. The shape of a horse drawn vehicle. I moved further back into the shadows, not afraid just cautious. It drew even with my tree. A hooded cloaked shape was at the reins as it slowly passed.

It was the hearse I had seen this morning at the carriage shed. There could not be two like it. The driver turned in my direction as if he knew I was there. A bolt of lightning lit the wagon for an instant showing the hooded driver but not enough to make out any details under the dark cloak. The figure faced forward again and passed on by. Another lightning flash briefly lit the rear of the hearse. I could definitely make out a coffin in the velvet lined interior. My apparition continued on the path towards the carriage house. Not waiting for anything further, I ran for the house, entered, and bolted the door.

I had to laugh at myself again. If there was such a thing as ghosts or spirits, a locked door was not going to keep them away.

There were no repercussions because of what I had witnessed. A generous sip of Cognac helped me unwind, then I went on to bed.

I slept in the next morning and didn't arise till eight ten. Over breakfast I relayed last evenings events to Joanne, who was very interested and did not appear to be bothered by my story.

Once breakfast was over we strolled again to the carriage house breathing in deeply the brisk autumn air. All seemed in order, the hearse was exactly where it had been all polished and shining. Now even the wheels were totally mud free.

"That's strange" I thought, just as Joanne asked,

"**D**idn't you say it rained last night ?"

She turned towards me holding a pile of wet cotton rags with traces of mud.

"**S**omeone must have wiped down the carriage last night because everything is clean and dry." I answered.

Joanne, not really talking to me, said,

"**S**omeone else is, or has been here then, but who ?"

Gazing directly at me now, she followed with,

"**I** thought we were alone here. I'm not so sure now.

I checked the inside of the hearse. It was clean and empty. Joanne, half smiling, commented,

"**I** know what we're going to do tonight"

Returning her smile I replied,

"**N**o! What ?"

We closed up the shed and were going back to the house when Joanne quietly remarked,

"**I** didn't know there was a cemetery plot on the property."

She pointed to some trees near the back of the carriage building.

"**I** guess I missed that in the dark last night." I said

We made our way over there to find a neatly laid out area about thirty feet square, outlined by a low rock wall. There were two crude wooden crosses indicating what was obviously two fresh burials ,one still quite muddy from last nights rain. I felt a little strange suddenly, I rejoined my wife took her arm and left the cemetery.

Nearing the house I said,

"There are two things I really want to do today. First we do some research at the library in town, and then this afternoon we are going to rent a boat and visit Light House Island."

"How romantic." she said. "You're going to take me away from a haunted estate to visit a haunted light house. What more could a girl ask for." She smiled. "When do we get started ?" I laughed as we headed right for the car.

The library was a small colonial house also quite old. They made good use of the rooms which housed more then one would have imagined. The librarian introduced herself as Emily Brown and knew right away who we were

"I'm sure you want to see all that we have on the old Tyler place. We collected so much stuff over the years we gave it, its own little room. Here we go."

She unlocked a door and ushered us into a dark musty smelling room stacked full of books, journals and loose papers.

"It's quite a mess I know but nobody ever seems to have an interest anymore especially after what that horrible man did years ago. That's why we keep it locked."

She pulled back some heavy drapes and flooded the room with sunlight. There was a table desk with two straight back chairs by the window and a single stuffed chair in the opposite corner.

"Have fun." said Emily as she closed the door behind her.

"Such friendly people here." Joanne sarcastically remarked.

She walked over to a large framed portrait hanging on the wall.

"This must be the old geezer himself. There's a larger version of this hanging in the den of the house."

I muttered a quiet "Uh Huh." Not really having heard what she said because I was already absorbed in a journal. I grabbed a pad and pencil and made some notes of my own. Joanne, I noticed, was also taking notes.

Three undisturbed hours passed, until my stomach said it was time to quit. My gracious lady agreed and suggested we continue the next day. Hiding our notes inside my shirt, we left our library dungeon. Emily cordially nodded on seeing us and asked straight faced,

"Find what you were looking for ?"

Not wanting to show any emotion I answered, equally straight faced,

"Interesting reading."

My wife followed up with,

"If it's alright with you, we may be back tomorrow. I would just love to find out more about the architecture of that period.

A sudden look of relief crossed Emily's face.

"Yes, it was an interesting period wasn't it. I may even have other reference books on construction in the seventeen hundreds." Emily volunteered.

"That would be wonderful." smiled my wife, "Until tomorrow then."

She followed me to the exit. We didn't say a word until we were in the safety of our car.

"There's something fishy going on here. I can't quite put my finger on it." I commented.

"I know what you mean. I felt a little uncomfortable in there." Joanne replied.

"That was a great cover you put on with that architecture bit." I complimented.

"**W**hy thank you sir. We do try our best." she replied sassily.

We had lunch at the house so we could discuss out notes in privacy. Lunch was kept short so we would have plenty of time for the light house.

The boat rental went smoothly and I brought along my fishing gear while Joanne carried a novel looking the part of a bored housewife. We did not go to the light house directly so as not to raise suspicion. Eventually we pulled ashore on the opposite side of the rock island. After securing the boat, we made for the light. For as old as the structure was and exposed to the elements it fared pretty well for it's years. Don't get me wrong, it still needed much work. Neglect had taken its toll.

There was only one door and it was securely locked. The lock was obviously old and thoroughly rusted. It showed no signs of having been tampered with. The door was solid and could not be budged. Joanne mentioned that there were no foot prints. The mud left after last nights rain should have yielded prints. There was not a trace. Joanne and I looked at each other, puzzled.

"**H**ow can this be." I said. "I know what I saw last night. I wasn't dreaming it."

"**I** believe you." Joanne said in a comforting tone.

"**T**here were lights." I went on. "There were moving lights, there had to have been people here. And then there's the big light up there. It doesn't just light by itself."

Joanne interrupted me.

"**I**t's getting late. We should get the boat back before dark. We can come again another day."

We returned to the boat and pushed off. We meandered back to the rental dock with my fishing line trolling along. Luck was definitely with me. I had a strike and managed to get it aboard. A good sized mackerel that would make a great dinner. It wasn't a bad cover story either.

Returning to the house with our prize catch, Joanne made dinner preparations inside, while I set about getting the grill fired up. The cold beer hit the spot while I was waiting for the fire and trying to piece together the days events.

After our superb dinner we retired to the living room, or drawing room if you will, with all of out notes. Joanne started organizing the library information in chronological order while I started logging all of my ghostly issues. In doing so, I felt a certain affinity towards these sightings growing within me. It was as if I was meant to see these things. Something beyond my comprehension was drawing me in. I had no fright or apprehension about it either. In fact, I felt rather comfortable with the whole thing.

Joanne made some progress also.

"What was that bartenders name ?" she asked

"Tom." I answered.

"No, his last name ?" she questioned.

"Oh, ah - - - Ashcroft. Tom Ashcroft." I muttered.

"That's what I thought." she mumbled back, then was silent again.

Within a few minutes she again broke my concentration.

"Tom, come look at this."

I put down the pencil and moved to Joanne.

"I'm sure there's a lot more papers to look through, if we can find them, but with what we have seen so far, I'm finding a common thread. Besides Thadeus Tyler, the name Ashcroft keeps popping up." she said puzzled.

"You shouldn't think that too unusual. There's a lot of old English families who stayed in one place. It's only the more recent generations who are moving on to bigger and better things." I lectured.

"I know, but I'm getting an eerie feeling about

this." she said.

"**Y**ou too ?" I questioned. "There's a lot of things about this whole house and town that just don't go together, and I have a strong feeling that we were sent here to find the answers."

"**W**hat do you mean ?" Joanne inquired.

"**I** can't really explain it but I just feel that's why we're here. Tomorrow let's hit the library again. I want to see what kind of records they have of the ships that were sunk. You keep digging into anything that has the names of Tyler and Ashcroft. There may be a connection that we're missing. Right now I'm going to take a nap. I have a feeling I'm going to be up again tonight."

I awoke about ten forty five. *"Good."* I thought, *"I still have time."* I went downstairs and found Joanne asleep in a soft chair, a book still in her hand. I touched her gently and whispered her name.

"**I**'m leaving now, I'll see you in the morning. I leaned over and kissed her on the forehead. She turned a little and grunted something unintelligible as I walked out the door.

The night air was a bit brisk but there were stars. I carefully picked my way back to the carriage house. As I came closer I saw that the door was closed.

"**T**hat's a good sign." I muttered quietly. "Maybe there won't be any activity tonight."

Still wanting to satisfy my curiosity, I peeked in the window with the flashlight I remembered to bring along.

The hearse was gone. I felt a touch of anxiety shoot through my body. Almost as sudden I calmed down as excitement filled my mind. The excitement of finding it and perhaps following it, to discover what it does and where it goes on it's nocturnal travels. Glancing down the path past the house I saw a distant flickering light.

"The light house." I said out loud. "Maybe there's a connection."

I moved as fast as I could heading for the cliff. Sure enough as soon as I neared the water I could see the dim glow from Light House Island. And again small moving lights around the island, just as before.

"Odd." I thought, "Our trip out there this afternoon showed nothing. I guess I'll have to risk a night visit, but not tonight."

I made myself comfortable on a rock and watched the light show and waited. Thank goodness it was a relatively warm night and not raining, although I could detect a light fog rolling in from the sea.

Apparently I was more tired than I thought. Being warm and somewhat comfortable I dozed off. A noise startled me awake and I found myself enveloped in a shroud of heavy fog. The light house could no longer be seen. Panicking slightly, I instinctively moved in the direction of the house. As I walked further inland the fog was less intense. For that I was grateful. It enabled me to see a little better and assured me of better footing. I finally came upon the trail to the carriage house. My timing, although just dumb luck, was perfect. I could hear the horse and wheels of a wagon again. Feeling less intimidated I did not fall back into the shadows this time. The hearse approached being pulled by a single, dark gray horse adorned by a black blanket and dark blinders. The driver was again draped with a dark hooded cloak. I could not distinguish a face. I turned on the flash light and because of the fog, the picture it presented was eerie and frightening, although I was not frightened. The hooded driver gazed slightly towards my direction and bowed his head as if in recognition or greeting. I stood there frozen, but still unafraid. The flash light, because of my frozen pose, was aimed up at the hearse. Even with the fog I could make out a plain box coffin resting inside. Then everything vanished into the shroud of mist.

I remained frozen for I don't know how long, suddenly realizing I should be following it. Regaining my composure I set off in the direction of the carriage shed. The fog grew in intensity making my short journey difficult. At last reaching the old barn, the door was closed, but peeking in the window I saw that the hearse was in it's normal place. Moving the flashlight I could see the back was empty

"**W**as I really losing my mind. Am I imagining all of this." I mumbled aloud. *"I have to stop this."* I thought. *"I'm talking more to myself lately than to anyone else."*

I turned to go back to the house, then remembered the graves. I reversed direction to behind the shed.

There were now three graves.

I checked the carriage house again, this time I went inside. The hearse had been wiped clean. There was a new dampish rag on the floor near the door. I examined it closely and discovered it was very old linen.

*"**W**hat a waste."* I thought.

I put it aside and as I was about to close the door I saw a shovel leaning against the wall. It had remnants of fresh dirt clinging to the blade. I left it, closed up the barn and made for the house.

Joanne was still asleep on the chair. I nudged her gently and escorted her to bed. I hit the pillow myself and don't even remember closing my eyes.

Seven thirty five, and I was staring at the ceiling with my mind going a mile a minute. Joanne was not in bed which was my incentive to get up. Coffee was ready so I filled my cup and made my way to the library. My wife looked up, smiled and said,

"**I** was going to let you sleep, you dirty stay out."

Laughing I kissed her good morning and sat myself opposite her. I told her of my nights activities between sips of coffee. She finally interrupted me to say she also was productive this morning. She handed me the journal she had been reading.

"Look at the name on this page." she instructed. "The last entry on the page."

> *"Oct. 29th., 1777. - - - If it had not been for my very good friend and trusted servant, Josiah Britton, I may never have uncovered this diabolical deed."*

It ended there. I flipped the pages but they were blank. Looking at Joanne, I asked,

"Are there any other journals."

"I haven't checked yet but I sure hope so." she replied."Did you have any relatives named Josiah."

"I honestly don't know. We would have to do a genealogy search. That takes time though."

I was silent for a few seconds, then continued.

"Today, instead of going back to the local library, let's make a visit to the county offices. There we can check the birth and death records of both Tyler and Britton."

"And Ashcroft." Joanne added.

"Yes, and Ashcroft." I repeated.

Breakfast was quick. We locked up, jumped in the car and made a beeline for the county offices. Forty six minutes later we were being escorted to a vaulted records room which turned out to be our home for the next six hours. It would have been longer, but the place closed at four thirty.

We started rehashing our research and comparing notes as soon as we hit the car. We were so busy with our notes, the drive home took no time at all. As we approached the private drive to the house, I thought I recognized the waitress, Lucy, from our first night here. She was parked some fifty feet from the drive on the opposite side. It was quite obvious she tried to hid from us as she drove away. The fact that she was even here was both good and bad news. The good news was we were on to something they did not want us to know. The bad news was we were on to something they did not want us to know.

In the house we put aside the notes and enjoyed a glass of wine before Joanne fixed dinner. When my wonderful wife went to the kitchen, I moved to the library. I sat alone sipping my wine and looking at the table full of papers, but not seeing anything. My thoughts were on tonight. I shifted my gaze to one of the book shelves containing a set of numbered journals. There had to be about thirty of them.. All were in numerical order except for sixteen and seventeen. These two were juxtaposed. I reached for number seventeen to set it in order when a loose page caught my eye. Opening the book to that page showed me that it was not a loose page but was an additional paper that had been slipped in. I unfolded it and read:

"The truth, now at last, has come
to the forefront of the situation.
 The shipwrecks off Light House
Rock having previously been
attached to my association are now
proven to be of other causes. The
greed of profit and sympathy to the
 Crown, have turned Edward Ashcroft
away from his own kind. It is
under his tutelage these dastardly
deeds have manifested themselves.
 I am apprehensive that foul play
shall fall upon me in the very near
future, for I, along with Josiah Britton,

*have located the cache of his ill
gotten efforts. Having so
located the aforementioned plunder,
we have taken it upon ourselves to
relocate same to a location
unknown to him. When this
diabolical assault becomes evident
to the proper jurisdictions, this ill
gotten plunder may be returned
to it's rightful owners and to our
cause of liberty.*

*Signed by my hand on this 3rd. Day of November
in the year 1777.*

*Your humble servant,
Thaddeus Tyler."*

I sat down devouring the paper with my eyes, committing it to memory. Joanne entered the room to tell me dinner was ready, but was alarmed by my trance like appearance.

"**A**re you alright Tom." she asked with concern in her voice.

Not receiving an answer she moved closer and gently touched my shoulder repeating her query. Tom, awakened by her touch turned to look at his wife and excitedly said,

"**Y**ou've got to read this Joanne."

"**W**hat is it." She asked.

"**J**ust read it." insisted Tom.

She carefully took the old paper from his hand and did as she was asked. When she finished reading she also sat down.

"**O**h my." Was her comment as she looked at her husband. She, too was digesting the papers contents. They both remained silent and unmoving. Joanne was the first to finally speak.

"You can't think clearly on an empty stomach, so let's eat and then talk.

Dinner was quick and they hardly spoke. Both were preoccupied with getting things straight in their own minds. Joanne was again the first to break the ice.

"I think we should go back to the local library tomorrow. There are a few loose ends I think we can put together."

"I agree." I said. "With this new information there are more details we need to clear up. Then, perhaps we can make some sense of this. Oh by the way, I want to check on the hearse again tonight." I finished.

"I'm going with you tonight." Joanne blurted out. "And there will be no arguments." she followed up.

There are times when one knows not to quarrel, and this was one of them.

"Okay." I answered, "But I want to leave earlier tonight."

"I'll be ready when ever you say." Jo replied.

A few minutes before ten we left the house heading straight for the carriage house. We took up positions behind some trees but close enough to observe the door of the shed. We waited silently. The night was partly cloudy, with a half moon that painted moving shadows on the landscape. The air became chilly, and I knew this meant fog rolling in from the ocean shortly.

Just after eleven we heard a disturbance in the underbrush from behind the shed. Bracing for the worst we waited some more. The quiet was broken with the soft sounds of horses hooves I had become accustomed to. My wife clasped my arm firmly. There it was the black and silver hearse passing in front of us, then disappearing down the trail. We let it pass before saying anything. My wife was awestruck and excited at the same time.

"Isn't this just wonderful." she whispered. My attention was on the door of the carriage barn. It was never opened. The hearse just appeared through it. I also observed that the back of the hearse was empty. There was no coffin. I mentioned this to my wife. Her only reaction was,

"That makes it even more exciting." she said happily.

We quickly followed our prey.

By the time we got to the cliff the hearse was no where to be seen, but the lights on Light House Rock were in motion.

"Let's go down on the beach to be closer." Joanne exclaimed.

"No ! Stay here." I cautioned. "We can observe more."

Surprisingly she listened. Again we waited and watched.

It was now nearing midnight and even I was somewhat impatient. I was about to give up when I saw the lights go out on the island

"Okay." I said, "Let's move a little closer to the trail."

We took up the same position I was in the other night and waited some more. We stood there in the foggy mist about a half hour, until I heard the familiar sound of the wagon wheels. I could sense my wife's anticipation. As it passed, the hood draped driver, guessing we were there, or knowing we were there, turned in our direction and nodded as he had done before. My main concentration was on the hearse itself, but the curiosity of my wife got the better of her and directed the flashlight she had on the driver. Her sudden intake of breath and tightness of her grip on my hand directed my attention to the now illuminated figure. The black cloaked figure was not that of a man but of a skeleton. The sudden light did not deter the driver, fore he continued on his mission undisturbed.

My wife seemed frozen in place, not in fear but in questionable wonder, her eyes still locked on the hearse as it vanished in the fog. Regaining her composure she looked at me and smiled,

"Come on, let's follow it." She stepped towards the trail.

"No need to rush, we already know where it is going." I replied.

Following the trail was difficult because of the decreased visibility due to the increasing fog density. By the time we reached the carriage shed all was in order as expected. Checking the window the hearse was in it's assigned place and the back was empty.

"The cemetery plot." I said to Joanne.

She followed me to the rear of the shed. There were now four graves. As I turned to leave Joanne held my arm saying,

"I thought you said there were just graves. You didn't say they had markers also."

"They didn't." I answered a bit bewildered by her comment. "Just crude wooden crosses.

Shining my light back to the graves, each one now had a wooden marker. On closer inspection, they each had a name roughly scratched into the wood.

"Jo, do you happen to have a pen and paper with you ?" I asked.

She reached into her pocket smiling and retracted them both.

"Ta Da." she said in a sing song voice.

Returning her smile I said,

"Knock off the theatrics and just write the names down."

"You're no fun." She laughed softly as she copied the names while I held the light to each marker. Finished for the night we went back to the house.

"To whom do those names belong I wonder." Joanne asked rhetorically."

"I have no idea but they must fit this puzzle some how." I replied. "I still have the feeling we are here for a specific reason."

My wife looked at me in a funny way.

"Perhaps you're right. All I know is that I'm suddenly very tired."

She started mounting the steps to the bedroom then called over her shoulder,

"Are you coming ?"

Killing the lights I followed.

We awoke the next day to rain. Well not really rain, but the early morning mist was so heavy it might as well have been rain. Breakfast was quiet, with both Joanne and I trying to sought things out in our minds. I started thinking out loud, not really addressing any one in particular.

"There has got to be more answers right here in this house. The trick is where to find them.."

Picking up my mug of coffee I went to the window looking out to the now quiet lighthouse. The mist was so thick there now I could not even see the bay.

"Just like the confusion in this house." I thought.

"That's it." I shouted.

I went back to the kitchen where my wife was still sitting.

"Today we stay here and start searching this

house from top to bottom." I stated.

"What are we looking for ?" Joanne questioned.

"I have no idea." I replied. "Papers, books, maps, any sort of hint. Anything that we think may tie in."

"Tie into what ?" Jo inquired again.

Looking at her sheepishly I answered,

"I don't even know that."

She smiled but seemed to understand my confusion.

"Let's start at the top and work our way down." I said.

Agreeing, we both headed for the tower room.

"Perhaps we'll find a secret panel leading to a secret room with all the answers." Joanne suggested.

"Don't be silly." I said. "This is not the movies." Down deep inside I was thinking the same thing.

The room was dusty and chilly, with not much in it. A book shelf containing only three books, and a small writing desk and chair. I went through the papers in the desk while Joanne flipped through the books, neither of which resulted in any information. I even knocked on the walls.

"Now whose being silly." harassed my wife.

"Who knows, maybe you could be right." I smiled in answer.

With no results here we moved down to the second level. There were five bedrooms here. Two large rooms on the south side of the house and three smaller rooms on the north side with a center hallway and stairs. Another half hour passed and still nothing. I went to one of the larger rooms while Joanne took the last small one. Within a few minutes she was standing in the doorway of the room I was searching.

"I think I found something Tom. Look at this paper. It's what would have passed as a newspaper two hundred years ago. Look at this column. It lists the names of the men who were drowned when their ship crashed on the rocks. It crashed because the light on Light House Island was extinguished. Maybe Mr. Ashcroft's story was true."

"Perhaps." I answered, "But I still maintain there's more to it than that. I'm convinced now more than ever that we were brought here for a purpose. I'm willing to bet that some of those names on that list match the one's we copied from the cemetery.

"I still have that list in my pocket." Joanne said as she retrieved it.

She compared the two lists, then with a surprised look turned to me and asked,

"How did you know ?"

"I wasn't sure, but if the rest of my theory holds true, we should have an answer to this soon enough."

"Care to enlighten me Sherlock ?" my wife inquired.

"Not just yet." I answered, "Because if you know what I was thinking, you would have me certified and taken away. Give me time to put the rest of the pieces together. Now back to our searching."

I know Joanne was disappointed. I also knew she understood me well enough and was willing to give me my space. The rest of the days search gave up many interesting documents. By themselves they meant nothing, but collectively they were adding up to prove my out of thin air theory.

At approximately five thirty we called it quits. I told Joanne to forget about dinner, that we were going to eat in town again tonight.

"Why would you want to do that ?" she quizzed.

"I need to get a feel of the locals again." I replied, "To see if my thoughts are making any sense."

We cleaned up, changed clothes and headed for

town.

It was a fun experience watching the faces as we entered the local eatery. The expressions were priceless. Lucy, the waitress, almost dropped the tray she was carrying. And of course, like the last time the place went silent. The bartender, recovering the fastest, put on a phony smile as he greeted us from across the room. We seated ourselves in the corner again. Lucy, I think against her better judgement, finally came over to us. Obviously nervous, she did, however manage to take our order. When she left the table side my wife snickered and said,

"You're enjoying this aren't you. ?"

With a forced smile, Lucy returned with our food, but uttered not a word. The usual whispers were going on along with the not so hidden glances. Almost finished with our meal, Tom Ashcroft came over to the table.

"Hi there folks, enjoying your stay in our quant little town."

"Yes, actually." my wife answered. "I just love that old house. It has such character, and I just adore the architecture."

"How true, madam, they just don't make them like they used to." was Tom's cookie cutter answer. "Have you been haunted out yet." He laughed that phony laugh once again.

"No, in fact it has been rather pleasant. I love the old carriage house." I smiled.

Tom A. did a good job of masking his expression, but I did detect a change.

*"**I** was right."* I thought. *"We did hit a point of interest."*

"Well that's great folks, that's just great. I better get back to my bar now, before they drink me dry." he quipped in his phony laugh.

Lucy returned with the check and seemed disturbed when we ordered two coffees, but I wanted to see everyone sweat some more.

"Now you're just being mean." said Joanne.

"I know." I replied smiling.

We finally left, leaving a very happy crowd, I'm sure.

"Looks like we'll be back just in time to go out for the night again." I said.

"Tom." said Joanne in a very concerned voice. "I think somebody is following us."

"I know." I answered. "Ever since we left the restaurant. They even turned their lights out."

"Thanks for telling me." scolded Jo.

"I didn't want to concern you unnecessarily." I replied. "I'm not worried about it. Don't forget we have those big security gates and fencing. Besides I don't think these locals are going to get involved in anything truly illegal. We know they are involved in something, but I don't believe we have to be concerned for our safety. Some of these puzzle pieces are starting to go together now.

"I'm glad you think so." Joanne said confused.

"The only mystery that still has me confused is our night time activities. What they represent and why has me stumped."

I turned into the drive, shut off the lights and waited. I didn't have long to wait. I could see the shadow of a car slow down as if looking, then satisfied we were home, took off down the road. Just past the fence line their lights snapped on as they increased speed.

"Just as I expected, they thought we might lead them some place else.." I said parking the car.

"And where would that be Sherlock." asked Jo.

"I have no idea my dear Watson." I answered.

We laughed, entered the house and prepared for

the nights events.

    Joanne wanted to join me again tonight. She had the excitement of a child. It looked like rain so Jo located her rain poncho. With flashlights in hand off we went. This time I chose to go down on the rocky beach. As luck would have it we made the right decision. No sooner did we settle ourselves when a soft noise caught our attention. Looking up the beach, barely lit by a sliver of moonlight between thickening clouds, I could see the shape of the hearse and horse traveling along the waters edge. It stopped at what I judged to be one hundred feet away. The cloaked driver descended from the carriage, walked to the waters edge, was met by other cloaked figures shown by the sudden glow of small lanterns. The shadow of a long boat appeared, collecting the hooded figures and departed for Light House Island. Other moving lights could already be seen on the island.

    "Oh how I wish I could be there." I whispered to Jo.

    The better part of an hour passed as we sat in the damp salt air. At last the long boat reappeared. The ghostly figures carried a box, obviously a coffin, to the hearse carefully putting it inside. The boat departed as did the hearse. Joanne and I headed for the cemetery as fast as we could but were hindered by the fog enveloping the land from the sea. By the time we reached the carriage house the reburial had already taken place and another crude cross marked the newly dug plot. The hastily scratched name also matched our original list of lost crew members from the fateful night of so long ago. My wife and I walked back to the house in silence, both contemplating what it must have been like on that night of tragedy.

    Things were now falling into place nicely, but more research was necessary to complete the puzzle. Both of us were exhausted when we reached the house, and without fuss went straight to bed. Believe it or not I had the first restful night since we arrived here.

I welcomed the sunshine the next morning and relaxed with my coffee on the cliff staring at Light House Island. There were a few important things left to be accomplished. A trip to the State Historical Society at the capital, a visit to the Boston archives if necessary, Perhaps even Mount Vernon. Secondly, a more detailed search of old burial records, and third a more accurate family history search of Tyler, Ashcroft and Britton. Last but not least to discover the cache relocated by Thaddeus Tyler and Josiah Britton. These things would also provide for the clearing of shame from the Tyler name.

Pleased with myself and my plan of attack, I walked back to the house. Joanne was up and had breakfast ready. We discussed my plan during our meal and Joanne showed her usual enthusiasm, even adding her own comments. To start with we decided to stay home this day and do some further research right here in the house. There were still many journals and books to sort through.

The decision to stay put was the right one. Although we were busy all day reading, it was relaxing at the same time. We took advantage of the afternoons warming sun and had lunch by the cliff. More reading after lunch proved quite fruitful. My wife was reading what was apparently Thaddeus's last days writings. She found it tucked away behind a row of books in one of the upstairs bedrooms. The entry was dated November 5, 1777. She found the note odd, and brought it to me right away.

"Tea time will tell all." and it was signed with the initials *"TT"*.

I read it a few times but could not make any more sense of it than she. We took an afternoon break and had some iced tea outside to take further advantage of the sun. I let my mind wander while looking towards the ocean. Joanne was jotting notes for a grocery list of things we needed. We finished our refreshments and returned inside. For no particular reason I glanced at the list as my wife put it on the table. The second item was tea, and she had underlined the word. This rang a bell in my head and I knew not why. We went back to our individual readings. Ten minutes later that annoying bell in my head rang again. I called to my wife,

"**J**o, where is that last journal you just showed me ?"

"**R**ight here next to me, why ?" she questioned.

I walked to where she was sitting saying I wanted to see it again. Opening the page she had flagged I read it once more.

*"**T**ea time will tell all." "TT"*

I stared at it a while before I made the connection.

"**T**hat's it.' I said aloud.

"**W**hat's it." asked my startled wife.

"**I** happened to look at your grocery list before and saw that you had underlined the word tea." I started to explain.

"**Y**es." she interrupted, "I used the last of it for our iced tea this afternoon and I didn't want to forget to get some more."

"**W**ell your underlining of tea sort of rang a bell with me and I couldn't figure out why until just now. Look at the journal."

She took the book and read.

"**Y**eah, so ?" she looked at me questioning.

"**T**he word tea." I explained. It's underlined. Not the whole word but just the letter T."

She looked again.

"**Y**ou're right, I didn't really see that till just now."

"**N**or did I." I said. "I think that would be probably anyone's reaction. We read the message as a whole and miss certain nuances. Your underlining tea on your list brought my attention back to the journal."

"You're welcome." she smiled. "We always like to help where we can."

"I guess I'll keep you around for a while." I laughed back.

On a serious note she asked,

"What do you think it means."

"It may be nothing." I replied. "But it may also be a way of telling something. The letter T only was underlined. Let's give this a shot and start looking at things with a T."

I think my wife thought I had really lost it this time from the look she gave me. Suddenly her eyes brightened.

"Downstairs in the library." she stated. "There's a whole row of books in alphabetical order.

"Good girl." I chimed as I ran for the staircase, Jo right behind me.

There was one book under T. "Theorems of Euclid"

"His interests sure were diverse." I thought.

I took the book from the shelf and started thumbing through the pages. Halfway through a small piece of paper fell to the floor. I retrieved it and read it aloud.

Treasures are not always what they seem
They are not given to everyone
But seek the clues and you shall find
Enough to break the ties that bind
When the rising sun falls on the tower
to the stars
Look to the west and between the bars
There marks a spot for those who care
But if not for liberty, then beware
Travel far for those who dare

"This has got to be a clue to where Thaddeus Tyler hid the ship wrecked cargo." I blurted out.

"That's all well and good as a theory, but what does it really mean ?" questioned Joanne.

"It's a riddle we'll have to work out." I replied.

Feeling one step closer to our goal I suggested we relax some more outside before the sun goes down. With no argument from Joanne we went outside to the warmth of the sun.

Our night time sojourns were becoming routine now. We check the carriage house, watch the lights on Light House Island, see the hearse drive by and discover another new grave. Routine but it remained fascinating.

We decided to repeat the beach visit for this night. The chances of a clear night were looking better and I was anxious to see the long boat action again. After dinner we relaxed with more journal reading until it was time to brave the brisk coastal air. The promised clear night allowed a greater visibility on the beach. We even dared to move closer to the action. The long boat was a marvel to see. It was it's true vintage of two hundred plus years. Only once before had I seen such a model at a maritime museum in Vermont. We again followed the hearse at a distance and ended our nights journey checking off another name from the list of lost crew members.

We no longer suffered any anxiety over our ghostly friends. We were without question, fully accepted. The why of it was still a mystery. We comfortably walked back to the house and to a peaceful nights sleep.

We were up at sunrise and on our way to the State Historical Society to learn what we could. It was a most enlightening day. After stopping for dinner we did not arrive back to the estate till well after dark. We chose not to trek out and after a relaxing cognac, hit the pillows early. I was awakened just after midnight by the familiar sound of the hearse on it's way to the carriage house. I just smiled, turned and drifted off to never, never land.

The results of our trip to the capital yielded many more papers, or at least copies of papers, all with bits and pieces of information we felt would help us with the story we were developing. Of extreme interest was a news article telling of the death, by unknown causes of Josiah Britton, just two days after Thaddeus Tyler was found Hanged. Josiah's body was found on the beach below the cliff fronting the Tyler estate. In his pocket was found ten pounds sterling, which was returned to his family who had no idea he had that much money. Rumors were started ,of course, as to how he came to have that much, which cast shadows on his good name also.

Joanne, checking cemetery records at the state uncovered the whereabouts of Thaddeus Tyler's grave. Apparently since he was considered a disgrace to the town, he was interred in a paupers grave yard a few miles outside of town. That, of course explained why we couldn't find any records of him at the local church burial site.

The next four days were spent in some serious genealogy research which proved most exhilarating. Tom Ashcroft, our local bartender friend, was a direct descendant of Edward Ashcroft The same man identified by Thaddeus Tyler. The next major discovery was disturbing, but also pleasing. Josiah Britton, truly was my ancestor.

Our collection of historical papers was growing. Joanne had even suggested that with this kind of information we could probably write a story. I totally dismissed the idea. Besides, who would read such a thing.

Our next step was a visit to Boston and review records of the Revolutionary War. Again our efforts were fruitful. Interspersed with occasional sight seeing, we had a great three day visit. On our return to our haunted estate we checked the cemetery plot behind the carriage house. As expected there were seven more names to check off the list of lost crew members. I felt one thing remained now, and that was to locate the wrecked ships cargo. Joanne and I reread the riddle left by Thaddeus time and time again. Over the course of the next two days we had committed it to memory, but to no avail.

Not giving up, but putting it aside temporarily, I was up before the sun the next day. To give myself a reprieve, I thought I would try my hand at photographing a sunrise again. I found myself on the beach as the first rays broke the horizon. I took shot after shot tracking it's ascent until it no longer looked mood provoking.   Turning back to the house I noticed a reflective glare on the window of the widows walk which in turn highlighted some of the balustrades. I froze in my footsteps. *"That's It."* I thought, *"That's the riddle. The sunrise, the tower, the bars. It has to be it."* I rushed back to the house. I had to give the news of my discovery to Joanne. I found her in the kitchen preparing coffee.

"I'm glad you're back she said excitedly. "I think I figured out the riddle."

"You too." I answered. "I just discovered it while on the beach.."

I don't know who was more excited. We were

like two children at Christmas.

"You first." Joanne volunteered politely.

I didn't argue, I just took the opening and described to her what I saw from the beach. I finished my story and she smiled.

"We must have been hit with the same idea at the same time." She stated. "I was here starting the coffee when a light out the window caught my eye. It lit up a spot on the hill behind us like a glass or mirror reflection. Then I realized it was probably a reflection from the tower windows.

"Then you put it together as I did." I interrupted, Rising sun, tower and bars."

"Yes." she replied, "but I'm not sure what the bars mean."

"The balustrades must be the bars." I said. "Look between the bars. So look at a certain spot only, I'm thinking."

"Of course." Joanne answered excitedly. "But which bars, it only lasted for about ten seconds."

"We'll have to wait until tomorrow, that is if we have sunshine again." I said. "Can you point out approximately where on the hill you saw the spot ?"

She described what and where she saw the spot of light, so we planned to have a look right after breakfast.

While eating it suddenly dawned on me that the sun angle changes constantly from day to day and month to month. That brought up the question of which were being referenced. We ate silently for a while, the wind taken out of our sails. Joanne put her fork down, looked at me and smiled.

"All may not be lost yet. Old Thaddeus was killed on November fifth. All we have to do is ascertain when the ship crashed. That will give us a time window."

"You're right !" I exclaimed, "And that window is most likely sometime in October. Right about now in fact. There's that same feeling. I know we were brought here at this time for a reason."

With our spirit soaring again we hurried through the rest of our breakfast. A half hour later we were trekking up the hill behind the house on our treasure quest. Doubts were being raised now. Two hundred and thirty years can seriously change the topography. The underbrush and rocks made our climb difficult and certainly not able to keep a straight line. Bits and pieces of the rock walls, New England is so famous for, were just one more hindrance. After an hour and a half we gave up disappointed.

Returning to the house we made a more thought out plan for tomorrow. We kept our fingers crossed for a clear day that would provide a good sunshine Not giving up our dream yet, we put it aside for more reading.

The mornings activities in the brisk air, a delicious lunch and constant reading in a comfy chair took it's toll on me. The price was a luxurious nap. I don't remember falling asleep but I guess that's what naps are. Whether I was dreaming or not I can not say for sure but my hooded, ghostly spirit friend was there in the room with me. Standing by the fire place mantle he was tapping on the intricately carved corner piece of the mantle with one bony finger. Aloud thump jogged me awake.

"I'm sorry Tom." Joanne apologized, "I was dozing myself and the book slipped from my hands."

"Did you see him ?" I asked.

"Did I see who ?" Joanne returned my question.

"Our hooded friend from the hearse. He was over

by the, Oh never mind." I cut myself short.   Shaking the
cobwebs from my head I stood up and went to the corner of the
mantle. I began tapping and fingering the carving that had been
shown to me.

"What are you doing ?" My wife asked.

Before I could answer the panel swung open. I
looked at Joanne and said,

"I guess you weren't so crazy after all."

A look of utter surprise appeared on her face as
she arose and joined me at the fire place. I reached in and
pulled out a beautifully designed wooden box. Placing it on the
table, we both sat down and stared at it and each other.

After a long pause I finally extended my hand to
open it. It was filled with papers. I reached for the first one and
read.

> *"November 4, 1777*
> *I have charged my trusted friend,*
> *Josiah Britton, to carry a letter by my hand*
> *to our Commander in Chief. The general*
> *must be aware of the plots by agents of the*
> *Crown against our newly formed Navy.*
> *I have provided Josiah with ten pounds*
> *sterling for the expenses of the journey*
> *to Boston to ensure no complications.*
> *I fear for my life, but must endure for the*
> *cause of freedom. I pray to the Almighty*
> *for his swift and safe journey and return.*
> *I will then - - - .*

That was all.   Obviously interrupted before he

could finish, he did manage to hide it away safely With a renewed pride and a tear in my eye I reached for the next letter. It was a tri-fold paper and of a much higher quality. Upon opening it my hand trembled a bit. The signature on the bottom was that of George Washington. Pausing to compose myself I handed the paper to Joanne. She smiled proudly and proceeded to read it to both of us.

> *"March 26,1776.*
> *My dear friend Thaddeus,*
> *My personal thanks for joining our*
> *cause for freedom. Your providing the*
> *schooner "Mercury" armed and with*
> *crew will not go unrewarded. Like*
> *me, I am aware you are not interested*
> *in personal gain. Running the British*
> *blockades and gaining supplies and arms*
> *for our justifiable cause is reward enough.*
> *Our fight for freedom will be hard won*
> *but we must endure to rid ourselves of*
> *the yoke of oppression upon us. Your*
> *patriotism fills my heart with pride and*
> *confidence we will succeed. My prayers*
> *and good wishes go with you.*
>
> *Your humble servant,*
> *George Washington"*

Now both of us were tear filled as my wife handed me a tissue. The other papers in the box all referenced the acquisition and arming and supplying of the ship.

Another letter from an unknown patriot out lined Washington's plan for this quickly thrown together navy. The Continental Congress was debating the merit of a war of independence and financing an organized navy. George Washington wanted action not words, so he took it upon himself to press into service lightly armed but fast ships which could outrun the larger, heavier warships of the Crown. Thaddeus Tyler was one of those who answered this call. This all took place in the fall of seventeen seventy five.

Joanne and I, now felt we had almost the complete puzzle solved. If the sun co-operated tomorrow we may have the last piece. We replaced the letters in the box and returned it to it's place of safety in the mantle hideaway. We straightened up the mess of our papers and retired to the outside to soak up the last warming rays of sun bidding it to return th next day.

Up before the sun, Joanne monitored the kitchen window while I climbed to the tower to observe the rays through the balustrades. The wait was not long but being as anxious as we were it seemed like hours. The light was suddenly there. I was almost in the way and had to jump aside before I ruined the day. The sun hit the window and bounced a perfectly straight beam centered between two balustrades, then on into the woods up the hill. I zeroed in with the binoculars till the light disappeared as fast as it occurred. The sun was now fully above the horizon and gave no hint of it's important signal.

My wife's observations from the kitchen allowed her time to choose several points of alignment, which she committed to memory. We hurried to put physical identifying marks on the points chosen.

As raring to go as we both were, we decided breakfast was in order first. There was no telling how long we could be on the hill even if we did locate the hiding place.

Collecting what we thought would be necessary, such as water, a small snack, flashlights and above all an ax and shovel, we started on our quest. Almost two hours passed, yet we found not a hint. Deciding to take a break, I sat down on a fallen tree and sipped some water.

"I'm sure this is the spot." Joanne said uneasily. "I double and triple checked my alignment points with the compass and I swear the light fell on this big oak tree. Just look at the diameter of that trunk. How could you miss it."

"That's it." I said in a louder than normal tone. "The big oak tree. It was probably nothing more than a sapling two hundred and thirty years ago. We should be looking on the other side of it."

Joanne was up and around the tree before I even got to my feet. The area of the other side was pretty much the same as where I had been sitting but a distance up the hill, where Joanne was already heading were various rock formations. I struggled to my feet and followed my wife. She had stopped and was checking her compass.

"About here we're still in alignment." she commented.

We separated and began a careful search of the ground. I noticed a rock wall. Not really a wall but more a line of stones of about four feet in length. More checking uncovered another such line. Joanne also found a line of stones. This was spread over an area of about fifty feet. Using these rocks as a sighting line, they all pointed to the same location. At that centralized spot stood a jagged rock out cropping, easily taken for ledge rock. On a whim I started digging where I thought a hollow might have been. I continued for an hour or so with

Joanne relieving me every now and then.

Working the shovel for another ten minutes my persistence paid off. It was like a dream come true. There was a hollow at the base of the jagged rock. Even though dirt and vegetation from over the years did a good job of masking, one could make out an outline of an opening. A large boulder had been rolled in front, with additional smaller ones. With some applied leverage and some broken tree limbs I managed to move the cover stone enough to squeeze in. Joanne followed with both flashlights. The small passage way slanted down slightly which we carefully negotiated. A few yards later we entered a large cavern. At least we could now stand comfortably. The approximately ten by fifteen room was filled with crates. Rather well preserved considering their age. Joanne was the first to uncover one of the crates. It was loaded with musket balls. There were about ten or so more just like it. A dozen long rectangular boxes held two dozen muskets each. There were many barrels of powder. In the back corner were five large wood and metal chests with secure padlocks. I did not want to destroy the locks because I felt they were a part of history.

"**L**et's check the house for keys." I said to Joanne, "Before we try to force them open."

I checked all five chests. The furthest one back had the padlock in place but it was obvious it had been smashed to open it. I looked at my wife and she nodded yes. I slowly removed the hasp from the ring of the trunk and swung the lid open. We were met with a vision of gold coins. It was filled to the top. I had no idea what dollar amount each coin represented but at today's prices of gold I know we had come upon a small fortune. Perhaps even a large fortune if all the other four chests were the same.

Joanne stood there absolutely quiet, a serious

expression upon her face. Slowly a tear started and slid down her cheek. Her mouth opened with the tear and almost in a whisper she said,

"**A**nd this was meant to help our revolution."

Neither of us touched the gold. I closed the lid and replaced the lock.

Joanne turned and exited the cave. I followed silently. We recovered the entrance and added a few branches to help hide our discovery.

We returned to the house without a word between us. It was now mid-afternoon. I poured each of us a glass of wine and we retired to the library. We sipped silently, both staring at the journals on the table.

"**C**hances are." I said softly, "Our local folk have been searching for this booty for over two hundred years, keeping the legend alive."

"**T**hat's why they're so leery regarding strangers." added my wife.

"**N**ow what do we do with all of this, including all of the paper work," I asked rhetorically.

"**G**ood question Sherlock." answered Joanne.

We lingered quietly a while longer, then rising from my chair I said,

"**L**et's take a walk."

Joanne followed already knowing where, as we walked toward the carriage house.

Arriving at the cemetery we counted. There were now fourteen graves, all named on wooden markers with their crude wooden crosses.

We sat on the low rock wall in the dappled

sunlight.

"These are the brave men who were fighting for what would be their new independent country. They have finally returned from the sea to be buried with honor on their hard fought for homeland." I said.

"Then their story should be told and added to the history books." suggested Joanne.

"Exactly." I answered. "Let's find out how we go about setting up this estate and light house as a National Historic site. Perhaps this gold can be used for the preservation of history and the restoration of Thaddeus Tyler and Josiah Britton as the true patriots they were."

Joanne smiled warmly and softly touched my hand.

"And what about our spirit friends ?" she asked.

"I have a feeling they will be satisfied now and return peacefully to their eternal rest." I answered.

We happily headed for the house, had a quiet dinner and a wonderful night's sleep.

~ ~ ~ ~ ~ ~

We did eventually meet with the town folks and told our whole story, without mention of our ghostly friends of course. They were disappointed about not finding the treasure themselves but were very gracious and accepting of our idea of an historical site. After all it would benefit their local economy I did feel bad for Thomas Ashcroft though. To suddenly find out that your ancestor was not a supporter of independence must have been quite a blow. But we did manage to get him involved in the supervision and management of this piece of history.

In the months following we did not find an answer to the last piece of the puzzle. Checking and rechecking the internet and physical addresses of the realtor, such a party never existed. The house had never been rented and our check had never been cashed.

A trust had been set up by the last surviving Tyler only to preserve the house, thus the fencing around the estate. The only gate remote was held by the management company in charge of security who only checked it every month or so.

On our last night at the estate before returning home we saw the hearse one more time. It stopped in front of the house just before midnight. Joanne and I went outside to meet it. The hooded Driver stepped down, faced us and bowed as if in thanks. Then both he and the hearse ceased to exist. They just faded into the mist of the night right before our eyes.

The next day I checked the carriage house and the hearse nor any sign of it was to be seen.

Oh ! By the way going back to the night before;

While we were standing there, not trying to figure it out but just accepting, I noticed the dark hooded cloak on the ground before us. I picked it up and in the pocket of the cloak was ten pounds sterling.

~ ~ ~ ~ ~ ~

The Beginning

IMAGINATION

A Short - Short story

by

K.J.Goss

Imagination

"Grampa, Why are you crazy ?"

"Why am I what ?"He answered his eight year old grandson.

"Crazy, why are you crazy ?" asked the boy innocently.

Suspecting he had said something to upset him, he added, everyone else in the family says you are crazy because you talk about strange things that can't be true."

"Well, how do they know that." the old man asked wanting to know how far this would go. "What do they mean by strange ?"

The grandson now looked confused.

"This was a good thing." Grampa thought. *"At least he's begun to think on his own."*

"Well," the boy said hesitantly, "They say you talk about being in different parts of the world and then they say you never left this small town. **Never in your whole life**." he emphasized.

"Let me tell you a few things, boy." said the gray haired old man. "First of all how do they know I haven't been where I said I was ? They weren't with me."

"But if you never left this town, how could you have been to all those other parts of the world." persisted the boy.

Ahhhh! - Now you have hit upon my secret, my boy."

"What secret." the boy asked even more confused.

"What books have you read lately ?" inquired his

silver bearded, beloved grandfather.

Not knowing what was really happening, Timmy answered innocently,

"I read a story about Huckleberry Finn and right now I'm reading about Tom Swift."

"Ah yes !" said Grampa, "I know them well."

"How can you know them, Grampa, they are just story's in a book.'

"Oh, really ! I didn't know that." answered Grampa, looking surprised. "Is that all they are ? I seem to remember going down a river on a raft."

"Yeah !, Huck did that with Joe, his black friend." said the boy excitedly.

"And I remember making an electrical connection using the lead from a pencil once.

"Yeah ! Tom Swift did the same thing in the book I'm reading now." Timmy interrupted again.

"Is that so !" said Grampa holding back a smile.

"Were you really there ? I mean with Huck and Tom..?" questioned the boy.

"What do you think.?" asked Grampa concentrating on stuffing his pipe.

You could see the young boy pondering this question. The old man let him struggle on a bit as he lit the old pipe. A small white curl of smoke rose from the bowl as he blew out the match.

"Let me ask you another question" said Grampa breaking the silence.

"But I didn't answer the other one yet." the boy said sadly.

"It's okay, boy, you can think about them together. Were you with Huck Finn going down the river ?"

"How could I be, I was on the back porch when I read about it." declared Timmy.

"That's too bad." replied Grampa, blowing a smoke ring and watching it float away.

"What do you mean, Grampa ? Timmy was looking even more confused again.

Grampa got up from the old wicker rocking chair,

saying,

"Come on boy, let's take a walk."

Happily, Timmy followed, going toward the path to the woods. The pair entered the woods with the Sun playing tag with the tree shadows on the trail. They walked silently for a while until they came to a clearing. A few cotton ball clouds could be seen floating over the distant hills. Stopping Grampa asked,

"What do you hear boy ?"

Looking up at the old man, Timmy answered,

"Nothing, everything's quiet."

Not looking down Grampa softly said.,

"Listen carefully."

They both stood there holding hands. A faint humming noise was heard growing stronger as a dragon fly crossed in front of them. Timmy's eyes followed until he saw a large orange and black butterfly going in the opposite direction. He was about to say something when the buzz of a bee around a wild flower distracted him. He watched the bee darting from flower to flower only to be interrupted by the distant caw of two crows calling to one another. Timmy looked off in the distance trying to spot the crows when to his left, the sweet song of a wren drew his attention. The old man was smiling now but he remained silent. The boy was again distracted by a few ribbits and a splash made by the frog in a small pond a few yards in front of them. Still holding hands with his grampa they walked to a fallen tree and sat down. Not a word was spoken. A woodpecker was drumming in a tree overhead followed by the rustle of dried leaves being carried by the soft summer breeze. A snake slithered quietly but could still be heard as he bent the blades of grass as he passed. The deep call of a Raven was answered by the chatter of two squirrels chasing each other up and down trees. The tree tops swayed in the upper wind carrying their melodies across the small meadow.A far away wail of a freight train whistle joined the chorus and the chirping of crickets at regular intervals as if they were regulating the beat of the serenade. This mixture of sounds repeated over and over until it became a symphony to the pair on the log.

"WOW ! Grampa, I never knew quiet could be so noisy, but it's a nice noise isn't it." Timmy said in a smiling whisper.

Grampa said nothing but picked up a few twigs,

bunched them together and tied them with long blades of weed grass. He took another twig, stuck it in the middle so that it stood up straight. On this he hung a leaf from an Oak tree and pretty soon it looked like a sail.

"Come boy." He said and left the log and walked slowly to the pond. Bending down on one knee he launched his raft into the water. Timmy was now on both knees with a longer stick pushing the raft.

"WOW, this is just like Huck Finn." He whispered excitedly, "And this could be the Mississippi River." he added.

A frog jumped off a nearby lily pad and made ripples in the water. Grandfather and Grandson watched their raft bob up and down on the waves till a breeze caught the sail and carried the boat out of reach.

"Where do you think it's going, grampa. ' asked Timmy.

" China perhaps, or maybe to England." replied the happy old man

"Naaaa! Said Timmy, This is the Mississippi. It's going to Mexico."

"I guess it is, Timmy, If you say so, then It's going to Mexico.

The two friends stood and watched the raft sail out of sight, then hand in hand walked along the trail to home occasionally stopping to listen to the music of the silence.

"Let me tell you about the time I took a Journey to the Center of the Earth" said Grampa. "And tomorrow I'll tell you about my adventure Twenty Thousand Leagues Under The Sea."

"Wow! You went to all those places Grampa ?"

"I sure did Timmy."

"You can go to all those places also boy - - - I'll show you how."

The End.

Reflections of a Small Town Santa

by
K.J. Goss

Reflections of a Small Town Santa

Truth or Myth

Did you ever stop to think about the magic of Santa Claus. No, really. I'm not trying to be funny. As adults we all tend to joke about Santa, especially when we are with our peers. "Oh it's just for kids.", "Isn't that cute.", What a sweet picture." Yet down deep inside each of us the magic of Santa still exists. It's a very personal thing and most grown ups try to hide it. It has been my experience over the years to see this magical transformation, particularly in adults, take place. We all have our coveted memories of special moments of our childhood. Once a year we allow these dreams to manifest themselves into reality and we do so without inhibitions. Why? Because we all do it together and the embarrassment that we would feel the rest of the year seems to melt away with the season.

Think about it for a moment. For the most part our personalities take on a change. Temporary though it may be, the change is real. How do I know this? Because I *am* Santa Claus. At least I have been for the last five years in a small town in Vermont. I have seen this change time and time again. Once a year, every year, friends and strangers alike exhibit these symptoms. Warmer and longer greetings, more eye contact, friendlier words, especially when they meet Santa.

Between Santa visits, occasionally I would walk the streets. There is not a car that goes by that doesn't honk it's horn, wave, or smile. Most even open their window to give a personal greeting.

It's the same thing with people that are walking. From toddler to senior citizen, the smile is bigger and warmer. Quite genuine, although some adults would not care to admit it.

The magic is there. You can see it in the eyes. The greeting is filled with sincerity. *The magic is there.*

The faces of the children actually glow because the magic is always there with them.

This is the age when the seed of the magic is planted. (The candy canes I give them doesn't hurt either.)

The teenaged girls become giddy and silly, but you can see the warmth of the magic in their eyes. Teenaged boys are the exception. At least they try to appear that way. When with their peers, they wisecrack a lot. But the eyes tell another story. When they are alone though, their reaction to Santa is much more respectful. They, too will fall prey to the magic of Santa as they mature and let loose their childhood memories.

We adults nurture the growth of this seed in all children. That's what keeps the magic alive. Again, why do we do this? Santa Claus is just a fairy tale figure, or is he? Fairy tale or not, he was very real to us during childhood.

That feeling of warmth and happiness from our youth, we seem to want to preserve for ourselves, so we do it through our children. This makes it okay. After all we are all adults and Santa is just silly kid stuff.

Which brings me to this silly kid stuff. This wonderful silly kid stuff. My own joy and pleasure has been heightened by being Santa Claus. I think down deep inside I'm just a child at heart. I never wanted to grow up and let go. Being Santa has allowed me to hold on a little longer. Listening to the children's requests stirs my own memories, and keeps them alive and even lets them grow. Oh the joy of childhood. We probably all would like to go back to it sometimes. I allow myself to do just that and I do it without regret. Through the vehicle of Santa Claus, I become one of those who sit on my lap. I am real to them because I am real to myself. The doll, the train, the truck the game. Silly stuff? Not really, because this is their world at this stage in life and Santa Claus lives it with them.

I have been fortunate to have a beard that grows out almost pure white and curly. This, of course enhances my own transformation as Santa Claus. My enjoyment of eating has not hurt this transformation either. Getting back to the beard, it really has made the difference with the children. We should never underestimate their young minds. They observe more than we, as adults, give them credit for. For instance, when it comes to Santa's beard, they know real from fake. I have always allowed them to pull on it if they choose to do so. Then I can enjoy the expression changes on their faces and especially in their eyes. You can feel the young minds at work. "Oh maybe he is real because the beard is real."

As far as children's observation of details go, the following is one of my favorites.

The start of the most recent holiday season was highlighted by the tree lighting ceremony in town. Santa arrived by fire truck and approached the darkened tree. With a few special words Santa threw some magic fairy dust in the air and the tree came alive with thousands of lights. The slight breeze of the evening, of course, deposited some of the fairy dust back onto Santa. Later, Santa was in his special chair listening to children's requests. One very cute little girl gave Santa a gift that she had made herself, which he greatly appreciated. Wanting to make the little girl feel special he sent a thank you note in the mail from the North Pole. She received the note and was thrilled. A few days later Santa and this little girl met again at another location. Her mother prompted the girl to thank Santa for the note but she said nothing. After parting she told her mother that I was not the real Santa because there were no sparkles on my belt, which of course was the remnants of fairy dust at our first meeting

Additional Favorites;

Friends of mine have three grandchildren who see Santa each year. Unknown to the children, I receive anecdotes during the year of their behavior, both good and bad. Knowing each of the children as they approach with their requests, I manage to remark about certain misdeeds that occurred during the past year. The youngest of the three has a mind that works with the speed of a rocket. He comes up with explanations and excuses faster than I can relate the stories that I know. As you might have guessed by now, he is totally innocent. It was always someone else's fault. He goes into such detail with his explanations that I have to interrupt him to ask what he would like me to bring. Even as he is walking away, his mouth is going non-stop about his innocense. The next oldest brother had a list so long that I had to tell him it would take two sleighs to carry it all and that it would be unfair to others. His quick reply was "Okay, then just bring me one thing." The oldest of the trio is as close to a model child as one can get, and when I mentioned this to him, he replied that he liked helping others. When asked what he would like for Christmas, he answered, "What ever I wanted to bring would be okay."

Then there was the little girl who wanted a Barbie Doll and some clothes. That was simple enough I thought. When I asked if she thought Mommy would like something she instantly answered, "Oh yes, Mommy wanted a Barbie Doll and a Barbie house." Not knowing when to quit I asked how about Daddy. "Daddy wants a Barbie Doll and clothes and accessories." Was her instant answer. "Don't you think Daddy would like some tools or something for his car." I asked further. "Oh no, He doesn't need that, he needs a Barbie Doll and her things." At that point I finally decided to quit. Giving the candy cane is sort of my cue for dismissal. Thankfully it works, and keeps me out of real trouble.

Sometimes I get too much information from the children, most of which I will not repeat here. A mild example would be, "Mom needs new front teeth." It does , however, show the thoughtfulness and caring on the part of the child.

There's always at least one heartbreaker, "I broke my glasses and we have no money to buy new ones. Could I please bring new glasses for Christmas." How do you answer that and still keep the child's dreams alive.

 ---"I really don't need anything. I just want everyone to be happy."

 ---"My brother doesn't deserve toys, just bring me stuff."

 ---"Bring Mommy and Daddy toys that I like."

 ---"Last year you didn't bring me everything on my list."

 ---"We don't have cookies. Do you like peanut butter?"

 ---"I have a new baby brother, but he's too small for toys so you can give his to me."

 ---"Why do I have to be asleep when you come."

---"I don't have a chimney." said through tears, of course.
---"How do reindeer fly."
---"Why did you come on a fire truck? Where's your reindeer?"
---"Is Rudolph's nose really red?"
---"My uncle is in Iraq. If I send you a letter, will you give it to him?"
---"Your elves don't do a very good job. Last year my toy broke."
---"How many elves do you have?"
---"What do you do when it's not Christmas?"
---"Why are you so fat?"
---"Do you really take toys away if I'm not good?"
---"My brother cries all the time, are you still going to bring him stuff?"

The list goes on and on. There are too many to remember.

~ ~ ~ ~ ~ ~

Visiting the hospital and senior care facilities is always a pleasure. Here is where you can see the magic of Santa Claus come alive. The smiles it brings, the memories it stirs, even if only for that fleeting moment. To listen to the stories they tell of their childhood shows me that Santa does exist. Their eyes are like a movie screen as they drift back in time. What ever discomfort or affliction they suffer from washes away with these memories. They are actually young once more. The biggest benefactor of these transitions is, I believe, Santa, or me actually. Being privileged to se these personal vignettes of another's world confirms for me that Santa does exist. How can he not?

Call me crazy or melancholy if you want, but Santa is alive and well. Some try to suppress this fact, but I say throw away those inhibitions and let him live in you as he does in me.

Merry Christmas
Santa Claus

Travel

A short story
by
K.J.Goss

Travel

The woman walked into the sun room that opened onto the garden. She saw her Father sitting in his favorite rocker facing the windows. It was late afternoon and she had just dropped by on her way home from work to check on him. As she drew closer to the chair she noticed a familiar trance like state on her Father's face. *"Oh no, not again."* she thought. She spoke quietly so as not to startle him.

"**D**ad." She paused, trying again slightly louder

"**D**ad." She waited patiently for a response before she tried for a third time. This time she accompanied her voice with a gentle touch on his shoulder.

"**D**ad." she repeated.

The seventy eight year old man slowly turned to his daughter with a smile of recognition.

"Oh, Hi Shirley, how's my favorite little Miss Temple today." She was named after Shirley Temple, whose movies her father liked to watch.

Shirley answered with concern in her voice.

"**A**re you okay Dad ?"

"**O**f course I'm okay, why wouldn't I be."

"**W**ell you seemed to be in a trance again when I came in."

"Nonsense." her father returned, "I was just visiting an old friend of mine in Atlanta. We were in the service together.

You remember I told you about my Cuban friend. We were just reminiscing about old times over a cold beer.”

“Cut it out Dad, you know I don’t like it when you talk like that. I’m very concerned about your...” She paused a moment to find the right word, “health.” she added.

Looking directly at his daughter and smiling, the father said,

“You mean my mental health.”

Feeling slightly embarrassed Shirley was quick to answer,

“I didn’t say that. I’m just concerned about you that’s all. You know I care about you but lately you seem to zone out more and more all the time.”

“Call it what you will, Shirl, but I’m just visiting friends and going to a few places I haven’t been before.”

“But Dad you haven’t been any where except this house in month’s. Why do you insist on talking like that. It’s just wishful thinking, your dreaming these things. I’ve read that dreams can sometimes seem real if you want to believe in them.”

The elder man smiled again and said,

“I feel sorry for you Shirl. You put too much drama into life and take it too seriously. You’ve got to learn to lighten up a little.”

Hurt and annoyed by his statement, the daughter looked at her father and in an angry tone stated that no matter what he said she was going to make an appointment with a doctor.

“That will be just fine.” answered her father, “Then perhaps you’ll be convinced that I’m perfectly alright. Let me know when and I’ll be ready.”

Quite angry and frustrated at this point Shirley stormed out of the room replying,

“You can count on it.”

She checked with the housekeeper then left the house. As she walked to her car she regretted having sounded off at her father. She really loved him but was totally frustrated with his travel stories, and his attitude about them.

With some insistence she managed an appointment

with his doctor three days hence. She notified the housekeeper of this and decided not to see her father until that time.

On the designated day she arrived to find her father smiling and ready. He gave no hint that there had been a rift between them. He willingly accompanied her to the car. On the ride to the doctor's he spoke of having seen some of the Anasazi ruins in the four corners area of the south west just the day before. He thought she would enjoy them also if she could get the time off and make the trip. Shirley chose to say nothing out loud but was thinking that he was really living in a fantasy land now.

The doctor's visit was fruitless. Her Father checked out to be physically in perfect health. In her private consultation with the doctor, he saw nothing wrong in a little harmless daydreaming. She tried to convince the doctor that she felt that this was more serious than just a little harmless daydreaming, that her father actually believed he was at these locations he dreamed about. Still not convinced of anything serious the doctor dismissed her concern as just part of the aging process and told her to not get so upset. Still confused and with no apparent answers she bid good day to the doctor and joined her Father in the waiting room.. She could tell right away he was zoned out again. She went through the usual three call process to bring him back to reality. As soon as eye contact was reestablished he said

"See, didn't I tell you I was just fine. Fit as a fiddle, just like I've always been. Yes sir fit as a fiddle."

"Yes Dad, in perfect *physical* shape." Shirley answered snidely quiet.

Her father picked up on her reference or lack of reference to his mental condition but chose to ignore it. *"She will learn someday."* He thought.

Walking back to the car she asked her father,

"And where were you this time, visiting China."

"Oh dear me no." he replied, "I was in DC with my cousin Pat and her husband. The cherry blossoms are just wonderful this year. By the way, Pat says hello."

Upset again Shirley chose to change the subject and spoke of her job and what was new in town. As they arrived home her father suggested she stay for dinner and she accepted.

After dinner she helped the housekeeper with the

dishes while Dad retired to the den with a glass of cognac. As Shirley was about to rejoin her father in the den the phone rang. She answered it to find cousin Pat on the other end of the line.
She was calling to make sure her father had made it home alright. Pat mentioned how much they enjoyed his visit and how beautiful the Cherry blossoms were this year. Before Shirley could inquire any further about her Father's visit Pat said she had to go and hung up. Totally confused now she remained by the phone trying to sort things out in her mind. She did not know how long she was there when the housekeeper alerted her that her father was calling from the den. Shirley entered the den only to find her father shivering.
        "Could you get me a blanket ?" he asked, "I'm afraid I stayed out in the cold too long.
        "But it's not cold Dad. It's spring and right now it's about sixty degrees outside."
        "Oh I wasn't talking about here, Shirley, I was just up in the Canadian Rockies, and I really wasn't dressed properly."
        She could see he was physically shaking as she covered him with a comforter. She then poured him another cognac, which he drank right down. He started rocking back and forth now while mumbling,
        "So cold, So cold."
        His voice seemed to be growing weaker. Shirley rushed to the phone to call the doctor. As concerned now as she was the doctor said he was on his way. When she returned to the den she found her father huddled in the comforter with only his face visible still moaning,

        "So cold, So cold."
        She held him close in her arms until the doctor arrived. After a preliminary exam he determined her father was suffering from exposure. An ambulance was called but exposure and exhaustion overcame the elder man before it arrived. He passed away in his daughter's arms, his final words to her,

"I love you."

Shirley mentioned his visit to the Rockies to the doctor. He looked at her but did not respond, his mind wandering through the events before him.

The funeral a few weeks now behind her, Shirley sat in her father's den going through a box of her father's papers she found in a lower, locked desk drawer. These were all receipts of airline tickets, car rentals and small souvenirs, each related to a specific "*DREAM*" her father had spoken of.

The dreams she had dismissed as hallucinations.

The End.

Big Foot

by
K.J. Goss

Big Foot

It had been raining for three days now. It was muddy. It was warm and I was miserable. Being a part time feature writer for a small wildlife magazine afforded me the advantage of pursuing my photography. I aspired to no special venue. I photographed everything and anything that caught my eye. If it moved me with that warm and special feeling inside I endeavored to capture it on film. I know digital is the fast track in the industry, but I'm old fashioned enough to still want to create moods with light and lens. Create being the operative word, from the heart and head. All that aside. I had the time for my passion but not the weather so I was feeling sorry for myself.

Now to top it off, I'm in my truck driving through the muddy rain because my editor called with a special assignment.

"You're going to love this one. It should really peak your interest, especially photographically." said he.

The only real reason I'm on my way there now is that my bank account developed a hole in the bottom.

"I've got to learn to keep better tabs on my finances." I said to myself.

My miserable drive ended temporarily and I was trudging up the stairs to my editor's second floor office. The niceties of greetings being dispensed with, I just asked bluntly,

"Okay, let's have it."

Tom, my editor, said with a half smile,

"Good morning to you also. Yes thank you I'm having a wonderful day."

I looked at him and laughed.

"You're right, I'm sorry. It's the rain that's getting me down."

"Well perhaps we can arrange for a change of climate." he said smiling.

"Come again." I answered, my interest being peaked.

"There's been another siting." He paused staring directly at me, "of Big Foot."

"Where this time." I asked with the annoyance not hidden in my voice.

"Oregon- - - - - again, where there have been many others over the years." Tom continued.

"When are people going to give up this crap." I half muttered.

Hesitating before I spoke again, I was thinking this could be a great opportunity for an expense paid trip to the northwest. It would give me the chance to photograph some new territory and who knows I might even find a decent story, other than Big Foot. I poured myself a cup of coffee without

asking as I continued to muddle over ideas that were running through my head. Tom sat quietly at his desk, doodling on a scratch pad, giving me my time. And I took my time. A whole cup of coffee worth. Draining the final drop from the mug, I sat in the nearest chair, looked at Tom and asked matter of factly,

"Okay, where am I going."

Without looking at me, Tom reached for an envelope on his desk, stretched his arm out in my direction saying,

"It's all here. Plane tickets, truck rental and cash."

"You S.O.B." I said half laughing. "How did you know I would - - - - -."

I was cut off mid sentence with,

"Close the door on your way out."

I had been politely dismissed.

"Oh well." I thought, *"I could use the cash."*

I walked down the hall to the elevator, pushed the down button and descended to the basement archives. Some preliminary research wouldn't hurt. Between the computer and some old index card files I spent about twenty minutes gathering information. There was more here than I thought there would be. A few more clicks on the computer mouse brought up an article I really did not want to see although I half expected it.

"Main stream scientific consensus does not support the existence of megafauna cryptids such as Big Foot because of the improbably large numbers necessary to maintain a breeding population and because climate and food supply issues would make such purported creatures survival in reported habitats unlikely."

There it was in black and white.

"I really am wasting my time." I thought, *"But then again I could use a road trip. Anything to get away from this weather."*

I collected my notes and headed for home.

I flipped on the kitchen light, dumped the papers on the table and went to dry off. I returned to the kitchen, grabbed a beer and a cold chicken leg from the fridge, sat and opened the envelope Tom had given me. Flight reservations, tomorrow, eleven A.M., Burlington to Eugene, Oregon, via Chicago, twenty minute layover at O'Hare. Not really too much time but because of what I do to earn a buck I always have a bag packed. One for clothes and one for my equipment. The latter being more important to me., I carefully double checked that one first. I added a few more film rolls from the freezer and was all set.

The next day it was still raining but I made my flight

on time in spite of it. Once we were airborne, I settled back and watched the miles sail by. The houses were specs, the rivers like sewing thread thrown on a rug. Except for the larger specs of cities, human life was undetectable.

"Wouldn't that be nice." I thought.

I drifted off dreaming of a land without people. The next thing I knew it was fasten your seatbelt time. We touched down at O"Hare and I ran for my connecting flight. I made it just in time, stowed my gear and settled back. Once again airborne I pulled out my stack of notes for review, still not convinced that Big Foot even existed.

There were many more sightings than I imagined. They were all over North America, but most prevalent in California and the northwest. They seemed to follow the Cascade range, which runs from California right up through Washington into Canada. The sighting dates ran a full range of years. Some as early as the nineteen twenty's. Who even knows of record keeping prior to that. I found my interest starting to grow in spite of my earlier attitude.

Reading the pages of descriptions, I started drawing a mental image. These descriptions varied somewhat, but the similarities were many. Six to ten feet tall, three to five hundred pounds, reddish brown hair covering most of the body. A few descriptions were slightly more scientific. They were listed as an apelike - bipedal humanoid. One very common theme among all of this was a strong, unpleasant odor.

"This sure does not describe someone I want to meet in a dark ally." I thought.

Viewing a map of the west coast, concentrating on the northwest, I suddenly realized this was mid September. The area I was to go had elevations of upwards of ten thousand feet. Dummy that I was I only packed summer clothes.

Note to myself, buy winter clothes and camping equipment.

"**T**his may turn out to be a fun trip after all." I said quietly, drawing the attention of my fellow passenger. "Sorry." I said, "Just thinking out loud."

He smiled and went back to his newspaper.

~ ~ ~ ~ ~ ~

We landed at Eugene, and by the time I retrieved my luggage and checked out a four wheel drive it was getting dark, so I checked into the nearest motel that had a restaurant and bar. After dinner and a few beers I retired to my room. The TV was the usual wasteland so I reviewed the maps again, watched the news and closed my eyes for the night.

Barely sunup found me already on route 126. It was proving to be a good day. A clear sky with temperatures slowly climbing. More than an hour passed when I finally reached the junction of route 242. Bearing right I followed 242 for another twenty minutes or so aware that I was climbing all the time. An area called Proxy Falls came into view which would have to be my destination for now.

I parked my rig and stretched my legs. There in front of me were the Three Sisters. Mountain peaks of ten thousand feet plus. A mantle of white crowned all three peaks.

Suddenly becoming aware of my surroundings, there were more people here than I anticipated. I wondered what was going on. Then I remembered it was Friday. With the weekend ahead, these were mostly thrill seekers come to catch a glimpse of Big Foot. This was not going to be a fun time. I appeased myself by looking at the beauty of the Sisters and the forest before me.

More people were arriving and groups were gathering. Curiosity got the better of me, so I wandered over to the closest group to listen to the man standing on the tailgate of his truck. It seems they were organizing scouting parties and communication signals. Quietly listening a while longer they were intent on capturing this thing. These people were from organized clubs that had been pursuing the Big Foot for years.

Identifying myself and my magazine won their favor and I was asked to join them so I could record the moment. I declined saying I was just here to do a follow up story and get a few pictures of the terrain. I was then seriously warned not to wander around alone. It was too dangerous. This creature was a wild beast that killed. No body was safe. It had to be destroyed.

I still declined their invitation to join with them and eventually wandered back to my own truck. I had this feeling in the back of my mind, that the danger warning was not necessarily given because of the creature.

I was starting to feel sorry for this thing, what ever it was and if it did exist. I lost myself in preparing for my day's hike. I changed into my favorite hiking boots and retrieved my special multi pocketed camera vest from my duffle bag. While I was loading the pockets with what I thought I would need for the day, three men approached me. I had a strange tingle on the back of my neck.

"Rather ornery looking." I thought, *"and very impressed with themselves."*

Their intent was obvious. Stay out of their way or else.

"So my original feelings about these guy's was right." I thought. I was polite but cold toward them when I assured them in no way would I jeopardize their mission. I continued looking directly at them until they turned and walked away. They were muttering quietly but I was unable to make out what they were saying.

I breathed a sigh of relief at being alone again. This trip was becoming more interesting all the time. I set up the tripod and captured a few shots of the Sisters. My ruse worked and I had the expected results. The group became disinterested in me and I guess having finished their plans, left for their search. I fiddled around with my camera a while longer to give me more space. I also took a GPS reading of the truck. A half hour later I gathered my camera equipment, locked the truck and started for the woods in a totally different direction from the mob.

The lower part of the climb was easy, but the deeper I went into the forest, the steeper the terrain. I was in no rush, so I stopped periodically. Not just to rest, but I managed to get a few shots of some very interesting flora. I wandered as I climbed and before long it was mid-afternoon. I grabbed a granola energy bar from my vest pocket. I really hate these things, but they're supposed to be good for you, so I'm told. At least they're easy to carry. I sat there not enjoying my energy bar when I heard two rifle shots to the north of me. That was the direction the local mob had gone this morning. This bothered me. If there was such a creature out there, why did they want to capture it ? Even worse why would they want to kill it ?

Because of the late hour there would be no time to head in the direction of the gun shots. I made my way back down the hill to the truck.

"Thank goodness for GPS." I said aloud.

I reached the truck about a half hour before actual sunset. I set up my tripod again and managed a few shots of the red ball disappearing. The local gentry were also returning, obvious by their loud joking and laughter. They looked at me snickering, then one by one departed.

Actually it was quite comforting being alone in the shadows of these three majestic mountain peaks. This area, according to the map, was called the "Three Sisters Wilderness Area." Judging by today's sojourn up the south Sister, A wilderness it is.

A park ranger pulled into the parking area. I told him who I was and showed my ID and asked about staying the night. He indicated that it would be okay but no fires. We agreed and he also recommended a good eatery a few miles down the road.

I had a tasty beef stew at the diner, then back to my sleeping bag. The day was starting to catch up with me and I was asleep before I knew it.

~ ~ ~ ~ ~ ~

Awake just before sunrise, back to the diner for a good hearty breakfast and returned to the parking area. I was in luck, none of the locals showed yet. I quickly gathered my equipment and off I went. This time I chose the middle Sister to climb. I believe that was where the shots came from yesterday. I was well into my climb and still had not heard any sound from the parking lot.

"A good thing." I thought, *"The more time I had before the locals intruded, the better."*

The climb was becoming more difficult. There was less and less open or flat areas. I must admit the photo op's were numerous and I took advantage of as many as I could. So much so that I almost forgot what I came for.

I was soon reminded though when I heard a distant scream. Not like a human voice. Not like any animal I ever heard, but definitely a roar of something disturbed. I listened quietly. A rifle shot rang out from a much lower elevation followed by that same weird sound. Only this time it was closer. I stood up, gathered my junk, hung the camera strap around my neck and moved toward the roar. I continued climbing as I did so. My strategy paid off. I could hear movement coming my way. It was definitely something or someone moving but it was ever so quiet. Almost imperceptible. We were on an intersecting course. I was now also hearing voices. The locals obviously were more used to this mountain than I was. I could distinguish one voice from the rest. It was of the same man that had quietly threatened me. Apparently he liked to intimidate everybody, his words were quite clear now,

"**C**ome on you guys, we almost got him now. We gotta kill this thing before he murders us all. Remember it already got one of my cows. Next it will be our kids, then us."

He had everyone fired up. It was like an old fashioned western lynch mob, one leader and a bunch of sheep like followers.

I was suddenly startled by a noise through the underbrush not twenty yards from me. A gorilla like shape but standing erect. At first glimpse I guesstimated it to be about seven feet tall. My mind was going a mile a minute in every which direction. This creature, this thing, this person halted and looked directly at me. Neither of us moved for what seemed like an eternity. Slowly I collected my wits and reached for my camera. Not wanting to move too fast, I brought my right hand to the shutter release and pushed ever so slowly. The camera was still hanging down by the strap and was about chest level. It seemed to be pointing in the right direction. I just prayed that luck was still with me.

A low grunt emanated from my unexpected visitor. Sort of like the character from Star Wars, what's his name - - - - - - Chewbacca, or something like that.

My eyes stayed locked with his. I no longer considered this a creature. To me he was definitely a humanoid. I felt a compassion I had not known before. I felt the need to communicate with him. But how ?

He started to move. Not toward me, but along the line he had been traveling. I moved also, not toward him but parallel. I was moving backwards so I could sustain eye contact. With my left hand I was slowly moving the camera up to my eye. I was bound and determined to get a good picture. I kept moving backward keeping pace with my new acquaintance. I could hear voices of the chase mob getting closer. Then it happened, my next step was on to nothing. I was falling. Sudden pain shot through my body. Then- - -
- - - - -.?

~ ~ ~ ~ ~ ~

Static, fuzziness, incomprehensible noise. The far away echo of Chewbacca talking to me. I could see but shadows before me.   All went dark.

Shadows, there were shadows again. I was straining to see but the fuzzy veil was reluctant to part. Dark and light were playing an alternating game with my mind. I gave up trying and with that the clarity of vision, ever so slowly returned. The shadows were taking on a more definitive shape. Finally, after what must have been forever, my mind cleared although my vision still seemed faint. Then I realized it was dark. It was night. A half moon shed some light but only enough to make out shadows. There were two shadows before me. My bare leg was being bathed with mud and leaves. My head was wrapped in wet leaves.

I was with them, "Big Foot." Now there were two of them. I was not a captive, they were caring for me. I tried to move and felt pain. My trying to move startled the one that was tending my leg. He jumped up and away from me. I apologized although I knew he would not understand me. The weak light of the moon caught the shadowy figure before me. He was a she. Even with the hair covered bodies, the breasts were unmistakable. This was definitely a female. I judged her to be about six and a half feet tall. I relaxed a bit, my mind swirling with questions and she resumed tending my wound. I drifted off to a restless sleep.

Awakened again with a not so gentle nudge, I opened my eyes to daylight. Judging from the angle of the shadows it was probably mid morning. The female handed me a leaf full of water which I gladly drank. Yuucckk ! It was not just water, there was something else mixed with it. The taste and smell was utterly horrible. I tried to push it away. It was rather forcefully pushed back. I thought better of arguing, closed my eyes and drank.

"My God, that was disgusting." I thought.

Looking around I saw we were in a natural overhang in the side of a rock out crop. Not really a cave, but enough to give shelter from the elements.

I was lying on a bed of pine needles, my back pack not far from me and I discovered my camera was still strapped around my neck. Seeing the camera brought back the memory of what happened. Not paying attention to where I was walking I stepped off the edge of a small precipice. I later discovered I fell about twenty five or thirty feet.

The two humanoids were communicating, not with words so much, but with hand signals and a kind of groan or growl. I was studying their faces which had slightly less hair than their bodies. They were definitely not like me, nor were they totally gorilla like. They had a pronounced brow ridge and low set forehead but the nose and mouth were more Neanderthal than ape like. I'm no anthropologist but this was almost like the missing link the scientists were always talking about.

I was shaken from my mind blowing questions by the sound of what I thought was a baby. The female went to a small niche in the rock side and withdrew a small short haired bundle. It <u>was </u>a baby. It clung to the mother just as chimps do. The baby instantly found a breast to suckle. My mind was whirling again. I was witnessing what scientists have been searching for, for centuries. This was a prehistoric family unit in the year two thousand nine.

I wanted to get up and started to when both adults looked at me, and made their growling noise. The female came towards me and again gave me a leaf full of liquid to drink. This time I did not hesitate. I just drank. It dawned on me that what ever was in the drink worked. I felt much less pain and could feel the strength returning to my body. I thanked her. Her features up close were not gorilla like, nor were the baby's She pushed me back down again, not quite as hard this time. I started to resist but felt myself drifting to la-la land again. When I awoke it was dark. Some crunchy nut like substance was pushed into my mouth followed by my not so favorite drink. Good night again.

It was the sun in my eyes that awakened me this time. I was totally out from under the overhang and propped up in a half sitting position against a rock. I felt amazingly well. There was no pain in my leg. Just a slight ache. I was still black and blue but I couldn't believe the pain was gone.

Mama was feeding her baby under the overhang. The male was chewing on a piece of raw meat. I had no idea what kind of animal he was eating. He offered me a piece which I declined. I wasn't that hungry yet.

These were intelligent creatures, no college graduates, but us about a million years ago. I could almost feel the trust between us. They obviously have seen a lot more of us than we of them.

I slowly and carefully raised myself to a standing position. Neither of them tried to stop me. I still could not believe how good I felt. I tried walking and that wasn't bad either. Feeling quite pleased with myself I retrieved my back pack and proceeded to set up my tripod. The two looked on with curiosity but did not appear to be afraid. As I finished attaching the camera to the tripod, the male made a very low growl. Both he and the female froze. The baby was put to the breast lest he should cry out. A few minutes or so passed in total silence.

I could hear it now. Voices. The locals were on the prowl again. I turned to my new friends and hand motioned them to hide under the overhang. It did not take too much to convince them. It was quite obvious they were frightened. I collected some downed tree branches and brush and did the best I could to camouflage the overhang. I hurried back to the tripod and camera. I could hear our visitors crashing through the brush now.

"They would make terrible hunters." I said aloud quietly.

Pretending to be concentrating on my camera viewer as if setting up for a picture, I half ignored the group as they stepped into the small clearing.

"Still taken your fancy piches ?" the leader remarked.

"I really don't like that guy." went through my mind.

"Yeah." I answered. "I have to bring something back to the magazine. I haven't seen anything ease."

"You didn't see that smelly animal killer come by here did ya." asked one of the other men.

"If I did, do you think I'd still be standing here." I said.

The four laughed about my answer.

One of them remarked, Naa, I spose not. You'd probably be back at your truck by now, drivin away."

They all laughed at this again. They turned and crashed away through the woods as noisily as they came, still making snide remarks about me. I continued fussing with the camera for a while just to make sure they were really gone. They truly weren't very observant. Me standing there with my pant leg ripped and my leg and head all bruised. Oh well, one track minds I guess. Their noise finally drifted away.

I returned to the shelter and removed the makeshift blind. The pair were huddled with the baby as far back as they could. The male had a large club in one hand and a rock in the other. My heart went out to them, having to live their whole life this way. They relaxed somewhat, knowing the others were gone.

~ ~ ~ ~ ~ ~

While the female tended to the baby the male was gathering things together. Large leaves, certain types of plants and roots and lengths of vine. It was as if they were planning to move. I busied myself with the camera, turning towards them and shot quite a few pictures.

"The world of science will be turning on it's head when they see these." I was thinking.

I finished that roll of film. Preparing to change film I noticed my large male friend getting ready to leave. I looked questioningly at him. As an answer he gave one of his low growls and put his hand to his mouth as if eating something.

He turned and bounded away silently. The female carried on with the baby as if I weren't even there. I guess some would have taken that as a sign of being ignored. I did not look at it that way. Actually I was quite comforted by the fact that I had their trust.

My thoughts wandered a bit. How many more of their species might there be ? Are there any more in this area ? How wide a range do they travel ? How far does their ancestry go ? How have they managed to go so long without being detected ? I don't mean these individual sightings either. Then again, if they were discovered earlier their innocense and way of life would most certainly have been destroyed. Just as we supposed civilized peoples destroyed the Native American cultures in both North and South America.

Destroyed ! All of a sudden the word destroyed rang a bell.

The local creature hunters were still at lodge. I should have been the one to go for food. If my large male companion is spotted again they will, in their ignorance try to destroy him. No sooner had these thoughts passed through my mind when two rifle shots echoed across the valley below. Twenty seconds later there was a third. My heart was in my mouth. I turned to the female. Fear filled her face and eyes as she clutched the baby close to her bosom. I indicated for her to get under cover of the overhang. She did as I directed without hesitation. I recovered the hideaway with the branches.

I stayed by my camera to continue my facade should it become necessary. Almost an hour went by without another sound. Even the forest was silent. The silence and waiting were frightening.

The female, quietly getting my attention was pointing in the direction her partner left.

"That keen hearing." I thought, *"Was one way that has helped them survive this long."*

A few more minutes of silence, which seemed like hours, culminated with the appearance of my large friend. He was bleeding, although it did not appear to bother him. He joined his mate under the overhang. You could feel the strong bond between them.

He let me look at his wound. A bullet had pierced his left triceps going clear through and catching the rear part of the rib cage. The wound was clean. The bullet was no where to be found. It had gone in and out. The female was already mixing up what appeared to be the same stuff she used on me. I then noticed some blood on his left leg. Upon further examination there was a hole in his left calf muscle. There too, the bullet had traveled clear through. Luckily, the locals were far from being expert marksmen. The female finished her first aid and was giving him my not so favorite drink. He sat back and rested. I guess because of his size he was not in la-la land as I was , but he did rest. I rebuilt the blind again on the overhang, just in case, then resumed my vigil by the camera.

I was angry and didn't know why. It wasn't just the ignorance of the four locals. I think I was feeling the ignorance and intolerance of the whole world. I felt frustrated because I knew there was not a damn thing I could do about any of it.

Suddenly I was feeling a chill. The wind was picking up and the clouds were thickening. The temperature was dropping fast. I figured this could be a good thing for my large friends. The locals would probably give up and head for the nearest gin mill. By now it was late afternoon. It would be dark soon, and there seemed to be no further disturbance from the forest, so I joined the others at the overhang.

The male was on his feet as if nothing had ever happened to him.

"Boy ! Would I like to bottle that miracle cure they use."

The pair were gathering up the few possessions they had. I knew this was good bye. My seven foot friend looked at me with his dark, deep set eyes as he pointed to the northern most Sister. I understood that's where they were going.

"Pretty desolate up there." I thought, "But probably a lot safer for them."

Our eyes still engaged, I could see a gentleness there that normally was well masked. He lay his large hand on my shoulder. That massage said it all. He then turned to go, followed by mother and child. As the latter passed me she hesitated a moment. I reached up and gently stroked her cheek, then touched the baby's head. I think I even detected a smile from her. She continued after the male, and all three disappeared silently into the forest. I wanted to go with them but thought better of it. It wouldn't have worked for either of us and I think we both instinctively knew that.

I starred at the forest for quite awhile.
It started snowing.

~ ~ ~ ~ ~ ~

I made it down to my truck, with the help of a flashlight, before it was totally dark. Just as I thought, mine was the only vehicle left in the parking lot. The park ranger pulled in as I finished packing up my things in the truck. We exchanged pleasantries and I told him thanks and that I was heading back east tomorrow. As I opened the door to get into the truck I said,
"**Oh** by the way, I didn't think you were allowed firearms in a state or federal park."
He indicated that was so.
"**Well** for your information," I continued, "I heard quite a few shots both yesterday and today."
He seemed upset at this and promised to look into it. We said our good byes and I started back for Eugene. I found a motel for the night and was lucky enough to catch a flight home the next day.

~ ~ ~ ~ ~ ~

We took off from Eugene and headed east over the Three Sisters. I looked down as we crossed and said a final fair well.

During the whole flight home my mind was a non stop review of what transpired over the last few days. I had been privy to something no man would probably ever see again. The story, the book, the TV appearances would be endless. I would be set for life.
It was early evening by the time I got home and I was tired from the last few days. I grabbed a cold piece of chicken and

a beer from the fridge and went straight for the bed.

Up before sunrise, I showered and took off for the magazine office. I couldn't believe it was still raining. I went to the dark room. I couldn't wait to process the film. As I held the film in my hand I again reviewed in my mind what had happened this past week. Mainly what I had learned and what I had felt, especially when my tall friend put his hand on my shoulder. Making a promise to myself never to divulge what I saw, I unwrapped the film exposing it to the overhead light. Feeling a certain satisfaction, I processed the other two rolls which turned out to be some pretty great pictures of the valley between the two northern Sisters.

By the time I finished, Tom was in his office. He looked up as I entered without knocking.

"Okay, what did you get." he asked anxiously.

I threw the proofs of the processed film on his desk.

"That's it ! Some pretty pictures. I could get them here." he commented, not too happily.

I could write a nice accompanying story if you want." I answered.

Further annoyed he questioned again,

"What about this Big Foot guy.

"Just a lot of local mumbo jumbo." I answered. "I told you there was nothing to it. No one saw anything. I even checked with the local park rangers."

Tom looked at me with a serious scowl on his face.

"I need some rest so I will be home if you need me."

I closed the office door behind me.

The End

"Quiet"

by
K.J.Goss

Did you ever stand still
And listen to the quiet of the forest
Quiet is anything but
You have to really listen to hear it
Which most of us do not
Quiet is unlike artificial noise
Which jangles the nerves and disturbs our poise
The noise of quiet can calm those nerves
Balance our mind, restore our poise
We accept man made noise as a norm of life
But do we realize It's gift of strife
It works on our body, our minds and our soul
It corrupts our rhythm, disrupts our goals
The noise of true quiet is a thing to behold
To hear it's beauty is like food for the soul
But listen you must to hear it at all
As loud as it is, most do not recall
The whisper of wind thru the limbs of the trees
The rush of the water over stones in the brook
Both caused by the flap of the butterfly wing
As it glides thru the air like a song that we sing
The calm that it brings is peace to the mind
The tension of the body begins to unwind
The longer we listen the more that we hear
The longer we listen the lessor our fear
It is truly stronger than man and his clatter
But you must truly listen to really make it matter
Open your mind, your heart and your soul
Let the noise in so you may reach your goal
So listen you must to the noise of quiet
It's good for the soul and your spiritual diet

K.J.G.

The Dead Living Mummy

by

K.J. Goss

The Dead Living Mummy

Chapter 1

I had always read about and was told how hot and miserable the Yucatan could be but I was still not prepared for what I was facing now. Coming from New England we had a few hot spells but they never lasted very long. I have been here at the Hotel Juarez for two days now and I don't think the thermometer has varied by more than one degree, night or day. I just wasn't used to one hundred and six degree readings with what seemed like four hundred percent humidity, but a job is a job and I had been waiting for just such an opportunity like this for a long time.

As an outdoor and wildlife photographer this was like a dream come true. For a crack at ancient history Eric Dexter could put up with a little discomfort. I was to meet with Frank Thurber, an archeologist from the University of Pa., who had just recently uncovered what could be another lost Mayan city.

I was anxious to get moving but there was a message waiting for me when I arrived informing me that Frank would be delayed a few days. I managed to get my film supply into the hotels's cooler which gave me one less worry, at least for the time being. Surprisingly the hotel food was quite good and the beer was cold.

The town of Oxtec was small, with two rundown

cafe's, a larger, what appeared to be a general store, and sundry souvenir
shops to capture the tourist dollars. In other words, there was nothing to do. I had checked my equipment countless times, so much so that I was afraid I was going to wear it out before I actually got to use it.

One of the few pleasures I discovered was an afternoon siesta. It was a small but pleasant escape from the oppressive heat of the afternoon. There was no air conditioning in the room but I did have a slow moving fan directly over the bed. That coupled with stripping to my shorts made the afternoon tolerable.

Chapter 2

It was day number four at the Juarez Hotel when I finally saw Frank Thurber checking in at the lobby desk. Boy, was I happy to see him. We exchanged pleasantries and he apologized for his delay. He finished signing in and I followed him to his room for a beer and he went right to outlining his plans and what equipment we would need, at the same time trying to keep it minimal because of weight restrictions. Having previously been here he already had a guide and porters lined up. Frank figured we only needed a day to get everything together, then we would be on our way. That was wonderful news to my ears. I was tired of watching the grass grow.

We spent the rest of the day acquiring the necessary supplies, food and equipment. The day was topped off with a great dinner, a few glasses of wine then we headed for our respective rooms in hopes of a full nights rest.

Chapter 3

Full sun, mosquitoes and a cool ninety eight degree day greeted us as we exited the hotel. Three porters and our guide, all locals, met us just outside the door. The equipment was divided up and our party of six headed for the river about half mile away. A crude flat bottom boat, that looked like an oversized John Boat, with an old outboard motor awaited us. We were barely settled as the boatman shoved away from the broken down dock. The motor was surprisingly quiet for it's obvious age.

Eight hours later put us quite deep into the jungle looking at another broken down dock. Thirty yards or so away stood our hotel for the night. A roughly put together, weather worn, boarded structure with a tin roof. This was to be the end of our creature comforts for a while, if that's what you call creature comforts.

It was good to stand and stretch after being cramped in that boat all day. No sooner had we unloaded our supplies when the boatman turned and sailed back down river again. As quiet as that old outboard had been the sound of silence really set in as soon as he was out of sight. At least I thought it was silent. Not having spent any time in a jungle before, I never realized just how much sound is generated by the unseen inhabitants. The quiet noise was not at all stressful as a busy city would be. It was more like a symphony of sound. Each note individual while blending for a chorus of nerve soothing natural music. I was suddenly aware of just how relaxed I felt. I smiled to myself thinking just how naive and silly I must look to others, but right now I didn't even care.

Every one turned to in setting up a quick camp. At least for tonight tents were not needed, only our cots and mosquito netting. Frank and I reviewed some maps while we still had some daylight and our guide and crew prepared dinner. We swapped some stories during and after dinner and again hit the sack early. I lay awake for a while listening to nature's nighttime symphony. It was different than the music of the day but just as captivating.

For whatever reason I was the last to get up the next morning. The cleanup had already taken place, some breakfast had been put aside for me. I just had to take my bunk down. Today would be another day by water. Just as I finished securing my cot away, two large dugout canoes arrived. From here on the river was too shallow to accept the motor traffic. We loaded our gear in short order and were soon on our way with the rhythmic swish of paddles. Because we were moving somewhat slower than yesterday I managed to take some great photo's of nature that few people ever get to see. The colorful bird life alone was worth the trip. The Caymans also are interesting in their own right. Most people know them as alligators but down here they call them Caymans. The power they possess is awesome and should command anyone's respect.

By mid-afternoon the dugouts beached at a large clearing. This would be our departure area. From here on our trek would continue on foot following our GPS. Frank decided that since we still had some daylight left we should take advantage of it and start into the jungle. Within minutes the sun was no longer directly visible. The jungle canopy provided an almost impenetrable roof. I thought that without the direct sun it would be cooler, but that same canopy prevented all air movement which made the heat seem even more oppressive.

After three hours of hacking a pathway we stopped for the night. We had only gone about a mile and a half. Now I understood why expeditions always took so long. With all of today's travel conveniences the only way to cross the jungle was just what we were doing. We set up camp and once I had my mosquito netting in place I fell exhausted in my bunk. I noticed the local chaps rigged up hammocks in the lower trees, netting and all. It certainly appeared to be a lot more comfortable. Tomorrow, I thought, I would ask about the hammock. Perhaps I could try that myself. I closed my eyes and let the orchestration of sound lull me off to sleep.

I awoke the following morning to a very different, yet as pleasing, serenade. The jungle was a never ending supply of music. One surely did not need a radio for entertainment. Surprisingly I was the first one up. I stoked the fire and put the coffee on. I was rested and raring to go. Breakfast was some sort of flat bread and fresh fruit which was quite filling. I inquired about the hammock and it was agreed the porters would show me how to hang it tonight. With renewed enthusiasm we set out on our quest for this new lost city.

The jungle is certainly not user friendly. At least not to a suburbanite like me. Almost every step is hard earned with the aid of the machete. I always thought I was in pretty good shape but this jungle sure makes you reassess what being in shape is. Nevertheless we forged on.

I learned to follow the others, that made it a little easier. At the end of the day I surprised myself with how well I had held up. I actually felt good. Not too tired and not too achy. Dinner was quite good. I don't know what we ate but it was filling. I almost don't want to know what we ate.

After dinned I learned to hang a hammock and netting. Frank and I then relaxed as he discussed what he hoped to find. I must admit I myself was anticipating great things. The day's trek was catching up to all of us so we called it a night. Again I drifted off to the songs of the forest.

As we started the next morning, Frank mentioned that two more days would possibly put us there barring any unforeseen circumstances. I was feeling the excitement of a kid at Christmas. I couldn't believe how anxious I had become.

Each day seemed to be a repeat of the day before. Nothing new, but everything new. I was actually enjoying myself. I would stop now and then for what I thought was an irresistible photo op. I got so carried away one time that I suddenly found myself completely alone. For some reason or other I wasn't alarmed. I probably should have been but I was having too much fun to think of my own safety. I put my camera away and ran as best I could to catch up. The path was obviously easy to follow. It's not like there are many people using machete's to blase a trail. I finally caught up to the group. Frank, of course expressed his concerns and suggested the next time I feel so inclined that I keep the guide or one of the porters with me. I agreed with him and we continued our pursuit for the lost city.

Around six o'clock we stopped for the night and I managed the hammock by myself under the watchful and smiling eyes of my teacher Diego. Dinner again was pleasant and Frank was extremely animated while talking about tomorrow's journeys end. His anticipation was contagious. I could feel my own anxiety building. We hit the sack in hopes of getting an early start for our final leg. I think I was the most enthusiastic of us all. I had never seen an ancient Mayan city before, not even one that had been excavated. To be present at the discovery or the uncovering of something that old was the dream of all dreams for me. I could not imagine what was in store for me. I felt like running the whole way just to get there to discover things for myself, though I really knew I couldn't do that. I was very familiar with methods of archeology and of course there are certain procedures to follow. That not with-standing, I still couldn't wait to get there.

Frank stopped a little after two with the announcement, "We're Here."

I looked around at nothing but jungle and unconsciously said, "We're Where ?"

"The lost City.", he answered, "You're standing in the middle of it."

I gazed around at thick jungle. Thicker than we had encountered before. I guess my confused look gave me away. Frank spoke again.

"Look around. Look carefully." he said.

I slowed my mind down and realized what they mean when they say, *"You don't see the trees for the forest."* I let my eyes wander slowly and then there it was. A small pyramid. So taken with this image, my eyes began to tear and my body trembled slightly. The facade was so overgrown with vines, roots, leaves and trees it was barely visible. But here it was right before me. I didn't move for what seemed like hours. I could feel the city, filled with people, moving to an fro, busy with their daily lives. Frank's voice shook me from my revery. He was staring at me smiling.

"I know how you feel." he said. "It struck me the same way when I first encountered it."

Turning to our four guides he continued,

"Okay, let's set up camp right here. I know there's some water about a hundred yards or so over there." He pointed easterly.

I was already shooting some pictures. Addressing me like one of his student's, Frank said

"There will be plenty of time for that later. We all help set up house now. This will be our permanent base for a while." Feeling slightly embarrassed, I knew he was right. Reluctantly, I put my camera away and joined the others with the work at hand. It took the six of us almost two and a half hours to clear an area and put together our semi permanent home. Tents and tarp's for shelter from the rain and storage for equipment and supplies. Frank and I continued with equipment checks while our four local helpers disappeared into the jungle in search of dinner. Although we were more than busy with our tasks I could not help but sneak peeks now and then at the wonderful structure before me. I was anxious for a closer inspection, but I knew it would have to wait. I guess after all these centuries, this magnificent building was not going to disappear over night.

The work of setting our base camp was more tiring than I thought. There were more details involved than I ever imagined. It was a welcome pleasure to sit down for dinner and rest. Dinner also turned out to be a surprise. At least to me it was a big surprise. I had never eaten monkey before. I was a little hesitant at first but after a few tastes I decided it really wasn't that bad and I ate heartily as the rest were doing. They all politely pretended not to notice my earlier discomfort at the start of the meal.

It was almost dark now and relaxing with a full stomach and a second cup of hot coffee we entered into an impromptu bull session discussing our plans for the work ahead.

This is where I found out that Mateo, our guide, was more than just a guide. He was an accomplished Mayan historian. A keeper of oral history dating back centuries. Years of practical study taught him to read and interpret Glyph's and writing. His own ancestry dated back to an unknown past. As he spoke, the pride in his people was obvious. He seemed to know how special they were based on the depth of their knowledge long before that of the Europeans.

     As fascinating as our discussion was, we all were tired and agreed to call it a night. I climbed into my hammock, listening to the music of the night and let my mind wander into the past.

Chapter 4

The aroma of fresh coffee tickled my senses as I slowly became conscious of the world again. I was comfortable and content and did not want to leave my world of peaceful dreams. The low voices of Frank and Mateo did manage to invade my private space and prod my mind awake. I swung out of my hammock and happily realized I did not have to take it down today since this was home for a little while. I finished my wake up job with some water on my face and followed the coffee smell. The work table, under a canopy, was covered with maps and other assorted papers as Frank outlined our days activities. We were to work in three teams of two, for obvious reasons, each man equipped with a hand held G.P.S..

After breakfast we were to fan out from our camp center to see what else, if anything, could be found. Carlos, one of the porters assigned to work with me was also a surprise. He was locally educated in his cultures archeology and was well versed in his own oral history. I was beginning to feel like, and actually was, the neophyte of the group. It didn't really matter though, I felt my excitement and enthusiasm could make my contribution worth while. Carlos and I headed out in an easterly direction and had not yet gone a hundred yards when we came upon rectangular blocks almost flush with the ground. A more careful examination revealed a regular pattern of these blocks. We carefully walked the outline, along with photographs and G.P.S. readings. Much to our surprise we were uncovering a large rectangular plaza which stretched before us back to our campsite and the vine covered pyramid. We would ascertain an accurate measurement after our findings were plotted on the maps but I guess it to be about fifty yards by one hundred yards. To me, in my uninitiated capacity, this indicated possibly a major city since we already had a large pyramid structure and now a huge plaza. I was excited to plot our find but was reminded by Carlos we were not to meet back at camp until mid-afternoon. We finished the complete plaza outline then continued in our easterly direction. We cut through another twenty five or so feet and were stopped by a wall. A man made block wall. We spent the next couple of hours doing a preliminary clearing of vines and underbrush exposing more of our wall, recording our slow progress with photographs. We guesstimated it to be about twelve foot high but it's length was still undetermined.

We finally called it quits around three in the afternoon. I was physically tired but my mind was still in overdrive. I can't ever remember when I was this stimulated about anything. Luckily it was a short walk back to base on an already cleared path. I was too exhausted to do much more hacking.

We arrived back to find the other four already enjoying a leisurely sit while being refreshed by fresh fruit. We collapsed into our portable deck chairs excitedly telling of our find. Feeling somewhat renewed we all migrated to the planning table and recorded our G.P.S. information. Frank had discovered two small pyramids a few hundred yards away while Mateo and Mario had uncovered a large living complex, probably of the more common people. The area was approximately two hundred yards squar. Proud of our day's accomplishments, we all showered,(*these portable showers are great)* and relaxed over dinner. Dinner was a choice of MRE's (meals ready to eat) but under the circumstances it felt like a feast. After dinner Frank had a surprise for us. He had secreted away in his pack a bottle of Remy Martin Cognac. We all had a shot in celebration of our fruitful day. We relaxed for a while longer letting the cognac do it's job and finally drifted to our respective sleeping area's. I comfortably lay there for a while allowing the sounds of the night work their magic on my overactive brain.

Chapter 5

The next morning Carlos and I headed east again back to the wall. Another hours worth of hacking at vines proved fruitful. We came to a portal that appeared to be about eight feet wide and seven feet high, the top arched and key stoned. I stood there marveling at the engineering feat when I noticed carved inscriptions along the top of the arch. I could not get to my camera fast enough. I needed to capture this before they disappeared. There I was being silly again. Why was I worried after they survived all these centuries.

I checked with Carlos about translating, but he was not sure and would leave that up to Mateo. Feeling that we wasted enough time already on our admiration of the magnificent entrance way we stepped through. Inside, were of course, more jungle vines, but not so the tall trees. Looking ahead and up, directly aligned with the portal we sighted the flat top of an extremely large pyramid. I judged it to be approximately five hundred feet away and well over fifty feet high. Snapping myself out of a trance I again reached for the camera . Carlos busied himself recording GPS numbers of both the wall, it's opening and was headed directly for the pyramid. We realized then we were walking on another plaza. Down on our hands and knees we clawed away at some dirt and grasses. Sure enough the same large, rectangular, flat stones came into view matching those of yesterday's plaza. I raised my head to speak to Carlos but didn't utter a sound. Looking behind and past him, I spied another smaller pyramid. I finally managed to get the words out and as Carlos looked up at me he said there was also one behind me. I snapped my head around and there it was. Both these smaller structures were peaked although they really weren't that small. By now my head was spinning. I almost could not believe what I was seeing. I wondered if Frank was having as much luck. Remembering some past readings the layout of these structures appeared to be classic in design. The plaza, large and small pyramids, and miscellaneous structures all on some planned celestial alignment. I made a mental note to check on the alignment and compare it to other known cities.

Carlos continued with his GPS recordings while I went camera crazy. We alternated our information gathering with more attacks on vines and grasses not even stopping to eat. At around two in the afternoon, energy drained and soaked in sweat, we called it quits. We rested in silence for a while before returning to base. The grandeur of the place just seemed to require stillness and respect.

We were first to arrive back at camp and were in the middle of plotting some of our GPS readings when Frank and the others returned. As a greeting Frank started right in, excitedly, about his finds that day.   There was obviously no interrupting his enthusiasm until he drained his head of all that he encountered. Carlos and I looked at each other smiling. We were listening to exactly what we ourselves had uncovered. Frank, half out of breath, reached for a cup of water which gave me a chance to tell our story. He was totally elated and speechless by the time I finished.

The next few hours were occupied with our plotting's and recordings. This was turning out to be the find of the century. From the looks of it, it might even be the largest city found to date.

That evening after dinner, Frank and the others made journal entries, as I busied myself, cleaning my camera and equipment, and storing away the exposed film. A quickly made up double lined box worked just fine to keep my precious film out of the excessive heat and harms way. Satisfied with the safety of my livelihood, I retired to my hammock and let my mind wander centuries back.

Chapter 6

We awoke the next day to a jungle rain. The thick canopy protected us somewhat from the heaviest of the rain but regardless of this small gift everything was drenched. I patted myself on the back for having the discipline of taking care of my film last night. The tarp's we erected over our work tables were doing their job quite well. The up side of the rain was that it gave us a day off so to speak. We all enjoyed the break and leisurely worked individually and collectively in updating our records and information. The rain let up early afternoon but by then we were all pretty much in a siesta mood Carlos and the other porters, Diego and Mario took advantage of the rainless afternoon to go in search for supper with fantastic results, returning with fish which they then willingly prepared and cooked. During our relaxing evenings repast, Frank out lined the next day's plan. To determine the full extent of our new found city, we were to fan out in all directions to try and set a size for this metropolis. Once that was accomplished we could then concentrate on some more detailed work. His plan was to do a partial excavation on one of the large, flat topped pyramids. That was like music to my ears. I had always wondered what it would be like to be the first to enter such an ancient dwelling. I went to sleep that night thinking of just that.

Chapter 7

Yesterday's rain only caused more humidity and discomfort. A quick breakfast and we were on our way. We had no idea how much territory we would have to cover today but we were anxious to get going. Compass directions were assigned and safety instructions were reviewed. It was hoped we could at least maintain visual contact. Just before eight AM our machete's were in action. I was happy to be in another direction thinking it would give me a greater chance of discovering something new.

The vines and undergrowth severely hindered our line of sight so periodic shouts were employed as a means of staying in touch. It was slow going, but necessarily so in order to be vigilant and not miss anything.

I was swinging away with my machete at an unusually thick clump of vines when suddenly I hit stone about three feet above ground. My arm went numb and my hand stung as I dropped the blade. I muttered a few expletives as I looked around to make sure no one heard me. There I go being silly again as if someone was going to be there. When I got feeling back into my hand and arm again I picked up the big knife noticing a nice sized chunk missing from what was once a sharp edge. I more carefully finished what I had started and to my delight was faced with a stelae. It stood approximately six foot high and twenty inches at it's widest. Of course I could not read it's message, but who ever it was dedicated to must have been very important fore it had Glyph's carved on all four sides. I recorded it with both GPS and film. I knew this was an important find and I'm sure Frank would be overjoyed.

As fascinated as I was with the stelae, I dared not delay any longer. I heard a signal shout and answered even though they were becoming more distant. My trek continued for what seemed like hours. Actually it was hours. By three o'clock it was obvious that all around me was just jungle. There were no signs of the slightest hint of previous occupation. It felt good to be returning to camp. I was hungry, tired and my arm still ached from the argument I lost to the stelae.

So much for what I thought was being thorough. In my trek back to base camp I came across what was possibly a small living area. I don't know how I missed it the first time. I took some quick readings of the location and the usual accompanying photo's. I noticed a few piles, somewhat buried in the undergrowth and vines, of small statuary broken and discarded. Perhaps this living area was for special artisans, but not being the expert I would have to discuss my idea with Frank.

Still deep in thought over my artisan theory, I was startled by Diego calling my name. Since I was long overdue at camp he was sent out to look for me. I indicated the find that was holding me up and he sort of confirmed my idea of artisans being special, and living away from the common man. I spoke of my discoveries as we made our way back to camp and he too appeared as excited as I was. It seems everyone had a run of good luck today and there would be much to discuss and chart tonight. We reached base and shelter just in time fore the rains started again.

Dinner was the quick and easy MRE's again as we had much work to do. The meal hit the spot as far as I was concerned. I found it quite good and filling and there was always plenty of coffee. Between the hard work and exercise along with the unwelcome regulated diet there would no longer be any worry about my growing waistline. I felt I had already lost five pounds in the last few days. Oh well, that's just the way it goes.

Due to all the successes of the day the energy was running high although there was a much relaxed atmosphere in camp tonight. We were all working but not very hard. It was more interesting to continue our conversations from dinner. Mateo was anxious to see the stelae I found because of the Glyph's. Even though I had thoroughly photographed all four sides he said he would shoot some Polaroids to give him time to study the writings. He was also going to attempt some tracings. I thought that was a great idea considering we did not have an artist as part of our expedition as so many in the past have had. It was then I found out I was wrong again. Diego was an accomplished artist and had also taught art and Mayan art history at the University of Mexico. He shared with me some of his sketches that evening. The detail he captured with just pencil and paper could have passed for photographs. I almost felt embarrassed thinking he was just a mere porter here to carry equipment.

A while later I had the opportunity to talk quietly with Frank. I asked him about Mario, the only one left I didn't know anything about yet. Sensing my embarrassment, he smiled and apologized. He was in such a hurry to get started when we first met at the hotel introductions had slipped his mind. As it turned out, Mario was a language and calender expert with numerous publications to his credit. I was truly the ignorant one in the group, although thankfully no one treated me as such.

The rain continued and our physical day caught up with us in spite of our enthusiasm. We all agreed to call it a night. As I lay in my somewhat dampish hammock my mind drifted back home. Everything seemed so distant and unimportant. There was only the here and now. I felt a contentment with what I was doing I had not experienced in years.

I awoke the next morning to the extreme humidity the rain left us with. I was fully rested and anxiously awaiting some new discovery. Frank was already at the planning table with his coffee. I filled my mug, grabbed a piece of flat bread and joined him. Staring at the area map for the first time in days it was then I realized how large our new found city was. I let out a low whistle as I looked for a scale measurement. Sensing what I was looking for, Frank volunteered,

"Three kilometers across, so far. I have a feeling we're looking at something even broader in scope."

"Is this what you expected ?" I asked.

"**I** expected a new find, but not something of this magnitude. I believe we may have to extend our search even further out than we are now.." He answered

"**T**oo bad you didn't have some aerial photography of the area, it might make this a little easier." I returned.

Smiling, Frank wandered over to his pack, retrieved what he was looking for and threw on the table before me a stack of nine inch by nine inch aerial photo contact prints.

"**T**hese are really useless, there's just too much jungle to see anything." he said. "This is the latest overflight I obtained from the government mapping department." he added.

"**I** don't suppose you have any stereo glasses." I inquired.

He smiled again and dug in his pack again and threw me a small leather case.

"**I** think you're wasting your time, but have at it." he said still smiling. "Everything is all the same, jungle and more jungle." he continued.

"**I**t's worth a try." I responded. "I was trained in the military in aerial photo interpretation, and quite successfully I might add. I have also been part of quite a few civilian endeavors using this expertise"

Getting more serious than I should have, I started mentioning various nuances of interpretation, such as spectral reflectance, foliage densities and colorations and so on.

"**W**hoa, slow down Eric, you're way over my head now. I bow to your judgement. Perhaps you can find something." Frank interrupted.

Laughing apologetically I said I would sit at the corner table and ply my trade. Who knows, and just left it at that. I suddenly felt pretty good about myself. Perhaps I could contribute something to this endeavor besides my photography.

After clearing the table, I first plotted the structures we already found. Now for the more difficult task of making comparisons and foliage studies. Alignment patterns also showed themselves. An hour and a half later I returned to the plot map Frank was working on with six probable locations. His earlier guess also seemed to be correct. These locations were all beyond the area we had already inspected. Frank looked at the map, then at me with a very doubtful expression.

"Okay my friend, let's go have a look."

Leaving Mateo and Mario at camp, we remaining four took our compass heading from the master map, a GPS fix on the closest site and off we went. Frank was giving me constant good natured jabs about how we needed the walking exercise anyhow. I made him promise that if we were successful I would get another shot of cognac tonight. The deal was agreed upon as we hacked our way through the undergrowth. Every now and then we would come upon areas that were more open then the others as if something hindered tree growth.

Carlos took to his hands and knees and started digging through the grasses. Turning his head up towards Frank with a big grin said,

"Looks like you're going to lose some of your precious cognac tonight."

Frank, with a befuddled look questioned.

"What do you mean by that ?"

"Well, if I'm not mistaken this is the remains of a roadway, a very old roadway." answered Carlos.

Now all four of us were on hands and knees scratching at the grass. A half hour passed and we stood back and looked at our labors. We had cleared a stretch about eight feet wide and ten feet long. There was no mistake about it. This was the remains of a classic Mayan roadway, gravel, stones cut blocks and all. Frank and I were both beaming smiles right now.

"But !." Frank said, "The bet was finding a structure."

I returned his look and countered with,

"Lead on McDuff."

We refreshed ourselves with some fruit and water before continuing.

We hacked away for another forty five minutes and as I checked on my GPS I heard Diego shout,

"Look 1 Look over there."

We all turned to where he was pointing. About twenty yards ahead, entangled with vines was a small Pyramid with a pointed top. Frank, smiling, almost laughing, asked if I wanted my cognac direct from the bottle or served in a glass. We started to clear some vines as I answered with great delight,

"In a glass and served on a tray please."

Everyone chuckled including Frank.

We continued to go through the routine recordings, measurements and photo's which kept us there for a while. Realizing there would not be enough daylight left to attempt a second site we returned to base. Our mood was light and jovial with Frank commenting,

"And to think for my whole career I've been doing it the hard way."

To make him feel better but still pleased with myself I said that this could have been just dumb luck.

"Perhaps my friend, but we will hold that decision until we check another site tomorrow." Frank answered.

Mario and Mateo had prepared a wonderful fish and fruit celebratory dinner, after which I received my cognac on a hastily made tray with much pomp and circumstance.

We made plans and chose a new site for tomorrow's search. Mateo and Mario chose to stay in camp again to continue working on the translation of the stelae Glyph's. It had been a wonderfully relaxed evening but I could feel the tired's coming on so I retired to my hammock. I finally felt good about being able to contribute something tangible to the expedition. I then lost myself in the all familiar symphony of the night.

I slept well and was fully refreshed th next morning. I couldn't believe how rested and invigorated I was. Secretly I hoped we would have as much success today as we did the day before although I was confident that we would.

We left camp a little earlier today knowing we had a further distance to cover. Our enthusiasm was high and because of that the jungle trek did not seem as difficult. We reached our destination around one in the afternoon, and yes there were two almost perfect pyramids connected by a causeway between them. They were also walled on three sides. This struck everyone as something different that no one had seen or read about before. Some serious study would have to take place to determine it's actual use. We had a quick lunch then routinely did our measurements before starting for base. The main topic of conversation on our return was speculation of this new structure. Of course nothing would be answered without extensive study. It was almost dark by the time we reached camp and again, Mario and Mateo had supper waiting for us. The evening bull session was stimulating. Apparently the home-body's had made some headway on the decipherment of the stelae but felt it a little premature to disclose anything just yet.

  Diego suddenly remembered something that had been haunting him all day. A drawing he had seen a long time ago done by Catherwood in the eighteen hundreds. It was of two small structures connected by a causeway and partially walled in. This of course piqued everyone's interest. Further details would have to wait until our return to civilization and the university's library. It was later than usual when we all turned in for the night. It started to rain again and the soft noise lulled me right into dreamland.

Chapter 8

      The rain continued for almost forty eight hours. We were obviously experiencing a tropical storm from the gulf. The winds, which usually do not affect us, were now a concern. We all worked fortifying our camp, securing everything possible. All we could do was wait it out. Our work went on only at a slower pace with a few more siesta's thrown in. We had rigged up a double roofed, double walled sleeping area which turned out to be quite comfortable and quiet. We enjoyed the forced rest but were really anxious to move on to hopefully new finds. Everyone shared their fields of expertise in such a way that we all benefitted from a new perspective of the whole. Frank even caught on to the use of the aerial photo's.

      On the third day we awoke to a literally steaming jungle, the humidity was so thick it was like fog. Nevertheless plans were made for checking out a third site I had determined from the air photo's. I had volunteered along with Carlos to be the camp watchers this time. We both welcomed the empty quiet camp and kept ourselves busy with what seemed like menial tasks, but were still important to the overall mission.

      Late afternoon we started preparing dinner and none too soon either. Our weary searches wandered into camp excitedly talking about another large pyramid they found. This one was about two hundred yards off from where I had indicated but it still confirmed my location technique. Frank was slowly being convinced that aerial photo's were certainly not the complete answer but had it's advantage as an additional tool that could possibly save field time.

Chapter 9

Rain again the next day forcing some more rest time. Although the downtime was welcome, it did put a damper on our overall enthusiasm of new finds. Mario and Mateo continued working tirelessly on the stelae translations. Lately though, they seemed more animated than usual. We all could tell something was up but they chose to remain secretive. When asked, Mateo would answer that he wanted more time to confirm or shoot down his suspicions. We all respected his expertise and thereby left him alone. We knew when the time was right he would let us all in on his findings.

Frank, as promised suspended our jungle treks for a while and was making arrangements for some preliminary excavation. It was just a matter of deciding what and where. Of course we all were allowed our input. Carlos and I both thought a good place to start would be the complex we came across by the archway. It seemed to represent a place of importance. At least it had that feeling about it. By the end of the day the consensus was also aligned with us.

Sometime during the night the rain ceased and we awoke to a much clearer day. The temperature had dropped to a cool ninety six degrees. We took this as a good sign as we prepared for an exciting day. At least exciting for me. I had never participated in a Mayan excavation before. Mateo and Mario chose not to join us on this first preliminary try but did travel with us for a while. Their plans were to visit the stelae again for some further confirmation of something or other. Details were still not forthcoming. Our journey seemed easy today and eventually the two Glyph experts parted company taking a heading for the stelae.

Approaching the archway and the complex it protected, we all became silent. It seemed the right thing to do in reverence for the secrets not yet revealed. Frank was wandering around making mental notes and checked some note book now and then. I occupied myself by taking a few more detailed photo's rather than the general area I covered last time. Frank, in a soft voice, broke the silence.

"This is it. This is where we start our cleanup."

He was standing in front of the large flat topped pyramid. He turned around checking the alignment with the archway. Satisfied, he made some notes in his journal, then indicated we all get busy clearing vines and grasses.

After nearly two hours of backbreaking labor we took a break and stood back to view our progress. We were all stunned by what we had accomplished. This structure was more magnificent than we had hoped for. The front facing the archway was stepped up to the flat top, while halfway up was a smaller flat area, guarded on two sides by intricately carved figures, half animal, half human. Set back in this alter area was a sort of portal, also intricately carved. I concentrated my lens on these figures to capture this wonderful detail. Diego, too, was busy sketching away.

Carlos and Frank were discussing possible interpretations of some Glyph's carved above this portal. After some animated bantering back and forth, Carlos climbed up a few steps and carefully edged his way over until he was above and in the middle of the portal. Ever so slowly he reached his hand down and grabbed a small protruding center stone, almost losing his balance.

"Wait a minute." cautioned Diego. "I'll give you a hand."

Diego also climbed the steps until he was just above Carlos. He managed a firm hold on Carlos's waist belt then said,

"Okay ! Now give it a try."

As if they were a professional mountain climbing team, Carlos, with added confidence again reached for the protrusion. With some applied force the stone turned slightly and pushed inward. He quickly pulled his hand away, so as not to get caught and we all listened to a slow growling rumble as the carved door, slowly, inch by inch moved outward allowing a two foot opening behind the door. All movement stopped, including our own. Double checking their footing Diego and Carlos climbed down and joined Frank and I in front of the door. I looked at Carlos and he must have read my questioning eyes before he softly answered,

"**I** remembered an old story passed down through oral history. Because of my modern university training I never put much stock in it. From now on I'll have more faith in my ancestors."

The smell of stale air emanated from inside the tomb. It wasn't just stale air. There was another acrid odor mixed in. None of us could identify it. It was like a chemical smell of some kind. Whatever it was it was strong. We hesitated entering, then decided to wait a while longer. After ten minutes or so the acrid odor dissipated. We wet our bandana's and tied them around our faces covering nose and mouth. Jesse James and his gang could not have looked any worse.

Since this was Frank's expedition he was first to enter. Each carried a battery lantern with wide angle heads. The light chased the darkness of who knows how many hundreds of years. Not a word was spoken as we entered what appeared to be an anti chamber. The walls were painted with muted color depicting various actions, one of which was a beheading. We assumed, for now, it was an enemy warrior. There were two stone benches flanking another large stone door. Glyph markings edging both sides and top. I know I should have been taking pictures but I was mesmerized by what I was seeing. Photo's would have to wait. Frank indicated with a nod of his head that we should try and enter. All eyes turned to Carlos, who was already studying the portal. A few minutes passed which seemed like hours, then Carlos carefully ran his fingers up and down the outline of both sides of the door. Making a choice he moved to the left side and putting his hands near the seam, gave a slight push. Nothing moved. With an obvious more exerted effort he pushed again, which produced a low sound of stone on stone, but not much movement. His next effort was to put his shoulder against the stone and use his body weight. The large stone indeed started to move but with much resistance. Diego quickly threw his shoulder against the stone and with a great effort by both of them the door slowly opened.

It pivoted on a center point and opened like a vertical louver. Again the stale acrid smell rushed out to greet us. Stepping back we turned away from the odorous attack. Once the air stabilized we returned out attention to the doorway with Frank leading the way. This room was considerably larger, which I judged to be about forty foot square. Our attention immediately went to the center of the room. On a rectangular stone pedestal was a mummified body.

We silently stood in awe, our minds working overtime processing what was before us. Diego was the first to move closer. As if it were a signal we all followed. The body was adorned with a cloak of feathers of many colors, although red was predominant. There were many strands of gold and jade around his neck. Bracelets of jade and other polished stones occupied both wrists. His right hand held a scepter of some kind, a design of which I had never seen, not even in books. A large feathered headdress encircled his head, highlighted also with jade. The facial expression was majestic and peaceful with closed eyes. There did not appear to be any sign of age as you see with so many mummified remains. Even the hands did not show aging.

Finally remembering my camera I recorded for posterity this magnificent figure from another age. Still not a word passed among us. I noticed the expressions of both Diego and Carlos had changed to sincere reverence and adoration. This was obviously one of their ancient rulers, and even after all these centuries they felt the need to subjugate themselves to his authority. It was fascinating to watch this transformation take place. Unseen hereditary knowledge took charge over their twenty first century behavior.

The room itself was exquisitely decorated with all the finery befitting a king. The walls were painted with all sort of life's scenes apparently indicating major events in this man's reign. Some were freestyle paintings, some stylized drawings filled with unimaginable color. Carved Glyph panels stood from floor to ceiling, which was about ten feet high. Even the ceiling was painted with the colors of the night, depicting celestial events and planet movement. One could read individual events, yet all blended together as one never ending sky, representing the infinity of the universe they seemed to understand. The pyre on which the body rested was carved on all four sides in stylized Glyph's, which we later learned from Mateo, depicted calender dates.

There were six stone benches scattered about the room, all strewn with finely woven, multi colored fabric. Woven baskets and stone chests occupied one corner, filled with objects of pottery and statuary, large and small figurines of all shapes, some definitely human, others half human, half animal. The animal figures were mostly identifiable while some defied interpretation, at least to us at this moment.

Children's wheeled toys were in a basket by themselves This seemed incongruous to their lifestyle. The Mayan were known for their great roadway system, yet they did not possess draft animals or the wheel except on toy's.

Again this would require extensive study and research. It appeared as if the whole of Mayan history was shown here in one form or another, pre-classic through post-classic. We were looking at a span of perhaps fourteen hundred years.

Chapter 10

For the first time in my career I actually ran out of film at a shoot. What we were looking at was beyond expectation. I would have to postpone any further documentation until I retrieved more film from our home base. Up to this point a word still had not been spoken by anybody. Almost two hours had passed before anyone realized the time of day. Frank, after checking his watch, spoke in a soft, almost undetectable voice.

"It's time we left if we want to make it to camp before dark."

We slowly exited the room feeling in *"I don't want to leave the party."* kind of mood. Carlos and Diego automatically pushed the door closed. It appeared as if Frank was going to say "Don't bother." But I guess thought better of it. After all, this was their history, not his.

Conversation was light on our return trip to base camp. Mostly *"Did you see this or did you see that."* The magical influence of the tomb still held sway over our thoughts.

Dinner was ready as usual upon our return. Mateo and Mario were acting like children with a big secret to bust out. Up till now we four had not spoken of our find except that we had an interesting day. Halfway through dinner Mario could no longer contain himself.

"We have something very important to tell you." he blurted out.

"I was going to say the same thing." answered Frank.

The table was all smiles now

"You go first." Frank and Mario said simultaneously. Mario did not politely wait any longer and proceeded with his story.

"It's about our translation of the stelae." He hesitated a moment as if thinking of other things. "We weren't trying to be secretive by not saying anything before this, we just were not sure of what we were reading. Now I think we are."

"At least we feel ninety five percent sure." interrupted Mateo. "The Glyph's, as far as we can discern, are speaking of some very high ranking personage. Perhaps a king, ---- a very old king."

Mario picked up from there again.

"The dated we are looking at are written using the long count. This is a rare use in classic and post-classic times."

"We won't go into detail now." said Mateo, "But this person we are talking about is probably from pre-classic times. Exactly how old we don't know yet, however he is very, very old."

Mateo joined in with,

"I have never come across this age before. It may even be the beginning."

Looking around the now quiet table all faces were sober. Frank's eyes were sparkling now as he took over the conversation. Gazing directly at Mateo and Mario he announced,

"I think we found your king. It fits, it all fits. We opened a tomb today. The one we agreed upon the other day. It was a tomb like I've never seen or heard of before. Inside is the mummified body of what appears to be a king or very high ranking ruler. There are markings on the pedestal that we could not read. You must come with us tomorrow. Gentlemen, we may be looking at the find of the century."

Everyone started talking now, each remembering something specific that stood out in their minds. We were all excited now. Frank retrieved the cognac bottle once more to toast our success. Carlos suggested we make journal entries individually of what we observed. A combined story could be put together at a later date. Mario and Mateo could do the same after they witnessed the tomb. It started raining lightly, though no one seemed to notice. The excitement and postulating carried on well into the night. I slipped away unnoticed and retired to the luxury of my hammock. I let my mind relax with the patter of the rain and drifted off to space unknown.

Chapter 11

I was up early and alone. I was actually pleased to be alone. I needed the time for my mind to settle and slowly accept and put in order all that had recently transpired. I mindlessly went about making coffee and other morning chores and finally sat down to relax in my portable deck chair enjoying my coffee and suddenly realized it was still raining. This was a good thing I thought. It would give us all time to settle and collect our thoughts. My own thoughts wandered away from the tomb and into the surrounding jungle. How cruel and hostile this environment could be and at the same time be so beautiful and luxurious. Micro ecological systems surrounded us at all levels, yet co-existence and dependency prevailed to make this one of life's greatest wonders. Right now I did not try to understand any of this, I just enjoyed where I was and what was around me. The gentle voice of Diego shook me back to reality.

It is beautiful, isn't it." He said reading my thoughts. Where ever I have traveled observing the wonders of our modern world, nature itself is still the most beautiful."

He filled his mug with coffee, joined me in a deck chair and we both listened to the noise of the silence.

Slowly the others drifted into states of consciousness and congregated around the coffee pot. The rain was actually welcome which allowed for additional planning. Frank suggested we set up camp at the tomb site to make things easier, which brought up another logistics problem. Our present camp was centrally located for our area of interest as far as the extent of this city was concerned. Setting up by the tomb would mean extra and inconvenient travel for boundary research, though it would allow for more hours of study at the tomb. A compromise plan was finally decided upon in early afternoon. We would split into two camps, leaving the present site as our main base. We would then set up a satellite base at the tomb to maximize our hours of study. Alternating people between sites to maintain a fresh approach was Diego's idea and well accepted by all.

By the end of the day Frank was riding high anticipating the research we would accomplish considering our small compliment. Mario and Diego set aside the necessary resources to set up our tomb side campsite if the rain ever ceased.

Chapter 12

     Two more days of rain had us all itching to be on the move again. It had been decided how a basic rotation was to work between the two camps and I was lucky enough to be included in the first shift at the tomb. This would allow me to finish my initial photos. The rain had given me time to reorganize my equipment and film supply. From here on my shooting would have to be selective in order to guarantee not running out of film all together. I knew I could manage this although it would prove difficult at times. Once my film and camera had been double checked I again turned to the air photos. I founds three more tentative locations that might prove fruitful. Of course they were in three different directions dictating three separate searches. Our city would now cover many miles of a never before known area.

     After five days we had our first reprieve from the rains as we awoke to a steaming jungle. By mid-day the first shift for the tomb camp departed. Frank, Mateo and myself, fully loaded, happily took to the trail. Carlos was to follow in short order with the balance of our supplies. Tomorrow, Diego and Mario would resume the search for new sites based on the aerial photo information.

     We reached the tomb with about an hour and a half of daylight left and chose a spot just inside the archway to set up camp. There were no large trees to hang a hammock from so we had to resort to the fold up cots with air mattresses. I was still working the foot pump filling the mattresses when Carlos joined us at the compound. By actual darkness we were pretty much finished with our camp layout and finally settled for some dinner around a small fire. The atmosphere around the fire was more somber than it had been for the last few days. Anticipating tomorrow one could feel the influence of the kingly figure casting his spell over us into the mysteries of the past. I for one could not wait to get back into the tomb to pick up where I left off with my photo documentation.

Supper was quick and we all turned in for the night. As I lay on my cot listening to the jungle I realized the sounds were different. Just as beautiful, but more serene as if they too were under the influence of the principal resident here. Sleep easily overcame me as my mind blended with the surrounding music of the night.

I was startled awake by a human cry only to find out Frank had just tripped over some vines and twisted his ankle. Luckily it was nothing serious as he apologized for waking us all. A quiet day was before us with traces of sunlight dappling through the overhead canopy. It almost felt cooler but I know that was just my imagination. Breakfast was light and none of us could keep our eyes from the tomb entrance knowing what awaited us again. Finally the moment arrived and with lanterns in hand we moved to the entrance to another world. I worked with Carlos to open the door just as he and Diego did days before. The escaping air was not as potent as the first time so we did not use our bandana's though we did have them at the ready. We allowed Mateo to be the first to enter, to behold what we had already seen upon our first entrance.

Again silence prevailed out of respect for the surroundings. I was the last to enter and was captivated by Mateo's frozen stance in front of the mummified king. So much so that it was the first photo I took. I then turned my attention to the other areas where I had run out of film. The four of us sort of did our own thing for a while with a few soft words mumbled here and there. My wanderings and shooting soon found me back at the pedestal of the king. I had not captured the carvings or Glyph's on the base yet and was about to set up to do just that when something caught my attention. Looking at the body before me, something was not right. I could not quite put my finger on it. I repeatedly scanned the figure from head to toe. Nothing seemed to gel. I dismissed it as my imagination again and returned to my camera.

I set up my tripod at a measured distance to the pedestal. This way I could move the camera parallel to my subject shooting at a set distance to attain overlapping exposures that could then be viewed in stereo at a later date. Very much absorbed in what I was doing, out of nowhere an image popped into my head. An image of the scepter held by the mummy. I stood slowly gazing again at the stately figure. I stared at the scepter but nothing registered in my mind. After a few minutes I shook my head to clear the cobwebs and returned once again to the camera.

I completed my task of recording in stereo the markings on all four sides of the pyre. I did not realize how much time had elapsed until my stomach reminded me it was being ignored. I broke down my tripod, gathered my equipment and stacked everything by the entranceway, exiting the tomb.

As fascinating as the kings room was it was good to view daylight again and breath some un-stale air. Carlos was already rummaging for lunch so we both settled for some fresh fruit we located just outside the wall. Reseated back at the table Carlos looked a bit preoccupied. We ate silently for a while, then looking directly at me he spoke hesitantly,

"This may sound silly, but there is something about the mummy that just does not sit right. I can't quite put my finger on it."

Half smiling I answered,

"I'm glad to hear you say that. I thought at first it was just my wild imagination. The same thing has been bugging me all morning. I keep having these thoughts about the scepter and I don't know why."

Quietly shouting excitedly he jumped up,

"That's it ! The scepter, that's gotta be it. Come on." he said as he headed back to the tomb.

I quickly followed nearly knocking Frank and Mateo aside as we rushed through the door.

"What's going on." Frank yelled as we passed.

"Don't know yet." I yelled back, "That's what we're going to find out."

Frank and Mateo retraced their steps joining us at the pedestal. Carlos and I were studying the mummy. Minutes passed with out a word when Carlos finally spoke in a somewhat subdued tone,

"**Y**ou were right ! It is the scepter. The other day it was in the right hand."

"**A**nd look here ." I interrupted, "the dust in the folds of the cloak has been disturbed."

Frank and Mateo looked at each other and then at Carlos and I as if we were crazy.

"**A**re you trying to tell us that after two thousand years this thing is alive."

Mateo and Carlos both snapped their heads towards Frank, a hurt look in their eyes. Catching their meaning of this instantly, Frank recovered with,

"**N**o disrespect meant."

I answered quickly,

"**W**e don't know Frank. I'm not even going to speculate on that. All we're saying is that something is different. We both felt it this morning. The scepter was in his right hand, and now as you can see for yourself it is in the left. If I had the film developed from the other day it would bear out what I'm saying."

All was quiet again as the four of us stared intently at the body before us. Frank quietly mumbled,

"**I** hope this is not some kind of joke you're pulling because right now I don't think it's very funny."

Understanding his confusion I assured him this was not a prank.

The four of us went outside again and sat silently while munching on some fruit. You could almost hear our four minds working to make sense of this. Frank sounding slightly annoyed questioned,

"**A**re you certain of what you're saying. This makes absolutely no sense."

"**H**onest Frank." I answered, "I'm not pulling your leg." I continued in a more serious tone. "I'm a trained professional Frank. It's part of my job to pay strict attention to details. Little things out of place could either make or break a photograph." I paused for a moment, then added "I'm quite confident and positive,

Frank, that the scepter was in the right hand the other day. Carlos even bears me out on this."

Frank's tension eased a bit and his body relaxed somewhat. He turned and looking directly at me, said;

"I'm sorry Eric. I'm not doubting what you are saying, It's just that this whole thing comes as quite a shock. I've never had an experience like this before."

"I think this is quite a shock for all of us. You're not alone in this." I returned.

Mateo, who had been staring at the tomb entrance, slowly and quietly inquired,

"Did any body leave their lantern on in the tomb."

Everyone automatically checked for their own lantern. We each had ours with us. Turning our attention to the opening in the pyramid, a faint, flickering light and shadow could be seen.

"Is it just me or do I see moving shadows." Mateo asked.

He was right. You could see slight shadow movements. We kept looking at each other and then back at the entranceway, each trying to figure this out in his own way.

"Perhaps Mario and Diego decided to join us." Suggested Frank.

"I don't think so." Carlos answered. "They were heading in the exact opposite direction this morning."

"Well there's only one way to find out." Mateo said already on his feet walking towards the pyramid.

The rest of us quickly followed single file. I was last in line preparing my camera as we went. The closer we came the more distinctive the shadow patterns became. This was not the light of an electric lantern. It was obviously the flickering light of some sort of torch.

Mateo, upon reaching the door did not hesitate but continued right inside. We three followed after him It wasn't until we were all completely in that we stopped, eyes wide in disbelief. An empty pedestal before us and standing just beyond that, his back to us was the king. Apparently hearing us enter he slowly turned and seeing us quietly uttered some unintelligible word. Carlos and Mateo immediately dropped to their knees bending forward at the waist, faces to the ground and arms outstretched. Frank and I looked at each other confused. The stately figure before us again grunted the same word staring directly at us. Mateo quietly mumbled,

"**I** would strongly suggest you both bow to keep him calm until we can make some intelligible contact."

We did as requested although this was not really my thing. You know what I mean - - - - *bowing to another person.* But considering the place and present situation, I went along with it for safety's sake. The ruler, king, or whatever he was grunted again and Mateo and Carlos stood up. Frank and I followed suit. Our resident host now spoke in sentences.

Without making any deliberate moves I slowly aimed my camera in the direction of the speaker and pushed the shutter button hoping the focus would be okay. Not wanting to push my luck I refocused my attention to the king. He was an impressive figure I judged to be about six feet tall. His chiseled features just added to his regal appearance. The most distinctive feature I found was his complexion. It was not the bronzed color that we know of today. It seemed to be more Caucasian white. Whether or not that was because of the mummification process I could not ascertain as of yet. He just did not fit the mold of Maya.

Carlos took the lead in trying to communicate with him with limited success. Luckily for us our king was a very patient man. It was almost as if he knew the time difference between our two worlds. In my opinion he showed his wisdom in that patience. After a few minutes of bantering back and forth with Carlos and Mateo and their limited language skills, the king held up his hand as a command to cease talking. Frank and I instantly prepared for the worse, but much to our surprise he smiled slightly and walked to a bench and sat down. Using his scepter to point he indicated that Mateo and Carlos should sit in the floor before him. When they were seated he looked directly at Frank and I , and again with his scepter waved us towards a bench on the opposite wall. It was obvious we were not of the same heritage. Satisfied that we were all settled, and ignoring Frank and I, he resumed conversation with Carlos with much difficulty. This word exchange went on for one half hour with a mutual recognition every now and then. I was totally lost by then. They could have been speaking Martian for all I knew. I did, however, manage to get a few more shots with my camera. This time I was sure of the focus.

With the king's assent Mateo stood and walked over to Frank and I . He looked both anxious and frustrated, speaking just above a whisper he asked that we go to get Mario. The king agreed to wait for the next sun to grant us an audience again. Carlos had made some headway but Mario was the language expert.

We stood slowly, not wanting to startle the king and headed for the entrance. It was only mid-afternoon, which meant ample daylight to get back to the main camp. Frank was not to eager to leave. He was completely taken in by the unbelievability of what was unfolding before our eyes. Although I was feeling pretty much the same I agreed to make the trip alone. I realized It was risky to go it alone but the trail was well marked and I felt confident I could make it safely. I passed through the archway and broke into a slow trot knowing Frank had already returned to the tomb.

Chapter 13

I surprised myself by running most of the way. I didn't think I had it in me any more. It's amazing what exercise and a healthy diet can do to a man who had become too used to the luxuries of urban / suburban life. I approached the campsite at the same time as Diego and Mario who were more than surprised to see me. Relaxing with some fresh water I told my story of our encounter with the mummified king. Neither wanted to believe it but both were drawn in by it's incredulous nature. Mario was all for leaving right then but it was already twilight and better judgement ruled for an early morning start.

We three had dinner while I continued to answer questions. Supplies and light packs were readied before we turned in for the night. The feel of the hammock was good for my weary bones as I was lulled to sleep by familiar sounds.

We were on the trail just as the first light dripped through the trees. We made good time on the now well worn path. Mateo had only asked for Mario but Diego was not to be denied. If what I told was true, it was a first and he wanted to be included. I don't blame him, I certainly didn't want to miss last night although we were obviously summarily dismissed by the king. Oh well, I guess it was more important for Frank and the real other scientists to be there.

It was just after ten A.M. when we walked through the archway. We were in luck. Frank and the others had not reentered the tomb yet. There were smiles all around and of course more

questions and few answers. Carlos immediately huddled with Mario discussing the language constraints. Mario, as if expecting this kind of encounter, reached into his pack and retrieved a small note book. He thumbed thru the pages excitedly, stopping about half way, ran his finger down the page and then grunted some sounds. Carlos, eyes aglow, jumped up almost shouting,

"That's it ! That's it ! That's what he was saying."

Mario tugged at his arm trying to get him back in his seat and to quiet him.

"This is definitely early Yucatecan. Probably from between one thousand and two thousand B.C. It most likely has not been spoken for some two thousand plus years on a regular basis. Frank, his attention caught by Carlos's outburst, questioned,

"Can you converse with him ?"

"I can try." was Mario's answer. "I have been doing a lot of research lately on the old original stems of the language. If this king is authentic as you seem to believe, then I think we can communicate. Enough at least to get his and give our stories."

"Great !" Responded Frank enthusiastically. "Now we just have to wait for his Excellency's invitation to go back in there."

"I'm glad you're waiting." commented Mario. "Long ago, as best I can figure out, there was a great deal of protocol and formality involving the *"CHOSEN ONES"* With this particular situation we sure as hell don't want to upset or piss off the Chosen One. I think the first thing I would like to try is to establish his name and tie it to a calendar date. That way, perhaps, we can fill in some blanks in our history."

Mario mentioning *"Our History"*, showed his great pride in his heritage.

You could tell the waiting was beginning to get to everyone. Nervous chatter was interrupting the quiet of the jungle. Diego had begun the makings of coffee when we heard an authoritative command echo from the tomb. Mario, understanding the command said,

"That's our call." then looking at me added, "By the way Eric, bring your camera with you but don't attempt any shots until I can establish an explanation of that little black box.."

I appreciated his warning. The last thing I wanted to do was to screw up this never before and probably never again opportunity.

We filed slowly into the great room of the pyramid. Our four Mayan friends immediately bowed, and with the king's eyes on us, Frank and I soon followed suit. Mario was the first to stand and uttered a few words. As I said earlier, it could have been Martian he was speaking for all I know, but what ever it was it registered with our host. A hint of a smile could be detected as he studied Mario and slowly answered.

With definite waves of his scepter he motioned Mario forward and the rest of us were relegated to the stone benches along the back wall. We sat silently and listened to the conversation that was beyond our comprehension. The slow exchange of words went on for almost an hour and then an abrupt lull. Mario turned and signaled for me to come forward much to the dismay of Frank. He actually looked hurt.

I approached cautiously not knowing what to expect. Mario whispered for me to bow as I neared the king, which I did, which obviously pleased the king. His eyes dropped to my camera as he pointed to it with his free hand while mumbling something quietly to Mario.

"Give it to him." said Mario

I snapped my head around to Mario in disbelief as to what he just asked. Yes I did have a back up camera but to turn over an expensive piece of equipment to a two thousand year old mummy who had no idea what it was, was out of the question. Why that was like committing heresy. That was like asking me to cut off my finger and give it to a head hunter as an appetizer.

Mario, starring at me with serious eyes, said,

"Don't let him think you mistrust him. Just give him the camera. Please !" I did as much explaining as I could. Trust me, he will not hurt it."

He repeated the "please" again.

I hesitantly slipped the strap off my shoulder and begrudgingly extended my arm towards the king. He reached out his hand, smiled and made a sound, I guess of approval, and accepted the black box from me. He then proceeded to put down his scepter and looked at the camera from all sides. I was surprised at how gently he handled it. I almost felt guilty about the way I was acting a few minutes ago. He looked at me, made a motion, grunted a few words and handed it back to me.

"He wants you to show him." Mario said quietly.

I looked at Mario, surprised again. I carefully took the camera, removed the lens cap, put the viewer to my eye and focused on the crew sitting behind us. I then offered it to the king, indicating that he also look through it. He accepted it back and drew it to his eye, but only for a few seconds. Suddenly he pulled his head back and looked with his naked eyes at Frank and the others. Returning to the viewer again he looked longer this time, a slight smile crossed his lips. He removed his eye from the camera, pointed to the four in the back and made a motion with his thumb and forefinger indicating a small size. I smiled and shook my head in the affirmative. The king now proceeded to look at everything in the room through the viewer. He alternated his naked eye with the viewer constantly. He viewed his scepter up close, pulled his eye away with a confused expression and shook his head. I realized it was out of focus and offered my hand for the return of the camera. Putting the viewer to my eye I turned the lens barrel to refocus on the scepter and returned the black box to the king. He gazed at his scepter again and then back at me smiling. He then proceeded to go around the whole room viewing and focusing.

He came back to me after a few minutes, mumbled a few words again and opened a small chest at the foot of the pedestal. Reaching in he retrieved three emeralds, each about the size of a silver dollar across, and handed them to me. I took them hesitantly and looked to Mario for an explanation.

"He is giving you a gift in trade for your camera." he replied.

"But my film, the shots that I already took. He can't take my camera." I pleaded.

"I'm afraid you can't refuse him." said Mario. "Let him have it for now. Perhaps we can work something out later.

Besides, from the look of the size of those emeralds you can but ten camera's just like it and then some."

"I know." I returned, "But that's my pride and joy, I don't want to give it up."

"I'm afraid you don't have a choice right now. I think you have just secured his full cooperation for us." Mario replied.

From the back of the room, Frank added,

"Let it go. You can use your spare camera for now. If this gives us an in with the king it will be worth one hundred cameras."

I knew he was right but I still felt like I just lost my best friend. Oh well, the advancement of science comes first I guess. Everyone was all smiles again.

The king was acting like a kid with his new toy. So much so that Mario was having a hard time getting his attention again. It took a while but he did manage to settle him down and they spoke for about another hour. This session also allowed Frank to join in with questions. The king finally picked up his scepter and waved it indicating the end of our visit. We were again dismissed. As we filed out of the tomb the king touched my arm and nodded as if to say thanks, but we were definitely dismissed.

Chapter 14

Once back outside at our hastily made campsite, Diego finished making the coffee he started hours before. Mario now became the center of attention. We all sat comfortably in a circle recording in our journals our own versions of what had transpired. Mario commented that he felt at ease with the king and that further conversations should prove fruitful. He did not yet learn the name or time period of the king, only that it was very early Mayan. He also felt that tomorrow would tell the how and why of him still being alive.

The balance of today's conversation was mostly about his people, their benefits and their future. How they once ruled the existing world and how they would again some day. This caught everyone off guard. No where in the history books does it say anything about Mayan rule of the world. Mario went on to explain that the way the king used the word rule did not mean as a regency or government, more like an influence on culture and knowledge. He spoke of his people as advanced in what we would call the sciences. According to the king, people in other lands grew up in ignorance. It was the beneficent influence of the Maya that brought them out of the darkness.

Wow ! I thought to myself. Talk about egocentric. He spoke as if the world revolved around the Maya and their predecessors. Then again, who was I to criticize. All the history I was taught growing up was from standardized texts. It wasn't until I was an adult that I realized a lot of what I learned as a child was not necessarily true. It was history as some self chosen people wanted it to be. Especially early history where we did not have the instant communication systems we have today. So much for getting lost in my own thoughts. Mario was still talking and I was missing some important information.

Frank wanted to know when he could actually meet the king, as we referred to him. Mario thought that would also be tomorrow, for the king also asked about Frank and I. I assumed that was because of our skin color and facial features. This pleased Frank and he now sported a large smile. I really feel Frank thought he was being left out considering this whole expedition was his idea.

The conversation then turned to questions and suppositions whose answers we would not know till our next audience with our strange new friend. I removed myself from the group, again lost in my own thoughts. I found my pack and dug out my backup camera, loaded it and proceeded to check it out by snapping a few shots of the crew still talking. Still drifting with my thoughts I almost failed to notice our old friend Mr. Rain stopped by for a visit . Safely covering my camera I joined the others in quickly setting up some tarp canopies. It's amazing how fast things go once you get used to doing them. In short order all was comfortably sheltered and each of us relaxed in his own way. Mine was to let my mind drift again to the sound of the jungle rain as I stretched out on my cot.

Chapter 15

I awoke to the smell of warming MRE's. It was still raining and darkness had settled in but I felt unusually content and at ease. I had slept a dreamless sleep for over two hours and was totally refreshed. I joined the others for supper and accepted the light chiding I received for such a long nap. It was a much relaxed atmosphere tonight even though we all looked forward to tomorrow. Diego was occupied with some pencil and charcoal drawings while Mateo continued on Glyph translations. Carlos and Mario studied more of the old language in order to formulate questions in a more understandable way. That left Frank and I to work on the map plots. Diego and Mario did find another small pyramid the day before, which meant I was batting a thousand so far with my air photo interpretation.

Frank could not be happier. If we could tie all these finds together some how, it would mean this truly was the largest community ever discovered. This we knew would take many years to excavate and record the discoveries found.

Now that Frank had contributed questions to the king he no longer seemed upset and we speculated some more on what else we could learn from him. I think what intrigued me the most was not who he was or where he came from but how it was after two thousand plus years he came back to life. Frank sort of agreed with me but was still more interested in the past history of the Maya and what led to their advanced knowledge. We kept our fingers crossed and hoped we would get both answered in further sessions with the king.

The hour was growing late and one by one the team

turned to their sleeping areas. Even Frank said his goodnights. I remained alone by the fire light still feeling refreshed from my afternoon nap.

Gazing over at the entranceway to the tomb I noticed a flickering light and moving shadows. I sat there mesmerized, my thoughts going wild. Curiosity overcame my better judgement. I knew I shouldn't go over to the tomb but I felt this strange magnetism I could no longer resist.

Leaving my lantern on the table I cautiously made my way through the dark toward the pyramid. Even the jungle was suddenly silent, warning me to stay away, but still I could not comply. Reaching the outer door I inched my way in as quietly as I could. The torch was flickering but I no longer could detect moving shadows. I hesitated, knowing I should not be doing this. My actions could anger the king and blow the whole mission. Frank would also undoubtably be upset no end. Should I listen to myself. Hell no and I moved forward, once more being drawn by a power my conscience could no longer fight, or did not want to, which was probably more the case.

I paused at the inner portal, my whole body shaking, not knowing what to expect. I could feel beads of sweat forming on my brow as I moved my head to the edge of the entrance. The pedestal was empty and I could not see or hear the king. Forcing myself further through the doorway I could see the flickering light of another torch which drew my attention to a section of wall that was opened. I hesitated again. Hearing nothing, I moved towards this new door ever so slowly. Finally able to see in to the anti chamber, the king was seated, his back to me, reading a scroll like document. The room was full of these scrolls. It was a library, I thought. Who knows what history it contained. I froze as the king reached for another document. He settled again, his back still to me. I retraced my steps to the exit, my heart pounding like a base drum.

Once again outside, I carefully made my way to my cot. I lay there shaking with excitement, not only from my discovery but from the adrenalin rush to get to the discovery.

Now I thought, do I admit my infraction to the others or do I retain my secret for a while. Rationalizing my thoughts, I chose to keep quiet about my night time prowl until such time I found it necessary to expose myself. My breathing returned to normal and I drifted off to sleep once more to my jungle music.

Chapter 16

A late and leisurely breakfast served us all well. A restful night and we were all ready to go. In between light conversation my thoughts kept going back to last night's intrigue. *" I wonder if we'll get to see that library? I wonder if we'll get any answers at all? Why was I having sudden doubts about this whole thing? Was this some kind of practical joke? Whoa boy, slow down. Why are you letting yourself go on like this. Get a hold of yourself."*

I suddenly realized some one was calling my name. Mario repeated his call,

"**W**here are you Eric? You seem to be somewhere in outer space. Come back and join the living, my friend."

"**O**h - uh Mario, I was just thinking - - uh - -uh, thinking about my camera." I answered.

"**I** know it meant a lot to you, but giving it to the king meant even more to this project." Mario remarked.

"**I** know that now. Let's hope it really pays off in that we can learn some unknown secrets of the Maya." I replied.

"**T**hat's what we are all hoping." he answered.

Apparently no one heard anything last night so I was able to relax somewhat.

We all went about our individual work with nervous energy waiting for the kings call which for some reason didn't come until very late morning. As before we filed silently into the anti chamber awaiting the kings direction. He indicated with his hand for us to look around.

I moved to the wall where I saw the door last night

trying not to look too obvious. Searching as closely as I dared I could not detect the slightest hint of the opening. Suddenly feeling self conscious as if I was being watched, I turned toward the king and found him staring at me. He smiled, almost imperceptibly and nodded his head. *"Did he suspect anything."* I wondered.

Raising his scepter he summoned me. Now all eyes were on me. As I drew near his smile broadened and he pointed to the camera that hung from my neck. He continued smiling as he reached down to the bench beside him and picking up the camera I had given him yesterday acknowledging that they were similar. He called Mario over to us and spoke to him. Mario relayed the kings message,

"**G**ive him the camera."

I was shocked again which I'm sure showed on my face. I started to protest but was interrupted as the king spoke again.

"**N**ot to worry Eric, he said he just wants to look at it." said Mario.

Quite relieved, I took the strap from around my neck and offered the camera to the king. This was a different make and possessed a different viewing system. I flipped open the top to reveal the square glass viewer and removed the lens cover.

The king seemed to know what to do after that and just like yesterday proceeded to look around the whole room with both the camera and the naked eye. After some five minutes or so he gently returned it to me smiling and nodding his head in thanks. While I was closing it up and returning the strap around my neck the king was saying something to Mario that made him look confused and surprised. The king faced the others signaling them to be seated as Mario whispered to me,

"**I**'ll talk to you later. The king just said something that really puzzled me."

I nodded agreement, and a seat with the others and returned my attention to our host who was looking at the wall where I saw the door last night. He then looked straight at me and tipped

his head slightly. *"He knows."* I thought feeling guilty again. I guess I'll just have to wait this one out.

The king, as if holding court, opened up the question and answer period by indicating that Mateo should start. He approached the king, bowed and then produced some Glyph tracings and through Mario asked some questions as to their meaning. Receiving answers that obviously pleased him he returned to his seat all smiles and happy.

Carlos was summoned next and he too returned to his seat quite satisfied after his session. Diego's interview was much shorter but he did receive permission to sketch a portrait of the king which he began immediately.

Mario and the king then spoke at length leaving Frank and I anxiously waiting. You could sense Frank's irritation which he was unsuccessfully trying to hide.

A little over an hour later Mario announced to us all that the king felt we should take a break and take some sustenance. He then bid Mario to fetch a basket of fruit from under the bench and pass it around. When all were served, indications were made that we should eat. Where he got the fruit from was a complete mystery, but then there was a lot of mystery surrounding this man.

Our rest period was over an hour which did nothing to sooth Frank's nerves. There was not much conversation during lunch which seemed to be the kings wishes. More than once the king made direct eye contact with me but for some reason it did not make me uncomfortable. In fact it was just the opposite. I could feel a growing connection to this man. What the common thread was I did not know but it was almost like a kindred spirit meld.

A wave of the scepter let us know the rest period was over. When the king settled on his bench his raised scepter finally pointed at Frank. In trying to play it cool he almost tripped over himself in getting to the king. Mario was already in place and so the questions began. Frank was taken completely by surprise for it was the king who was asking the questions. They were talking quietly so we really could not get the gist of the whole conversation. We did, however, catch the king's question of where did Frank come from. Was it across the sea to the east. Taken aback by this, Mario tried to explain about North America. He was waved silent and told the king knew all about the land to the north because he had been there before, but the people there were primitive and lacking culture. The king further questioned Frank's ancestry. As it turned out he traced his heritage back to England. Late- comers to the world of culture according to our Mayan celebrity. The king then went on to say he knew about the light skinned people from over the sea to the east. He further stated they were late learners of the arts and culture. He was referring to the sciences when he used the word culture.

Frank was becoming irritated, not a good characteristic for a professional man. The king sensed this and allowed him to ask a question.

His first question was not a good one I thought. It was too challenging, however I was not the one asking.

"What do you mean when you say these people were late learners ?" Frank asked.

Even our four Mayan friends stiffened at the question.

The king settled back considering the inquiry as if it had been asked by a child. He was trying to find the right words to answer the child. Showing his wisdom and patience, the king slowly smiled and spoke in a quiet and reserved tone.

"Let me give you an example. There are a few pyramids on the south continent over the eastern sea. We, indicating himself as all the Maya, taught them how to build them. Ours, waving his arm to show the surroundings, were here before they were children."

He continued to smile and stare directly at Frank, who suddenly seemed humbled. He knew he had been bested and realized his attitude had been too pushy. Instantly back peddling he assumed a proper demeanor for a professional scientist. The king in turn picked up on this and adjusted himself to reflect his acceptance of Frank as a scientist.

"I know you have a lot on your mind." remarked the king, "I hope we can come to a mutual understanding on some answers."

"I wish that also." answered Frank. "You seem to be aware of the world as we know it but where did you yourself come from ?" he continued.

"**I** thought you would get around to that." the king smiled. "My world was once the center for all culture. Knowledge of the stars and planets we inherited from those who went before us. They gave us Art and Stories and Design to build things. We learned to meld with the creatures who did not speak. We learned to work with the growing earth and seas, not control it. It cannot be controlled, they will always return to their original form. Universal powers beyond our limitations and comprehension have set things in motion that must play out on its own accord. There were those from my world that sought to control and thus brought on their own destruction. Eruptions from within the planet caused the seas to engulf the land and swallow it forever. I and others alone were allowed to escape so we could teach the ways of culture and live with the land."

We were all hypnotized by his words like children hearing their first fairy tale. I have to give Mario credit for his translation efforts of the king's words. I don't imagine it was easy deciphering phrases that were thousands of years old.

I guessed he was talking about a legend and myth that has survived for eons but no one really believed. Anticipating our thoughts the king said the magic word.

"**M**y world was called Atlan. After its upheaval we few came here and so started our new world. Over the centuries we traveled the planet enlightening peoples as we went. However, here is truly my home where the land provides all needs that matter."

Standing, scepter in hand, he announced,

"**I** must rest now, the air grows thin and I must rejuvenate."

We all knew dismissal was at hand and even Frank accepted this although a thousand more questions were begging to be asked.

As we were leaving our king spoke softly to Mario. The words could not be heard but I did see Mario glance at me and nod affirmatively to the speaker.

We left in an orderly procession quietly

contemplating what we had just witnessed. No one spoke as we assembled around our all but dead fire. Carlos poked the embers and added kindling. Diego took advantage of the new flames to reheat our now cold coffee.

Before I sat down, Mario drew me aside and whispered that the king wished to see me later tonight, alone. I attempted an explanation to Mario but he just smiled and said he didn't want to know. I then changed thoughts and asked Mario what he meant when he said earlier that he would tell me later.

"**O**h that." he answered, now using a regular speaking tone. "The king said something to me referring to the cameras. He was describing to me that long ago he saw an image projection through a hole in a wall in a reduced size, only it was upside down."

I was both shocked and elated on hearing this. Mario looked at me curiously.

"**W**hat did he mean by that ?"

"**T**his is unbelievable if it's true. What he was describing was probably the first discovery of light characteristics that would later become lenses and then cameras. He may have been present at the first demonstration but that took place thousands of years ago."

Mario interrupted with, "He did say it was on the southern land mass across the sea to the east."

"**I** can go into detail later if you want." I answered. "But right now this is definitely journal information."

Joining the group near the fire they were already occupied with that very task as had been our habit. Mario and I started our own entries.

Paper work temporarily done with we moved to our debriefing phase while eating our standard MRE's. Apparently Mateo's preliminary decipherment of the stelae's Glyph's were correct as confirmed by the king. They referenced an extremely early date, what Mateo called the pre-pre classic period. It was definitely using the long count and was most likely highlighting the beginning. Naturally it was decided a greater and more detailed study of the stelae would be done to try and fix the age of the carving and thus date the stone. Here is where my stereo pictures would be of value.

Carlos admitted the king shed a great deal of light on previously unknown history. He said we Maya have even more to be proud of than before. Carlos hoped to be able to gather more history if he could speak with the king again. It seems that's what everyone wants, more time with the king.

Diego acknowledged his interview was brief but received what he wanted most, permission to do a portrait of the king. He passed around his preliminary sketches. They were extremely life like and captured everything that was the king. I only hoped my photos would be that good.

Mario took his turn at debriefing. His discussion with the king was naturally centered on language and the history tied to it. He admitted that he himself would now have to do further study. The growth of the Mayan language encompassed many stems from middle eastern and far eastern nations. They were mixed and bastardized over the millennia into something unrecognizable even by the original language the stems were derived from. The king was most cooperative and helpful though and taught him many things regarding language decipherment.

Apparently finished with what he had to say he turned his eyes to Frank. We all followed his glance. He appeared to be deep in thought still digesting the kings words. Finally realizing we were waiting for him, he spoke humbly,

"There's no need for me to say much right now. You all witnessed my exchange with the king and I really don't have anything to add. I gather by listening to this session that you all garnered some valuable historical information. Let's just hope the king will continue to enlighten us before we awaken from this dream come true. I guess we can go back to our journals. We must record as much and as accurately as we can."

Just then a call emanated from the pyramid. It rang out a second time clearly understood by Mario who instantly took off running for the entranceway. The rest of us remained by the fire, curious.

Not even ten minutes passed when Mario returned. Looking directly at me but announcing aloud,

"**T**he king wants you Eric, in about an hour. He also wants me along to translate. Oh, and bring the camera."

"**I** guess it's your turn Eric." Frank said not looking too upset, then went back to his journal. Mario was the only one intrigued by the night time visit. I do believe he suspected something between the king and myself, but also respected my personal space. I decided I would explain what I new to Mario when I got the chance later.

It was now eight o'clock and almost dark as Mario and I walked to the great room and the king. He was waiting at his usual bench, scepter and all. Mario and I bowed in respect which visibly pleased the king. He briefly spoke with Mario, who in turn faced me;

"**H**e wants you to explain how the camera works. He is very astute and quick to understand. I have been dismissed but I will return with pencil and paper for you to illustrate with."

"**W**hat do you mean you've been dismissed. How do I talk with the king without you ?" I questioned.

"**H**e said the two of you could manage. These are his wishes. I'm afraid it's out of my hands." answered Mario. "I'll see you in a few minutes." and off he went.

There I stood, not knowing what to do next while in the back of my mind I also felt for some reason that the king and I could manage without a translator.

The king waved his hand, motioning me to sit down on the same bench as he. I was a bit surprised by this but did as

requested. He reached down under the bench and brought up the camera I so reluctantly gave him. He made a gesture toward the one I had around my neck indicating I should open it to show. I lay the case aside and removed the lens cap just as Mario returned. He bowed to the king, handed me the pad and pencil and retreated without a word.

I heard the king let out a small sigh, relieved that we were now alone. He held the camera to his eye, made a motion with his finger as if clicking the shutter, smiled and pointed to the pad and pencil. It was obvious to me that Mario must have been doing some preliminary instructing.

I hesitated. Well not really hesitated, I paused collecting my thoughts. I never before taught someone who did not understand English. Finally deciding on a starting point I held the camera in one hand and with the other pointed first to my eye and then to the camera lens. Drawing a lens representation on the pad. I then pointed to the opposite wall and made a line on the pad away from the lens figure. I drew another line, smaller and closer behind the lens. The king was watching intently. My next step was to connect the two lines through the center of the lens, top of one to bottom of the other and visa- versa. The king was then all smiles, he pointed to the opposite wall then turned his head as upside down as he could. He straightened up and looked at me questioningly. He pointed to the wall again, then touched the back of my camera. I smiled, almost in disbelief, and nodded affirmatively. Mario was right, the king understood completely and instantly. I wish my other students over the years caught on as quickly.

What to do next stumped me and I could see the king anxiously waiting. Then it dawned on me. My wallet, I had pictures in my wallet. I dug it out and removed three different ones to show as samples. A portrait of an old girlfriend, a vase from Mesa Verde and a landscape scene on the back of some ones business card. One by one I went through the motion of pointing to an object, clicking my camera, then holding the picture at the back of the camera. Again the king smiled broadly pointing to the wall, the lens and the photo. This was almost too easy I thought but we were getting along fine.

Questions and answers were becoming complex but overall it was still easy teaching. He understood before I was halfway through the answers. An hour had whizzed by unnoticed. The king hand signaled to put the camera down and follow him. He moved to an earthen chest by the pedestal and retrieved some fresh fruit. *"How does he do that and where does it come from."* I wondered. We ate silently both feeling at ease.

Now refreshed, he bid me follow him as he moved to the wall that opened. Indicating that I should close my eyes, which I did, I then heard stone moving on stone. A light tap on my shoulder told me I could open my eyes. There before me was the library.

There had to be thousands of scrolls on the shelves of stone and sticks of a type of wood I could not identify. I turned to the king who was smiling knowingly.

*"**H**e knows."* I thought. *"Of course he knows stupid but for some reason trusted me not to have told the others."*

I nodded to him letting him know I understood. He also nodded slightly in return. It was amazing how well we understood each with a span of some two or three thousand years between us.

The king chose two scrolls from different places and returned to the big room. He stretched them out side by side on the bench. Employing hand signals again, he made it clear one was very old and the other from when he lay down on the pedestal. Now it was my turn to interrupt him, which I did not feel uncomfortable doing. I raised my hand to halt him, and he nodded approval. I returned to pencil and pad again and between that and hand motions I managed to get my question across, which was basically,

"How was he still alive all these years on the pedestal sealed in."

It took a while but he did comprehend what I was asking. He smiled and again touched my shoulder as if patting it. Taking my pad and pencil he drew two suns and then said quite distinctly, "Mario." Then making three lines he pointed to the first, then to himself, the second then to me, finally the third and said

again Mario. Nothing could be clearer; in two days the three of us would meet and my question would be answered. I shook my head yes.

The king, very unceremoniously, put his arm around my back and gently guided me back to the library. He bid me wait there as he returned to the great room. Twenty seconds later he reappeared with my camera. He said a few words, which of course I did not understand, but simultaneously employed hand signals. Opening a scroll flat on a stone, he aimed my camera at it, made the motion of clicking the shutter then with one of the photographs I had showed him went through the act of removing it from the back of the camera. Holding the photo in an out stretched arm to no one, said

"Mario."

Not knowing whether to laugh or cry I looked at him, shock, I'm sure showing on my face.

"Was he saying what I think he was saying." I wondered aloud.

The king was looking right into my eyes showing a quiet smile and as if anticipating my thoughts said clearly in English, "Yes."

I repeated his motions with the camera and photograph, including the act of handing it to Mario, and in answer the king again said yes.

My mind started spinning a million miles a minute. What a find ! What a discovery ! to be able to copy all these scrolls for later study. How much time would it take ? I don't have that much film with me. Which do I copy first ? How do I get more film here ? How long will it take not only to get the film but to actually shoot every scroll ? Can I start now ? Can I come Back at another time ? Will they still be here ? Will the king still be here ? Do I stay here ? The questions in my head were coming so fast I could not even fix on one when it was forgotten and replaced by another.

I felt the king's hand on my arm as he led me to a bench and made me sit. By his own example he had me breath deeply to relax. He sat down next to me, the low smile still fixed on his face. It took a few minutes, but I did calm down somewhat, even though the excitement was overwhelming. Lost in my thoughts again I was not aware my new friend left the bench and closed the wall to the scroll chamber until he returned and was standing before me. Handing me my camera and papers he looked to the passageway out. Our session was over. He placed his hand on my shoulder, smiled and proudly said yes again as we walked to the door. A few feet from the opening he stopped as I continued towards the outside.

The night was pitch. Thank goodness for the glow of the fire embers to lead me back to my cot. The others were asleep. Checking my watch as I fell to my bed, It was three forty in the morning. I started to review what had just transpired but everything went black from exhaustion.

Chapter 17

The heat was intense as the flames engulfed the pyramid. So much so that the stones themselves were melting. I ran to the telephone booth only to find it occupied by some woman gossiping with a friend.

"**P**lease get off the phone." I yelled, "This is an emergency."

The woman ignored me and turned her back to me. I banged on the glass of the door to no avail. Then I heard a voice behind me.

"**N**othing doing pal, you're not jumping ahead of me, I'm next for the phone."

"**B**ut this is a real emergency. Can't you see the whole jungle and pyramid are in flames." I pleaded.

"**S**o, what's that got to do with me." was the answer I got.

"**N**O ! NO !" I screamed. "This can't be happening to me." I ran over to the bird bath, tried to scoop up some water when I felt a hand on my shoulder and my name being called.

"**E**ric, Eric." Diego's voice said softly. "It's okay man, you must have been having a nightmare."

I looked into his eyes and could feel my body shudder as it slowly came back to life. I sat up feeling a little woozy.

"**T**ake it slow." Diego said, "I'll get you some coffee."

I thanked him as he returned with the black coffee.

"**W**hat was that all about." he inquired.

"**I**'m not sure I even know myself." I lied, a little embarrassed. "I don't remember much at all."

"**P**robably from staying out carousing all night. I understand the night life around here is pretty hot." Diego chided.

"**W**here is everybody." I asked looking around.

"**F**rank and Mario were summoned to the king, and Carlos and Mateo went fishing for supper." Diego said. "Frank and Mario have been gone since eight o'clock."

I looked at my watch. I couldn't believe it said almost ten thirty. I guess all that excitement of yesterday plain wore me out. I walked around a bit looking for something to eat when I heard Diego say,

"**W**hat do you think" referring to a charcoal drawing at his table.

I wandered over and was stunned. This man was truly an artist. I thought his preliminary sketches were good but this was the king himself ready to step off the paper.

Mario and Frank walked toward us looking quite pleased. Seeing me led to remarks about sleeping late and staying out so late.

"**B**y the way Diego, you and I are to return to the king this afternoon, and bring your artwork.." commented Mario.

Frank, a bit more serious now questioned politely,

"**I** understand you have something to share with us ?"

Mario added, "It's okay Eric, the king said he shared something with you that you are to share with the rest of us."

Smiling myself now I said I was very anxious to give out my information, but in all fairness I would like to wait for the return of Mateo and Carlos. Frank reluctantly agreed but was obviously a little annoyed.

"**B**y the way." he asked, "How did you manage with the king not knowing the language at all."

"**I**'ve been asking myself the same question. I don't really know. We just seem to have a mental connection. It's almost like we can read each others thought's Trying to switch back to a lighter note I commented,

"**Y**ou're really going to like what the king shared with me. Oh and while we're waiting, did you learn anything new today."

"**A**s a matter of fact we did." smiled Frank. "Thanks to Mario's translations we learned some interesting history about our new found city. Apparently this was a central repository for knowledge."

These words of his triggered an internal smile in me.

"Only the very elite resided here. Knowledge, or culture as the king says, and governing emitted from this very temple. This particular pyramid housed the highest authority of all. So our king may be "The King" and so far everything points in that direction."

"**H**ey! Look at that, our party boy is finally awake. joked Carlos.

"**D**on't talk so loud." joined in Mateo. "He may have a hangover."

All five joined in the ribbing for the next few minutes. There was not much I could do but take it and smile and accept it the way it was meant.

"**O**kay you guys if you don't knock it off I won't tell you my secret." I threatened.

Frank took over from there explaining to the others what the king said and how I was to share the news. All eyes were on me now. I took a swig of coffee and was about to start when Mateo interrupted,

"**W**hoa, wait till I take care of these fish."

He held up a catch of four good sized fish I dared not to ask the name of. With in five minutes he was back as attentive as the others. So I began my tale of the camera and library.

"**W**here is this library and how do we get to it." inquired Frank.

"**I** know where it is but how to get into it I have not been made privy to. At least not yet. But. And this is the crowning jewel, he said I could use my camera and copy all the scrolls for future study, but they can not leave the tomb."

E very one was stunned to silence, even Frank. Then as if it was ice melting smiles began to appear. Mario was the first to speak,

"I guess I have my life's work already planned for me."

This drew a few chuckles. Questions poured forth from all five at the same time.

"Okay guys, slow down." I asked "Yes, I have been in the library, and yes I have seen the scrolls. There must be thousands of them. From what I can gather from the king this is history going back before what we know as recorded time."

"This will be the biggest breakthrough since the Codex. Even bigger then the Codex." stated Mario.

"This could possibly rewrite history itself." said Carlos.

Eyes fell to Frank

"I'm thinking of the papers, books, appearances; this may be a hard thing to sell. No one likes to think that the history we have known for centuries is wrong. These scrolls may be the truth, but the establishment minds are not going to change over night just because we produce a few scrolls. Especially only photographs of them. They are going to fight and question everything we may say."

"Right now who cares about them. Let's just do the job we are all trained to do and do it to the best of our ability, gathering help and support as we go and let the pieces fall where they may." preached Mateo. "Fearing something that has not happened yet will only hinder our work. Let us accept this gift of gifts and educate ourselves."

Silence reigned for a time while each digested Mateo's words. All agreed and all were happy again. Frank came over to shake my hand,

"I don't know how or what you did Eric, but history, myself and all Maya will thank you and will be grateful for all eternity."

I thought this was going a little overboard but I

accepted his thanks and was glad there were no hard feelings between us.

Chapter 18

$\mathbf{M}$ario's name was being called,

"$\mathbf{O}$h geeze ! I almost forgot. Come on Diego, grab your stuff and let's go." said Mario.

$\mathbf{T}$hey arrived at the great room to find the king all smiles. They started to bow but the king bade them stand up. They looked at each other questioningly. Then in total surprise the king said to them, still smiling,

"$\mathbf{C}$ome sit." as he pointed to the bench. "Have you made any progress with your art ?"

$\mathbf{D}$iego unrolled his charcoal portrait proudly. The king moaned a sigh of approval, reached for a large scroll of his own and opened it. It too was a portrait. Mario and Diego stared at the two drawings side by side. They were almost identical. The king still showing his approval said something to Mario using words of the Long Count time. Translating for Diego he said,

"$\mathbf{H}$is portrait is just over three thousand years old. It was done by one of the court artisans as a present for him. He also asked if he can keep the one you did after you sign it and date it.."

$\mathbf{N}$ot wanting to part with his work, he also felt honored, so Diego agreed reluctantly.

"I can always do another." he mumbled.

$\mathbf{T}$he king picked up the camera he had and pointed to the outside asking for a name of the other man.

"$\mathbf{E}$ric." answered Mario.

"$\mathbf{E}$ric." repeated the king quite correctly. He then continued to say that Eric can copy both portraits with his camera.

Explaining this to Diego resulted in a broad smile. The king then took them around the whole room describing the events the wall paintings depicted. Stopping at a blank space about five feet wide he turned to Diego and said ,

"This is for you."

At first Diego did not understand. Mario then explained that the king wanted Diego to draw this event for posterity, just like the others. Diego was humbled, yet overwhelmed with emotion. He bowed in thanks. The king touched his shoulder, smiled and said,

"Yes."

Diego was instructed to start tomorrow early and for now they were both dismissed. As they were leaving, the king handed Mario the pictures from Eric's wallet he had left behind.

Outside it was raining heavily and the pair made a dash for the tarp shelter. Relaxing out of the wet Diego related his encounter with the king and his commission to draw this event on the wall.

Mario spoke with me about shooting both portraits with his camera.

This expedition was turning out to be a huge success. Much more than was anticipated. The evening turned into a mini celebration along with the fresh fish dinner.

Later, lying in my cot, I could not believe my good fortune. I smiled to himself and let the rain lull me to sleep.

Chapter 19

Diego, not wanting to go against the kings wishes was up early and out on an expedition of discovery. Luckily for him, his knowledge of prehistoric art and study of Mayan art gave him a firm basis of what natural ingredients he needed to make the colors he would need for his wall art. He wanted to keep in the tradition of his ancestors and match as close as possible the already existing art work. By noon time he was satisfied with what materials he found to fulfill his needs.

He and I had a quick lunch out of necessity and excitedly walked to the pyramid. The king was waiting and acknowledged our presence without words. He pointed with his scepter and Diego went to his assigned wall and immediately got lost in his own world.

The king turned to me smiling, put his arm around my shoulder and led me to the already opened library vault. Leading me to a back corner I interpreted his motion to mean this was the beginning. I was almost afraid to touch the scrolls for they seemed so fragile and delicate. He encouraged me to proceed as I slowly and gently extended my hand to touch one. I was surprised and amazed to see how sturdy they were. Whatever their process was for producing this parchment like material, it was light weight and appeared extremely strong. Gaining confidence because of this I lay it on the flat surface provided by the king, and secured it with long flat stones. I set up my camera on my light weight travel tripod and snapped my first exposure. The torch light in the room burned with an amazingly bright light that almost had a blue white hue to it. It was well suited to do the work ahead of me. I was soon into a regular step by step routine of copying these priceless treasures. Apparently the king had complete trust in me as I soon found myself alone. No matter, I was too thrilled and involved in what I was doing to really notice or care.

In the meantime the other four members of our team had been summoned and a history question and answer period had begun. As usual Mario had been invaluable. I found out later it wasn't just Mayan life being discussed, but the king seemed to have extensive insights into other parts of the world of old.

Afternoon arrived sooner than expected and I was instructed by the king that my time was up for the day as it was also for Diego. I wanted to keep going but I knew better than to counter the kings wishes. I packed up my equipment and joined Diego in the great room. We bid our farewell and headed for the exit.

It was only mid afternoon and both Diego and I were disappointed about leaving early. The others were also surprised to see us leaving the tomb. Our usual debriefing took place with everyone more than satisfied as to how the day went. The chat was short and all took to doing their own thing. Frank was well buried in his journal, Diego was mixing more color while I was doing a film count. Mario and Carlos were playing a game with small pebbles, and old Mayan game I assumed, which caught my attention but I did not have the time right now.

Supper was light with everyone just sort of picking at whatever was available. The conversation was light also, mostly speculation on what do we do next. Everything seemed to be working out so well. Too well I thought. Something started nagging at the back of my mind. I couldn't quite put my finger on it. I just felt like the bubble was going to burst any minute now. I kept these thoughts to myself because the others seemed to be taking everything in stride. I did, however, enter these doubts in my journal as a foot note. I could always just scratch them out later if nothing came of it. Remembering tomorrow was a special day, the king was going to reveal his secret of staying alive. I reminded Mario, who was also anxiously awaiting.

Finishing up with my camera equipment faster than I expected sort of left me hanging without anything to do. Everybody else was otherwise occupied so I decided to take a walk. I grabbed my camera, made my intentions known to Diego and left the compound through the archway.

Once outside I turned left for no particular reason. I lazily followed the compound wall though I was at a distance of thirty some odd feet. Enjoying the dappled light and thinking of nothing in particular, a sudden sound caught my attention. It was not the usual jungle sound. I froze, listening, remembering that there are large jungle cats that appear now and then. I stood silent for at least three minutes not hearing a thing. Deciding to dismiss the whole thing, I took a step and heard the noise again. I froze again and could feel my nerves tense and tingles run down my back.

"**I** should not have come out alone." I thought. I didn't even have my knife with me. "Stay calm." I repeated to myself. I heard it again, this time behind me. Trying not to move too fast I slowly turned my head. Standing there was the king. A slight smile crossing his lips. My whole body instantly relaxed although my breathing was stall a little rapid. I bowed my head in recognition, the king returned the nod. It was obvious he saw the question on my face as he reached down for a basket by his feet filled with jungle fruit. He turned away from me but signaled for me to follow. We had walked about a hundred feet when he stopped at a large boulder. It moved exposing an opening that revealed steps leading underground. I followed blindly as he descended. I counted ten steps, then a narrow passageway about twenty feet in length, then again ten steps up which opened to the great room. The wall door swung closed, again leaving no trace of seam. Once closed, the king turned to me sporting a large smile. He seemed to sense my curiosity. He pointed to the wall that was no longer and shook his head in a negative manner. To me the message was clear, don't tell anyone about the rear entrance. I confirmed what he had said and took my leave, questions filling my head. That uneasy nagging feeling was there again.

"What was wrong with this picture ?" I kept asking myself. Perhaps there would be some answers tomorrow.

Back at the campsite, I mentioned nothing to the others of my encounter with the king although I still had uneasy feelings about what was happening lately. I settled in a seat away from the others, journal in hand. I opened the now dirty book but did not see the pages. My mind was preoccupied in another zone.

As much as I liked the attention from the king, there was a disturbance there, a gut feel if you will, that was very unsettling. Was this all a hoax ? Some kind of big joke ? Could the king really have been asleep all those years ? Was he even really a king ? Who was he and where did he come from ? More importantly, why ?

I was startled back to the present by Diego who was handing me a cup of coffee.

"**W**hat a great day this has been." he said cheerfully, "I can't believe our good fortune."

I smiled and agreed with him, trying to hide my real feelings of disturbance. We chatted for a while about his art, particularly what he was doing now in the tomb. I was happy for him but still plagued by uneasiness. For Diego's sake I hoped my feelings were wrong.

Darkness was fully upon us and Diego said good night. I moved to my cot and welcomed the night and the chance to be alone again.

Chapter 20

I awoke to a relatively bright day. At least it was not raining, and I wasn't feeling too bad but I remained a little apprehensive about yesterday's darker shadows that had crossed my mind. I made a conscious decision to dismiss those feelings as best I could.

Breakfast was fruit and coffee and fun conversation. Everybody was in an upscale mood. I was with Frank when the king 's call came, summoning Mario and myself.

"**T**his is it." I said to Frank. "Perhaps we can get some answers now."

I grabbed my camera and met up with Mario and started for the pyramid.

Once inside, the king, as usual, was seated in the same spot. Next to him on the bench were a few scrolls and an earthen cylinder of sorts. The king indicated with his ever present scepter a nearby bench. We settled ourselves while the king spoke a few words to Mario. He then looked at me and nodded. There seemed to be a twinkle or sparkle in his eye divulging a hidden secret between us. His gaze did not go unnoticed by Mario who looked at me with a half smile.

As the king spoke, Mario translated.

"**S**o, my friends, you want to know how I came to be here. If I did not know the things I know, I would be curious also. I like that in a person. Since you are curious I'm guessing you do not have too advanced a knowledge of the sciences as of yet. I would

have thought that by now you would have learned of such things."

Mario and I looked at each other a bit bewildered. Here we thought we were so advanced only to be politely criticized by someone who was over two thousand years old.

The king smiled at us and continued,

"These scrolls here", as he reached for one, "tell of the preservation process and the need to do it."

Again Mario and I looked at each other questionably. What did he mean by ***"The need to do it. ?"*** I thought. As if reading my thoughts again, the king pressed on.

"Our scholars realized long ago the need for the preservation of our scientific knowledge. Many of our ambassadors traveled to distant parts of the world meeting peoples of all kinds and knowledge. We determined the necessity of collecting this world wide learning and having it repose in one place. We also determined it would be up to us to keep this history because the other societies around the globe were not stable enough to maintain them without destruction. A man called Alexander, a long time ago, had the foresight to try this only to have his storage place destroyed by short sighted peoples. This act only confirmed what we already knew and further cemented our resolve. The future of this cosmic orb is on shaky grounds, more so now I'm sure than the last time I walked the nations. Even our own people were destroyed by those who thought themselves superior when in fact their knowledge of the sciences was lacking to the point of destruction of others and eventually their own self annihilation. We on the other hand, have managed to endure through our use of the sciences in a way they were meant to be employed."

The king paused here and refreshed himself with a vessel of water. He ignored us while he reread the scroll in his hand. He put it aside and reached for another. We watched a tear form in his eye as he read this second scroll. We were anxious for more of his tale but dared not disturb him. Finally looking up at us he made no excuses but continued as if there had been no interruption.

"I and others like me were put into a preservation state throughout the world, each of us a keeper of the collective sciences. Whether or not the others have survived is yet to be determined. That will be my quest once I have found persons responsible enough to handle this knowledge of the sciences. I only pray that I am not too late."

I looked at Mario who appeared to be shaken as he finished translating the last few words. Gazing back at me Mario said,

"It's obvious the king does not know the state the world is in today."

"You mean because of the wars, pollution and greed that controls the planet today."

"Exactly." he returned. "Do we dare tell him."

Turning again to the king and noticing his expression as he listened to us I said,

"I think we just did."

The king waved us silent, and ignoring our interruption, continued his discourse.

"This," again indicating a scroll, "Contains the secret of our preservation. When you opened this resting place of mine you most likely detected an almost unpleasant odor. This was not stale air of long ago. It was a gaseous substance that kept us in a suspended animation state for later discovery and release. You have triggered my release so that I may hopefully continue my work of sharing our long collected knowledge. A goal that is only meant for the good of all peoples, not the destruction and control. These scrolls in the wrong hands could mean the ultimate annihilation of the living things of this planet as has happened so many times before."

The king paused again letting us digest his words. The silence was frightening as our minds and imagination worked on what we just heard.

Then came the question.

"Can you be the keeper and the teachers of this collective information and not let it's power influence you to control others ?"

This wasn't just a question, it was the question of all time.

How does one person, or even a few people maintain

such a wealth of knowledge and not be tainted by it's power ? How does one protect this knowledge to be used for good against those who would use it for world domination ? How does one protect himself against others who would destroy life itself to gain access to such knowledge which in turn is power of control ? The questions were without end. The answers were not forthcoming. The king obviously knew this as he watched both of us struggling, knowing he put our minds in turmoil. He smiled a knowing and understanding smile. Neither of us spoke for quite a while because there was probably no real answer. It was a question that has plagued mankind since the beginning of intelligence. I began to doubt there even was an answer. I suddenly decided I needed more information. Here we were contemplating the future of mankind but still did not know the scope of the sciences the king referred to, so in my innocense I asked directly,

"What exactly is it that we do not possess that you feel would corrupt and destroy us."

The king nodded his approval of my inquiry. Directing our attention to the scrolls he answered,

"This is the knowledge that can change the future for all persons from all nations. It is beyond the comprehension of most but the discerning few,"

I immediately pictured in my mind Steven Hawking. A mind beyond most now residing in a physical host which was of no value to him in the way of movement. I pushed my inquiry further stating,

"I understand what you have just said but that does not tell me what that knowledge is specifically. Can you give us an example of what you are referring to. A demonstration if you will. I find it difficult to make an intelligent decision on something I have no knowledge of."

I hoped, deep inside, I did not offend the king with my directness but I felt we were being taunted with riddles. The king paused considering my request. Fearing I pushed things too far I was about to rephrase my question when the king extended his hand and retrieved his scepter. Now staring directly at Mario and I he moved his arm outward away from us all and appeared to squeeze the trunk of the scepter. The room was instantly filled with a blue white light. It was almost blinding and at the same time was soft and very acceptable to our eyes. Daylight had been duplicated in the room. There was no noise or heat from the light source. Mario and I were stunned into silence, in awe as to what was before us. The king spoke calmly and matter of factly without emotion.

"This is an unlimited and unrestrained power source. It can be used to power anything at no physical or monetary expense. It is all but harmless, however, with a slight modification it can destroy instantly all matter. This entire planet could be vaporized in a matter of seconds. Does that answer your question, my cautious friend ? This is only one of many things these scrolls tell of. So I will ask again. Can you be the keeper and teacher of this collective information and not let it's power influence you to control others."

I felt as if the weight of the world was just dumped on my shoulders and I'm sure Mario reacted the same. Finally finding courage I answered the king.

"I think I or we could be the keepers," I pointed out to Mario, "But I feel that once the secret of this power source was known we would most likely be in great danger, and that is something I don't know if I can handle or would want to handle. I don't know what you remember of your time before on this planet but today's world is not an ideal situation."

"I'm sure you are right my friend, the paths that some men follow are not always the right ones. This has always been the nature of man. Now you know why we have kept this collective of knowledge, hoping some day it could be used to benefit all peoples. It could provide unlimited heat to those who live in the dark frozen lands; power water pumping for those in the dry lands, cooling in the heated jungles. But by what you are saying though, the same mind set that existed thousands of years ago, still exists today. If that is truly the case then I can understand your hesitation. But being of positive thinking and attitude is what has kept us going as a people. We have always known that we were advanced beyond all others but were willing to hold ourselves back in order to bring others out of the dark. Our willingness to wait these few thousand years has not been totally in vain. I have encountered the two of you and Diego. This has given me much hope. Perhaps, before I go further with this gift of knowledge you could enlighten me on the scientific status of your world today."

The king paused a moment obviously contemplating before he went on.

"As anxious as I am to learn this information, it shall have to wait another sun. I am growing weary as I know Mario is also from translating for both of us."

I put up a mild protest, but to no avail which is what I expected. Talking to the king was sometimes like watching a serial movie when we were kids. Just when things got exciting, it was continued next week. In all fairness though I knew Mario was getting tired. It was quite a struggle at times for him to find the right words in translation to make sense of the Old Mayan words or phrases.

"You may send Diego to continue his art. He will not disturb me."

We knew now we were dismissed. Bowing respectfully we left the king and once again entered the daylight. It was early afternoon and the air was very refreshing. We drank deeply of it hoping to clear our minds. Mario and I lingered just outside the tomb doorway both mentally reviewing what had transpired with the king. Mario spoke first, echoing my own thoughts.

"I don't think we should tell the others all that we heard and saw. At least not just yet."

"I agree." I answered, "What we witnessed was almost too much to believe."

"That scepter thing I found downright frightening." replied Mario.

"Yes it was a bit scary." I said. "I wonder though, was it real or just some kind of trick ?" Do you really think that it is some kind of energy source ? If it was it's potential is unbounded."

I looked at Mario who had a look of disbelief on his face that I could question something the king had presented.

"Don't get me wrong Mario, but before I believe

everything completely I think I would like more information and further demonstrations. If this energy source is what he says it is, it's way beyond any technology that we possess today and yet it is thousands of years old. How can this be ? What happened to man all those years in between. We, or at least what we know of history, were still throwing rocks when your ancestors had this potential to change the world. This is what I find so questionable. The fact that this potential is now being offered to us, I find downright frightening. How do you go about using this for all mankind when there will be those who would kill and destroy to possess and control ? What safeguards will we have against such movements ?"

Mario continued to look at me though acceptance of what I was saying could be seen in his face.

"At least we have time now to reflect on what we have learned so far." I continued, "Perhaps we will know more tomorrow. Please go with me on this Mario, this is far too important to make hasty decisions."

He smiled in answer as we turned and walked to the others.

Frank was the first with questions as we neared the group. Mario and I explained the gaseous preservation state but avoided anything more. Frank was pleased with the information we gave him but you could tell he wanted more. He seemed annoyed that he could not have more direct contact with the king. He was even a little jealous of Diego having more time in the tomb. I had a lot of respect for Frank as an archeologist, but he was one of the people I had in the back of my mind when I spoke of control. He would not mean to control on purpose but I could see it happening, especially under the influence of others. I did not want to bring this up even to Mario because loyalties can make unsuspecting bedfellows. Mario relayed the kings message to Diego who happily gathered his art materials and was on his way whistling cheerfully.

Questions having been answered somewhat satisfactorily I wandered back to my cameras. I needed time to think. Too much was happening too fast and it all had to be sorted out. I cleaned my lenses and cameras, sorted out my film and performed other meaningless tasks almost as an involuntary reflex action while my mind was mired in the clutter of the last few day's events.

For the rest of the day I tried to keep to myself as much as possible. I really needed the alone time. Diego returned just before supper, his usual happy self, Frank instantly cornering him, but to no avail. He had no new information. In fact he said he had not even seen the king until he was dismissed. Frank was becoming impatient and everyone knew it. After a quiet dinner he joined me at my sleeping area. Trying to act nonchalant he asked,

"So Eric how goes the picture taking ? Do you have all the scrolls copied yet ?"

"Hardly." I lied, "It's not as easy as it sounds. They have been rolled so tight for so long they have to be handled with kid gloves." I exaggerated. "It's going to take a lot of time, if I even have enough film."

"I know, I know." He answered, "I'm not rushing you, I was just being curious. Tell me, when you talk with the king do you get much information from him." he pried. "I thought for sure, once we met him that we would have all the answers to a lot of old mysteries. I have to admit I feel quite disappointed so far. I feel like I'm back in Anthropology 101. We sure could use a break with some new historical documentation about now."

"Boy, if he only knew." I thought to myself. Pretending to be interested in what he was saying, I sympathized with him and counseled him with the fact that it has only been a few days and that we should give him time to learn to trust us. Surprisingly, this appeared to make him feel better. We continued with some polite chit-chat and he finally said good night.

I was happy to be alone again but I was not happy or pleased with myself for withholding information the way I did. I rationalized my feelings by telling myself all will be disclosed soon enough. I soaked my head with some water and lay down looking forward to my night time symphony.

Chapter 21

It was a restless night. Even the jungle orchestrations would not sooth my troubled mind. Each time I would start to doze off I was taunted by the king's words. *"Why me ?"* I kept thinking. *Why is the king favoring me to be the keeper of his secrets ? I am not a scientist or a political leader or statesman. I have no influence on world happenings."* My thoughts returned to my earlier doubts. I believed the king, yet I didn't believe him. If he has all this power and knowledge, let him use it himself. Suddenly it dawned on me. Perhaps he can't use it. Perhaps his time is limited because of the preservation technology. Perhaps even his sciences have limitations. I started racking my brain for a candidate to be the keeper of this future world. No matter how hard I tried, the answer always came up the same. *"No One."* The few that would even be close that I could think of would easily be overcome and destroyed by the greed and power hungry many who existed in today's world. The responsibility is far too great for any one man, or for any one group for that matter. The king seemed to be referring to an ideal world. I personally don't know if that could even really exist. Knowing the world as it exists today to me would make it an impossibility.

My next question for the king is how extensive is the science he is always referring to. Maybe it's just another form of control that has reared it's ugly head time and time again through the centuries. What ever it is I feel it's beyond my capabilities, or am I just making excuses for fear of failure. Failure of what though ? Now I know I'm thinking in circles. For all I know the king may not even be thinking of me as a successor. Perhaps he is just using us to lead him to the right person. Now I feel I'm back to where I started from. Suddenly my head cleared and the only thing I heard was my favorite night time serenade. I could feel the stress leaving me as I let myself be drawn into the music.

Apparently I slept. I don't really recall when I dozed but the smell of coffee tickled my nostrils enough for me to open my eyes to daylight   I sat up shaking off the cobwebs of the night. Carlos was the only one awake and he greeted me with a salute with his coffee mug. I nodded in return, still not quite awake myself. I made my way to the coffee pot and drank deeply of the hot black syrup. I was really becoming addicted to the black stuff. I breathed an unconscious sigh as the coffee went down and Carlos laughed quietly.

"**I**t does get to you after a while doesn't it."

I just smiled in answer and sat down at the table. Carlos sat across from me and after the time of day pleasantries he became more specific.

"**I**'ve been meaning to ask out of curiosity, since you seem to have spent more time with the king, has he ever mentioned possessing powers that were beyond the understanding of most men ?"

"**W**hy do you ask ?" I questioned in reply not wanting to divulge any information yet. He took another swig of coffee and quietly responded.

"**W**ell, I recall years ago reading a report by an archeologist, I can't remember his name at the moment, who had been doing some Mayan research and mentioned just such a thing. Supposedly he had found a letter in some church archives in Spain, written by a missionary who came over with the early explorers. Remember, one of the purported missions of Spain at the time was conversion of all the heathens to the Catholic faith. Anyway, in this letter he talks of a scroll he had seen with some strange markings, almost like writing. It was translated for him by one of his local converts, talking of this power. Of course this priest dismissed that such a thing could exist, but nevertheless he did mention it in his letter to the Spanish home church. He also reported that he had that scroll in his possession. What has since happened to it is anybody's guess. It was reported the priest was working in the Uxmal area well north of here.

"That's quite a story. Do you think that letter still exists today ?" I asked..

"I really couldn't say." Carlos replied. "The archeologist's report was from the early nineteen hundreds, so I guess it's possible that it still resides in the archives of the church of Spain. Which particular church and where would have to be determined."

I was excited by what Carlos had told me but did not want to reveal anything yet.

"I had not heard any stories like that so far but perhaps I could ask the king if the opportunity arose." I responded. I wonder what this so called power was." I said rhetorically.

"I've wondered about that for years but I must admit I never pursued it any further. Maybe I should have." Carlos answered.

Mateo was now awake and after filling his mug with coffee joined us at the table. He spoke of going fishing for dinner again and I was glad for the change of subject. After a few minutes I excused myself, returning to my cot. I sat down fumbling with my camera so I could reflect on the conversation with Carlos. This information shed new light on what the king said. Perhaps he wasn't totally out to lunch. It was known that some of these old missionary's were extremely reliable in their reporting, and tolerant and understanding of the people they had conquered. I will definitely mention this to Mario. Hopefully we can talk with the king about this power, or knowledge as he calls it, again. Not this soon though, I thought. I still need time to collect my thoughts.

By now everyone was up and our little camp was busy with routine activity. I had already made arrangements with Mateo to go fishing in the afternoon. This was the perfect excuse for me not to see the king today. I found Frank at his writing table and convinced him to see the king. I could tell he was excited with the thought even though he did not pre-arrange the meeting. I was also counting on the king's hospitality and congenial nature not to turn Frank away.

Right after a light lunch Mateo and I started off for the river, fishing gear in hand, while Frank and Mario headed for the tomb. Diego was already there working on his event mural. Carlos was now alone working on his writing which I'M sure he was happy with the alone time. I know I would be.

Learning new ways to fish from Mateo was a welcome relief from the pressures of my visits with the king. No mention at all was made of our searching expedition, just light conversation of river fishing techniques entertained us both. It was like a day off and a very welcome one.

Late afternoon and a bakers dozen large fish to our credit, Mateo and I returned to camp. Frank and the others had been dismissed an hour or so earlier by the king. I braced myself for a scolding as I noticed Frank walking towards me.

"I see you had a good day also." he said indicating our string of fish.

"Yeah, we did pretty good." I replied.

"My day was great." Frank said excitedly. "I'm glad you urged me to go. I have a lot to share with everybody."

"Can it wait until supper Frank ? I promised Mateo I would help clean the fish and do the cooking tonight."

"Sure thing Eric, I want everyone to hear it at the same time anyway. I'll catch you later."

That being said Frank turned and went back to his table. I sighed quietly to myself. *"That's a relief."* I thought *"I guess he had a good time with the king. I wonder what little tidbits he learned to make him so happy. The fact that he's happy again is the important thing. Now perhaps he won't bug me for a while."* Feeling better myself now I cheerfully attacked the task of fish cleaning while Mateo prepared the fire.

As it turned out I wasn't the only one affected by Frank's good mood. Everyone benefitted and the atmosphere at dinner was light and jovial. Frank, of course, dominated the conversation with a few fill ins by Mario. The king shed some new light on not only this city but others as well. This was actually the oldest, though not the most elaborate in design. Why this had not been discovered before was a puzzle to all. He pointed out that some of the engineering and art work, as good as they were, were not as advanced and sophisticated as in other temples and cities. Frank went on for what seemed like an hour. The fish dinner, by the way, was as good as his new information. With dinner finally over and the stories at an end everyone drifted to their journals to log the day's activities.

Mario joined me shortly thereafter.

"The king was not happy with your absence." he said. "He is not accustomed to being put off that way by one of his subjects."

I think Mario anticipated my reaction because he instantly put his finger to his lips in an attempt to quiet me. I understood his meaning and looked around to make sure I had not disturbed the others with my sudden outburst. Lowering my voice I ranted at Mario, who politely listened, that I was not one of his subjects. My tirade finally over Mario spoke,

"I'm just the messenger Eric. I understand how you might feel. You must remember though, the king is from another era when things were different."

I looked apologetically at Mario and replied,

"I'm sorry my friend. Forgive me for making you the blunt of my anger and you are right, the king is from another time. I think we both have a lot to learn from each other."

Calm having returned, Mario finished his message that the king wished to see me first thing in the morning. I looked directly at Mario and said,

"Check with me again in the morning and I'll tell you then if I am going to comply with his wishes."

Mario agreed but I could see he was disturbed by my answer. I think he also knew it was useless to continue any further discussion. He politely said good night and left me alone with my thoughts. As I watched him walk away I realized I was no longer upset, in fact I felt rather pleased with myself and sat down with my journal before going to bed.

The next morning our old friend Rain was back. A good reason not to get out of bed. As I lay there listening to the rain I started thinking about the king's proposal. In my mind we seemed to be pretty well advanced. That is the collective we of course. Yet the king spoke as if we were almost primitive. It dawned on me then that this should be my next discussion with the king, to let him know

just how advanced we are. After all, not being around for the past
few thousand years I'm sure he has no idea.

This trick he performed with the scepter could have been just that.
A trick, something to keep the masses in line. But then again I
shouldn't judge without all the correct information, nor should he.
I decided then to see the king again. We must have this discussion.
I don't know how long I lay there thinking but the sound of voices
mingled with my thoughts, enough to realize that others were up and
about. I dragged myself out of my cot, washed and headed for the
coffee pot. Mario was already there and showed no signs of anger
from yesterday. I was thankful for that. I mentioned about seeing
the king and why, which pleased him. We had a quick breakfast,
notified the others of our intention and took off for the tomb.

     As we entered the outer room we caught the king, as
the expression goes, with his pants down. Apparently not expecting
us this early, he was finishing up his morning toilet. Dressed only in
a sort of loin cloth, his torso was a surprise to us both. He was
sinuously lean, with muscles that seemed to dance with his every
move. The skin was taut without an ounce of fat to be detected. I
judged him to be about one hundred and eighty pounds on an almost
six foot frame. He reminded me of a sleek panther when he moved.
The whole scene just added to the confusion in my head as to how he
could have maintained such physical shape while having been asleep
for two thousand years. I did note however that the scepter, as usual,
was not far from his reach. I made a mental note to investigate this
further at another time.

     The king did not appear to be annoyed or distressed
at all by us seeing him this way. In fact, I think I detected a show off
quality in his behavior that may have been meant to intimidate us. I
filed that away in my mind also for possible later use.

     The king maintained his usual reserved friendly smile
while his eyes continued a non-readable look. His ever present
mysteriousness remained. Mario and I bid our good mornings and
proceeded on to the larger chamber while the king finished dressing.
We took seats in our usual place not saying a word to each other. A
few silent minutes passed before the king joined us, scepter and all.
As he seated himself on his chosen bench he looked directly into my
eyes, a half smile on his lips, almost a sneer, as if to say, *"See you*

did come at my bidding. " but at the same time I saw a glint of respect which I assumed was because of my refusal to appear the day before. I think we were both finally on the same page and on equal standing. He was not my king and now we both knew it.

Once we were all comfortably settled I wasted no time in starting the conversation and I spoke rather bluntly and direct without being completely disrespectful.

"You seem to think of us as primitive by comparison. Apparently you are not aware of our scientific accomplishments over the last several thousand years."

Without letting him interrupt I went on to list the most startling of these breakthroughs. Astronomy, Gunpowder, Mathematics, Internal combustion, Flight, Under water travel, Engineering, Space travel, Nuclear power, Communications, and finally Computers.

The king listened patiently, his demeanor being quite calm. I finished with a few minor discovery processes and sat back feeling quite proud of myself in the game of one upmanship.

The king, without showing any signs of distress, reached into his ever present basket and handed each of us a piece of fruit. He also served himself and proceeded to eat quietly. His silence was agonizing but I let him have his time. When he finished eating he wiped his hands on a cloth, sat back and spoke my name aloud in perfect English. He smiled slightly as if proud of himself and I smiled back in recognition of his effort to communicate. Now it was his time to list accomplishments, or should I really say counter list. He used my listing in the exact order and proceeded to answer or again should I say tear apart what I had presented. Starting with astronomy the king said they studied the stars long before the Greeks and actually introduced them to the heavens. Even before the Greeks were known as Greeks.

Gunpowder, after having it explained to him, he said he would reserve that until last.

Third on my list was mathematics. He reminded me that they invented the zero and also how much more accurate their calender was. Other mathematical advancements were beyond my comprehension at this time. He then moved on to internal combustion which he said was unnecessary and would explain that further later on.

Flight and underwater travel he sort of laughed at and as before put it aside for a later demonstration.

"Now I've got him." I thought to myself. *"He can't keep up with our achievements. Their advanced scientific knowledge he was always spouting was just a lot of hooey, lip service so to speak."*

As for engineering he used his hand to span the structure we were in and the complex that surrounded it. He reminded us that no mortar of any kind was used and has survived what ever nature could throw at it.

I had to give him that one, what with all the sliding doors and passageways we found and all without cement.

Space travel and nuclear power was again, as before, put aside for future demonstration.

I still wanted to give him his equal time but I felt this was becoming absurd. He obviously could not explain away the more challenging ideas I had presented

Communications was simply done with the power of the mind, no matter what the distance. The king felt this use of the brain must have slowly dwindled away over the course of time and non use.

I knew of ESP, but what the king was saying seemed very far fetched even for an enlightened one.

Computers, he stated, were just advanced mathematics employed by functions of the brain, much too advanced for us to understand.

This I started to challenge and vehemently object to. I had enough of his holier than thou attitude and I let him know it. The king calmly smiled and held up his hand,

"Please Eric, let me finish my demonstration and then if you still find fault with what I have said, further discussion can take place."

As incensed as I was I knew he was right. He did listen patiently to me, I should at least return the courtesy.

"**A**ll right." I answered, "But we are definitely going to further discuss this." I said authoritatively. I sat back on the bench and with a wave of my hand indicated he could continue.

Mario in the meantime was in a state of shock that I would talk to the king in this manner. While looking at me in a scolding glance he apologized to the king for my behavior.

With a wave of his hand the king dismissed this and smiling a placating smile he stood and retrieved his scepter as he did so.

"**F**ollow me." he said softly walking to a wall. A gentle touch on a certain part of the painting and the wall moved back and angled slightly revealing a passageway. Indicating again that Mario and I follow him, he entered the darkness. After a few steps into the dark a small but extremely illuminating light appeared from the tip of the scepter. It grew in intensity till all seemed like daylight. The walls of the corridor were also painted. Scenes of unbelievable beauty and style with a combination of shades and color I had not witnessed before, even from some of the old masters. The scenes depicted were not just Mayan, but were representations of ancient Greece, Rome, Babylon and who knows what else. It would take time to research all they resembled. Further on were detailed renditions of European sailing ships of the fourteenth, fifteenth. and sixteenth centuries. Sprinkled among the European paintings were those of early Viking and Chinese vessels. What particularly caught my attention were representations including large Chinese junks along with obvious European ships. There were harbor scenes with trading taking place. Another large painting showed what I guessed to be Phoenician sailing vessels sailing side by side with log and bark ocean going rafts definitely of South American origin.

Mario and I were so taken by these paintings that we almost forgot what our mission was. A blunt reminder from the king brought us back to reality. A reality I definitely wanted to follow. I was anxious to show this king up for the charlatan he may be. Although seeing these paintings did add a dimension of doubt to my thinking the way I was..

Reluctantly we again followed the king with the corridor now descending and also becoming more narrow. The paintings stopped also and I assumed it was because of this narrowness. After what I judged to be about fifty feet the walkway was on the assent as the walls widened. Paintings appeared again. I lost track of exactly how many but it was obvious they would fill any big city gallery and then some. Unfortunately they could not be moved. What a loss to the world, particularly the art world. Perhaps a video documentary could be done in the future so the world could see this magnificent art.

Eventually we approached a set of stone steps going up. There were six steps that ended at a large flat stone slab not dissimilar from the last jungle entrance the king made me privy to. It seemed to magically open at the king's touch. We had to stand aside as dirt and debris rained down on us, evidencing it had not been opened for some time. When the dust settled the three of us exited to the jungle.

Mario was all smiles by now and remarked quietly,

"**I** have read about such things but did not know they really existed."

I nodded in agreement as we followed our host to a small clearing. There was even a break in the canopy showing us blue sky. Deciding this place would do the king turned his attention to us, mainly me. I was the one questioning his knowledge. The king spoke slowly and quietly, Mario translating word for word.

"**A**s for your gun powder Eric." He smiled at saying my name again. "This is why we found it unnecessary."

Lifting his scepter and pointing it directly at a nearby stone of about two and one half feet in diameter his hand moved almost unnoticeably, and with that a rose colored ray emanated from the tip and touched the stone. Instantly the stone disappeared.

"**I**t is now part of the matter scrambled in the universe." the king explained.

Mario and I looked at each other in disbelief, both our mouth's hanging open. The king smiled smugly. Forgetting the king's smugness I tried to review in my mind what I just witnessed. There was no sound, no explosion, no flying shrapnel, the stone just vanished. It vanished while I watched it. I walked to where it once stood, saw the depression where it lay which was the only evidence of it's previous existence. The grasses surrounding the area were brown and black tipped having been singed by something extremely hot, yet there was no heat felt by the observers. I turned to look at Mario who was still just staring. My gaze moved to the king who spoke quietly. I had to shake Mario from his trance to translate.

"Now you know why we found your gun powder without use.." he stated. "Before you ask any more questions, let me show you one more demonstration. I believe it will dispel any doubts you may still have as to my credibility. I acknowledged his request with a nod of my head and stood silent with Mario.

The king stepped away allowing more distance between us. Facing us again, still with that half smug smile, his hand moved to the center of the scepter, held it in front of him parallel to his body and slightly away and tightened his grip. There was a hesitation of a second or two then he lifted off the ground. Still there was no sound, no air movement, just a single body rising into the trees. Suddenly there was a drastic increase in speed as we watched the king grow smaller. In less than a minute he was just about out of sight.

Mario and I both started to say something but nothing passed our lips. Then as quickly as the king disappeared he reappeared descending slowly to touch the earth directly in front of us. It was then I felt the sensation of a disturbance. Exactly what, I couldn't say. It wasn't a breeze or wind but an unseen movement. My mind started working overtime to analyze what I was experiencing. Paranormal thoughts were crowding me as if they were the answer. I told myself I was more rational than that. It then dawned on me that I may be feeling a molecular disturbance caused by the scepter.

"You are correct Eric." I heard the king say.

I had been looking at him and his lips had not moved nor sound of any kind came from him, yet I heard him clearly in my own language.

"Do not doubt your thoughts Eric, your assessment is correct. I knew you would be the one to contact." the voice in my head continued.

I looked quickly at Mario, who still seemed to be in

a state of shock and bewilderment. I could tell he had not heard anything. My eyes returned to the king observing an imperceptible smile.

"**O**nly you can hear me." came the voice again. "Mario is not ready yet."

Is he reading my thoughts ? I asked myself. Could we actually communicate this way ?

"**O**nly if you allow it." the king answered.

I shook my head hoping for a return to reality. Anything to get away from this dream. Mario's voice helped pull me back.

"**A**re you alright Eric ?" he questioned. "You seem to be in a daze. I'm kind of in a fog myself. I guess it was the shock of what we just saw. We did just see the king fly, didn't we ?" he asked

confused.

"**N**o you're not crazy Mario. The king did leave the ground and with no apparent means." I answered.

Avoiding my eyes the king addressed Mario in his native tongue for him to translate.

"**D**oes that answer all your questions my skeptical friend ? I can travel as well under water. There are no bounds to this power we have harnessed."

"**I** concede to you my doubts on the specific topics mentioned but this brings up a whole different set of questions even more relevant to what we just witnessed." I answered.

"**I** thought it would." the king stated. "I would have been very disappointed if it had not. Before we go any further I must ask you both not to reveal anything that took place today. This was for your eyes only and I'm sure you understand why."

I looked at Mario and after a short hesitation he nodded in the affirmative. I agreed but with reservations. We must discuss this at great length. The king agreed enthusiastically. As we turned to go back to the pyramid I caught a glimpse of the king again squeezing the scepter around the middle. The grip was less than a second. It was as if he was turning a flashlight off.

"**I** must learn more about that scepter." I thought.

"**Y**ou will soon enough my friend." answered the king, of course, like before , was only in my mind.

Mario was still oblivious to these mental conversations.

Chapter 22

We entered the tomb from the hidden jungle entrance and slowly retraced our steps to the large chamber. The flight demonstration was temporarily forgotten as we viewed the wall art for the second time. The color, detail and style were incomparable. To me, the subject matter was the most eye catching. Their knowledge of contact between peoples of different parts of the world and of different era was mystifying. The intricate detail with which the ships were painted could only have been done with first hand knowledge. Perhaps the king has been right all along. Maybe they do possess a superior intellect and maybe they were the teachers of other civilizations. All of this, of course, led to other questions.

I soon found myself in shadows as the others had continued to the chamber along with the light from the scepter. I had to hurry to catch up and realized they had not even noticed I was delayed.

Back in the chamber with the passage door sealed again the king sat and reached for fruit. I declined this time, still standing where the door was. I could not detect any seams. This baffled me bringing in the question of their engineering. Here I was bragging how advanced we were then I see something like this, which defies logic. I guess I had been put in my place.

I rejoined Mario and the king settling myself on a bench. The king addressed both of us saying,

"I know you have many questions, as well you should but I ask your patience with me. I grow weary and wish to rest. I will enlighten you as best I can at another time. With another sun perhaps I will be rejuvenated. I wish you to take your leave now."

He spoke with a sincerity I had not heard before and he truly looked rather tired. Mario bowed and headed for the entranceway. I nodded my head and followed.

Once outside we took deep breaths, not necessarily for the air, but to clear and settle our heads. The events we had witnessed were almost to much to believe. Had we not been there I would have doubted such a story from anyone else. We stood in silence for a while out of sight of the camp.

Mario spoke first, echoing my own thoughts.

"I haven't always agreed with you but this time we definitely should not tell the others what we just experienced. First of all they probably would not believe us. I'm not even sure I believe us. Secondly there is too much going on in my mind to be sorted out to even discuss it further with you right now."

"Exactly my thoughts my friend." I replied. "We both need time to evaluate and consider. I think a few days separation from the king will fare us both well."

"I do not disagree with that but I don't know if that's a good idea either." Mario replied. "I get the feeling he's anxious to continue and for whatever reason he seems to want to continue with just you. The rest of us are only getting fragments of information, but with you he seems to bare his soul."

Mario said this without malice or jealousy. It was his own observation. I did not answer this but started to slowly walk back to camp. We both remained silent. We were met, as expected, with the usual questions from Frank to which I responded that we discussed more about the scrolls.

"I notice you don't have your cameras with you, have you finished copying them ?"

I laughed lightly and replied that I guessed only about ten percent had been photographed. Frank was disappointed with my answer but could see I was not in the mood for further questions.

"I just need some rest right now Frank. Let's review this after dinner, shall we ?"

It was more of an ending statement than a polite request but nevertheless he got my message and walked away. Mario turned away also saying,

"Catch you later, I need to think."

I went straight to my cot and sat with my back to the camp resting my head in my hands. Suddenly feeling sorry for myself I thought I would not be in this position if I just stayed home taking pictures. Who are you kidding Eric, you're enjoying every minute of this, I argued with myself. I lay back in my cot with both hands folded behind my head staring at the overhead canopy hoping for sleep to overwhelm me. I was trying to blank my mind but there was just too much attacking from too many directions.

"Okay." I said to myself out loud. "Let's try and make some sense of this. Perhaps if I put things in some sort of order then I can deal with them one at a time."

As I was saying this, still talking out loud, another thought slipped it's way into my conversation.

"I wonder if the king can still read my thoughts. He said only if I allow it. Well right now I don't allow it." I said determinedly. "I hope it's that simple. I'll have to do more research into this mind stuff. Now where was I ? Oh yeah, putting things in order. Geeze Eric you must be losing it, you're only having a conversation with yourself and you still can't keep up. I'm glad the king isn't listening in right now, he may change his mind about me. Which leads me back to where I want to be. What do I do about the king situation." I stopped talking aloud having convinced myself no one was eavesdropping. As fascinating as today's demonstrations were they were ultimately frightening. To have control of that kind of a power source, unharnessed, could lead to the complete destruction of the world overnight. When you think about it, we're doing that to ourselves now anyway, just at a slower pace. I drifted to thinking about all the benefits such power could yield. Heating and cooling with out the use of fossil fuels. That alone could make a difference in our planet. Lighting, agriculture, manufacturing would also be enhanced greatly. Then there is the opposite side. War, weaponry, enslavement would increase exponentially. The evil of greed, at least in my mind, I'm afraid would win out in the long run. Apparently the king knows this or we would have already had such mechanisms in place for the good of all. Apparently the king's own era went through the same thing otherwise why would he still have the scepter and be trying to find a new keeper of the knowledge of the ages. That leads me to contemplate what happened thousands of years ago to have put this off. Probably the same evil greed, I posited to myself. I had not even thought of the how and why this source of energy was discovered and why, after thousands of years it had not appeared again? What was this special thing ? It appeared awfully simple, yet manifested itself in a manner that was unthinkable. The control of this unknown thing is what frightened me. Who ever controlled it would be the target of all sorts of unsavory people the world over. That brings me to my next question. If the king already controls this wonderful thing why has it been a secret for all these many years, and why now does he want to give it to me or whoever he feels is right.

Then like a flash bulb going off in my head my thoughts exploded. I had to see the king and **now** I thought. I jumped out of my cot, looked for Mario, who did not seem to be available and decided to head for the pyramid anyway. No one else seemed to notice or even care that I was going back alone.

I found the king resting on the bench, eyes closed and breathing slightly irregular. Not really wanting to disturb him, yet I felt this was important. Important for both of us. I did not want to shock him awake so I avoided touching him. This is a good time to try this mental stuff I thought, Let's see if he is receptive to me. I concentrated my thoughts and directed them at the king. "Please hear me." I repeated a few times mentally. It only took about half a minute when the king opened his eyes. He smiled softly and nodded in recognition. It was obvious he was in a weakened state although he tried to hide it. Again communicating only with my mind I stated,

"**I** had to see you. We must talk. I need to know some things."

"**I**t's okay." He answered. "I expected you would be

back."

"**W**hat a great way to communicate." I thought.

"**Y**es it is." came a clear answer I didn't expect.

"**O**nce your mind is open, it is open until you choose

it not to be.

By now the king was sitting upright looking some what refreshed but I could still detect an air of weakness about him.

"**Y**our assessment of me is correct my young friend and it is only you who knows this."

I read his meaning without him having to spell it out. My mind was racing again. I know I was fighting the clock. I decided the best way to get answers to my questions was to skip the formalities and just blurt it out.

"**T**his power source, the scepter, What will happen to it if you do not find anyone to pass it on to."

Hesitantly, and with a sadness in his expression the king answered,

"**I** guess it will just have to be destroyed. It can not be left without the knowledge of it's use.

"**C**an it be destroyed." I asked curiously.

"**O**h yes, quite easily and safely." He answered calmly.

Now came my most important question.

"**Y**ou're dying aren't you ? Your time is limited here on earth. That's why you are in such a rush to pass on your secret. That's why you singled me out from the others. But why me ? I'm no scientist or a world leader. I'm sure there are thousands of others eminently more qualified to be the caretaker of this knowledge."

"**I** am sure you are right about that Eric but I am not looking for a world leader, or scientist or even a statesman You are correct, I am dying and a successor must be found. You are that man Eric. It is true you are not Mayan, but you possess all that is Mayan, the Mayan of old. I can read it in your heart, in your eyes. You care Eric. You care greatly. You possess fairness and reason. Your whole being is compassion. I believe in fate Eric, and it was fate that brought us together. As much as I respect the others for what they represent, Mayan or not, they do not collectively have what you have in your heart. A little history if you will."

I sat before him, humbled and still confused, yet I nodded in agreement to listen to more.

"Eons ago." the king continued, "Our race of people, as advanced as we were, also succumbed to the evils of greed. The true ways were being thrown aside and replaced with a thirst for material possessions. It slowly advanced to taking what wasn't theirs to take. They found it easy to conquer other peoples and eventually turned on their own for the sake of control and power. It was then that a group of The Chosen Ones, as we were called, decided to put to sleep this beneficial knowledge. We would wait for a better time when acceptance would be forthcoming. There were originally five of us. Each went to different lands through out the world, the thought being, as people grew in maturity, the handling of this discovery and it's benefits for all mankind would be more easily welcomed. Each of us five had our loyal followers who administered the life suspension gasses. The fate of the other four is obviously unknown. The period of time of our ultimate death after reawakening was never established. There was no way to know or test it. It was hoped to be lengthy to allow a proper time to find the appropriate caretaker. On this point we greatly misjudged."

The king paused as if out of breath even though he was not physically talking. He slowly drank of the water I provided. He thanked me and proceeded further.

"I would like to fulfill my mission Eric, and you can help me do that. From what you tell me of your advancements I'm sure the peoples of the world are ready for this knowledge."

The king paused again to rest. I started reviewing in my mind the world's history as I knew them forgetting he could and did read my every thought. The positive highlights were easily overshadowed as I recalled wars, enslavement, and genocide that was still going on to this day. I portrayed to the king that as much as we have learned over the thousands of years we still have learned nothing. Greed and power existed now as it did then. The king became extremely saddened as he listened to my thoughts.

"My choice is clear then." He answered sadly "This power source must be destroyed. I have waited all these years with high hopes for mankind only to find nothing has changed."

I could tell he was deeply distraught in having to make this decision but I had to agree with him. The world was still not ready for such advancements.

"The scrolls."I asked, "Must they also be destroyed ?"

"No, they are yours to study. They tell only of our history and contact with other nations. The formula of our discovery was never recorded for obvious reasons.   Once the scepter is destroyed it will never be found out again. Of that I am confident. It will truly be a loss for all time to come. Will you help me Eric. I feel my time is growing near. Come, we must go outside to the wind."

I helped The Chose One up, he grabbed his scepter, and we made our way to the wall. He opened the wall and with his lighted scepter we slowly walked the passageway past the magnificent paintings of the past. Outside he instructed me to hold his free hand. He then squeezed the scepter and we rose in the air. I was startled at first, but realized there was no sensation of flight. We traveled through the canopy overhead and in no time at all were standing on the beach of the gulf.

The head of the scepter was removed and a powder like sand was thrown to the wind and was carried out over the water. Sudden panic overcame me and was answered by the king.

"No need to worry, my friend, there is enough of the original source to return us to my home. The scepter was closed and once again the king reached for my hand as we lifted off the beach.

In no time at all we were back at the outside entrance to the pyramid. As soon as we touched the jungle floor the king squeezed my hand even harder and reached his other arm to steady himself against me. I put his arm around my shoulder and assisted him down the steps to the painted corridor. Once back in the great room I made him as comfortable as I could on his bench.

I heard Mario's voice behind me,

"Is he alright ?" he asked.

"For the moment." I answered.

The glance between us told the whole story. He had come to the same conclusion I had and when he could not find me in camp rushed here to the tomb. The king himself confirmed Mario's suspicion and suggested he get the others for a last talk. Mario turned as he was bid and left us alone.

"Quickly my friend get me that small earthen jar. The one with the cover."

I retrieved the small vessel and set it beside him on the bench. The king then proceeded to open the scepter again and emptied the remaining sand mixture into it. Covering the jar he handed it to me.

"This is yours my friend and yours alone. Put it out of sight before the others return. Do not attempt to analyze this, it will do you no good. The elements that make up this mixture no longer exist, or shall we say will be impossible to locate. You will know what to do when it is time."

I secreted the jar away knowing there was only minutes before the others returned.

"I am sorry I could not help the world with our knowledge. It saddens me greatly but I do understand your reluctance to accept the responsibility as caretaker. Our decision was for the best for all. Perhaps some day people will learn to coexist without greed and hatred. Your efforts should always be toward that goal. I hope you see that day Eric and when you do, remember me. I feel we could have been true friends and wish we had more time together."

Not knowing what to say at this point I took his hand with a gentle pressure. Our eyes met and words or thoughts were no longer necessary.

The king slowly smiled as Frank and the others entered the room.

"Come sit and let me answer your questions." The Chosen One said through Mario.

Diego was the first to speak inquiring about the mural.

"Can I add you to this event drawing."

Touched by his sincerity the king answered,

"Paint me as I once was, not as I appear before you now. The world is not ready for such contradiction."

We all knew his meaning. Frank jumped in on the king's last word.

"Can we still have access to the scrolls."

Sensing the discomfort and annoyance in his Mayan descendants at this question being asked the king slowly smiled, looked directly at Frank and said,

"I'm sure Eric can arrange that for you when you are ready."

Frank's anger was obvious at this answer as he snapped his head around and glared at me. Our four Mayan friends were extremely attentive to the king discussing his final time and burial wishes. They assured him all would be done according to tradition. Frank again made an inquiry about the ancient history. Before the king could answer, Mateo being unusually stern, turned and answered,

"Now is not the time Frank."

He continued his stern look for a few seconds before returning his attention to the king's needs. Words were now being mumbled in their native language that neither Frank or I understood..

"I will miss our discussions." I thought to myself.

"As will I my friend." came an answer in my mind.

I turned my attention to the king and realized those were his last words. The serenity of peaceful sleep overtook the king's face. I shed no tears but felt a sudden loss.

The room remained silent for the next five minutes or so. The quiet was only broken when Frank turned to go not seeming to care what happened next.

The four native Mayans, after an appropriate period of time, automatically went about the task of the king's burial according to what they knew of tradition. The body was stripped and washed then redressed with the finery befitting a Chosen One. The feathered cloak and headdress along with bracelets and necklaces were the perfect finale to salute this king.

I stood respectfully aside watching the four administer to their ancient king. I thought about asking if I could be of help in any way but decided against it and remained silent.

Carlos was studying the stone pyre where we first discovered the king and after a few misplaced touches found the key stone that slipped aside and the cover was moved away length wise. It was the king's already prepared coffin, lined with finely woven cloths of many colors. Precious gemstones, although mostly Jade, were strewn about along with gold and silver jewelry pieces. A most curious trinket that captured everyone's eye was that of a horse made of gold mounted on a stand with wheels, with a finely woven gold chain attached like a child's pull toy. I always thought horses were unknown to the Mayan culture. This would make the perfect picture I thought but again out of reverence of the occasion I restrained myself.

When all was ready and preparations completed the four friend most gently lifted the body of their ancestor and carefully placed it in the stone casket. The only thing left now was the scepter. Mario picket it up from the bench and carried it forward to the pyre. Here he hesitated and looked at the others as if for approval. The three nodded affirmatively. Mario walked to me and held out his arms offering me the ritualistic scepter.

"The honor is yours." He said quietly.

Without thinking I reached and accepted the symbol, overcome with one last feeling of a connection to the king.

I walked to the king's now eternal home and lay it across his chest and joined the hands around its base and stood back reverently. All was silent again as final farewells were silently spoken.

Frank reappeared and joined us at the pyre and with proper humility bowed his head. Mateo uttered a few words in his native tongue and the phrase was repeated by the others. The stone lid was then slid back in place and Carlos re-locked the small key stone.

We lingered a few more minutes, then one by one left the pyramid. As Frank left he gave me a look that showed he was not happy. I equated it to a child who did not get his way and chose not to let it bother me. Mario and I were now alone. He searched my eyes inquisitively.

"The scepter." He said quietly. "What about the scepter. Since he and I were the only ones privy to it's amazing power I made sure no one was within ear shot. I related what happened between the king and I and his decision to destroy the advanced knowledge of centuries past rather than let it be used for domination. He looked relieved when I told him this. As good as it could have been he feared this power for obvious reasons.

"How do you feel about it's destruction." he asked.

"I was in favor." I replied. "Like you, I could see the many benefits but what I feared most was it's control by the wrong people. I know that would happen no matter what you and I personally thought. I truly believe mankind is better off without it, at least for right now. Perhaps some day such a thing will come to pass and be justified but I doubt it will be in our lifetime. The world is just not ready for peace and harmony."

Mario was actually delighted right now that this decision was made. We both pledged our secrecy that this matter would never be revealed. We paid our final respects to this wondrous man and left the tomb which it truly was now.

Chapter 23

Walking back to camp we agreed to tell Diego of the corridor of paintings. All would know after that and arrangements could be made by Frank for it's video recording for all the world to see. This, we thought, would satisfy his ego and give him the world recognition he seemed to be yearning for.

The camp that night was somber. Only absolutely necessary conversation took place. Frank stayed pretty much to himself. He definitely avoided me. There was no real dinner, everyone fended for themselves if they even ate at all. I know I welcomed being alone. It started to rain again which added to the heavy mood.

Rather than be accused of stealing a precious artifact I emptied the contents of the earthen jar into an empty film box I had. Tomorrow I would return the jar to the tomb. I viewed the strange silky sand for a while wondering what gave it its unique character. No matter I thought, at least it would not be used for any evil purpose. I resolved then not even to tell Mario of this gift from the king. I closed the box, sealed it with some tape, and tucked it away deep in my personal pack.

I lay down, relaxed by the rain, thinking of my encounter with this man from another world.

Chapter   24

  I was startled awake, as was everyone else, when Carlos dropped the empty coffee pot.

  "Sorry guys." He mumbled

  It was still raining only now it was more like a heavy mist. We all automatically went through our morning ritual before breakfast. Frank acted as if nothing happened yesterday, planning for the day's activities. He spoke to me like an old friend asking if I could continue recording the scrolls. I said I could as long as my film held out. This satisfied him. He then went on to assign tasks for the others. Mario took me aside and suggested we discover the painting passageway today. That way it would eliminate any curiosity as to why only we two were shown this hidden treasure. I agreed and relayed to him about where I thought the king touched the wall to open it. He said he would try to do it in the presence of Diego. Pleased with our plan we attended to our other chores before going to the pyramid.

  Mateo was the only one to stay at camp. He was working on Glyph translations Diego could include in his mural. The remaining five of us entered the great room to continue our research. The missing presence of the king lent an air of emptiness to the room, at least for me it did. I went about my recording work with the scrolls almost without interest, thinking about the king's dedication to a world of peace. Wouldn't that be something.

  I heard the excitement of raised voices. I smiled to myself knowing they just discovered the paintings.

  Carlos shouted to me,

"Eric, you have to come and see this and bring your camera."

I took advantage of the distraction and returned the small earthen jar to its place. I then joined the others and was surprised to see the beauty of the wall art. Even though I had seen them before I was still genuinely captivated by them. Mario was as excited as I was now that we could study them in a more relaxed manner. He winked at me acknowledging our little secret. The excitement of our find overcame even Frank. I took this opportunity to suggest to him the video idea. Mario and the others supported this thought which Frank then took and made it his own. I walked away, laughing to myself and went back to the scrolls. The rest of the day was routine for me. Eventually, Mateo joined us and was also amazed by the paintings. Diego was acting like a child at Christmas as he studied the art work. I never saw anyone so completely involved in art before.

The next few days followed routine almost to the point of becoming boring. Without the king's unique presence things became predictable. I personally missed him more than I thought I would.

The rain became more frequent and at times was getting heavier. It was decided to end this particular expedition. It had been a success beyond ones wildest dreams. Further excavation and research of this new city would have to wait for next year's dry season. Frank was already discussing plans for the next venture, wanting to have more crews at more sites.

We carefully packed our gear and sadly resealed the tomb and pyramid. It was like leaving an old friend. Speaking of old friends, my favorite camera was returned to me by Mateo. It was like another connection with the king for me.

Chapter   25

      Our trek back to civilization was totally uneventful and anti-climatic though I still found the jungle fascinating and mysterious.

      We held a celebratory parting dinner in Mexico City and relived our adventures.   It was at this dinner I presented Frank with two of the jade stones the king had given me. I offered them to help finance next years expedition. For once Frank actually appeared humbled, and I was glad he accepted my offer. Whether or not I would be asked to go along again, or even if I wanted to go again, I did not know yet. I kept the third piece of jade as a memento of this wonderful but strange journey.

      We all parted reluctantly but had to go back to what would now seem our mundane lives. I promised Frank I would follow up with all the photography as soon as I finished the processing and logging.

      My   return flight to Vermont was tiring and thoughtful. I relived the whole experience in my mind and was not unhappy with it. Once back home I took my time unpacking and caught up on some much needed sleep. I transferred the king's gift of the silky sand to a clear glass container and placed it on the mantle. It would always be a reminder of exciting times.

      For reasons unknown to me the glass jar constantly drew me to it whenever I passed. Once, just before going to bed , I stopped to study it for the umpteenth time. Holding it in my hand I remembered the king's actions. I was quite tired and was thinking that I should be going upstairs to bed. Unconsciously I squeezed the small jar and instantly lifted off the floor and floated up the stairs without touching a single step.

~ ~ ~ ~ ~ ~

And so began my next journey.!!

~ ~ ~ ~ ~ ~

Keeping an
Old Fashioned Christmas

by

K.J.Goss

Keeping an
Old Fashioned Christmas

Chapter 1

"Scrooge was better than his word. He did it all and infinitely more; and to Tiny Tim, who did not die, he was a second father."

With these words and others Dickens puts an end to probably the most widely recognized Christmas story of all time. Everyone seems to know this tale and usually quotes a line from it sometime during the Christmas season or if you're like me you quote from it all year long.

Christmas means many things to many people and for me this story and it's setting ignites a warmth of feeling that make me long for that period in time. Now in my later years I often allow my thoughts to drift to my own childhood at that special time of year. I also mix my own children's early Christmas's with mine and we share that individual fondness for the Dickens era.

There is just something I find unique in that period setting. The rushing to and fro of that last minute shopping. Not so much for presents, though they are also fun, but the last minute addition of a decoration for the house or room or that particular finishing touch for the holiday meal. In my case it's not so much the finding of that last minute treasure but the utter enjoyment of searching for it. The hustle and bustle of the busy streets and shops, the gayety and happiness that all seem to share, each with their own design on what makes that feeling unique only to them.

I consider myself lucky to have lived my youth in just such a setting. No, not in Dickens Old London Town, it was a more modern version in a very small village that still maintained the same warmth and coziness that Dickens portrayed in his "Christmas Carol" I believe I was able to relate this to my own children. At least I succeeded in my own mind. Perhaps I was trying to relive my own youth through them. It worked for me anyway. The warmth and sharing of the immediate family at this season gave me the most joy and pleasure I have ever known.

All of this brings me to my little fairytale. I say fairytale because I don't know if I even believe it myself. It started a few Christmas's ago. Living in rural Vermont has many advantages and living on a hillside in the middle of a forest is one of them. Anyway this one fine winter day about a week before Christmas I headed into the woods to gather some evergreen branches to add to my indoor decorations. I guess I had walked about ten minutes and was well out of sight of the house. I was enjoying the brisk air as my thoughts drifted to the Scrooge movie I had watched the night before. Wouldn't it be nice I thought to live in a quaint village as they pictured in the movie. You know, with all the varied shops capturing the merriment of the season. Even my own old small village where I grew up would do about now. I was smiling as I reflected on some childhood memories when suddenly an unfamiliar noise caught my attention. Unfamiliar for the middle of the wood that is. It sounded like distant voice Up ahead was a light foggy area which seemed odd to me on such a clear day. I approached slowly until I was totally enveloped by the misty air. After a few more steps it thinned out again and I found myself standing at the edge of a street that led to a Dickens Old London Town setting. I hesitated in a confused state till I heard some one bid me a Merry Christmas. I quietly returned the greeting felling almost shy. I walked forward timidly now recognizing signs above shop doors and on the sides of buildings. This was it. Old London Town of the eighteen forty's. I was in Dickens era London at Christmas time. I could feel my heart beating faster with excitement. The more people I passed, the more cheerful greetings were exchanged. I found myself looking in the toy shop window with the anxious enthusiasm of a child. I marveled at the open meat stands with the variety of hanging fowl for all to choose from. The sweet perfume invading the air from roasting chestnuts. Fruits of all kinds on display in front of the several shops. I reached the end of the street, the gaiety fading along with the light. It was then I noticed there were no more gas lamps at the end of the village.

I checked the clock in a shop window noticing a little more than an hour had passed. How can this be I thought. I just left my house less than fifteen minutes ago. Obviously this is some sort of dream my sensibility's told me. I guess I can wake up now and collect the pine branches I came for. Nothing happened. I was still at the edge of a darkened street in Old London Town. I turned and was drawn back to the excitement of the shoppers. I wasn't afraid or upset or even concerned at not being in my own world. As I rejoined the hustle and bustle I thought I might try some roasted chestnuts. It was then I realized I did not have the coins of the time. As if reading my mind the peddler smiled saying;

"**D**on't you worry Gov'ner. It's Christmas, have a few on me and a Merry Christmas to ya."

He scooped a few from the fire and put them in my hand. I thanked him rather embarrassed but he was already serving another patron who had real money.

As I continued along the street it began to snow. There was already four or five inches on the ground, nevertheless this added to the atmosphere of the season. I took my time meandering thru the many shops and alley's forgetting about the time. I at last found myself at the edge of the wood where I had entered. I hesitated and turned back to look at the village and was lost again in the warmth and happiness of the scene before me.

A most pleasant middle aged woman with two children approached me.

"**I**t's okay sir, you can go back. We'll always be here for you. Merry Christmas to you and your's."

I returned the sentiment and the two children echoed the same.

I invaded the mist at the edge of the forest and retraced my path to home. Within minutes the mist was gone but it was still snowing. As I drew nearer the house I glanced at my watch. I was only gone a total of twenty five minutes. How can that be I wondered again. It seemed like I was there for hours and on top of that I forgot the pine branches I set out for. Oh well, there's always tomorrow.

As I entered the house my wife inquired about the greens.

"**I** couldn't find anything I liked." I lied.

I certainly did not want to reveal what I had experienced. She would probably have me carted off to the loony bin. I busied myself with some outside lights so I could be alone and think about what I had just witnessed. Maybe I was losing my mind. In the meantime I made the decision to return there tomorrow to determine the severity of my mental state.

Chapter 2

I awoke the next morning to a beautiful mantle of white. There was only six days until Christmas and the snow was just perfect for the season. I puttered around the house tending to odds and ends in the morning knowing my wife was going shopping with a friend for the afternoon, a perfect opportunity to check out my Dickens apparition.

After a quick lunch I made it a point to collect some pine branches and stacked them by the trail entrance to the woods. Satisfied that that was taken care of I chose my course to that special place in the forest. The new snow in the woods was absolutely mesmerizing in it's silent beauty. The hush that encompassed the frozen scene actually added an undetectable warmth to my little world. The familiar mist appeared again and I was drawn to it with out hesitation this time. As the shroud dissipated I again saw the same scene as yesterday, different people, but the same shops. I checked my watch, same as the day before, it took about ten minutes to get here.

Though my clothes were different no one gave notice, or if they did they were too gracious to say anything. As yesterday, Christmas greetings were on everybody's lips including mine. I felt totally at home here and felt like I wanted Christmas to last forever.

While standing at a bakery window marveling at the varied cakes and breads, a voice called to me.

"**Y**ou there Sir, would you care to give this lady a hand, she has too many packages for those too small arms."

"**B**e glad to." I replied and found myself loaded up with parcels following this very round lady down some less crowded back streets.

"**H**ere we are kind Sir." she said as many children poured from the house and relieved me of my burden.

"**A**nd this is for you Sir and have a Merry Christmas." as she dropped a shilling in my hand. I tried to tell her a tip was not necessary but before I completed my sentence she disappeared behind her closed door. I remained there a moment debating what to do and then wondered what I could buy with a shilling. *"There's only one way to find out."* I said aloud and I set off back to the shops.

It was still snowing but that did not dampen the excitement of this Yule season, in fact one could say it heightened the enthusiasm. It truly was a time for children of all ages.

Once back to the main street of shops I paused to listen to caroler's who were making their way up the busy street. I followed them for a bit thoroughly entranced by the Old English Carols till I found myself at the bakery again. I finally went in and inquired about a small plum pudding on display. Pleased and surprised by the answer I purchased the wonderful delight for less than a shilling. I put the change in my pocket, then savored my newly acquired prize even without the flaming brandy. The taste was pure enjoyment. The look on my face was a dead giveaway of the pleasure of my taste buds as people smiled and nodded as they passed. A few even commented about their equal love for this tasty delight. I was beginning to feel like I belonged here.

A local church bell tolled the time. It was four PM and the lamplighter was now making his rounds. The glow of the lamps added more magic to the picture. Still happily stuffing my face I walked back to my entrance portal and entered the fog.

Maintaining my state of enchantment and humming the recently heard carols I found myself back at the house again having passed the pile of pine branches I lay at the far edge of the yard. Laughing at myself I walked back to retrieve them.

Thinking that it was late and my wife would return from shopping soon I checked my watch only to find it the same as yesterday. Twenty five minutes had passed. This had a very sobering effect. These incidents had to be day dreams, wishful thinking on my part. I went into the house and poured myself a small glass of cider. I sat and contemplated my disturbing day dreams. Only they were not disturbing, they were extremely pleasurable. I could still taste the plum pudding, even over the cider.

   I guess I nodded off for the next thing I knew my wife was calling to me from the kitchen reminding me I left the cider on the counter and did not put it away. She rambled on about her shopping day while I just smiled to myself convinced my day was far more enjoyable.

Chapter   3

       Five days till Christmas, and as much as I wanted to get lost in my Dickens village, it was just not possible today. I spent the morning finding and cutting a tree for the house, then the rest of the day I spent decorating it. It was a beautiful tree, but then again, to me every Christmas tree is a beautiful tree, even Charlie Brown's.

       My disappointment of not getting to the woods today only heightened my anticipation for tomorrow's visit. My wife's annual Women's Club Christmas party would keep her out most of the afternoon and on into the evening. This would give me more than adequate time for my daydreams. My wife commented on how happy I seemed to be that evening, listening to Christmas music and spending more than the usual time on the tree and wrapping presents for the grand kids. In reality I was just trying to make the time go by as fast as I could.

       Morning finally arrived and I couldn't believe how excited I was.   I was acting like a kid just before Christmas. Come to think of it I was a child at heart and it was just before Christmas. I consciously tuned myself down but even with that my wife made remarks about how different I was acting. I told her it was just the excitement of Christmas, which was partly true.

       Early afternoon arrived and none too soon. I was running out of things to occupy myself with. I said goodbye to my wife and wished her a fun day, then watched from the window as she left the driveway. I couldn't get out of the house fast enough. There was a light snow which added to my excitement as I made my way to the woods. I quickly gazed at my watch upon entering the maze of trees. One forty in the afternoon. I had plenty of time I told myself although it really didn't matter based on my past two visits. I wound my way through the now familiar trees at last reaching the small cloud of fog. I chose not to enter immediately, instead I observed this magic mist. It appeared to be about twelve or fifteen feet wide with no apparent end if I looked upward. It was like a breathing mass as if being disturbed by a light breeze. I stretched out my arm and penetrated the vapor and lost sight of my hand in the vaporous wall. There was no sensation at all. Retracting my arm I checked my jacket sleeve. There was no sign of dampness. The material almost felt warm. I looked at my watch. Fifteen minutes had passed since I left my yard. So far everything seemed to be quite real and I was not dreaming.

I took a few steps into the fog and stopped. Observing nothing, I turned a complete circle. Still nothing changed. I was no where. A few more steps and my Dickens village lay before me. Enough of this research stuff, my excitement drew me to the shops. My mind was happy and free again. I strolled slowly taking in every detail I could. Smiling greetings came from everyone who passed which I happily returned. I paused in front of a quartet of caroler's and without thinking reached into my trouser pocket, found two quarters and dropped them into a cup held by one of the singers. She nodded her thanks and continued singing.

I moved on thinking of the Scrooge story but I saw no one like him. I observed both people of refinement and those less fortunate and all were cheerful with the season.

The toy shop caught my eye again and I stopped to view the window. I felt the presence of someone else near me and looked down at a young boy's saddened face.

"Why so sad young man." I inquired.

His eyes caught mine when he answered; "I wanted to get my little sister a dolly but I don't have enough money."

"What do you need." I returned, trying to be friendly.

" I need another tuppence." said the boy sadly.

It was then I remembered the change I had from my shilling the other day. I searched my jacket pockets and sure enough it was still there. I offered the tuppence to the boy.

"**O**h no Sir." He answered quickly. "I could not take your money Sir. I did not earn it."

He averted my eyes by continuing to look in the window.

"**O**h but you can earn it." I said trying to mimic his voice inflection.

He looked at me quizzically.

"**C**an you direct me to a pawn shop young man ?"

A twinkle grew in his eyes.

"**I** can take you there Sir." he answered excitedly and reached for my hand pulling me up the street. Weaving in and out of people we came to an alley off to the right. Another fifty feet or so he stopped before a large handsome door. A sign hanging from an iron bracket said;

PAWN SHOP,
JONATHON DRINKWATER – PROPRIETOR.

"**H**ere you go Gov'ner." the boy blurted out.

"**S**o it is." I answered gratefully. "And here's your tuppence my lad and a Merry Christmas to you ."

"**T**hank you Sir and a Merry Christmas to you to Gov." he yelled as he ran to the street. "And a Happy New Year." he screamed as he turned the corner and disappeared.

I laughed to myself and felt quite content.

The inside of the pawn shop was not unlike the shops of my own era. A pleasant looking gentleman appeared from behind a drape, obviously a back room, his age I took to be mid to late forty's.

"**M**erry Christmas to you Sir. How can I be of help."

I felt myself turn shy, I guess embarrassed would be a better word.

"**W**ell - - - Well." I found myself stuttering. "I was wondering if I could get some money for my watch."

"**I**'m sure we can make some kind of arrangement,

may I see it." The shopkeeper asked quietly.

I extended my arm and slid the expansion band off my wrist. The man gazed at me with a rather puzzled expression.

"How unique." he said as I handed him the watch.

Looking at it as if he did not believe it was a watch the light of recognition finally showed on his face as he saw the time. He checked the time against his large, by comparison, pocket watch.

"Very good." he said. "Only twelve seconds difference." He was all smiles now while examining every detail, particularly the expansion band.

"How interesting." he mumbled. :This sort of idea might catch on."

"It already did." I offered, then realizing I probably shouldn't have volunteered that information.

He looked at me strangely but did not pursue it any further.

"Are you staying with us very long Mr. Thomas."

Now I was the one with the bewildered look.

"How did you know my name." I asked confused.

He wore a big smile now while showing me the back of the watch.

"It's engraved right here, William Thomas."

I laughed with him, saying

"Oh yeah, I almost forgot."

Feeling a little more at ease now, I continued,

"I hope to visit as often as I can. I like it here."

"We like having you. Any one who loves Christmas as much as you do belongs here." he answered.

Changing the subject quickly,

"Back to the business at hand." he said inspecting the watch again. "I can give you four and six."

Knowing a pound sterling was a lot of money in that period I accepted gratefully. We exchanged Christmas greetings again and I exited to the street with renewed enthusiasm. Now I could really partake in the shopping frenzy.

My first stop was a clothing shop. I just had to have a long great coat with the shoulder cape attached. If I was to take part in the local merriment I wanted to look the part. Satisfied with my purchase I rejoined the festivities in the street smiling my best smiles. Christmas had never been such fun for me and I intended to savor every moment. I located the chestnut peddler and this time I proudly paid for my snack. From there I walked to the toy shop exchanging Seasons Greetings with everyone.

Entering the toy shop was like a childhood dream. The coal fire in the corner fireplace instantly negated winters chill. The scent of evergreen and cloves invaded one's senses and filled you with Christmas whether you wanted it or not. I scanned the shop and was drawn to a carrousel as it went round and round. I was as much taken with it as the children that surrounded it. When it stopped I could see that most of it was hand carved. The six horses were magnificently detailed. This was not any plastic junk. You could feel the love the craftsman put into it. I imagined the wind up mechanism was equally flawless. I just had to have it, but I waited for the children to leave so they would not be disappointed.

The shopkeeper most generously provided a box and wrapped it beautifully with colored paper and ribbon. I gladly paid him and received my change. He was most thankful. I could see the light fading as I left the shop. I remembered then that I pawned my watch so I could not check the time. I slowly walked to the foggy entrance very much enjoying the sights and the day. I entered the misty woods not wanting to be there on total darkness. Much to my amazement when I exited the cloudy mix I was greeted with sun and blue sky. *"So much for Christmas snow."* I mumbled.

I reached the house in the usual ten minutes and once inside I looked at the wall clock. I was only gone less than one half hour. Now I was really confused. I know I was there for a good couple of hours. Is this really a dream, am I losing my mind altogether ?   No! Of course not. I answered myself. To convince even myself I viewed myself in the full length mirror admiring my great coat. I reached into my pocket and looked at the coin of the realm I still had.

"The Carrousel" I said aloud. "This is another real

proof that I was there."

  I was now thoroughly convinced but what about the rest of the world. This would have to be my secret for a while longer. I returned the money to my pocket but I hid the coat in the back of my closet under some old sweaters. The carrousel I put on top of my desk in the den so others could see.

  I fixed myself some dinner and poured some cider, this time remembering to put away the bottle. I sat and enjoyed the Christmas tree and watched the Scrooge movie again.

  My wife was home around seven thirty and noticed the Old Carrousel almost instantly.

  "**I** see you went shopping today." she commented. "Where did you get this ? In some antique store ?"

  "**I** guess you could say it was an antique store." I answered smiling to myself.

  "**T**he kids will like that." she said

  "**I**t's not for the kids." I answered "It's for me. It's a rare antique not to be abused by children."

  She chose to ignore my replay and rambled on about her party and friends.

Chapter 4

Over the next few days I found it difficult to get to my Christmas village even though it took less then a half hour. I remained happy and content though knowing it was there for me. Christmas Eve I did manage some time and I'm glad I did. Excitement abounded and I knew a more peaceful place would not be found anywhere else on earth. Church bells were softly ringing while strolling caroler's sang Silent Night. I did not stay long but silently bid my Christmas wishes to all as I left through the mist.

Christmas eve day brought my daughter and family to be with us for a few days . My three year old grand daughter was a delight but there was even a stronger bond between my eleven year old grandson and me. My daughter used to love watching or reading Scrooge with me and now my grandson took her place. When he and I were alone I would talk about my visits to my Dickens village. He was fascinated by the story's I told but I could tell he had his doubts about the truth of them. I could tell he wanted to believe but did not have enough faith in his own imagination yet. I guess he just humored me and I was alright with that for now.

Christmas passed but my love for the season did not. The winter blessed us with heavy snow which made it next to impossible to visit my special place. It was spring before I could get there again. Nothing had changed. It was forever Christmas there. Over time my visits became less. Not because I wanted it that way but my advancing years and physical frailty would not allow it. I lost track of time after a while but my Christmas love did not diminish.

A surprise visit by my now twenty year old grandson

and a feeling deep inside me convinced me I had to make one last trip. It took a while to talk him into it but I could not do it alone. I pleaded with him to humor me and allow me to show him my Dickens village. Down deep inside I knew he loved Christmas as I did but would not allow these childlike emotions take over his now adult life. However he did relent and give me my last wish.

It was slow going, instead of the usual ten minutes it was more like twenty minutes before we reached the misty cloud. A confused smile showed on my grandson's face. He tried to hide it and I pretended not to notice. We stopped for me to rest and catch my breath.

"I always thought you were making it up." he said shyly.

"Making what up." I answered seriously pretending not to know what he was referring to.

"Oh, nothing." he answered embarrassed.

"Oh." I said in a non committal tone.

I loved messing with his head.

"I'm okay, we can go on now."

I took a step into the cloud pulling him with me. Inside the dampness he held my arm a little tighter. Soon we were out looking up the street of Old London Town. I turned to look at my walking companion and saw only a wide eyed, open mouthed young boy. He was frozen in that position for at least a minute. I smiled quietly knowing what he was feeling. I stood there unmoving, letting him take in this magnificent spectacle. I could sense the spell invading and taking over his whole being. I was very happy to have someone to share my precious secret with.

Shaking off the hypnotic hold the scene had on him he turned to me half smiling, half laughing and said,

"This is what you were always talking about. You've been talking about this for years but we all chose not to believe you. It's true. It's all true."

He was giddy with laughter now. I smiled at his recognition pleased that he would now see Christmas as I did..

"Come on Grandpa, I've got to see more." he said pulling me along.

"Slow down boy, I can't walk that way any more.

You go ahead, I'll catch up."

"**A**re you sure ? Are you alright ?"

"**Y**es, I'm sure and yes I'm alright. Oh by the way when you get back to the house look in the back of my closet under some old sweaters. There's something special for you. Now go on ahead. Scoot."

I watched my grandson run on ahead and get lost in the maze of shoppers. I was happy now knowing that Christmas was now in good hands.

I walked towards the church and many old friends from the Dickens village escorted me inside. We wished each other Merry Christmas and as the church bells pealed out a carol I felt myself fade away taking my place in this forever Dickens Christmas.

The owner of the pawnshop spoke of William Thomas with love and great respect. He was talking to Bill Thomas's grandson who was looking at a familiar watch preserved and displayed in a glass case.

"**A**nd the one next to it was his fathers, and next to that is his grandfather's" said the shop keeper. " There is still room for another if you so wish."

*R*emember if you truly love Christmas
we'll always be here for you.

The
Mysterious Wagon Wheel

by

K.J.Goss

The Mysterious Wagon Wheel

Chapter 1

The trophy room could be accessed from the main part of the somewhat spacious log home, or from it's own outside entrance way. The room was part of the house but separated the main house from the three car garage. It wasn't really a formal trophy room but that's what Luke, the owner, called it. It housed an eclectic collection of things he took a liking to and had gathered over the years. His pride and joy, believe it or not, was a large, a very large, old wooden wagon wheel. It was handed down to him years ago by his uncle. With it, to his surprise and great pleasure was a box filled with all sorts of hand written notes. Paper of all sizes and shapes contained scribbling's, some readable and some, because of the years I guess, took some concentrated effort to decipher. There were two notes that weren't even on paper. One was tanned deerskin and one looked like a well preserved piece of birchbark.

Except for the initial perusal when he first received it, he never looked into it in detail. Finding time one winter evening, Luke spread everything out the large table he had in the trophy room. His uncle had hinted at some sort of history, years ago, but he never paid much attention to it then. Well, after a cursory inspection, Luke determined it was just that. A history of this wagon wheel. It took him a few nights to chronologically put things in order, being that some papers were so difficult to read, but he was finally successful.

Now he assigned himself the task of trying to read this history and perhaps write the story of this survivor of a couple of hundred years. Would you believe it, this one lonely wagon wheel weathered centuries of use and hardships and pulled through to look as good as it does. Luke imagined all sorts of story's that went with each piece of writing. But that was it, just story's from his imagination. As he viewed each bit of paper, it was a history, provenance, I believe they call it, and it did tell a story, no matter how incomplete.

   True, this wonderful wheel had a history, unfortunately not enough of it was written by it's various owners or users. The wheel itself only knew the complete story and whether or not it was exciting or dull. The only guarantee we know of was that it was witness to many years and could probably tell us of many interesting tales.

   Oh, if only inanimate things could talk. Then again, inanimate is only what we, as sentient creatures, label things we can not converse with. Perhaps, if we seriously concentrate and listen closely, we could feel it's life's story's. A gentle touch might garner us communication with it's innermost self. Whoa, listen to me , now I'm trying to talk to things. But then again, the very makeup itself of this wondrous wheel once had life. It was constructed of wood. Some of the finest and strongest wood available at the time of it's birth. This very wood was once part of a tree. A living, breathing tree. It went through a pre-determined cycle of birth, growth and death, as do we. It suffered disease and illness as do we. In it's death it contributed part of itself to help us in our life. Why shouldn't it have a story to tell.

   So join me, and open your mind to the world around you that we tend to ignore. Listen, as this wheel tells it's story to his new young friend. This new friend is a wheel also. Only a newer and much smaller one. It was part of Luke's first wagon he had as a child. The wagon was accidently destroyed, this small wheel being the only part to survive unscathed. This was one of those little things that meant a lot to Luke, therefore it won a place in his trophy room.

   Listen as these new friends first meet.

Chapter 2

Luke was leaving the trophy room, having just given the small wheel it's place of honor. The little wheel looked around his new home and spotted the wagon wheel mounted in the center of the wall across from him.

~ ~ ~ ~ ~ ~

"**W**ow ! You sure are big. You look pretty old too and I might add kind of ugly also."

"**S**ay what you want, little one, I've heard just about everything in my lifetime."

"**I** didn't mean to offend." offered the small one immediately. "I have a habit of saying what I think before I think of what I'm saying. I bet you could tell lot's of story's if you're as old as you look."

~ ~ ~ ~ ~ ~

Luke had returned to his precious trophy room and made himself comfortable at the table where he had put the papers of the wagon wheel's history. They were neatly stacked in a protective box in date order. Luke was also supplied with a large note pad. He hoped to be able to organize an interesting story of his wonderful wheel

With pencil in hand he reached for the first paper from the box. It appeared to be a bill of sale. The heading on the paper read "Townsend and Son. – Wheelwrights." It listed an address as Beacon way, Liverpool.

Holding the paper, he felt a sensation running through his body. A tingle would describe it best, but there was no actual physical feeling, just a warmth of recognition. It was as if he was in Liverpool. He felt strange, having never encountered anything like this before.

As Luke held the paper and stared at it, the proud wagon wheel answered his curious new companion.

~ ~ ~ ~ ~ ~

"You're right. I do have a story. I have lot's of tales to tell, and since you seem to be interested, I'll start at the beginning. I was first brought to life in Liverpool, England. It was a large seaport town, a very busy place. A man and his apprentice son had acquired some of the best Oak and Elm and Locust woods available. With this they fashioned my main spokes, slightly flared at one end. Even my hub was made from a combination of all three woods. They took great pride in their work. I've always believed their care in my construction at the very beginning is why I have survived so long."

~ ~ ~ ~ ~ ~

Strange thoughts were running wild in Lule's mind. He felt like someone was telling him the story. He put the paper down and started to write some notes on the pad before him. Within seconds the tingle disappeared but the thoughts remained. Luke dismissed this as part of his imagination and continued to write. Suddenly the thoughts ended. There was no more to write.

"I'll try again later." he thought. *"I have chores to take care of."*

Both wheels were also now silent.

It was days end and post supper when Luke was able to return to his favorite room. He reread what he had written earlier and wanted to continue, but his mind was blank. Puzzled by this, he sat back in his chair and as he did so reached for the original bill of sale. It was then he noticed the date, September 7, 1740. The paper in his hand reignited the tingle he experienced earlier. His head was once again filled with thoughts just as the wagon wheel resumed his story to little wheel.

~ ~ ~ ~ ~ ~

"They, themselves were so proud at how I turned out, they almost did not want to sell me, but they honored their original agreement and before long I was aboard ship bound for the colony's

"You mean here in the United States." questioned the small wheel.

"Yes, here, but it was not the United States then. It was only a colony under the King's rule." explained the proud wheel.

"What happened when you arrived here." the little one further questioned.

"Nothing special for quite a few years. I was put on a big wagon that hauled heavy loads around the docks of Boston harbor. It was hard work, but I was new and strong. Then came talk of a revolution in 1776. My wagon ended up hauling cannon to Dorchester Heights outside of Boston during the sea blockade of the town. George Washington was in charge of the Revolutionary Army. The British finally gave in and left Boston. They had to. Our cannon worked day and night, and we cut off there food and supplies. (1) The wagon I was on did such a good job, and I was so strong that we were kept with the army."

~ ~ ~ ~ ~ ~

The large wheel rested after his tale and thoughts no longer flowed through Luke's pencil. Luke put the bill of sale on the table and the flush of a tingle left his body. He marveled at this affect but again wrote it off as being exhausted and retired for the night.

The next morning before Luke left for the day, he

stopped at the table where he was writing and picked up the 1740 bill of sale. There was no feeling, no sensation, no tingle.

"Just as I thought." He said to no one. *"My imagination has gone haywire. Of course there can't be a feeling from a piece of paper."*

He threw the paper down and left the house, he had fences to tend to.

No words passed between the two wheels.

That evening, after a good hot meal, Luke decided to do a little more writing. He walked to his special room and stood for a while admiring his wagon wheel.

"I bet you have a lot of story's buried in that magnificent wood." He said aloud to the wheel.

Luke looked around then making sure no one heard him talking to a wagon wheel. He moved to the table, sat down and reached for the next paper in date order. This said "Trenton – 1777." He read the not too long essay and as he did so that tingling sensation ran through him again. He tried to ignore it and continued reading. He wanted to understand the gist of the paper to be able to further record his history of the wheel.

~ ~ ~ ~ ~ ~

The wagon wheel again spoke to his new acquaintance.

"You see, the man who owned me, well really the whole wagon, stayed with and became part of the army. Not too much as a soldier but as a wagoners. You know, moving supplies, hauling cannon and of course, carrying the wounded.

Over month's, in constant skirmishes and travel, they found themselves in New Jersey. In May of '77 - Washington moved his army away from Morristown to Middlebrook. That was truly a busy time for me. You see, the army had grown to over seven thousand men by that time.[2] Because of my size and strength, my wagon was assigned to General Knox, who commanded all the artillery.

$\sim\sim\sim\sim\sim\sim$

The short essay Luke was reading basically followed the same tale being told to the small wheel. The paper was short on some details but it was following a history. Luke, wondered again, about this feeling he was experiencing. The historical record he was trying to reconstruct seemed to flow more easily in his thoughts as if someone was actually telling him what to write.

"**N**o harm done." he thought, "At least I'm able to put together a story."

Luke placed the antique essay back on the table, yawned and stretched. As he did so the funny sensation left him and the wagon wheel ceased speaking

Day's passed before Luke could get back to writing his story. Ranching does not always leave a lot of free time. It had been raining for a few hours and did not look like it would let up for a while, so Luke decided to give himself the afternoon off in his favorite room.
He grabbed a cold beer and settled down at the writing table. He took a swig from the bottle while looking at the wooden wheel.

"**W**ell, my friend, what are you going to tell me today." He said jokingly to himself.

Pencil in hand he stared at the large pad in front of him. He reread the last few paragraphs he had written a couple of days ago, but it still did not trigger any new thoughts. Frustrated, he threw down the pencil, sat back, beer bottle in hand.

"**I** don't know why I can't come up with anything, the other day I couldn't stop the flow of words. At least not until I - - - -."

He paused, thinking.

"**N**aaa, that's not possible."

Picking up the pencil again, he addressed the paper in front of him. He wrote a few words, then scribbled them out.

"**T**hat's not right." He thought.

He settled back again, drained the beer and reached for

the next note from the box which happened to be by the same author who penned the previous essay. Luke was flushed with that now all too familiar sensation. The tingle as he referred to it. The date at the top of the paper read September, 1781.

~ ~ ~ ~ ~ ~

"**Y**ou mean you stayed with the army for four years." asked little wheel.

"**O**f course. At least my owner did and he needed me to do his job." answered Wagon Wheel. "Never mind your questions, just let me tell my story."

"**B**ut where were you for four years." persisted the little one.

"**I** did a great deal of traveling, from as far north as West Point in New York, south through New Jersey, Pennsylvania, and Delaware on down to Virginia. It wasn't always easy going either." commented the large story teller. Three of my spokes had to be repaired. in New York. They were smashed by a small cannon ball. My iron tire was replaced twice, just from all the rough terrain we crossed. Even my hub was partially rebuilt in Pennsylvania. I'm glad they had a good wheelwright there. He did as good a job as my original hub. Well we finally ended up in Virginia, just outside of Yorktown. (3)We had th British, commanded by General Cornwallis, totally surrounded. The cannon I had been hauling started firing and kept on for three or four days. Eventually Cornwallis surrendered." (4)

The warm tingling feeling kept Luke writing for quite some time, to the point where his hand was cramping. He had written a great deal more than the paper exposed to him. He marveled at how much seemed to flow from his mind to his hand. Putting the pencil and paper down to massage his stiff fingers, he realized the tingle ceased, and his mind felt used and drained. The wheels on the wall were silent once again.

Luke was now convinced something out of the ordinary was talking place. He did not ordinarily believe in story's of the paranormal but this present situation was certainly challenging his mind. That puzzle would have to wait for another time to be worked on, he was just too tired tonight. Luke made his way to the bedroom and was asleep in a matter of minutes.

Dreams took over his restful sleep. He was seeing and conversing with people from two hundred years ago. He was living their life. He was part of the Revolution. He became the wagon wheel, traveling through rain and mud. Hitting a rock buried in the mud, startled him awake. *"What was happening to him ?"* he thought. He usually slept well, dreamless, most of the time. He sat up in bed and turned the lights on. Right away his mind drifted to the trophy room and the box of papers. What mystical powers did they possess. It certainly wasn't harming him, except right now by keeping him awake. He remembered the busy day ahead if him, and his head seemed to settle, he lay back and sank into a deep repose.

Chapter 3

The north wind was bringing the colder Canadian air along with snow which kept Luke busy for a spell. This was the only down side of being a rancher in Colorado, he told himself. After many days of making sure his cattle had enough food resources, Luke gave himself a rest period. It was still snowing and there was not much else for him to do, so he welcomed the warmth of his fire in his favorite room. With a hearty bowl of beef stew in front of him along with a cold beer, he was finally able to relax. Savoring the stew by the spoonful, he gazed admiringly at the old wagon wheel.

"What is this mysterious power you seem to have over me, my friend ? What is it that draws me to you ? Are you really trying to tell me your story ?"

Luke suddenly realized he was once again talking aloud to the wheel. He shook his head as if to clear it, took a long pull on his beer and thought

"I must really be losing it, yet I can't seem to help myself."

Luke finished his meal, returned the dish to the kitchen and grabbed a second beer. Determined to finish the story of the wheel, he tried to put the conversation out of his head. Returning with his drink to the trophy room he settled himself at the work table. He took a quick upward glance at the wheel, smiled, and reached for the next paper in the box.

~ ~ ~ ~ ~ ~

"**W**ith the war over." continued the large wheel to his smaller companion, "I was put to work with a stage coach company. I was carrying delegates from Williamsburg to Richmond for the Virginia convention. It was a meeting about ratifying the new Constitution. You see, Richmond was the new capital of Virginia. They moved it from Williamsburg in 1779 because of the war. There was fear of naval attack with Williamsburg being so close to the sea." (5)

"**O**h." mumbled the small wheel, not really knowing what his friend was talking about.

Luke almost welcomed the familiar tingle now, for he knew it enabled him to resume his writing. He laughed quietly to himself, thinking that this tingle was like an umbilical chord to the wheel itself. How else was he able to come up with the tale he was weaving. He wrote uninterrupted for another forty minutes, amazing himself at the continued flow of words.

The wagon wheel became silent when Like returned the aged paper to the box. *"Enough for today"*, Luke thought as he looked out the window at the still falling snow.

The following morning exposed a mantle of white as far as the eye could see.

This would give Luke another day of R&R which he so desperately needed. He took care of a few household matters before he settled himself by the fire in the trophy room. He found himself looking forward to the now familiar tingle, as strange and mysterious as it still was. The next piece of history he chose now found the wagon wheel on a medium sized farm in northwest Virginia. Luke relaxed with his tingle friend while reading the next part in the wheels life.

~ ~ ~ ~ ~ ~ ~

"**A**fter the convention was over I was taken out of service and sat in a barn with others like me for many months." big wheel continued. "I was finally traded to a farmer who took me to another part of Virginia. Work there was quite easy compared to what I had been through for all those years of war. I was used mostly for hauling hay or produce into the local town, and even that was not too often."

"Is that where you stayed until you came here." asked the child's wagon wheel.

The answer he got was a subtle laugh.

"Since we have a lot of time, and I still have a lot of story to tell to bring me to this place why don't you be patient my young friend and enjoy."

"I only worked on the farm a few years, when the wagon I was on was sold and I was headed for Ohio. That was back in 1790."

"Boy, you really did move around." commented the Little Wheel.

"That's only the beginning, Boy. Wait till I really get going with my tale." chuckled the big wheel in answer.

The laughter of the old wagon wheel transferred to Luke. He did not know why, but a flush of comfort suddenly overcame him. Returning the short note to the box, Luke leaned back in his chair and allowed himself to drift into restful sleep. The two wheels gazed at Luke and remained silent.

~ ~ ~ ~ ~ ~

The heavy snow lasted for a few days, which gave Luke much needed rest. He also used the time for equipment repair and general maintenance in the two large barns. The physical, but mind satisfying exhaustion kept him from his writing, but then again , what's the rush for a story after two hundred plus years.

A week passed before Luke returned to the wagon wheel. His fondness for the wheel was becoming stronger. He laughed at himself for having an attachment to just a wagon wheel. But was it just a wheel ? The mystery shrouding it seemed to be drawing him in deeper. Luke sought out the next chronologically ordered piece of paper from the box and welcomed the tingle.

~ ~ ~ ~ ~ ~

"**Y**ou see." said the big wheel, "The Ohio Valley had just been opened to settlers, every thing west of the Ohio River. My new owner was in the freight hauling business. I made countless trips from Richmond to Pittsburgh and on through to this newly opened territory. Settlers flocked by the hoards to make a claim on new homesteads. Of course, this did not go over too well with the Indians who were already settled there, which in turn caused many problems. At that time, Native Americans did not know of individual ownership of land. Their Ohio Valley was opened to, and used by all with respect of other peoples use at the time. These new settlers were cutting down forests, clearing the land and fencing off large areas however they were taking land that truly was not theirs to take. There were constant struggles and incidents between the two factions. I myself, still have scars from arrows and burn marks from these hostile flare ups."

"**W**ere you seriously hurt." asked Little Wheel."

"**N**o, not that time. I guess I could have been but remember I told you I was built quite strong. For twenty years or so I made those back and forth trips between Ohio and Virginia till I was sold again and taken further west."

~ ~ ~ ~ ~ ~

Luke found what he was writing, intriguing. The historical notes he was reading were like an outline of the wheels life. The actual story he was writing based on this information was of course, fiction, or was it. The words poured from his head almost without thinking. As silly as he thought it was, Luke was now convinced he was now connected directly with the Wagon Wheel. He returned the paper back to it's place in the box knowing he would lose the tingle. Sitting back, he gazed intently at the Wheel.

"**I** wonder what else you have to tell me old friend ?" he said out loud. The wheel and his smaller companion were mute. Except for the ticking of an old grandfather clock the room was silent.

Luke couldn't wait to see what the next adventure would be, but for now, he had other things to attend to.

There was finally a break in the weather and again it was days before Luke was able to return to the Old Wheel. It was like visiting an old friend when he got back. He wasted no time in reaching into the box to see where the wheel would take him.

~ ~ ~ ~ ~ ~

"It was now around 1810 or so and I found myself in a place called St Louis. It was right on the Mississippi River. The place was all hustle and bustle. There had to be thousands of people there. You see, this was the starting point for wagon trains crossing the river and heading west into the unknown wilds."

"What did you do with so many people." asked a curious little wheel.

"Oh, my new owner kept me quite busy hauling the extra heave freight from one part of the town to the other, so the people moving west would be well supplied. Not every one traveled west though. Some stayed right there in St. Louis opening shops and supply houses. As many blacksmiths as there were, they were all kept busy for obvious reasons."

"You mean because of all the wagons." interrupted Little Wheel.

"Exactly." was his answer

"Although there were also a number of people who turned back east again."

"How come." inquired the young one.

"Story's" answered Wagon Wheel. Story's about hardships, and Indian trouble."

"Indian trouble." exclaimed an excited Little Wheel. "Did you have any Indian trouble." he inquired.

"I had my share, maybe even more than most, because I made so many trips back and forth. I was burned numerous times and had untold small repairs, but I always managed to come out alright."

"Where actually did you go when you went west ?"

pestered the little one again.

Frustrated, the Wagon Wheel finally scolded gently;

"Just let me tell my story, small fry and then you can tell me yours later."

"Sorry." said Little Wheel slowly and sadly.

"To answer your questions, most of the wagon trains took up a course into the Kansas and Oklahoma territory's. They were all dreaming of a homestead of their own. Some trips were pleasant and peaceful, while others were filled with anguish and fear from Indian raids. Most of all they were all long and weary journeys.

All was suddenly still.

~ ~ ~ ~ ~ ~

"How interesting." thought Luke replacing the paper in order in the box. He reread what he had just written, not knowing where it had come from. He raised his head up looking at the Wagon Wheel.

"You really do know how to get inside my head, don't you, old friend."

Talking out loud to no one seemed to be common place now.

"So long as I don't see the man in the white coat, I guess I'm alright for now."

Putting his writing aside, Luke's attention turned to other matters. Finally retiring for the night he drifted into dreams about past history.

Chapter 4

$\mathbf{B}$etween the harsh winter and the holiday season, months had scooted by before Luke could return to the trophy room, with signs of spring beginning to show as he did so. He could feel a comfort in the room as it welcomed him. His pad and pencil, in the same place where he left them, were calling to him. Happily, he reached for the special box retrieving the next piece of history. This brought him to southern Kansas. The wheel was now owned by a small hauling company trading mostly in farm equipment. Luke's fingers started to tingle as the pencil smoothly glided across the paper. He smiled at the feeling, knowing more history was about to be revealed.

~ ~ ~ ~ ~ ~

"Suddenly there was talk of war spreading through the town." said the Wagon Wheel. "Both North and South were gathering arms and supplies. I was purchased by a local branch of the Confederate Army and put to work hauling cannon again. It was long hard work, but nothing new to me. The weeks swiftly passed and before you knew it I was involved in the shooting war. My wagon took a direct hit from a Union mortar shot which left me lying in the mud apparently the only piece surviving the hit. One of my spokes was splintered a little but other than that I was in good shape."

"Were you frightened." asked the little one, thoroughly fascinated by the story.

"Not really." commented Wagon Wheel. "After all, I had already been through the many years of the revolution. A few days later the advancing Union forces found me, cleaned me up, and put me on another wagon. Now I was moving cannon for the North."

Laughingly, Wagon Wheel commented that he had served both North and South during the Civil War.

"Which side did you like best." inquired the small one.

"I had no special allegiance to either side." he answered, "I just did the best job I could. I was built strong and I was proud to serve. That was my job."

"My life was never that exciting." remarked the Little Wheel sadly. "Luke took very good care of me until one of the ranch hands ran over my wagon with a truck. Like you, I was the only wheel to survive. I guess that's why I'm here now."

"The war was over in 1863 and my wagon's driver took me back to his home in Texas.

Luke's thoughts were interrupted by a visitor. He hated to lose the tingle sensation but he knew it was necessary for now as he put down the aged note. The wheels became mute.

~ ~ ~ ~ ~ ~

The business of earning a living in the method he chose kept Luke away from his beloved trophy room for extended periods. This made his joy all the greater when he was successful in stealing an hour or so now and then. The wheels story had him totally captivated. He was the one writing the story, yet some how he felt the wagon Wheel itself was dictating more than he was gleaning from the bits of historical papers. The next peek at history told of the long journey back to Texas from Virginia.

"There were three other wagons besides mine and a total of ten men. They were all anxious to return to their loved ones. The first part of the journey went well and was somewhat easy. Then as we passed through Mississippi and Arkansas things got rough."

"You mean there were mountains and things." asked Little Wheel, interrupting again.

"No." replied a slightly annoyed Wagon Wheel. "Going

over mountains was almost the easy part. It was people that gave us trouble. Some of those Southern folk were still bitter about losing the war and did not like my owner because he fought for the North. Then there were others who lost almost everything because of the war. Times were tough and some folk turned to robbing others, especially if they knew they were Yankees. And if that wasn't enough trouble, there was always the Indians who were losing out no matter who won the war. I don't know which of the encounters was worse, the white man or the Indian. We did, however, manage to reach Texas. I picked up a few more burn marks on my spokes from Indian flaming arrows but all in all I came through the experience fundamentally in tack."

"There he goes again." the little wheel thought. *"I wish I knew what he was talking about. My history is so limited, I wish I could be more like him but on the other hand it looks like I have known more peace in my short life than he has in two hundred years. I guess I'll stick to being me."*

"In the beginning, Texas life was easy, but then came the trouble with the Comanche Indians. Many Indians chose not to stay on the reservations because of the way they were treated, and also the lack of game to hunt. It was the Comanche Nation that literally stopped the Spanish expansion north from Mexico and the French expansion west from Louisiana.   They were said to be the most powerful Indian tribe in America. My wagon ended up in part of the Red River War against the Comanche. It was in 1874 when they were finally subdued. (6) When the peace in Texas was restored I was again used in hauling heavy freight between New Mexico and California.

Luke could feel the day's efforts catching up with him as much as he wanted to pursue his fascinating story, he had to give in to his body's need for sleep. Reluctantly he put down the paper from the box and allowed the tingle to leave him. The wheel looked totally innocent in it's silence on the wall.

~ ~ ~ ~ ~ ~

Waking early, Luke felt totally refreshed and knowing he was near the end of the wheel's story, decided to stay in the trophy room until it's completion.

"**O**n my final routine trip to California I was again sold to a large enterprise and was taken to Death Valley where I was used to carry heavy loads of Borax." continued Wagin Wheel."This was almost as hard as hauling cannon. Death Valley lived up to it's name. It was nothing more than parched sand and rock. It never rained and rivers and streams dried up long ago. I felt sorry for the mules used to pull the heavily loaded wagons. Death was common place in Death Valley for both man and beast. Again my superior strength saved me although I did start to dry some what."

"**H**ow did you get here." questioned the little wheel.

No longer minding the interruptions Wagon Wheel patiently answered.

"**I**'m getting to that little one. After delivering the Borax from my last trip, The wagon I was on was really in bad shape. They took me and the other wheels off and used the wood of the wagon for fire wood, and we were stored in a barn. I rested in that barn for years and was finally chosen for a wagon heading for Colorado.

Luke was both excited and sad at this point. He picked up the last hand written note. This was the one on deerskin. It told of the three year journey from California to Colorado.

" **T**he wagon owner was an old prospector who searched for gold during the whole trek to Colorado. The prospector never struck it rich but did manage to get enough to live on. After reaching his destination the wagon was worthless although he did sell the wheels. It was Luke's uncle who purchased them. I was the only one he finally kept. I believe it was because I was built so well from the start. I was kept in a shed and never had to work again. It was years ago when Luke brought me here. I've been on display here ever since. I still have years of work left in me but I would rather be resting here."

"**W**ell, I'm glad you're here also. It's my pleasure to know someone with such an interesting life." said the small wheel. "I hope we can stay together from now on."

Luke reorganized the papers one last time securing them in the box. As he put the box away in a cupboard he realized he still felt the tingle. He returned to the table and without consciously thinking picked up the pencil and started writing. The words seemed to just appear beyond his control. The pencil stopped and he read what had been written as the tingle faded away.

*"**I** am just a wagon wheel. There are many like me. I am nothing special but I am very special. You look at me as just a thing but you do not see my history. I see and feel but you do not see me see and feel. I have witnessed history you only read about. You pay not attention to what I feel or what I have seen. You assume things that are not true. The real things you do not see. If you could know me you would understand. If you could understand me, you would know the truth. I am not governed by emotions. I accept what is real. If you could accept what is real, you would not wander. When your emotions do not wander reality becomes a certainty. Certainty brings peace of mind and understanding of why. I am just a wagon wheel who is finally at peace. Will you reach the joy I possess. It is yours to grasp, if you understand.*

I am just a wagon wheel."

The end of the beginning.

The Movie

by

K.J.Goss

The Movie

The hideous scream pierced the night with such force that even the trees were quivering. The cry was un-mistakenly human yet at the same time too shrill to be human. It was like someone turned the volume on an old TV thriller to maximum. Those gathered around the movie set froze in place.

"Cut, – cut, –cut." Shouted the director. The annoyance in his voice was more than obvious. "Who the hell is working sound effects. Get his or her ass over here right now."

Talking to any one and no one he ranted on,

"Like I don't have enough problems, what with four days of rain, broken scaffolding, half the crew down with food poisoning. Geezes, what next.

"I'm sorry Mr. Turk, I was about to - - - -."

Kurt, who was the sound man was cut off mid-sentence.

"You're sorry !" yelled Turk for all to hear. "You're sorry ?" Here we are three weeks behind schedule with the first good day to shoot in a week and you're sorry ? You're really gonna be sorry when you have no job. Now tell me what the hell is going on."

Now equally angry, Kurt shouted,

"I'm trying to, but you won't shut up long enough to let me speak."

Totally taken aback by this assault, Turk snapped his head around with a look of hatred and fire in his eyes. Standing his ground, Kurt stared right back and in a firm, strong voice repeated,

"I was about to turn on the scream recording when

that hideous scream started. My equipment remained off. It is still off.

"Then what the - - - -." Started Turk who suddenly froze with all the others. There it was again. The same hideous scream that cut through the jungle so shrill that all else was silent. The pitch of this second scream had a much deeper tone but was as blood curdling. A direction could not be ascertained, it was all encompassing. Harry Thurber, the man hired as their jungle guide approached Turk, rifle in hand.

"Do you really think that's necessary."Turk said sarcastically.

Harry answered quite calmly,

"I've lived in the jungle long enough to know that it is always necessary."

Turk did not like his answer but did not comment further. The screech sounded again and as before it was at a different pitch but of a shorter duration. The crew of forty three people were looking around in all directions but a definitive location could not be determined.

"CUT." Sounded out loud and clear.

This was followed by the deep booming voice of the director, Sam Caldwell.

"Okay people, I don't know what's going on here but now you have one too many screams. Let's try and keep to the script. As it is this movie is too long. Let's try it again." he finished in a frustrated voice. Before he could return to his position behind the camera's, the sound effects man, Ed Jenkins intercepted.

"They didn't do it Sam, and neither did I. That last scream came from the jungle. The real jungle, not our effects machine. As a matter of fact I think all three came from the jungle."

"That's not possible. The screams are in the script and the timing was where it was supposed to be."

Cutting the director short the sound man said,

"I know the timing was perfect, but I'm telling you we did not manufacture those screams. I know that for a fact because, well, I didn't want to tell you but my equipment isn't even working. Tom and I have been working on it for the last half hour to get it fixed."

The director looked at him as if he could not believe what he was hearing. Angrily, he shouted,

"Am I running this film or not. Everybody knows more about what's going on then I do. It would be nice if people told me these things."

Ed meekly answered,

"Our electronic screams aren't as good as what we just heard."

Sam stared at him, eyes burning and nostrils flaring. Before he could speak there was a forth scream even louder and more shrill than the others. This was a deep masculine cry.

"Cut." came an echoing out of the megaphone, followed by the quiet but stern voice of Josh Granger.

"The idea of making a film about making a film of making a film sounded intriguing but would someone here please tell me what happened to the original script. Because so far nothing that has happened in the last twenty minutes even slightly resembles the pages that I'm holding."

He paused looking around, about to speak again when a runner, part of the native guide entourage, came yelling from the jungle to the clearing of the movie set. He pointed in the direction he came from. Excited words were exchanged followed by the guide directing his men to positions surrounding the filming location, rifles at the ready, while he and three others ran into the jungle where the runner had come from.

The runner then approached Josh, and in broken English told of finding four bodies hung upside down not too distant from the set. They were all members of the movie crew. Three women and a man. He then retrieved four tarp's from the supply tent and rifle in hand followed the trail he ran in on.

Quiet panic ensued with cast and crew gathering in a tight circle in the center of the posted guards. The conversation naturally turned to suppositions and questions about the happenings.

A fifth scream, more hideous than the others quieted even the noise of the jungle. The circle of people moved even closer to each other. A few of the women were in tears now. Gun shots could be heard off in the distance. The silence that prevailed was eerie. People's breathing was all that was heard. The runner returned, gathered more men and left immediately.

It was another ten minutes, then all returned. They carried five bodies wrapped in tarp's. The carriers were stained with blood.

The guide related the story of finding all five bodies hung by the feet upside down from trees. All five had been obviously clawed open and the blood almost completely drained.

A few of the cast and crew members fainted. Others were starting to panic. A sixth scream was heard which sounded even closer. Some of the native guides lost control and started shooting wildly into the jungle. The guide had all he could do to stop the frenzy. Once a semblance of calm was restored, Josh speaking through the PA system, tried to assure that everything was under control and that they should all start packing up.

"We'll cancel the shoot for now." He said, "Until we can find a safer location."

A closer, softer scream was then heard. It came from their midst. A woman's voice yelled out,

"Where's Jenny, she was right here next to me. She just disappeared."

A shrill scream sounded from the jungle again followed by a lesser scream from the woman who asked about Jenny.

Josh spoke again through the PA system.

"Please keep calm, we'll leave immediately. Forget the packing, just take some food and water."

"Roger just disappeared right in front of me." some one shouted.

Minutes later the jungle scream was repeated. People wanted to run now.

"Which way do we go." seemed to be the cry.

The guide organized them as best he could before starting. Suddenly the guide vanished while everyone was watching. He just wasn't there any more. They all waited silently and as expected the scream came.

"This way someone yelled, let's take this trail."

"No !" somebody countered, "I remember we came in by this trail."

People started running. A few were pushed and fell to the ground. It made no difference to others. They still ran. Josh tried to help some woman up. She disappeared as he reached for her. Her shrill scream was heard a few minutes later.

A native guide and the director stayed at the site. Both were armed, although Josh realized it would do no good. What ever it was out there must be something supernatural. More hideous cries could be heard. Some were more distant now. Perhaps this being was following the mob. Perhaps they alone would survive and be saved. They stood back to back their eyes searching the jungle in all directions. Screams were even more distant now.

Eventually all went quiet. Slowly the natural sounds of the jungle returned. It was as if nothing had happened. The two men turned toward each other, the look of relief on their faces. They had survived. How, they did not know. The tension left their bodies as they disappeared before each others eyes.

"Cut." The assistant director yelled. "That's a wrap folks. Great job. This is going to make one hell of a Saturday night thriller. Let's get something to eat, then pack up and go home.

The End.

A Special in the Woods

by
K.J.Goss

A Special Place in the Woods

The old man rested in his reclining rocker on the porch of his mountain cabin looking out over the green valley. He was slowly nursing a cold beer in one hand while the other hand absentmindedly clicked a lantern light on and off repeatedly. His thoughts drifted back to earlier days when he first met Caleb Montgomery. Caleb changed his life dramatically although most who knew Nick would not consider him any kind of great success. He started reliving that time period as he drifted into a semi-dream state while staring at a slight concave depression area of green just a few yards from the porch.

~ ~ ~ ~ ~ ~

Chapter 1

It was the heaviest rain I had ever seen in all my years of coming to this cabin. I was glad I had plenty of food stashed away. Even with four wheel drive there was no way I could get down the mountain in this mud. And if I did get down there is no way in hell I would get back up. Might as well just sit back and wait it out. I had plenty of books and magazines and there is always my writing. Writing short story's had become a favorite pastime recently though

I would probably never do anything with them.

It was too early for supper and I already had plenty of dry wood cut but with this severe rain I was really confined to the cabin. It was dark because of the weather although it was only early afternoon. I took off my boots, grabbed a magazine and stretched out on the bed.

Thunder roared as a prelude to a massive bolt of lightening which struck just outside the cabin. I was shaken from my drowsiness as I felt the whole structure shake. It was pitch black outside except for the few seconds of brightness from the lightening strike. I suddenly smelled the distinct odor of burning wood and leaves. The cabin was intact and on looking out the window I saw the source of the odor. A patch of ground about six feet in diameter was smoldering as a result of the electrical discharge. The flood of rain left no threat of fire but the spot of the strike, revealed by my flashlight, was now a crater three or four feet deep. The rain now appeared to be heavier if that was even possible. What used to be dry ground was a maze of rivulets running helter skelter. This storm was already over fourteen hours and there did not seem to be any end in sight. Apparently even the radio waves were in a disturbed state because static was the only thing heard on my trusty old transistor radio. Oh for the good old days of a wind up Victrola. At least then I could have some music.

I came up here to relax and finish the research report I was working on. I guess now's as good a time as any, I thought. I dug out my papers, lit a candle and reread the little I had written. I decided it was badly worded and boring and I'm the one who wrote it. This was doing no good. I just could not get my head into it. I turned to stare out the window and exactly then another bold of lightening struck the exact same place as before. As I watched the smoke dissipate I recall the old adage *"Lightening never strikes the same place twice."*. So much for supposed theory's . I was just witness to a science changing event. I laughed at myself. Look at me, I'm a big deal nothing. Who the hell would believe me.

Thunder rolled again and another strike in the same crater. Now I was starting to get frightened. All I could think of was the cabin might be next to be struck. Ordinarily I would have bugged out, but where would I go in this monsoon. I sat back to think. The best thing to do was to stay put. This had to be over soon. I grabbed a cool beer, thank goodness for ice coolers, and made up my mind to relax. Just as I picked up a magazine thunder and lightening attacked for the fourth time and again in the same place. This is getting ridiculous, I thought. "There must be a reason for this." I said aloud.

Looking out as best I could with the now fading flashlight the crater now appeared deeper. Not wider, just deeper. There was also something reflecting the soft light of my flashlight. *"I have to search around for the extra battery's."* I told myself. Probably just some quartz or mica I answered myself about the reflection.

I will further investigate the hole as soon as the storm lets up, I thought, more importantly I will have to fill it in before someone falls in and gets hurt, namely me.

The storm carried on well into the night and did not really let up until just before five AM. Sometime a little after midnight a flash of daylight lit up the cabin as yet another strike aimed for the crater. This was obviously something more than a freak accident. There has to be a reason for this and I intend to find out. My curiosity overcame my fear. I was more than anxious for daylight to come. Exhaustion finally took it's toll and I willingly fell asleep in my only stuffed chair.

A stiff neck along with bright sunshine streaming in the window brought me out of my much needed sleep. The clock read eight fifteen. Well three hours sleep is better than nothing.

Chapter 2

The sunshine was of course a very welcome commodity. Gazing out the window I saw nothing but mud and debris. What ever was surrounding the cabin except for large trees was relocated elsewhere. My new surroundings came from father up the mountain. The perfect opportunity to try out my new boots.

I had a warm can of juice and skipped actual breakfast. I laced up my boots, threw on an old denim shirt and went straight for the crater.

I approached carefully not knowing how soft the edges were going to be. Looking down, the view held me spellbound. There appeared to be some sort of platform about twenty five feet down. It certainly wasn't wood, it almost looked like a metal. The parts that weren't covered by mud had a sheen to it. This must have been the reflection I saw last night.

I went back to the cabin to get a flashlight. I also grabbed my hunting knife, some rope and remembered the old apple ladder hung up on the back of the cabin. I lowered the ladder to the platform which turned out to be quite solid, but short of reaching the top where I was standing. I secured the rope to a tree and let it dangle in the crater by the ladder. Carefully I lowered myself till I managed a foot hold on the apple ladder. Soon I was standing on the platform. *"Could be an old mine shaft."* I wondered. *"Looks pretty Hi-tech for a mine shaft."* I tapped it with the butt end of my knife. It sounded extremely solid. "Must be thick." I thought. Using the blade I made a scratch, or at least I tried to scratch it. The blade left no mark. I tried again putting my shoulder into it. I did not mark it in the least. All I did was to remove some caked on dirt. That's really odd I thought. I know of no alloy or metal that is so hard you can't scratch it.

Making a closer inspection of the platform I walked off some quick measurements. Roughly sixteen by twenty feet. The edges of the stage were rounded as in finely made furniture. There were no sharp corners at all. I stood on the edge and looked down into the hole the lightening dug. The platform had sides, or at least one side. It obviously went farther down than the dirt disturbed by the electrical discharge. A lot further down than I could reach with what equipment I had with me. I tried scratching it one more time to no avail. I stood silently for about five minutes observing everything I could and finally climbed up and out returning to my cabin.

I made some coffee, filled my mug and sat by the window staring at the crater trying to put some pieces together. It suddenly dawned on me. No wonder there were so many repetitive strikes on the same spot with a hunk of metal that size being so close to the surface. *"I've got to cover it up until I figure out what this thing is."* I thought. *"I've got to cover it up so it's safe and at the same time leave access for myself."*

I finished my coffee and wandered over to the old shed where I kept a small tractor. Amazingly it fired up after only a few tries. I found some beams, logs and some old canvas tarp's

By dark I had finished what I considered to be a satisfactory cover. Not the prettiest piece of landscaping but it would suit the purpose. It was now too dark to do any more so tomorrow I would concentrate on access for myself. I could think about that while I had some dinner. Perhaps I could sleep tonight.

Chapter 3

Sleep still did not come easily no matter how physically tired I was. Excitement of what may lay ahead played games with my mind. I finally argued myself away from those unrealistic day dreams and let nature take control of my body. Undisturbed sleep was the reward.

I awakened to a clear blue sky and the suns rays filling the cabin with warmth. Quite a change from two days ago. I relaxed with a good breakfast knowing I had all the time in the world to pursue my search of what ever it was occupying the hole in my yard. It obviously was there for years another lapse of an hour or so was not going to matter. After all where was it going to go. I laughed to myself as I cleaned up after breakfast. I couldn't believe how good I felt. It's amazing what sleep can do to renew ones energy and outlook.

Outside I gathered some basic tools, picked up my trusty apple ladder and rope, then went directly to the tarp covered opening I provided myself the day before. I managed, with some difficulty, to slide down the side of this curiosity. I found myself standing on some rock outcrop but realized I was not yet at the bottom of the mysterious shaft. Obviously some more digging would have to be done which I was not in the mood to do. Trying to ignore what I had to do I started a closer inspection of this bronze colored structure. Managing a few hazardous steps I maneuvered around to the opposite side. I established what I considered a safe footing and as I raised my head up was surprised to see some incised writing. At least writing of some sort. It was a form I had not seen before. Using my flashlight I scanned the wall to pick up as much detail as I could. The script was definitely inscribed into the surface. How that was accomplished was beyond me. I could not even make a scratch with my knife.

I guess rather than script it was more like hieroglyphics. A similarity to Egyptian but definitely not Egyptian. That I was basically familiar with from past studies. Unfortunately I did not bring my camera down into the hole with me. *"Oh well."* I thought, *"It's not like this thing is going any place soon."*

After a bit of struggling and dirt scratching I was able to move to another side where again I was met with more strange looking symbols. These were totally different than what I had just witnessed and just as indecipherable. I was becoming intrigued now. I could feel the curiosity growing.

This second set of marks, for lack of a better word, seemed to be inscribed in somewhat of a vertical fashion, or better yet, it ran curvilinear from horizontal to vertical as if pointing down. This would absolutely require more digging now.

I realized I could do no more today with what I had with me and it was still early enough to get to the local library. With some difficulty I exited this great hole and promised myself to rig up something better and more permanent for future use. I re-covered the entrance way and cleaned myself up for my trip to town.

Here at the library I sat staring out the window. I came here to do research but now that I'm here I'm not sure what I'm researching. I don't ever recall reading about any such thing that was in residency in my yard. I guess about the only thing I can check on now will be hieroglyphics.

The next two hours zipped by as I went from one book to another. I was surprised at how much there was about Glyph's and I had not even tried the internet yet. It was early closing day for the library so I reluctantly tore myself away from the books and decided to have an early dinner here in town.

I arrived back at my cabin just in time to see a beautiful sunset. I sat down with a cold beer and proceeded to make a list of what I might need for tomorrow. Besides the list I slowly collected the sundry tools and items. Finding myself pleasantly tired I lay on my bunk with a magazine and reflected on the day's activities.

Chapter 4

I must have been really tired. I awoke with the sun still in my clothes and magazine in hand not remembering a thing. I took my time for a nice breakfast and two mugs of coffee. I remembered to make a snack for lunch because I just knew I would be busy all day. By eight o'clock I was already digging. I made the opening wider with a more permanent ladder system for an easier up and down. I accidently dropped the shovel point side down and watched it bounce off the strange shaft. As I made my way down I checked out the point of impact. Not a dent or scratch to be seen. To me this defied all logic. Having remembered the camera, I too some shots and wrote some notes with date and time. I moved on to the inscription side. I repeated the procedure. Satisfied with that I looked into further digging to enable myself to go deeper and determine just how big this, this thing is.

Much to my surprise, the digging was relatively easy. I guessed with all that rain the dirt was still soft and there was very little in the way of rocks or stones. It dawned on me then, that however this thing got here there had to be some excavation done. That alone would have helped, depending on how long it had been here. Allowing my mind to take off on it's own I further speculated that it might not have been here too long. I felt the dirt was far too soft for it to have been here for any great length of time. By great length of time I was meaning decades, not centuries.

As soft as the dirt was it still took many hours to make any progress. There just wasn't any maneuvering room. The larger problem was what to do with the dirt. I took myself a snack break because I needed time to think. I definitely needed help but I dared not. I don't know if it was selfishness or fear of ridicule. I just felt that I did not want to share this, what ever it was, right now. So what do I do. I dug myself a comfortable seat in the dirt wall and sat back to relax. I stared blindly at the mysterious shaft before me. Some mud clinging to the bronze colored wall drew my attention. I moved to the wall and brushed aside the dirt. More strange markings came into view. Directing the light from the extension cord I rigged up I saw they were again different from the other two sets I previously viewed. These were totally unique. They appeared to be random but uniform sets of parallel lines, both vertical and horizontal interspersed with quarter circle marks. I had no clue as to what it represented. These particular marks covered a more extensive area than the other markings.

My interest piqued again and I went back to digging, which I did for another hour before I climbed out of my self imprisonment.

There was still daylight left which allowed me to rig up a pulley system to help with my dirt problem. It really slowed my work down, but then again, what's the hurry, at least I did not have to share my crazy secret.

My aching muscles told me I had enough for the day. I covered up my pit of pain and went straight to the cabin. I downed a cool beer as I prepared a fantastic dinner of franks and beans topped off with a Twinky. A quick hot shower and I collapsed in bed. I tried to update my day's notes but the sandman had other ideas.

Chapter 5

I awoke to the unwanted sound of rain. Without thinking I threw on my jeans and ran outside to check the tarps. Surprisingly everything was pretty well covered. I amaze myself sometimes, considering how tired I was yesterday, I still did a fair job of covering my secret. Luckily the rain was light but it would still prohibit any extensive digging. With that decided I grabbed my laptop and headed for town. I stopped at the "Country Kitchen" and grabbed a table in a back corner, ordered breakfast and flipped open my computer.

A two hour breakfast search netted a whole lot of nothing. I had gathered tons of information but as of now it seemed nothing was of any relevance.

Feeling disappointed I paid my tab with a good tip for space rental and wandered out to my truck. I sat there in the parking lot trying to decide my next move although nothing came to mind immediately. For now I guess more digging would be my only route. I headed for my mountain home watching the rain slip from the wipers thinking of absolutely nothing. When I reached the cabin the rain had increased slightly but the radio promised some clearing in the late afternoon. I glanced over at the tarp's as I walked to the shelter of my humble abode. Still a bit weary from yesterday's workout I lay on the bed again drifting off to sleep.

I awoke to sunshine but to my chagrin it was morning sun not late afternoon sunset. Although I had no need I was a little embarrassed. I was also very hungry. Juice, bacon and eggs soon satisfied that.

Tools and camera in hand I entered my underground world. I was again filled with wonder looking at this marvelous structure. Now all I had to do was to figure out what it was, who built it and what it was for. " No big deal I have the rest of my life in front of me yet." I laughed.

The digging was much slower now but was actually easier since I rigged up the pulley system. Yesterday's rain was of no hindrance for which I was thankful. Another four feet down uncovered more markings. After cleaning them off as best I could they struck a familiar note in my head. I stared at them for a while when it suddenly dawned on me. This was a star constellation. Off hand I couldn't remember its name but I had seen it before. My excitement grew again. Perhaps now I could get a toe hold on some kind of clue to what I was confronting. I took a whole mess of pictures and even made a few sketches for later study. Remembering my last encounter with star studies I made some quick measurements of the distance between the placement of the markings on the bronze wall.

It was then I noticed one dashed line led away from the main cluster and continued further down into the dirt. Frantically I started digging again not caring where I threw the dirt, which of course created a problem. Because of my haste I had to cease shoveling and sort out the mess I made. "I guess that old saying, "Haste Makes Waste." was coined for a reason." Well at least I learned my lesson this time. After losing about an hour's time I finally made it back to my extended line, my enthusiasm dampened somewhat but it was still there. My shovel work resumed, just more carefully and slower. The line I was following seemed to go on forever as did the length of this shaft. Eventually I gave myself a break, the end of the line not in sight yet.

I glanced at my watch. Four nineteen glared back at me. No wonder I was hungry again. Of course my aching muscles did not consider this too much fun. I decided to quit for the day.

With cleanup and re-tarping it was after five when I reentered the cabin. Supper and some quick note updates was about all I could handle before I hit the sack.

Chapter 6

I was up with the sun and felt surprisingly good. Coffee mug in hand I stood at the edge of the pit. I was already down about forty feet or so and my work space was growing narrow. This would never do, and I still had not come to the bottom of my mysterious structure. I stood there a while till I remembered an heavy equipment rental place just the other side of town. Was all this really worth the expense. I went back inside to refill my mug and think. By the time I finished the coffee I had made up my mind to make the big leap and go for it. I finished dressing, jumped in the truck and headed for town.

Two and a half hours later I was back on my mountain, Bobcat in tow. Thank goodness I did not have any neighbors. The last thing I needed was someone satisfying their curiosity about my secret project.

The afternoon was spent doing some preliminary ramp building, or should I say digging. I started about twenty five feet out from the shaft to give me a comfortable angle down. Now my hand digging would be a lot easier.

As anxious as I was to continue I chose to wait and have a fresh start tomorrow. *"I should have rented this Bobcat to start with, I might even be finished by now."* I thought. *"Oh well, such is life."*

I was feeling pretty good about what I had just accomplished so I decided to treat myself to dinner in town again. I had passed an Italian place on the way to the rental. That and a glass of wine will top the day off nicely.

Chapter 7

  I welcomed the early morning sun with renewed enthusiasm and energy. I was anxious to get started but listened to my stomach and kept it happy with a full breakfast.

  The digging did seem to be a tad easier though it looked as if this shaft had no bottom. I alternated between the Bobcat and hand shovel all day and the only thing I uncovered was another inscription. This also appeared to be some sort of star chart, at least it impressed me that way. This one, though, I could not recognize. I did my usual pictures and sketches. Another trip to the library would be in order, but not today. I wanted to take full advantage of this rainless day.

  The more I dug the more I pondered over this metal giant. What was this thing? More importantly, who put it here? Here out in the middle of nowhere Vermont on a basically deserted mountainside.

  I shoveled some more while my mind was wandering to thoughts I really was trying to avoid. The thought of extraterrestrials had been in the back of my mind since I first came upon my find. I always believed somebody else was out there but I never imagined I would personally have any contact with such beings. "There I go again, getting carried away, just what I did not want to do." I scolded. I went back to digging pushing my wild thoughts back to the archives. I was now at about the forty five foot level and because of the low sun of the late afternoon it was becoming difficult to see. I called it quits until tomorrow.

  There was no way I could cover this massive excavation up so I just threw the tarp's over the very top of the shaft and hoped no one wandered around here in the dark. And that pertained mostly to myself.

Thanks to my handy transistor radio I found out clear weather was mine for the next three or four days. That put some much needed energy back into my tired bones. Perhaps in that time I could find the bottom of this thing. The library would have to wait until a rainy day.

By mid-day something caught my eye. I thought it was another symbol marking. It was that and more. Below these new symbols, which, of course, made no sense to me, was a visible seam, about four feet long running horizontal on the shaft. I double timed my digging my excitement driving me. I know there was no hurry, I just couldn't help myself. The anticipation of discovering something new could not be contained.

After some clearing, the seam showed itself to be running vertical also. There were three of them. The outline reminded me of elevator doors. Could I be so lucky I thought. I kept digging frantically until, *"EUREKA."*, I think I finally hit bottom. I was tired, my arms and back aching but I couldn't stop now. I had enough dirt cleared to make a closer inspection. I was definitely at the bottom and this definitely was some kind of entrance. My heart was thumping while my hands were shaking. I was so excited that tears were forming in my eyes as they rushed over the seam outline. No buttons or handles were visible that I could detect. I took a deep breath trying to settle myself. I realized it was getting late because the light was dimming again.

I traced the seam outline with my hands hoping for a hidden switch. No such luck. Remembering the crazy shaped symbols above the door and thinking that may be the key I began pressing each individual one. Disappointment was again the answer. I stood back a little trying to clear my head. Shadows from above were becoming darker which convinced me that my work day was over. It was truly dusk by the time I climbed up and out of my sub basement. Feeling a touch of self pity I grabbed a cool beer as soon as I entered the cabin. I downed that quickly and grabbed another from the cooler. *"Note to my self; get more beer since there were only two left. Just as well."* I thought. *"I needed a clear head if I was to figure this puzzle out."*

I finished the second brew while fixing some supper and talked myself out of a third. After piling the dirty dishes in the sink I grabbed my notes, which was mostly loose pieces of paper, sat at the table and concentrated on some sort of organization. I surprised myself at how many notes I had. There was quite a pile. I started to feel better thinking that just maybe I was being efficient without even thinking. Roboticly I arranged my loose notes by date and time, matched each up with photo's and just like magic, a folder materialized that could almost pass as real research. With my organizational skill no longer in question I turned to the real question. "What's next ?" I decided on another beer and again talked myself out of it.

Perhaps the answer, or at least a clue rested behind that door that I found today. Again my mind was making suppositions. Maybe it wasn't a door at all but just more design marks. I know it was late and quite dark but I chose to go back to my bronze question. With both flashlight and extension cord light I made my way down to the door in question.

Things looked different in the dark with just artificial light. The strange symbols took on a mystical quality that hadn't appeared in the daylight. Moving the light back and forth to view the markings, something different caught my eye. A minuscule reflection, blue in color. Using my shirt sleeve I brushed away some dirt residue. Bringing the light closer while repeating the back and forth motion I saw the blue reflection. It was a tiny jeweled object in an egg shaped circle. I carefully searched the other symbols for anything similar with no results. Returning to my blue jewel I studied it more closely. It almost looked like a tiny sapphire, but then again, since I'm no expert, it could be just glass, or some other weird element from outer space.

There I go again, bringing in something I am trying to avoid.. I've got to dismiss this space stuff. I sat back staring intently at the blue crystal like object. "Do I dare touch it." I thought. I hesitated a moment. "Of course I'll dare touch it." I said out loud. "How else am I going to find out about this quandary. I extended my arm and index finger touching the azure colored stone. I was startled by its warmth and jerked my hand back. There was a hum, almost undetectable, as the large doors parted as in an elevator that I thought of earlier. Slowly a dim light glowed from within. There did not appear to be a particular source, just an internal luminance. Now there was no hesitation on my part. I was drawn in like a magnet. As I stepped across the threshold the light intensity increased enabling me to scan the interior. The walls were lined with what appeared to be banks of computers, lights blinking in a variety of colors. I shook my head to clear my eyes. I could not believe what I was seeing. I scanned the interior as much as I could. There were narrow metal staircases leading up to different levels, which all housed machines of a sort that were unidentifiable to me at a first glance. Looking up I could see clear to the top. The center was totally void of anything. It was only the outside walls that held equipment or computers or what ever these things were. "This has to be a dream." I whispered. "Why am I whispering. It's not like there is anyone else here to hear me. That's funny." I thought. "There is no echo. This humongous empty space made of metal and there is no echo.. Pictures, I've got to take some pictures. Oh great." I scolded, "I left the camera in the cabin. Tomorrow would have to do. I'm not leaving now I'm even more intrigued now than I was a few days ago. "What is this place or thing ? I asked myself out loud. Again there was no echo. I yelled for a good five seconds. Still no echo. My thoughts were running a mile a minute with mass confusion. Lots of questions but no answers.

I moved to one of the computers on the wall but dared not touch it.   There were symbols on the switches and buttons matching what I saw inscribed on the outer hull, a language unidentifiable. The space theory crept into my thoughts repeatedly. Could this be from another world ? If so, was it manned ? If it was piloted then where is the occupant now ? I shook my head to dislodge the silliness.

I climbed the stairs to the next level. Buttons, switches and screens of all shapes and colors leading me to no answers. A small walkway traversed the whole perimeter and there were no windows to the outside, just these strange looking computer screens with buttons flashing.

I ascended to the next level where there was more of the same just less of it. Up again to the last level. This was quite different. There were boxes about fifteen inches square and four inches deep extruding from the bulkhead. No buttons, no screens only more strange markings as meaningless to me as the others.   I continued walking finally seeing something recognizable. A wheel.

A steering wheel, or at least it resembled a steering wheel to me. On the wall was some sort of a movable pointer, a diamond shaped tip directing ones attention to a quarter circle screen filled with symbols.

Hesitantly my hands moved to the wheel. There was some minor resistance but it did turn which moved the pointer and started a whrrring noise along with some tinkling sounds. Not a very adult description but that's what it really sounded like. There was a soft flash of light which alarmed me so that I dropped my hands from the wheel and jumped back a few feet, then watched as the pointer resumed its original position. All was quiet now.

I could feel myself trembling slightly. I didn't know if it was from excitement or fear, but whatever it was it convinced me that I had enough for one night. I made my way down to the bottom level and walked to the doorway the lights dimming as I went. Once outside I turned to close the door only to see the lights were totally out already. "This thing has a life of its own." I commented to no one.

Back in the cabin I grabbed for a beer but changed my mind and poured a large Cognac instead. I felt I needed it. I plopped down in the chair, took a healthy swig, put my head back and closed my eyes. "This isn't happening." I thought. "This is absolutely incredulous. I've got to be dreaming." I opened my eyes, looked around with everything the same and realized this was all for real. What do I do ? Who do I tell ? Do I tell anybody at all ? Of course I have to tell someone sooner or later. Why do I have to tell someone ?

I finished my drink and poured a second just as stiff. I needed some sleep.

Chapter 8

I looked at the sun foggy eyed, listening to the birds thinking how lucky they were not to have Cognac in their lives. I stood gazing out at my guest house from who knows where. I know another trip to the shaft was necessary, with a camera this time, in order to further validate my discovery even if only for myself. Breakfast first though, I had more thinking to do.

While eating it suddenly dawned on me to check with the previous owners of the property. Just maybe they also knew of this thing in the yard or possibly shed some light on who else owned the land. Pleased with myself for thinking along these lines I took the time to wash the dishes and generally clean up the kitchen. While tending to the household chores I recalled the woman I purchased the land from. It had been her father's, who had since been relegated to a home for seniors. I knew I had her information somewhere in my records but I would look for that later. Right now I just had to get back to my mysterious shaft.

I finished the dishes and put everything away. "I must be slipping." I thought. "Since when did I become that neat." I grabbed my camera and assorted other things I might need and went straight for my newest and best brainteaser. I pushed the magic blue gem and watched the doors quietly open and like yesterday the lights came on as I crossed the threshold. Immediately I started taking pictures of everything and anything. I watched the computer lights blink their multi colors and wondered what they were actually computing. Perhaps they were analyzing my presence. I advanced to all three levels taking pictures as I went. "This is just too good to be true." I heard myself say.

Before I knew it one P.M. rolled around. I did not discover anything new since my first visit. That was actually quite disappointing. I decided it was time to leave that I may pursue this mornings idea. I could not get over the amazement I felt watching the lights turn themselves off again. Checking to see that the door was secure I walked up the ramp to the cabin .

Chapter 9

I found the old records of the house sale without much trouble at all and copied the woman's name, address and phone number. Making myself look presentable, I jumped in the truck and pointed towards town and a telephone. Twenty five minutes later a woman answered. I explained who I was and asked if I could indulge on her time to ask about the history of the property. We agreed to meet the next day at a quiet luncheonette halfway between our respective locations. I figured it would be approximately a two hour drive for each of us. She said she was going to that town to see a friend which is why I agreed. I did not give her any details about my inquiry for fear that she would think I was some kind of nut. Who knows, perhaps I am.

I treated myself to lunch in town and then spent the afternoon at the library. My research there was educational but fruitless. I could find nothing to shed any light on my special project

Hoping for some enlightenment from tomorrow's meeting I stopped to pick up some beer before returning to my mountain. I used the last few hours of available day light reviewing the various symbol markings. No matter how I looked at them, whether horizontal, vertical or reverse they still gave up no clues as to what they meant. Frustrated at my lack of progress I gave up, went back to my cabin, opened up a beer, sat and felt sorry for myself.

My pity party did not last very long. I remembered tomorrow's meeting and the hopes it held reignited my enthusiasm. I reviewed my notes in case I would need them and tucked everything neatly in my briefcase. I relaxed to some music on the radio and thought that this would probably make good material for a book, or at least a short story. Finally mellowed out, I went to bed.

I arose early feeling totally refreshed. I showered, shaved and even put on some decent clothes so I didn't look like a total bum.

I arrived at the restaurant a few minutes ahead of schedule and chose to leave the briefcase in the truck only bringing a note book and pencil. As I closed the entrance door I noticed a woman sitting alone in a back corner booth. I guessed her to be in her mid fifties, not unattractive but looked to me like a typical housewife

"**M**rs. Powers ?" I asked.

"**W**hy yes." she answered. "And you must be Nick Townsend, please sit down and call me Janet."

We exchanged the usual pleasantries and then ordered lunch. Coming right to the point Janet asked,

"**E**xactly what is it about the property that you want to know ?"

I'll have to admit she sought of caught me off guard with her directness.. I paused for a moment my mind racing to find the right words.

"**W**ell -- -." I said hesitantly. "I was wondering if you knew anything unusual about the land. It seems to be so pristine. Perhaps some history that I'm not aware of."

Looking me straight in the eye, Janet answered immediately.

"**Y**ou're either writing a book or you're sounding just like my Dad. He's the one who used to live there, not me."

"**E**xcuse me ?" I questioned politely, "You sort of have me at a loss."

"**S**orry" she laughed. "It's my father really. He's been going on about that land for years."

"**W**hat do you mean." I asked confused, not trying to give myself away."

"**W**ell to be perfectly honest with you, he's really not to stable anymore.   Let's just say his mind is always drifting off to who knows where. He seems to be paranoid about the government, you know secrets and the like.

"**O**h! I see." I said for the lack of anything else to say.

Recovering I asked if she could be more specific. She looked at me curiously but continued.

"**H**e was always mumbling about technology, secret technology, and that the government people did not appreciate or listen to him. He knew things and they did not want to listen. You see he, my Dad, was always a tinker type of person, but after a while he was believing in his own dreams. Especially these last few years. He started talking about space technology and how he could help NASA, but they just shrugged him off." She suddenly stopped talking and apologized for going on so. Smiling she added "I'm afraid I'm becoming like him and just rambling on about nothing. So what is your real interest in this particular piece of property ?"

Thinking fast I said, "You were right from the beginning." I lied. "I'm doing research for an article or story about rock walls of New England, particularly Vermont. And since you are a native I thought you might have more historical information. You know folk lore etc."

"**I** thought so." she answered pleased with herself. " I was always pretty good at figuring people out." she smiled. "I was never too interested in that sort of thing but I can give you some names of people who will probable be of much more help."

"**T**hat would be great." I replied trying to sound sincere.   I took out my note pad and went through the motions of collecting her information.

"**W**hat about your Dad." I inquired matter of factly.

"**Y**ou can try." she said innocently. "But I'm afraid he won't be of much help. He's in a home now and kind of lives in his own world." She paused as if thinking, then continued, "Sure why not. He might enjoy having a visitor other than me."

She proceeded to give me his name and the senior home where he resided.

"**B**ingo." I thought and had to contain myself not to show my enthusiasm.

We finished lunch continuing to chat about normal mundane things. I picked up the tab, which she seemed to be genuinely pleased about, and thanked her for her time and information. We said our goodbyes and parted in different directions.

Chapter   10

I arrived back at my own little town mid-afternoon and stopped at my favorite telephone booth. I dialed the number for the senior home where Janet's father was living. I inquired about visiting hours and whether or not my cabin predecessor, Caleb Montgomery, was up to visitors. I was informed visitors were welcome and that would be everyday between one and eight P.M. I let them know I was a friend of his daughter's and that she was aware of my intentions. I added that it would most likely be tomorrow. With that accomplished I aimed my truck for home and a rest.

I had forgotten I cleaned most everything, and was surprised how good the place looked. Maybe I would try to keep it that way but I knew myself better than that. I was going to rest but something in the back of my mind pushed me out to my bronze shaft again.

Small things amuse me I guess but I was still intrigued by the illumination system in my mysterious structure. There did not appear to be any power source. The other question had to do with the length of time this thing sat here and yet the lights still functioned. Hopefully tomorrow's visit will bring some answers.

Being bolder than in my previous visits I thought I would attempt a try at the computers. What the heck, all that can happen is I blow up or take off into space. I really did not expect either to happen but I was going to push some buttons.

I stood watching the colored lights flashing for a while and finally raised my hand to the keyboard. The keyboard itself was rather simple having only fourteen keys. I pushed one at random in the middle. There was some clicking sounds and the large monitor lit up in a pale green color. It stayed that way about thirty seconds then resumed its dull gray shade. I pushed a second key and watched the process repeat itself. I clicked on a few more buttons only to watch the same thing. Puzzled I moved to another computer. The same situation existed with a different color on the screen. I tried a third, fourth and fifth machine with the same results. I either did not have the right combination or they were non functional which also did not make any sense.

Climbing the stairs to the last level I made a closer inspection of those weird fifteen inch boxes on the wall. Nothing new presented itself. They remained a total mystery as to their function.

With nothing more to look at I returned to the house and thought about dinner.

Chapter 11

    I gave myself a treat and slept late knowing I did not have to leave the house until eleven thirty-ish. I had a lazy breakfast and just lolled around daydreaming about various uses for the shaft. My thoughts did drift to yesterdays conversation with Janet Powers. I felt a little guilty deceiving her but I did not want to reveal my hand just yet. I guess I will call and interview the names she gave me. Who knows, perhaps there is a story in rock walls.

    I arrived at the senior home at twelve fifty. It was quite an impressive layout. It reminded me more of an old English estate than a nursing home. I checked in and was directed to the second floor room of Caleb Montgomery. I was surprised at the spaciousness of the room.   It was like a mini apartment. Mr. Montgomery was seated in an easy chair by the window reading. He looked up as I knocked quietly. For ninety two years old he looked very alert.

    "You must be Nick Townsend. My daughter called yesterday and said you might be around. You really interested in rock walls or something a little more scientific."   He asked with a sly smile and a twinkle in his eye.

    "Nothing like getting right to the point." I thought.

    "I don't know what my daughter told you about me, but what ever it was it was wrong. I'm as sane as anybody else.

    "My eyes gazed down at the book he put aside. He was reading about Quantum Physics. Caleb noticed where my eyes went.

    "Hogwash."   He blurted out, referring to the book

"These young pups today want to make a big deal out of everything. I hope you're not one of them.

I felt like I was on the defensive and I hadn't even said anything yet. I looked directly at him,

"No, I'm not one of them and it looks like you already know why I'm here.

Caleb chuckled slightly with an impish glint in his eye.

"Sit down my friend, I'm sure we have a lot to discuss."

I relaxed myself now and took a seat across from him.

"Can I get you something to drink." He asked all smiles. "Of course they don't allow me any booze but I can offer you a soda or juice.

"Sure, why not." I answered.

"The frig is over there." he replied. "Don't mind if I don't get up and grab me a juice while you're there."

"I think I'm going to like this guy." I told myself. Once settled again with our respective juices, he took a sip of his mumbling,

"This would be a lot better if it had some Vodka in it. Well Nick! Can I call you Nick, yes of course I can." He answered himself. "Well Nick, I guess you found the metal box. I know that's not what you told my daughter, and that was a smart move, but I knew when she called what you really wanted to talk about."

I was dumbfounded at his uncanny insight and decided he was not like any other ninety plus year old that I knew.

"Yes I found it purely by accident though. It was during the storm we had a week or so ago. Lightening struck four or five times in the same spot and created a large crater."

"I knew it finally would." He interrupted. "I thought I would finally get some attention."

Looking and probably sounding confused I asked,

"What do you mean you would finally get some attention."

"I haven't really lost my marbles no matter what my daughter and others have said." he answered. "Before I answer your question let me ask you some questions.

"You found my box, right ?"

Yes was all I could answer because he just continued talking.

"What did you think of it ?"

"Quite interesting." I started to answer.

"Did you manage to get inside ?" he asked more slowly his eyes showing anticipation of my answer.

"It took some time to figure out but yes, I did get it open."

"Good, good, excellent." he replied, excitement in his voice. "And did you go inside? Yes, of course you went inside, who wouldn't go inside, everybody's curious. And what did you find inside ?"

He stopped talking because I think he was out of breath.

"What looked like many computers with flashing colored lights."

"Oh good, then it's still working." he interrupted.

I went on to describe all that I observed, this time without interruption, right down to the variety of symbols. I ceased speaking taking a sip of my juice and waited for his reaction.

"Excellent observations my boy, yes excellent, very good." he said pleased with himself. I'm glad to see someone else has finally seen my creation."

"Your creation." I exclaimed a little startled.

Caleb looked at me questioningly.

"Oh that's right you didn't know. Okay, I guess I'll answer your question now."

I could feel the excitement building anew down deep inside. "I.'m finally going to get some real answers." I thought.

"I guess maybe I'll start at the beginning." said Caleb. Come let's walk outside.

He stood up out of the chair almost better then I could. Spry was not even a good enough word to describe his actions. I should be that nimble. I followed him out of the room, passed the elevator and down the stairs. Stopping at the visitors desk he informed them he and his young friend were going for a walk but would be back for dinner. He turned to me saying sarcastically

"You can't even poop in this place without someone recording it. We'll be okay for a few hours as long as you're with me."

We wandered outside to a lightly wooded area and sat on some rather comfortable padded benches about one hundred yards from the main building.

"We'll have some privacy here although I'm sure they will keep tabs on us. My daughter doesn't think I can handle things on my own, but as you will soon see there are many things she, nor anyone else, does not know about me."

He paused as if collecting his thoughts looking pensively at a bee on a flower. He turned to me, his face now relaxed saying,

"Now back to my creation. Sixty years ago whin I arrivv- - - , when I came to Vermont, I started on my special project. I chose that land in the mountains because of its seclusion. I wanted to keep my work as secretive as I could. Janet's mother supported me completely, unfortunately she died of cancer when my daughter was only about five."

It was obvious by his expression that he cared deeply for his wife.

"I raised Janet as best I could, with the sometimes help of her mother's sister. Neither took an interest in what I did, in fact it was just the opposite, which explains my daughter's attitude today."

He paused again clearing his head.

"Now, back to my box! I completed its base structure a year or so after my wife passed. Now fast forward a bit, I spent many, many fruitless years trying to convince the Air Force, the Government and yes even NASA that I had something they could use. A few things actually. But everything I said fell on deaf ears. The only answer I received, which really wasn't an answer, was it was not possible to have what I said I had. I could not even get a representative from any group to come and look at my results. They pushed me away as if I was some kind of kook. It finally came down to the point where I could not even get an appointment to talk. I was totally shut out."

He looked at me as I started to speak.

"And to anticipate your next question, Why didn't I try some place else ?   What I have here was for the betterment of mankind, for peaceful use only. I could not, or did not want to trust any other group or country to use what I have for what it was meant."

He stopped talking and resumed staring at the few scattered flowers on the ground before him.

"Wow." I thought, *"That was some mouthful to swallow."*

He chose to remain silent for a spell, as I did.

"Janet sure did have her father wrong." I said to myself. *"He talks and acts more in his right mind than a lot of people I know. I have yet to learn how and why. Do I just ask him ?"*

Caleb, leaning his elbows on his lap, turned his head slowly moving his eyes to mine, with that wry smile on his lips.

"Now you want to know the how and why of it, am I correct ?"

"I'm beginning to think he can read minds." I silently told myself.

Caleb Montgomery perked up again continuing his story.

"The how of it I care not to tell at the moment. There was a formula to make the metal which I have since destroyed years ago. As you saw for yourself it is harder and more durable than anything else here on earth."

My overactive mind registered for a second time a reference to something or somebody not of this world. As soon as these thoughts passed through my mind I could detect a twinkle of recognition in the old man's eyes and the slightest hint of a smile came to his face.

"It will withstand the extreme cold of space and the highest temperatures the sun can throw at it. It is virtually indestructible, to date that is. Why did I destroy the formula ? Because no one would believe it. If someone had accepted it, knowing the government scientist as I do they would probably try to analyze it and change it. There was nothing to change. It was perfect. I won't explain how I know that, just accept it as I have stated."

"**P**lease don't get me wrong." I replied immediately. "I'm not questioning anything you have done. I'm trying to find answers to satisfy my curious mind. I find the whole matter totally fascinating and intriguing, so much so that I'm trying to learn everything and anything I can so that I may understand fully what you have accomplished."

Caleb put his hand up to stop me and spoke in a lower voice,

"**I** know you are my boy, I can sense your sincerity. Why do you think I'm telling this story. It's refreshing to be able to converse with one who is not judgmental. I can answer the other big question on your mind. It is the power source for the lighting I believe. Am I correct ?"

I was again dumbfounded and could only nod my head affirmatively. He smiled, that twinkle highlighting his eyes again.

"**T**here is no power source per se."

Caleb was looking directly at me when he said this amused by my expected reaction. I don't think I disappointed him either.

"**T**he light units them selves generate their own power."

"**H**ow can that be ?" I asked foolishly. "I'm not totally ignorant about power sources. I keep myself up on the latest technology and to date I have not heard of such a thing. Do you mean to tell me that the power source is itself perpetual ?"

"**T**hat's exactly what I'm saying, my boy." He replied happily.

I sat there with my mouth open not wanting to believe what he said, only I did believe it. I don't know why but I did believe him.

"**T**his principle was developed a long time ago." he added.

"**T**his would solve the world energy crisis we face, it could eliminate fossil fuel dependence." I blurted out.

"Yes it would." he said. "However there is one serious drawback."

"How can there be a downside to something that could help the world be a better place ?" I asked stupidly.

Caleb was silent. He stared into my eyes smiling all the time, letting me think about what I had said. It took a while, then suddenly the light went on in my thick head. "Control." I whispered aloud. "It would be a control thing, and control is power."

My new mentor smiled approvingly. We were both silent now for quite some time. My mind was racing as before trying to put all of this in place, although nothing seemed to fit. My extraterrestrial thoughts were creeping in no matter how hard I tried to push them away. Half joking I told myself that Caleb was not from this world. I was arguing with myself attempting to push these thoughts out, but not trying too hard.

"No I'm not." Caleb said quietly.

At first it didn't register, when it did I snapped my head around to look at my new found friend. He stared back showing no emotion and repeated, "No I am not." as clear as a bell. I instinctively knew he was being open and honest with me. A flush came over me and I suddenly felt privileged. I stared not knowing what more to say.

"Now that you know perhaps you can help me."

I found this amazing. Here this man from another place, advanced beyond us by who knows how much, was asking me for help. I willingly answered, "Of course, but what can I do to help someone of your advanced knowledge.

Chapter   12

Caleb smiled saying,

"I knew someone like you would come along sooner or later. Someone with an open mind, willing to learn and understand. That metal box, or shaft as you call it, and I have been here close to sixty years now without having made any progress with the people of this planet. It's time to leave."

"You can't leave now." I interrupted I just met you. I want to learn more."

I must have sounded like a child whining and feeling sorry for himself but I felt a great loss of something I had barely found.

"I must leave. We all must leave."

"You mean there are others." I shouted.

"Yes there are seven of us total throughout the planet. Our mission is finished and has been a failure I'm afraid."

"Why must you leave now ? Can the others leave and you stay a while longer and teach me."

"Teach you what ?' he returned.

"Everything you know." I went on like a child.

Caleb laughed lightly.

"And how would you use this knowledge ?" he asked patiently. "You would be sought after by all. You would not have any privacy. You would end up unhappy and controlled. Unhappy because you are controlled and you would not be able to do anything about it. We have a vast experience in this very thing and this is one of those times it will not work. Don't get me wrong, I believe in your sincerity and honesty though you are only one of a few out of millions. No it is better this way. It must be."

I sat back feeling dejected. Not a word passed between us for some time. Caleb was allowing me time to think. His instincts were correct, fore the more things I considered the more I realized he was right. We sat quietly for a while longer until at last I broke the silence sheepishly asking,

"**H**ow can I be of help."

Caleb smiled gently, his eyes saying he was genuinely pleased.

"**H**ow about staying for dinner. We can talk further then. The dining room is far from being a gourmet palace, the food however is good and of course nutritionally well balanced. We both laughed and proceeded to meander our way back to the main building.

Dinner was as Caleb predicted and at this point I didn't care. My thoughts were more focused on his plan to leave. Not too much was discussed while we ate and I became aware of my anticipation building. We passed on dessert and returned to his room for privacy.

Once inside the room Caleb closed the door indicating we sit by the window overlooking the estate gardens. He retrieved two apple juice boxes from the cooler and joined me by the window.

"**Y**ou asked how you can help. You can help me in several ways he stated. The first is you can help get away from here."

"**Y**ou mean help you escape from here." I challenged.

"**N**o. I'm not going to escape." He answered. "I'm going to die." he added, then waited for my reaction, which of course he got.

"**Y**ou mean you want me to help you die ? I'm sorry I can't doo - - - ."

He stopped me mid-sentence.

"**D**on't get upset my boy, let me explain and I'm sure you will understand."

Embarrassed by my outburst I remained quiet nodding

my go ahead for the explanation.

"**I**'m not really going to die, not as you perceive it."

Now I felt myself looking confused. Caleb smiled and continued,

"**Y**ou see where I come from I have not yet reached halfway in my life span. I may physically appear old by your standards ,but all that is, is our ability to adapt our appearances as necessary.

"**Y**ou mean you made yourself look old." I said incredulously.

"**T**here are many things we have learned to master over the millennia of our existence, which is why I said I am going to die."

I think I was beginning to understand, though I was still confused.

"**S**o as not to draw attention we adapt to the cultures we visit and as is your way of life you age and then cease to exist. That is what I plan to do, however I will not actually stop functioning. I will slow down my bodily activities and will appear to everyone as if I have passed. Your assistance will then be needed."

"**I** still don't quite understand." I countered.

"**I** know this may sound bizarre but I would like you to pick me up at the cemetery after the final services, which I'm sure my daughter is going to require because that's just the way she is."

"**I**n other words you can revive yourself from the trance state and be normal again." I replied.

"**T**hat is correct, my boy. That is basically what I meant. You can then pick me up at the cemetery and drive me back to my ship."

"**T**o your ship ?" I said surprised

"**T**o the shaft or box if you prefer, and thanks for digging it out for me." he said smiling as always.

"**I** hope I didn't damage anything in doing so or by playing with the computers." I returned experiencing a sudden rash of guilt come over me.

"**D**on't worry, you could not hinder any of its functions." Caleb quipped. "Getting back to my pickup, obviously it would be better at night. There is no sense in pushing the risks. We can work out the details as things progress."

Settled back to normal now I felt more relaxed.

"Do we have time to discuss the box." I inquired, still anxious to learn something.

Caleb glanced at the clock on the wall and answered affirmatively.

"What exactly are you curious about ?"

"Everything." I replied, " but to be more specific," I hesitated then trying to phrase my question. "You talk about blending with our culture, which obviously you are successful doing after sixty years, yet won't you be attracting a lot of attention when you leave in the box."

My older friend, although not so old, laughed kindly at my naivete.

"There is no need to worry about that, my friend. Our propulsion system is unlike your own. It is basically silent and no explosion to start."

"But rockets are far from silent." I blurted out.

"Who said anything about rockets, my young friend."

Embarrassed for a second or third time I laughed at myself.

"You're right. I should have known better. I keep forgetting who you are. What is your secret ?" I asked.

"It is no secret, not to us anyway. Have you ever heard about magnetic propulsion ?" Caleb inquired.

I thought for a minute, then something finally registered.

"I remember reading an article a few years ago but there was nothing definitive."

He replied, "We use magnetic propulsion for almost everything. It is efficient, quiet and more importantly, always there. The magnetic pull between planets, stars and even solar systems provides a never ending source of energy. We have harvested this specific power and with it can traverse the universe without restriction and with unlimited variations in speed."

I must have looked like a manakin sitting there frozen in my seat trying to absorb all that he threw at me. Caleb chuckled quietly letting me have time. My mind was going wild, the possibilities unlimited. My dream state was rudely interrupted by a P.A. announcement advising that only fifteen minutes remained in visiting hours. Caleb was already up throwing away our juice boxes.

"Come on." he said, "I'll walk you down."

Now I know why he is so spry despite his aged appearance.

Our final goodbye's were cheerful with a promise of more contact very soon.

Driving home was automatic, my mind still a jungle of new thoughts and longings. Once home I grabbed a beer and went out to the box. I let myself in with what seemed like a more comfortable familiarity.

"So you are really a space ship." I said out loud to the large metal shaft. I slowly sipped my beer viewing the interior in a whole new light. Twenty minutes later I was back in the cabin getting ready for bed my mind still working overtime.

I lay in bed staring at the dark wondering what it would be like if I was to go with Caleb. I'm sure it was totally out of the question for numerous reasons that even I could think of. I tried to imagine being the first human to set foot on a world light years away. Would the inhabitants be like us or something strange. I wonder what Caleb actually looks like or is he really a similar form. I dwelt on these thoughts a few moments then decided to switch the lights on again. Maybe if I read awhile I can relax my mind and get some much needed sleep.

Chapter 13

The next couple of weeks were agony. They dragged on and on. Each day was a week long. I tried keeping myself busy with normal mundane chores. Chopping wood, laundry and house cleaning were not my idea of productive or interesting things to do, though they did help pass the time. The cabin never looked so good, at least for the time I lived here. I did some additional digging around the bottom of the bronze box slash shaft hoping to make it easier for Caleb.

The thought did occur to me that Caleb could have been pulling my leg with the all time stunt of the century. After pondering this for a while I dismissed the idea. I genuinely felt he was being sincere.

I was glad I started a journal recording every thing that had occurred to date, although even with the diary I don't know if people would ever believe such a story. No matter, I probably won't have the gumption to tell anybody anyway.

Two days into the third week I received a telegram from Janet Powers notifying me that her father had passed away peacefully and could I please meet her at Foster Funeral Home on Friday.

"This is it." I told myself. *"I just have to wait now for further instructions from Caleb."*

I almost felt like I was taking part in some kind of top secret enterprise. I guess when you think about it, it actually was.

Friday took a long time to get here but when it did I was ready for it. Up early I went through the normal grooming routine, I even put on a jacket and tie. I figured I should at least look the part. That finished I was on my way.

The three hour drive was boring with my mind almost stagnant not knowing what to expect with Janet. I made up prepared answers depending on which way the conversation went.

I reached the funeral home parking lot at the prescribed time noticing that only a few cars were there. I reviewed again my statements and went inside. Janet must have seen me pull in because she met me at the door. She did not appear to be grieving too much but then again at ninety plus years this sort of thing was expected. She greeted me with a friendly smile and a warm hand shake.

"You must have made quite an impression on my father." she started. "He considered you a friend and after only one visit. He didn't usually make friends too easily you know, not really being with it all the time."

Her statement hurt a little. She obviously did not know her father or perhaps she just didn't care. I let her remark slide and answered with a smile.

"We found a lot in common to talk about."

"I'm so glad for him." she said in a phony way as she reached into her purse for an envelope. It was sealed and taped.

"He wasn't taking any chances." I thought.

"He said this was lists and history of the rock walls you were discussing. He thought this might be of help to you."

I took the envelope and thanked her and put it in my jacket pocket while asking about a rest room. I could not wait to read Caleb's message.

With the door securely locked against sudden interruptions I carefully opened the message I had been waiting for.

"Nick, my boy.

I hope you are taking my passing well. (Ha-ha). This is the most rest I've had in a long time.

The wake is Friday which you obviously know since you are reading this. Saturday is the cemetery bit. Of course you will come to see me off. That's what friends are for, right ? I figure on leaving this humble abode about two in the morning. That should lower the risk considerably. I have already done some preliminary study of the cemetery and will leave via the north side. Trees are quite numerous and will give me the most protection from prying eyes. I figure if you drive by the middle gate at two fifteen with parking lights only that should about cinch it. If perchance something go awry just keep going back to the cabin and I'll catch up with you there later.

Wish me luck my friend, I'm starting to get anxious to get home.

Caleb.

PS. Be careful what you say to my daughter or she'll have you tagged as a nut case also.

I relaxed now knowing the final arrangements. I returned the letter to my pocket, put on a smile and went out to face Janet Powers.

Other people were arriving when I went back to the lobby. I tried to stay in a corner as best I could but Janet kept seeking me out to introduce me to Mr. what his name or Mrs. So and so. Do you know how hard it is to act somber at a funeral when you know the person you're mourning isn't dead. I finally managed an excuse to get out of there but promised I would be there for the cemetery services.

What a relief to be back in my truck heading away from there. I stopped at that Italian place again and had a nice leisurely dinner and a few glasses of wine. It would all be over soon and I had no idea what I was going to do then. Everything else would seem dull.

I met with the others at the funeral home on Saturday morning and took part in the usual short ceremony before the trip to the cemetery. I felt like such a hypocrite putting on this facade although I was the only one. By one o'clock everything was finished. I said my prolonged goodbyes to Janet with the usual sorry for your loss thing, though she looked almost glad it was over. Let's face it, she just didn't get along with Caleb. She had closed her mind to what should have been a wonderful, loving relationship.

I now had approximately twelve hours to kill before the next chapter in my adventure opened. I decided to go home even though it was a three hour drive. At least the drive back and forth would eat up time.

At home I checked on the metal box one last time. It hadn't hit me before but this interior sure was lacking in creature comforts for something that traveled such vast distances through space. That last thought got me to wondering more about the real Caleb. Perhaps he actually was a completely different being. If so what does he look like ? Do I really want to find out ? I started visualizing all kinds of shapes, sizes and weirdness. *"Now I am getting carried away with stupidity."* I thought. Perhaps I will ask him directly but I also decided I would not push the issue if he was inclined not to approve.

Pleased with myself I went back to the cabin for some journal updating. Too excited to take a nap I prepared a light dinner, cleaned up and headed out to the truck and set out for the cemetery. I made a few stops at convenience stores to help waste time and re-stack my pantry and other than that I just drove slow.

My timing worked out well as I neared the cemetery about five minutes to two. I pulled into a local gas station to top off and kill the last few remaining minutes.

Back in the truck I steered for the north side center gate. I turned on to the north side road at two twelve dimming my headlights to just parking light. I crept slowly keeping close to the curbside. I approached the afore mentioned gate and a shadowy figure cane out from behind the trees and hurried to the truck which was stopped by now. Caleb jumped in as I accelerated before he finished closing the door. My eyes scanned the area. There was no sign of life. *"Of course not dummy, it's a cemetery."* I thought trying to make a joke of it. Caleb sat there smiling. He looked at me saying,

"It was funny if you think about it. Remember, not everybody walks out of a cemetery like me."

We both laughed and enjoyed the ride back to the cabin making jokes about the cemetery.

At the cabin Caleb was very animated, pleased that he was free and going home. He joined me in a glass of Cognac mentioning that he was going to miss this part of Earth life. I believe he enjoyed the Cognac as much if not more than I did.

Warmed and relaxed by the drink and looking directly at me he asked;

"I sense you have a few questions yet to ask."

"Yes, actually, I do." I answered feeling comfortable and confident. The important one, to me anyway, is what you really look like. You know, in your home planet form."

He smiled but lowered his eyes, the smile slowly disappearing.

"I knew you would come to that sooner or later." He replied quietly. I can also sense you will not rudely push me on that point."

"You are correct in that assumption." I returned respectfully. "We humans are basically curious creatures, me in particular."

A slight smile returned to Caleb's face as he nodded.

"I gathered that a long time ago. There is a difference in some people though. You, Nick, are curious and I understand that, most humans are just plain nosey."

Our laughter merged and further solidified the bond between us. Caleb returned to being somewhat serious saying;

"You don't want to know what I actually look like. Let it suffice to say that from our vast contact experience we have learned to not show ourselves in our original form. Please accept that.

"I absolutely do, with disappointment of course, but I respect your position and wishes.

"Good." Caleb said happily, "Now on to your other curiosity."

Before I could say anything, again he read my mind.

"The writing or symbols or Glyph's as you call them, imprinted on the box , most of them are genuine language markings designating historical events and dates."

Raising my hand a little to get his attention, I quietly interrupted.

"Most ?" You said, then what are the others ?"

Caleb gave his little chuckle with that special glint in his eye.

"That, my friend, was an inconsequential folly of mine. They represent absolutely nothing. I copied symbols from where I could find them and mixed them. Some are from the far reaches of the universe with some right here from your own past civilizations."

"Why did you do that ?" I asked.

"Nothing but a whim. I was counting on meeting someone like you who would understand me and my mission, but in case I didn't, I wanted to leave a confusing message that would keep your scientists puzzled for centuries."

"I think you succeeded." I smiled in answer. "The symbols that are genuine, where are they from." I further inquired.

"No place that you know of. They are from galaxy's far beyond your own, totally unknown even to your astronomers. You star charts, as far reaching as they are, fall short of the actual size of the universe we live in. Perhaps that's a project you could work on." He said jokingly. "That way they can call you crazy also."

I poured each of us another shot and looked at my watch.

"When are you going to leave." I asked reluctantly.

Caleb looked at me, hesitated before answering then sheepishly answered,

"I thought I would spend another day here with you, that is if you don't mind."

"Mind." I exclaimed loudly, "I think that would be wonderful. I would love nothing better."

Caleb's grin grew bigger. He looked relaxed and genuinely pleased.

"After all." He remarked, "After sixty years what's one day more or less. And since you are agreeable can I be so bold as to ask for one more refill." He held up his glass. "I think there's a hole in my glass."

$\mathbf{I}$ willingly filled both our glasses and toasted to his successful and safe journey home. We sat there relaxed and I took advantage of the pause.

"**N**ow that I think of it I do have another question."

"**S**hoot." Caleb replied.

"**Y**ou mentioned your magnetic propulsion as being silent and would not draw attention. That's all well and good, but how do you get around the radar defenses. You're talking about a four story building weighing who knows how many tons lifting off and traveling through the atmosphere out into space. You are bound to be seen by somebody, possibly even from another country."

It was quite obvious from my voice that I was concerned.

Caleb went through his quiet chuckle again.

"**F**irst of all to answer your concern." He commented, "Even if I was seen by anyone I would be traveling much too fast for them to do anything about it, but going beyond that, do you remember the TV series Star Trek ?"

I nodded that I had.

"**A**nd do you recall both the Enterprise and the Klingons had cloaking devices aboard their ships.

I looked at my guest suspiciously, "What's he going to tell me next, that he has a cloaking device." I asked myself.

"**T**hat's exactly what I'm going to tell you." my mind reading friend volunteered.

I must have had a look of stupid amazement on my face.

"**I**t's true you know." continued the old man. "Your science fiction writers possess fertile but accurate imaginations. I can see you are finding this hard to believe so I am prepared to show you ahead of time."

I guess I still had a look of disbelief about me.

"**C**ome, I'll show you." said Caleb as he stood. He emptied his Cognac glass first then proceeded to the door. I stood and followed silently. As we approached the Box Caleb told me to wait outside while he opened the hatch and entered closing it behind him.

A few minutes passed and the Box faded from view. I stood frozen for a moment then moved forward reaching out. I touched something. Something that wasn't there. Not that I could see anyway. I was suddenly startled as the hatch opened. I could see inside, the same interior I had seen a dozen times, but that's all I could see. I was looking at a rectangular picture of the interior only surrounded by the landscape of my mountain beyond. It was surreal. I could not believe what I was seeing. I couldn't move, I just stood there mesmerized.

"Nick, Nick, Nick."

I heard a voice calling from a distance but I could not answer. I felt a touch on my shoulder and then saw Caleb standing in front of the closed door of the Box. The complete Box. I could not see through or around it. The whole thing was there right before my eyes. Caleb took my arm;

"Come my friend, let's get you inside."

By the time we reached the cabin I was fully recovered.

Seated inside once again Caleb went on to explain, not only visually was the ship not seen but also electronically it disappeared as well. No radar or tracking device could pick up a signal or image. He could come and go at will and never be detected.

"What a weapon of warfare that would make." I stated.

"Now why did I think of that first." I asked myself.

"Now perhaps you see my position with more clarity." answered Caleb.

Feeling ashamed for my line of thinking I answered;

"I see what you mean. I don't usually think along those lines, I don't know why that popped into my head."

"I know you don't Nick." Caleb comforted. "But so many others do think that. I hate to say this but your planet is just not ready yet for advanced technology. Maybe it is best if all peoples find out things at their own pace as destructive as it may be at times. We learned the hard way, a long time ago, not to interfere with normal growth advancement."

"Then why did you try to push your Box or the metal formula." I queried.

"Good question, my boy, good question." said Caleb animatedly. "You already had your space program and have been trying to out reach, but not without problems and casualties. We felt a small help with your design was not really an interjection of our advanced knowledge. And you know the results of our offer. Total rejection because of disbelief."

"What if you had shown yourselves the advanced people that you are ? Would that not have made an impact." I asked.

"What you say is quite logical my boy, but reality dictates otherwise. Fear of someone or thing more powerful than you leads to distrust. That distrust gives birth to insecurity which leads to further distrust and so on. No, we learned our way is better. We check on other worlds periodically and when we think they are ready we make ourselves known to them and welcome them to a universe of peace. Nothing is truly infinite, so we foster making the most of our finite existence."

Caleb finished speaking and I sat in silence digesting the few words he spoke. No one could disagree with his words but who knows how many years and lives it would take for us to smarten up and realize we are our own worst enemy.

Silence presided a while longer as we watched the sun come up. Caleb in a cheerful voice aroused us both,

"This cabin has not changed much you know, it still gets hungry here in the morning."

Smiling in return I got up and walked to the kitchen.

We enjoyed a light breakfast then proceeded to the bronze shaft. Following his instructions enthusiastically we commenced the final preparations for his departure. It was a most pleasant day. We joked as we worked with no more serious talk I learned a few more things about the symbols and computers as the day went on, a knowledge I would keep to myself which Caleb already knew I would.

The ship, finally ready and buttoned up for the night we headed out for a farewell dinner at that Italian place I found a few weeks ago. We enjoyed a great dinner and just enough wine to keep us happy. At home we topped off the evening with generous portions of Cognac for both of us, allowing us to sleep without interruption.

Chapter 14

Breakfast was simple and subdued, almost anti-climatic. Neither of us wanted to face the obvious. Leaving the dishes on the table we wandered outside breathing deeply the crisp morning air. We stood there quietly, not a word between us. Caleb at last took a step toward the box;

"Come with me, my boy."

I followed without hesitation watching him open the hatch. Without further urging I trailed him inside and up to the fourth level. Caleb went straight for one of those rectangular boxes I was curious about. Magically it opened and he withdrew a small lantern. He clicked it on then off and offered it to me.

"Now you will never be without a light." he quipped.

I accepted willingly knowing I would cherish this as long as I lived. It would truly be the only tangible thing I would have to validate this meeting. All else that happened no one would ever believe. Even the secret of this lantern would die with me.

We returned to the first level and I stood by the exit. Caleb extended his hand which I grasped firmly and warmly. We held the clasp for a spell when he finally said;

"It will take about twenty minutes of your time."

Nothing more was said but I knew what he meant. I exited the Box, went to the porch and sat in the rocker staring at the bronze shaft.

At about eighteen minutes later I heard a small electrical click and my shaft vanished, leaving only a few seconds worth of shimmering waves, the kind you see from a black top road on a hot summer day. There was no sound, no disturbance of any kind, just quiet country mountain air.

~ ~ ~ ~ ~ ~

I *gazed at the large hole left by the lightening strikes of weeks ago, clicking the lantern on and off.*

The End.

Halloween

by
K.J. Goss

Halloween

Ahh–! Yes, Halloween. What a great time of year. As far as I'm concerned it's the official start of the Holiday season. Cool crisp air, cooler nights and days warm enough to enjoy chasing falling leaves and marveling at the color Mother Nature so graciously throws at us.

For me though, it is extra special. Now that I'm well into my seventy's, it is a time of reflection and nostalgia. I guess it's expected that most older folk always go back in time trying to relive better times I suppose. Me, I don't consider myself old. Age is just a number and I refuse to be categorized. I have always believed if you keep the brain alert and functioning you can live forever. Well, perhaps not forever, but young enough until your time here is up.

Speaking for myself, I'm still a child at heart. I love children. I love being with them, watching them learn and learning of and from them as they learn. I learn more from teaching children than they learn from me teaching them.

But I digress - - - Back to Halloween.

It truly is a special time of year. The change in the air reminding us of the warmth of a fire place that will soon be lit. Biting into a crisp apple fresh from a tree. The special perfume of burning leaves filling the air. The pile of leaves you ran through or rode your bike through or just jumped into before your Dad burned them. That special smell as you rolled around in them would stay with you for hours.

Then there's the desire now to go back in time and enjoy that feeling all over again and you suddenly realize that your generation was special. It was a time before you regulated yourself out of the simple pleasures of life. They are some of the things the younger folk, today, will never have the pleasure of experiencing.

Of course there was always Trick or Treat. The beauty of it was that it was never organized. Sometimes you even went out alone, but it seemed to double your fun with a few friends. Candy, homemade cookies, fruits and nuts were the treats you collected. A super special treat was if you got pennies. Trading treats with friends , and eating too much before supper was always the plan of the day. The tricks came after dark, but never anything destructive. Daring things, - Ha Ha - such as ringing doorbells, then running to hide, even doing it a few times to the same house. There were even times that you, yourself were scared, for example, by a homeowner, who sometimes participated in the fun.

Costumes were all self made, nothing store bought. Hobo's, pirates, ghosts and clowns to name a few. All neat stuff.

A house party after dark was always fun. Dunking for apples, even dunking your friends was always part of the excitement,. and having candy apples and cider just added to the fun.

Then came telling all of your exploits the next day in school and comparing all the goodies you collected.

If Halloween fell on a weekend it was super special. You got to go all over, all day long, stopping home a few times to empty out your bag so you could collect more. Listen to a ghost story being read by a parent or grandparent at night before bed. Then going to bed and thinking how great a day it was. Each year was better than the last and how you would have to wait a whole long year to do it again. It was a long day that always ended too soon. Of course, being lucky enough to have siblings to share their loot with you if you were sick and couldn't go out was a good thing also.

There was more nuts and fruit then there was candy, but it was all good. Home made cookies or fudge was really the best. One year I collected thirty six cents. Do you know how much that bought ?

Then you grew older and faced the realization that it

was just for kids. Perhaps you still wanted to go Trick or Treating but now you were too embarrassed to do so. Teenagers went to party's. Sometimes in costume, but mostly to impress the girls or the girls went to find a new steady,

When you were older and married with children, you tried to pass on your fun traditions, but this did not always work. A tradition is made by the young folk themselves. They can't relive your life and you can't live theirs. Each generation will have it's own memories and no two are alike.

Oh well, I guess that's life. I'll just have to be happy with my own memories. They are mine and no can take them from me. They are unique only to me.

Happy Memories.

The Little People

by

K.J.Goss

The Little People

Chapter 1

"**H**ey! Let me go!" said the little man in the bright green suit. The jacket was short cut in front with three large shiny brass buttons. The back of the jacket was knee length and tapered to form two tails as in a tuxedo.

"**I** thought it was next to impossible to catch one of you." I said curiously to the frantic squirming little person with bright the green top hat.

I had hold of the jacket tails as he struggled to get away.

"**W**hy are you being so mean to me ? I haven't done anything to you Ken."

Calling me by my name took me totally by surprise. So much so that I almost let him get away.

"If I let you go will you stay and talk to me ?" I asked.

"Of course I will." was his grumpy answer.

"I'm obliged to ?" He added. "That is our code and always was ?"

I released my grip and my little friend stepped away while straightening his jacket and large green bow he was wearing as a tie. He was mumbling to himself quietly.

"How could I have let this happen to me ? Me of all people ? Shamus O'Flaherty you should be ashamed of yourself ?"

Satisfied with his appearance he looked up at me.

"And who'd be giving ye the right to be grabbin me like that ? And you of all people Ken ? We thought you knew better than that ?"

I answered his questions with a question.

"How do you know my name. We've never met before."

"And wouldn't ye like to be knowin our secrets ? You with you pushin and grabbin attitude ?" Shamus said in a slightly aggressive manner.

"I sincerely apologize Mr. O'Flaherty. I meant no ill will. I don't usually do things like that. I think it was just the challenge of the moment. I never expected to see one of you, although I wanted to."

"We'll be lettin it go this time, seein that it was you ?" Shamus answered calmly.

"Getting back to my question, how did you know my name ?" I quizzed again."

"Surin we keep track of all believers, didn't ye know ?"

"What do you mean believers ?" I asked.

"So now ye are goin to make me explain everything,

are ye ?" Shamus replied.

"**I** didn't mean to offend, I'm just curious."

"**A**nd didn't you think we knew that. Of course ye are curious. You're a believer, and all believers are curious ? If ye were not curious ye would not be a believer ? And now to be answerin your question ? Aye, we have special ways of knowin who is receptive to, shall we say things that do not appear normal ? We know of your interest in things that most people don't believe in ? And if given the opportunity we like to cultivate relationships with these people ?"

"**A**nd just how do you go about that." I asked

"**A**nd surin there ye go again, pryin into things ye need not know. Suffice it to say that we missed you the last time ye were here ?"

"**T**he last time ? I questioned.

"**A**ye! We could not show ourselves because you had someone with you ? You were looking at a lot of rock walls. You almost caught me a few times but I managed to hide just in time ? I dared not show myself to a non believer ?"

I reminded my little friend that I was with someone again on this my second trip to Ireland.

"**A**ye, we know that but surin ye are alone now ? And will ye be gettin a chance to be alone again ?" asked Shamus.

"**T**hat's hard to answer," I replied. "My wife and I are here to enjoy the beauty of your ancient home and want to do it together."

"**C**an she be trusted ?" Shamus inquired.

"**T**rusted to do what ?" I said.

"**W**hy surin to be quiet about meeting us Little People ?"

"**T**hat you have my word on sir. She already thinks I'm a little daft and now she can be part of it."

Shamus laughed at this with a sparkle in his eye that

looked like a twinkle of the stars. His smile showed off his pure white teeth outlined by his red short beard that rimmed his cheeks and chin.

"Aye! So be it then my boy, we'll be meetin up with you real soon."

Shamus turned to go.

"Wait, don't go." I yelled. "Don't you owe me something."

Shamus O'Flaherty stopped and turned slowly a cunning glint in his eye and a sly smile on his lips."

"And what would someone like me be owen the likes of you ?" he said.

I answered with a sly smile of my own;

"By your own admission a short while ago you said it was your code and you were obligated."

"Aye, I said that?" he replied with a glint still in his eye. "And you would be lettin me go and in turn I spoke with you?"

Shamus started to dance away laughing a giddy laugh.

"Not so fast." I called after him. "I believe you still owe me something."

I still smiled but my voice was a little more firm. My little friend stopped, cocked his head and with one eyebrow raised asked as if a challenge;

"And would ye be mindin in tellin me what that would be ?"

"A wish." I answered. "In fact three wishes. I have it on good authority that if an outsider catches you, you grant three wishes if he lets you go and promises not to tell of your where abouts."

The little man's expression changed to something more serious though he retained the sly smile.

"And it seems to me you were trying to get away without fulfilling your commitment."

"**O**h! Is that what you would be thinkin now ? And with me bein an elder and outstanding member of our clan ?"

"**B**ut I'm right, aren't I." I further questioned.

His sly smile changed to a broad grin and ignoring my question he in turn asked;

"**A**nd now what would ye be wishin bein the fine lad that ye are, you bein a believer and all ?"

"**I**'m not quite sure yet." I answered, "But meet me here tomorrow at about noon and I'll have an answer for you."

"**H**a - ha, that's an easy one ?" Shamus said dancing away singing some old song in the Irish.

~ ~ ~ ~ ~ ~

There I stood, alone amidst giant rocks at the edge of a cliff overlooking the ocean. I had come up here alone to do some photography while my wife finished preparing for our day's sightseeing along the western coast here in Ireland.

I had never expected to meet one of the little people I've always heard so much about. It's also true what Shamus said about me being a believer. I have always let my imagination mingle with reality. Most people shrug off what they can't see and if they can't physically see it they do not believe. Myths and legends must start from something so why not let your imagination be part of your life. You might be surprised at what things can be revealed.

Back to reality I thought as I headed back to the B&B we were staying at.

Chapter 2

As my wife and I drove along the coast heading north to Ballyvaughna, I tried to casually bring up my appointment for tomorrow. I mentioned I had seen some special sights I thought she might be interested in and that I wanted to do some more photography on the cliff. I used the sun's position as the excuse to want to be there about noon. Understanding my love for my work she reluctantly agreed. I promised she would not regret it and that we would still be able to see all that she wanted in the time we were here. She doubted my statement but did not argue. We were both happy to be here and wanted to enjoy our time together. Little did either of us know what was in store for us.

The next day dawned with a beautiful sunrise and looked like we would have a perfect day ahead of us. We just finished our heart attack on a plate breakfast that Ireland's B&B's are noted for and relaxed on the veranda reading awaiting my appointed time. Eleven forty five rolled around and we made our way to the car and started to the cliffs. I silently thanked my wife for her indulgence as she sat there fingering a map trying to reconfigure our itinerary so that she could get to see all we came for. I quietly smiled to myself knowing what one of my wishes was going to be.

I parked the car and we meandered our way toward the cliff edge. I sighted in on one of the large rocks I recognized from the day before but saw no sign of Shamus O'Flaherty. We reached the rock destination and stood gazing out to sea listening to the crashing surf below.

"**I** thought this was going to be a special photo shoot." remarked my wife, Jeanne, somewhat annoyed. "I imagine it will be a little difficult getting photographs without a camera."

I looked at her a bit embarrassed and then I heard it. We both heard it. A raucous belly laugh from behind the rocks. My wife was startled but I recognized the laugh and taking my wife by the hand I walked to the largest of the rocks. We walked around the boulder only to find no one there, but the branches of a bush were still moving. There was no wind this day.

Subtle giggles were heard behind us by another rock. We moved to the sound only to find nothing again. Dancing feet and a louder laugh were evident at the first rock again. We turned and looked up to see Shamus doing an excited jig and laughing out a melody.

My wife's look of surprise soon turned to a broad laughing smile. She no longer appeared to be annoyed with me. Taking my wife by the arm and extending the other to my little friend I announced;

"**T**his, my dear is Shamus O'Flaherty."

"**T**he one and only Shamus O'Flaherty himself ?" he joined in while making an exaggerated bow, his top hat in hand showing his bald head ringed by the same red hair as his beard.

"**S**urin tis a grand thing to make your acquaintance me lady and I'm a hopin you'll not be tellin a soul about meetin me ?"

"**I** won't say a word." smiled Jeanne in answer.

She watched in awe as Shamus lept about from rock to rock putting on a show of his agility finally ending up on the level ground where we stood.

"**S**urin you've never seen the likes of me before lass, and chances are you never will again." said Shamus still showing off with a little jig.

"**I** didn't know you even existed." commented Jeanne.

"**A**ye, and we like to keep it that way ?" was the little

one's quick answer.

At last a calm overtook Mr. O'Flaherty as he settled on a nearby stone. Out of nowhere he produced a long white clay pipe, lit it and immediately generated a series of smoke rings that encircled his head, each one larger that the one before.

Jeanne laughed deeply watching the rings grow larger and dissipate high overhead.

"So ye be likin me smoke circles now do ya lass ?" Then you'll be liken this even more ?"

Shamus took a long drag on the pipe and exhaled a large ring that just seemed to hang there. He put his arm through the ring, made a few motions and instantly there appeared an Irish Harp made of smoke that grew larger and larger till it disappeared in the air above.

Jeanne smiled broadly mixed with Ooo"s and ahhh"s at the smokey visions before her which triggered another outburst of giggles from himself who was rolling on the ground in fits of laughter.

"Are you always so silly." asked Jeanne.

"Surin tis not bein silly lass, we call it enjoyin life ?"

"Enough with the nice nice you two." I interrupted. "What about my wishes."

"Aye, your wishes." repeated Shamus in a remotely more serious tone still carrying the twinkle in his eye and sly smile on his face. "And you'll be wantin three of them ?"

"Those are your rules, not mine." I challenged in answer.

"Surin ye'd be drivin a hard bargain Master Ken and what will ye be wantin for your first wish ?"

"My first request is more for Jeanne than myself, but it's still my wish." I stated

"Aye go on with ye then, ask away ?" Shamus returned.

"**W**ell, Jeanne has many more places to see and things to do than we have time for before we have to return home."

I hardly finished those words when Shamus laughingly interrupted.

"**A**nd that's a grand thing you'll be askin my friend. Done and done ?" He said as he spit lightly on his hand and extended it toward me. I accepted his hand and in one exaggerated pumping motion we shook and set the deal.

"**I**'ll be goin now ?" said Shamus as he moved quickly and disappeared behind the large boulder.

"**N**o wait." I yelled after him. How will I find you again."

"**W**hen you need me just say my name and I will be there ?" came Shamus's words from above us.

Looking up we saw him sitting cross legged atop the rock exhaling shamrock shaped smoke rings which totally encircled him and he disappeared from view in a fit of laughter.

Chapter 3

Jeanne and I stood there bewildered gazing at empty space and a few wisps of smoke where Mr. Shamus O'Flaherty once stood.

"What about my wish." I thought to myself. "Oh well, I know Jeanne's anxious to be on our way, we have a lot of ground to cover and limited time to do it."

We laughed about the antics of our little friend as we walked to the car.

Driving north following the west coastline, we enjoyed all the sights we had on our list and even added a few as we went. Nothing was rushed. We probably spent more time than necessary at each of our stops but it was not something we thought of or were concerned about at the time. The excitement of what we were experiencing of the landscape and the friendliness of the wonderful people far outweighed any concern for a restriction in time.

Late afternoon we found our B&B sight and planned our evening. Over dinner at a local Pub we reviewed our day's progress. It was then we realized we had seen almost twice as many places as we had planned spending many hours at each location. What should have added up to roughly twenty hours we had accomplished in just over seven hours. To our added amazement we were not even tired. Smiling at each other Jeanne and I realized our wish had been granted. The funny little man had kept his promise. We ordered another Guinness to celebrate our good fortune.

Leaving the Pub to return to our B&B Jeanne mentioned that she wished Shamus was here so she could thank him. She opened the car door and there sat Shamus O'Flaherty gigling with his eyes a twinkle.

"Surin ye are very welcome Miss Jeanne, tis me pleasure to serve the likes of you ? And you Ken, have ye been thinkin of your other two wishes ?"

"That I have my little friend but I'm not prepared to ask them yet." I answered.

Shamus just laughed, exited the car, did a few somersaults and disappeared into the tall grass of a nearby field and was swallowed by the dark. Jeanne was certainly enjoying the antics of our new found friend, she talked and laughed about him the rest of the evening.

The next day was as fulfilling, going places and seeing things that were never planned for. We spent what seemed like long hours at different places that caught our interest yet time appeared to stand still. Our most fervent wishes were being manifested because of a fairy promise. Not that the "Little People" were actually fairies but they were part of that whole other world that only children believed in. In any case I was not about to argue with whatever it was that was giving us the happiness we were experiencing.

~ ~ ~ ~ ~ ~

The following day a light rain greeted us rather than the sun. Wet though the weather was it did not dampen our spirits. We made our plan of tours and sights we wanted to se and much to our surprise all were rain free, at least while we were there. I guessed, and later confirmed correctly, that Shamus had a hand in our good fortune. We had a picnic lunch that day, pleasantly supplied by our gracious B&B hosts.

Sitting on the cliffs overlooking the ocean we were in an isolated dry place. As we relaxed enjoying our lunch we found out there was a price to pay for this dry luxury. As I reached for a piece of cold chicken I discovered it was all gone. Assuming my wife had finished the meat I settled for an apple. In the meantime Jeanne assumed I had finished the block of cheese so graciously provided to us. Neither of us said a thing until we heard a rather loud belch from behind a nearby rock.. This was followed by a raucous laugh.

"Shamus O'Flaherty what have you been up to." my wife and I said almost simultaneously. The laughter grew louder as our little man dressed in green rolled from behind a large boulder.

"You naughty little imp." my wife scolded. "I was looking forward to that cheese all morning seeing as how our hostess raved about it last night."

Shamus laughed even louder yet as he danced a twirling jig and was singing;

"Chicken and cheese,
Chicken and cheese,
Yum, Yum,
Chicken and cheese."

He stopped dancing, looked directly at Jeanne, his eyes twinkling;

"Surin don't ye know that we should be sharin ?"

"Sharing is one thing." replied Jeanne. "But you're not sharing, you just took and when we weren't even looking. Shame on you." She added with a smile.

"Aye, but I be sharin my wishes don't you know ?" commented Shamus.

"That's not sharing either." Jeanne returned. "If I understand the rules correctly you're obligated due to the fact that Ken caught you."

Shamus bowed his head with a tilt exposing that sly smile knowing he had been caught in one of his exaggerated lines recovering with;

"Surin ye can't blame a lad for tryin now can you lass ?"

"That's another thing." Jeanne said in her continuing verbal assault; "A lad you are certainly not. Just how old are you Mr. O'Flaherty."

Shamus's eyes started to twinkle once more while he danced his little jig and laughed heartily.

"That I'll not be tellin ye lass. Let's just say I remember the time before the first kings ?"

His hat was now on the ground as he did a toe tapping scissor kicking dance step around it humming a tune to himself. I was astonished as Jeanne when I heard this, that is if he was telling the truth. The Little People's reputation for overstatement was well known.

"Well now that our lunch is finished." I said looking at Shamus in the eye, We might as well continue our touring."

Shamus stopped dancing, smiled and exclaimed;

"Well then! Surin I'll be seein ye fore supper ?"

With that he clicked his heels together and actually disappeared before our eyes. Jeanne laughed as usual. I smiled with her saying;

"If nothing else he is entertaining along with being a nuisance."

We packed up returning to the car and continued our sightseeing.

Dining in a quant pub that night was relaxing and enjoyable. At least for a while it was. Our drinks were being switched time and time again and when we moved to switch them back food would disappear from the plates. Jeanne was becoming upset and I was losing patience. Pretending I was preoccupied I waited for a glass movement again. I did not have to wait too long. I sensed a disturbance and heard a very low snicker. Shamus was at it anew. Judging the direction of movement I reached out and grabbed at the air. My guess was correct. I now had Shamus by the coattails. Being caught like that naturally made him physically appear. Startled and embarrassed he tried to hide as best he could. Lucky for us we had a corner table with minimum lighting. No one else saw our little struggle. Hiding on the seat between us Shamus was frightened and upset at being caught a second time by the same person.

"Now my little friend do you want to be exposed to all here at the pub or are you going to behave." I whispered still clutching his coat.

He ceased struggling starring at me with frightened eyes. Being caught was bad enough but being exposed to the public would lower his status tremendously. Credibility with his own kind would become non-existent. My intimidation worked, he promised not to bother us any more this night if I would let him go. For once his plea seemed genuine and I let go of him. He vanished instantly and we both knew we would see him no more on that night. As much fun as he could be we welcomed the alone time to enjoy the evening on this magical Isle of green.

Chapter 4

The luck of the Irish was with us weather wise for the next few days. We enjoyed each day more than the last which was so much more exciting then we expected. This trip was any persons perfect dream vacation in spite of Mr. O'Flaherty's antics.

A weather front moved in from the west carrying scattered showers that could dampen most tourists spirits. We of course had Shamus and true to his word the rain surrounded us but it never rained where we were visiting. It was funny to hear the remarks of others who happened to be at the same places we were. We quietly laughed and of course did not reveal our secret.

Shamus, being the forever clown did not restrict his tricks to just us. Jeanne and I relished the confusion he sometimes caused for others nearby. Not everybody is open minded to the pranks of the Little People.

The days rain ended toward late afternoon giving way to an absolutely beautiful rainbow. It had to be the largest and most vivid I've ever seen. It was this colorful vision that gave me the idea for my second wish. We walked to a secluded place away from prying eyes and I called for Shamus. It took a few calls to get him away from his pranks on others but he at last appeared. He relaxed himself on a rock wall and proceeded to light his pipe. He made a few Shamrock smoke rings, his eyes ever twinkling and finally asked why he was called.

"I have decided on my second wish." I informed him.

"**W**ell have ye now. Surin it's about time lad ?" he answered.

He took another puff at his pipe producing a small Irish Harp as he exhaled.

"**A**nd what is it ye be wishin for ? Some more sunshine perhaps ?"

"**I** want to see the pot of gold at the end of the rainbow." I stated firmly.

I never saw an expression on someone's face change so fast. Levity and mischief were gone. They were now replaced by seriousness and alarm. Shamus's body language showed sudden panic and shock. It took a moment for him to compose himself, then he stated strongly, trying to intimidate I guess, that it was not possible. As an afterthought he half jokingly added;

"**A**nd now who ever heard of such a silly thing ? A pot of gold at the end of a rainbow ? And where do ye be gettin such story's from ? A pot of gold indeed ?"

His nervousness showed in his voice and body movements.

"**I**t's one of your legends, not mine." I replied calmly.

"**A**nd now surin who is going to believe silly legends ? They're just fairy tails in the wee one's story books ?" Shamus retorted, trying to put on a smile again.

"**A**hh yes." I returned. "Then if it's just a fairy tail, how come I see you here before me. Your existence has been a legend for centuries. If you're just a fairy tail why are we talking. Jeanne sees you too. Catching you and being granted wishes I guess is also a fairy tail or myth. It's a very realistic myth since I'm already enjoying one of my wishes. Watching and experiencing your antics and tricks is another very realistic myth. How do you account for that Mr. Shamus O'Flaherty."

His expression changed once more. This time to one of submission and defeat. His eyes averting mine he slowly put his pipe away. There were no more happy smoke rings. He remained silent as he inspected the shiny brass buckles on his shoes. Shamus raised his head, looked at Jeanne, then turned to me;

"Tis true what ye say lad. Tis all true. You have caught meself in lies. Tis the shame ye have put on me ?"

He was really wallowing in self pity now or it might have been one of his acts.

"Hold on a minute." I interrupted, "I never said you were lying. You may have been avoiding the real truth, but I never said you were lying."

"Surin tis a kind thing ye be sayin lad, but never the less tis the shame I'm feelin ?"

Jeanne showed a look of sadness as she suddenly was feeling sorry for Shamus.

"Never mind that." I addressed Shamus again. What about my wish ? What about my rainbow ?"

Instant seriousness overcame Shamus again. He paused looking for words.

"Tis a thing I don't know if I can do ?'" he answered quietly without any snicker.

"But you have to." I pushed. "Is that not the rules."

Shamus was thinking again then he replied.

"I'll grant almost anything in it's place ? Now wouldn't that be just grand. Anything you and the good lass want Then we can all be happy ?"

"The rainbow." I said softly but in earnest.

"Oh, let him be." Jeanne said touching my arm. "I think you've teased him enough."

Hearing this Shamus's eyes became a little more alert, hoping for a change of heart.

"No." I answered Jeanne softly. "That is my wish and I know he can do it and he knows I know."

Our little friend was now pacing a small circle, his hands clasped behind his back, his head down, brow wrinkled in thought. I waited patiently. He quit circling and stood before me.

"**T**is true what ye be sayin Ken ? I can grant this wish but not without some hardship on meself ?"

Now I was the one taken by surprise. It had never occurred to me that there would be difficulties.

"**A**nd what kind of hardship would that be." I asked in a friendly manner.

"Now perhaps we can have a real conversation." I thought to myself.

Shamus sighed deeply staring at the ground.

"**I** had me some trouble once before by granting such a wish and I have tried to stay away from it ever since ?"

"**W**hat kind of trouble." I persisted.

My little friend repeated his deep sigh.

"**B**elieve it or not such a wish is rarely asked, and tis only the grand council that can approve it ? And surin wouldn't you be knowin Shamus O'Flaherty meself granted such a wish without approval ? I thought it was goin to be makin meself a better man says I ? But no says they ? It put me in a most unfavorable light it did ? They took away most of my wishin powers ? I was only allowed to play tricks. Even those were limited and supervised ?"

"**B**ut you granted my wish. Is everything okay now?" I inquired.

"**A**ye, tis now or was up until now ?

The little man for once appeared to be genuine in his concern.

"**I** must stand before the council again and ask for their blessing ? How well that will work out I can not foretell. After me last infraction it took me almost two hundred years to get back in good graces with the elders and get me wishin powers back again ? Then they assigned me you because you were a believer. Ye are my first people in that two hundred years and now meself will be back at the beginners school ? Aye, tis the shame that is upon me ? I'll go before the council now and get ye your wish then maybe I can find some little glen to live out me life alone ?"

Shamus started to walk away.

"**W**ait." I called after him.

He stopped but did not turn around.

"**I** know what I want for my third wish." I said calmly.

"**L**eave him alone Ken. Haven't you made him feel bad enough already." Pleaded Jeanne almost in a whisper.

"**I**t will be okay, just wait. I answered quietly

"**W**hat is it that ye be wantin ?" inquired Shamus. I can't be in any more trouble than I already am ?"

"**M**y wish is to go before the council with you." I stated.

Shamus turned quickly around to face me, that look of panic blanketed his face once more.

"**W**hat are ye tryin to do to me lad ? Why not just run me over with your car ?"

"**W**hat do you mean." I replied half smiling.

"**S**urin an outsider seein the council ? It's just not done ? Tis not allowed ? Said Shamus in a shaky voice.

"**H**as there ever been an outsider to see the council." I further pushed again.

"**W**ell y-y-yes." Shamus stuttered in answer. "A few times, but that was a long time ago lad ?

"**S**o there you have it then, if it was done before then it can be done again." I said in a very happy tone.

My little friend was now sitting on a rock his head bowed in his hands, slowly shaking it back and forth.

"**T**is the end of me life ye be askin for lad ? The end of Shamus O'Flaherty himself ?"

"**N**onsense." I stated confidently. "If I'm not giving up why should you my friend. We'll both see the council together. Everything will be alright. Trust me."

"**T**is grand that ye call me your friend, but then ye go and stab me in the back ? Tis the ruin of meself that ye be makin ?

"**O**h stop being so melodramatic." I said laughing.

Shamus looked up at me open mouthed;

"**W**hat ye be sayin to me lad. ? As if shocked in all innocence.

He quickly turned to Jeanne for support, eyes pleading.

"**Y**ou are overdoing it a little." she remarked taking the wind out of his sails.

Shamus stared at Jeanne a few seconds then shifted his gaze back to me and locked eyes for a moment. Back to Jeanne and returned to me again this time with that sly smile of his.

"**O**kay lad ?" He smiled. "Im still going to be in trouble because takin outsiders to the council is frowned upon ?"

"**A**h ! But not forbidden." I interjected.

Shamus, still with his sly grin offered in return;

"**T**is me punishment that they assigned me you ? They knew all along ye would be trickin me ? Me, himself being outdone by an outsider ? Me pride is being dashed on the rocks ?"

"**H**ere we go again." whispered Jeanne, but loud enough for Shamus to hear.

He looked at her, the hint of a twinkle in his eye, "Aye, so ye are not buyin it lass ?"

"**N**o" she answered out loud.

Shamus shot up from the rock, brushed himself off turned to his left and started to walk.

"**W**ell tis best we get started then ?"

"**W**here are we going." I shouted after him.

"**W**hy to see the council of course ? Surin is that not what ye wanted ? Stay close now, I don't want ye gettin lost in the woods. There are tricky little Leprechauns about who could try to lead you astray ?" he giggled and danced about.

We hurried hand in hand not letting Shamus out of sight.

Chapter 5

We wound our way through trees, rocks and brambles, up and down small hillocks covered with lush green and crossed a few babbling brooks. Almost an hour had passed when we finally stopped at the base of what looked like a shear cliff hidden by tall climbing vines and underbrush.

"We're here now lad ? Tis sure ye be wantin to do this now ? Tis not too late to be changin your mind ?   I could make ye a nice bouquet of flowers for the lass and we could all be goin our separate ways ?"

Shamus was now all smiles. Not wanting to give in I asked;

"How much further till we meet the council."

Losing part of his smile Shamus replied in a mumble.

"Tis a stubborn man ye are Ken. A stubborn man ?"

He pushed back some vines revealing a cave entrance. Just inside Shamus picked up a shamrock shaped lantern which instantly emitted an eery green glow illuminating the passage walls. The litle man giggled as he tip toed along the narrow path. We had not traveled far when daylight suddenly appeared. We stood viewing a lush green valley from which came the sound of music. As we stepped from the cavern pathway surroundings, voices and laughter could also be heard.   It sounded like some sort of party or celebration.

"What's the occasion for the celebration." I asked.

"**T**is no celebration ?   Tis just everyday life ?" Shamus answered happily.

We followed him down to what appeared to be a village center, like a village green that is so common to many New England rural towns though this was a bit more rustic. There was a large fire burning in the center of a rock pit. A center spit held a hefty sized pig being turned over by two men. Little people of course. Their coats were off and shirt sleeves rolled up. A third man, similarly stripped was basting with a brush almost the size of himself. The aroma wafting from this succulent roast would taunt anybody. Wee tables were about the green, each occupied by both men and women. This was a whole community of little people. The music filling the air was from four men off to one side of the park. Two fiddles, a concertina and a small Irish harp made up the quartet. A few couples were doing an intriguing dance to the captivating sound.

Women dressed in long green skirts, green waistcoats emphasizing rather full bosoms barely covered by white, off the shoulder, puffy sleeved blouses. Some wore white flat caps, others displayed magnificent full heads of hair, a majority dark red, sprinkled here and there with auburn or black. Not one blond was to be seen. A few of the younger ladies, which in this case is a very relative term, were serving both food and drink. The others mixed with the men rather well in eating and drinking. A more boisterous group of men were gathered at the opposite end of the park area where we noticed four large wooden kegs, obviously the cause of the louder voices. I didn't really make a count but a quick guess would put their number at about one hundred plus or minus. It looked like a fun time.

"**F**ollow me now ?" said Shamus, "And don't be puttin any more shame on me now then ye already have ?"

We slowly wound our way to the far side of the glen to a sort of isolated table occupied by four pipe smoking gentlemen. The smoke rings above them showed all sorts of shapes and designs. They were dressed much like the others except each had a large shamrock in his left lapel.

This I assumed was the council. The elders you might say but who could tell how old any of them were. Once we were spotted walking with Shamus the celebratory din began to fade. The closer we came to the council table the quieter it became until there was total silence.

Shamus stopped about four feet from the main table. Hand in hand Jeanne and I stood behind him quietly observing the surroundings. Shamus removed his hat and bowed. It reminded me of the story's and movies you would see depicting the royal courts of Europe century's ago.

The four elders looked at Shamus, then at Jeanne and I and then back to Shamus. Each man puffed at his pipe, blew large smoke rings that rose and interlocked with each other and drifted upward and out of sight.

One man removed his pipe from his mouth and with a remarkably deep voice for such a little man addressed Shamus.

"And what sort of trouble ye be bringin us now Shamus O'Flaherty ? Must we remind ye again of the rules of outsiders ? And two outsiders at that ? Do ye not like your life here with us ?"

"Tis surin I can explain, Colm ?" Shamus interrupted. This is no ordinary outsider ?"

The booming voice spoke again while pointing his pipe in a menacing fashion at Shamus.

"I'll not be takin your silly explanations Shamus ? You know the rules ?"

"Then perhaps you'll be taking my explanation. I said as I stepped forward slightly.

The once silent onlookers gave out a combined loud intake of breath that echoed across the green. At the same time an expression of shock covered all their faces. The women folk timidly moved behind the closest man.

"And who be given ye leave to speak ?" Colm replied

looking directly at me.

"**I** don't need any ones permission to speak when I think something is unjust." I answered.

Again the mass intake of breath. The whole community was shocked that anybody would talk to the council this way.

"**A**nd now ye be accusin me of bein unjust ? Tis a bold man ye are ? A bold man ?"

Colm, was now standing, his whiskers twitching with irritation.

"**A**ll Ken is asking is for you to listen." Jeanne said calmly.

She stepped closer to the table.

"**I**'m sure that's not too much to ask of distinguished gentlemen such as yourselves."

The silence was deafening, but Jeanne's plea fell on receptive ears with such a calming effect that Colm had reseated himself.

"**K**en, did you say ?" He asked directing the question to Jeanne.

"**Y**es." she answered smiling. "Ken Goss and I'm Jeanne."

"**A**ye, tis a grand name, Jeanne lass." Colm smiled in answer.

Raising his voice he turned to Shamus;

"**A**nd why did ye not say so Shamus ? Here ye be gettin us all upset for nothin ? In a much friendlier voice.

"**S**it lass, sit down and rest ?" said another elder as he raised his hand in signal.

Within a minute two women appeared, one with a tankard of dark foam, the other with a plate of scones. A third woman followed with a tankard for me.

"**H**ave a wee drink and relax ? It will do you good ?"

"**W**hy the sudden change of heart when you heard my name." I inquired.

"**A**ye tis true what you say Ken but we know all about you. You're a believer and there are not many anymore." answered Colm.

"I still want to explain because I'll not let any trouble befall Shamus because of something I caused him to do. I wanted to come before you to plead my second wish. My third wish was that he bring me here." I stated plainly.

"**A**nd what was so important about your second wish ?" Colm asked.

"Shamus said he would need council approval before he could grant it." I answered.

"Could be he was just tryin to trick you ? Tis only one thing that needs council approval.? Liam another elder replied.

"Then that is what I must have asked." I replied.

Liam looked at me questioningly, almost a bit confused as did the other elders.

"I wish to see the pot of gold at the end of the rainbow." I continued. "If there really is such a thing."

My answer not only startled them but shocked them as well.

"**W**hy of course there is such a thing." all four answered in unison before they realized what they had divulged.

Embarrassed by their mistake, Colm answered for them.

"**S**urin tis a tricky one ye are Ken ? Not only are ye a believer but ye are clever enough to be one of us ?"

"**T**hanks for the compliment." I replied while bringing my tankard to my lips. I took a few deep swallows and was more than pleased. Licking the brown foam from my lips I commented;

"**I**t tastes like Guinness."

"Surin, and why shouldn't it ?" Liam responded.

"I would have thought you made your own brew." I replied.

"Aye but we do lad, we always have ?

"Then how come it tastes like Guinness." I asked again.

"And now who do you think gave them the recipe ? Tis a grand thing we did for them ?"

For all I know he could have been right. As the legend says the Little People have been around a long time and I am now witness that they do exist, so who knows?

~ ~ ~ ~ ~ ~

"No more of your tricks now Ken ? Tryin to distract us with your interest in our brew ? Surin we should get back to the matter of your wish ?" Colm stated. "What ye be wantin with our pot of gold ?

"Just to see it." I replied "Curiosity I guess to see how you get there. Rainbows always appear to be so far away, almost never ending. The closer you get to them the farther away they appear."

"So ye not be wantin to take any of our gold ?"

"No." I answered as convincingly as I could. "I've been chasing rainbows since I was a kid and people have always talked about the legend of the pot of gold at the end of the rainbow. Now that I'm here at the home of the legend I just wanted to see for myself. The question is, can you really get to the end of the rainbow. Science today takes it to seriously and of course their answer is that it's not possible. You say I'm a believer and I think I am also. So show me I'm not loony and believing for nothing. You can keep you gold, I just want to reach the end of the rainbow."

I ended my little speech and looked directly at each of the four elders. Detecting nothing in each of their faces I figured my

argument was for naught. The four council people whispered with
each other for a few minutes. I turned to Jeanne and shrugged my
shoulders. She smiled sympathetically and mouthed the words, "You
tried."

Colm at last turned to me saying;

"Tis time we be needin and privacy if ye don't
mind ?   Shamus, tis entertaining ye should be showin your friends
now ? We'll be dealin with ye later ?

Shamus led us away from the council table to the
center of the park where tables were filled with culinary delights.

"Me thinks I'm in trouble again ?" he mumbled.

"Nonsense." I answered. "We'll do everything we
can on your behalf to prove your innocense."

"In spite of what you have been trying to do to us."
Jeanne added smiling.

Shamus looked at us both with a broad grin.

"Ye would do that for me ? Tis grand people you are.
Surin now I almost feel guilty for playing tricks on you ?"

"I notice you said almost. You should be ashamed of
yourself Mr. O'Flaherty." Jeanne added.

"Aye, you're right lass, tis the shame I'm feelin. Now
how about something to eat ?" Shamus offered.

"You can change the subject fast enough, can't you
Shamus. You must have had a lot of practice over the centuries.
Jeanne answered.

"Who me lass ?" Shamus replied in all innocense.
I have no idea what ye be talkin about. Here try one of these scones,
they're delicious ?"

Both Jeanne and I were now laughing. Shamus
O'Flaherty was surely one of a kind.

Chapter 6

We were enjoying ourselves at the food table, I even managed to fill my tankard a few more times. The women of the Little People were most gracious hosts and kept us engaged in delightful conversation. I felt genuinely welcome. I was about to ask for another refill of brown ale when a messenger arrived to say the council was ready for us. Jeanne and I enthusiastically headed for the other side of the glen with Shamus not so excitedly trailing behind.

The four elders were trying to act all proper and official but you could see the impish twinkle in their eyes. Colm struggling to remain serious addressed us in a formal tone.

"**T**is a most unusual request ye be askin of us lad ? But since you've come all this way and seem like a decent enough fellow, and the lass of course, and we bein of a generous nature have decided to grant your wish ?

I glanced at Jeanne who was all smiles and started to reply only to be quieted by Liam's raised hand.

"**O**n one condition." He stated firmly.

. "**Y**ou will take no gold ?" said a third man.

"**A**nd ye will take no pictures ?" said the forth member.

"**A**greed." I answered cheerfully. "If you remember I myself stated that earlier. I'm not interested in your gold.

I paused, then added, "When do we leave ?"

"**T**is a hurry you're in now ?" said Colm. "Slow down

lad. You'll not be seein anymore rainbow today. Enjoy the evening with us and ye will be havin your wish on the morrow ?"

"**A**nd one more thing." Interrupted Liam. "You'll not be goin alone."

I turned to look at Shamus.

"**A**ye, Shamus will be there to look after you, and Timothy Flynn will be there to look after Shamus ?"

Shamus quickly jerked his head around to the council, a look of surprise in his eyes.

"**B**ut that was a long time ago and a different circumstance ?" He pleaded guiltily.

"**W**e'll not go into that again Shamus." replied Colm firmly. "That is the council decision ?"

Shamus pushed no further, turned toward Jeanne and me , sheepishly mumbling, "Family squabble."

We were both smiling knowing the imp that he was.

The Little People entertained us with music and dancing and of course food and drink for the rest of the evening. At last we parted company and returned to the B&B. I was looking forward to the next days showers so that we could have a rainbow.

Shamus stayed with us all the next day, not always visible but we knew he was nearby, particularly when we found half of our lunch missing or when we heard a not too well disguised belch followed by a sneering laugh. True to his word though we were able to see more than we had planned for in the amount of time available.

Luck was with us still, fore around half past three in the afternoon we were subjected to the usual showers. Feeling the first cool drops of rain on my face triggered an excitement I had not felt in years. My hopes were high for a short period of showers followed by the ever popular rainbow and of course the magical pot of gold. Jeanne sported a childlike smile as she squeezed my hand in anticipation of our upcoming adventure. We sought the shelter of some trees so as not to get thoroughly drenched. Some twenty minutes later the soft patter of drops on the leaves slowed it's music until eventually the natural symphony ceased replaced by the sound of silence. Gradually the sky lightened allowing the sun to reappear. In quiet anticipation the three of us stepped out from the protection of the trees glancing to the east. It took a few minutes but eventually it was there. Our long awaited color streak, barely visible at first, which was a disappointment, but it's intensity gradually strengthened as did it's length increase. Now before my eyes was the most magnificent rainbow I had ever seen. The color was deep and the width was beyond my wildest imagination. I looked at Jeanne but could not speak. Her reaction was the same.

I was suddenly aware that we had been joined by a fourth person. Timothy Flynn appeared next to Shamus much to his disappointment. Shamus may have been annoyed but it told me this was the real thing. I looked directly at Shamus, childlike excitement filling my eyes.

"Aye lad, I guess we should be on the way ?" he said.

Timothy chimed in; "Follow me then before we lose the day ?"

Off he went toward a thickly wooded area. We walked for some twenty minutes with Timothy checking on the rainbow periodically. Eventually coming to a small clearing we halted. I looked for the rainbow through an opening in the trees.
It was there more vivid than ever. I noticed it was the lower part of the arc with the color bands the widest I've ever seen.

"Now." Said Shamus, "Tis time for the hands ?" as he reached out to take Jeanne's hand, who in turn clasped mine. Timothy moved to a position behind me and grabbed my hand. Off we went again Shamus in the lead. I quickly glanced at Timothy questioning with my eyes.

"Tis normal procedure lad. This way no one gets lost in the brambles and marsh ? Tis protection for our gold ?"

I nodded in understanding without saying a word.

As we continued winding our way about I did notice tangles of thickets and heavily vegetated wet lands. Trying to take in all that I could as far as land marks I finally gave it up as a lost cause. There were just too many twists and turns to remember. Coming to my senses I admitted to my self there was no need to know anyway. We would most likely not return to Ireland but the memory of this trip would last us the rest of our lives. After all how many people ever got to see this magical sight. Let's face it no one would believe it anyway.

Our chain of hand holding people meandered for another hundred yards or so till we were stopped by a rather large fog bank. Although the fog seemed to have a light yellow hue, there was an aura about it that even felt strange.

Timothy Flynn called out; "Tis time for the closen of the eyes ?"

I could feel Jeanne's hand tighten around mine. I looked to both Timothy and Shamus for an explanation.

"Tis the rule ?" Shamus volunteered.

"Aye, tis the rule for us all ?" followed Timothy. "No harm will come to ye. If ye want to visit the rainbows end the closen of the eyes is a must ?"

I turned to Jeanne and nodded my approval as I clasped her hand firmly in a reaffirming gesture. She smiled and closed her eyes. My own followed suit. Our individual breathing was all that broke the silence. A tingling sensation swept over us accompanied by the soft touch of a warm mist. Jeanne and I tightened our grip some more, not really in fear but more in excitement. The warmth of the sun could be felt again as Timothy instructed us to open our eyes.

A deep intake of breath emanated from Jeanne as she viewed the massive pot of gold, the sparkle in her eyes matching, if not out doing, the glitter of the coins.

"How beautiful." Was the only thing she said beaming her pleased smile.

I felt myself joining in her excitement without the obvious display of emotion. As I took in the overall scene My attention was drawn to the golden yellow mist shrouding the large, what appeared to be bronze pot, and extending it's rays to include the whole wooded glen and the end of the rainbow.

There was a joyous giggling behind us and as we turned to look, Shamus and Timothy were arm and arm dancing around in a funny sort of jig. We also were suddenly in a giddy mood so we joined them in a made up dance of our own. I didn't let it last too long because I was curious about the pot of gold. Actually I was more curious of the rainbow's end. It really did end at the bronze pot.

Gazing up at the vivid colors I followed them down as they lost their saturation and blended with the coins to form the golden mist. You could almost feel it's magnetic pull. Finding Timothy I asked;

"Can I touch."

"Aye lad, ye can touch but ye must return all to the pot."

Thrilled with the idea I moved slowly to the caldron of gold, fascinated by it's glow. Shamus was beside me hand outstretched.

"Not you Shamus ?" Timothy said loudly. "You know the rules ?"

With a guilty expression on his face and cheeks he answered;

"I was just guiding the lad so he did not fall and hurt himself ?"

Timothy drew closer and Shamus pulled back. Jeanne joined me at the pot still maintaining that wonderful smile. Now that we were closer I guessed it's size to be about three feet across and about three and a half feet deep at it's widest bulging sides.

Hesitantly I extended my hand and watched it fade into the mysterious mist. I picked up a coin. It was the size of a silver dollar, perhaps a bit larger but twice as thick. It must have weighed a good five ounces. The coin itself was inscribed on both sides. One had the design of a small Irish harp, it's opposing side looked to me like symbols or letters of Gallic. Jeanne reached in and picked a coin also. It's design was different on both sides. We retrieved others finding no two coins alike .

I looked around to find our two guides sitting on a rock, both puffing away on their clay pipes. I asked Timothy about the difference in the coins.

"**A**ye lad, each and every one is different. Tis part of the beauty of our pot of gold. Tis something you can not put a price or value on. We add a few coins every year ?"

"**A**nd where do you get the gold from ?" I questioned.

The pair of little men laughed and put a finger along the side of his nose.

"**T**is a secret ye will never know ?" answered Shamus. They looked at each other and laughed again.

Jeanne and I returned the coinage to it's rightful place and continued to explore the area. It all looked like a Disney animated fantasy. The golden mist began to fade as did the magnificent rainbow. Dusk was setting in across the magic glen. Minutes later, right before our eyes we were standing in an ordinary forest clearing. No rainbow, No gold, no golden mist. Even Jeanne appeared to be quite disappointed with it's passing.

"**O**h well." She said with a smile, "You had your wish and I was glad to be part of it."

Timothy arose, shook out his pipe and approached us.

"**S**o tis not a total loss, the council authorized me to give this to you."

He drew from his pocket a golden coin and offered it to me. I looked at him questioningly.

"**N**ot to worry lad, It's real. I drew it from the pot earlier ? Tis not for spendin now but for the rememberin ? A story ye can tell your wee grandchildren some day ? And may the luck of the Irish be with ye always ?"

I examined the coin happily and passed it to Jeanne

who treated it like the treasure it was.

"Come now." Said Shamus, "Tis gettin late and we must be gettin back while there is a little daylight left ?"

Hand in hand we wound our way out of the darkened wood. We found ourselves back at the car. Timothy Flynn, being the true gentleman, doffed his hat and bowed graciously and faded away. Shamus, however, jumped into the back seat of the car and settled himself comfortably. As I drove back to our B&B Shamus spoke sweetly to Jeanne.

"And now lass will ye be showin me the special coin ye be holdin. I should check it out for you to see if it's the real thing? Can't be too careful you know ?"

Jeanne , alert to his scheming answered in his own manner of speaking.

"Tis agreeable I be to showin ye the coin but I'll be keepin it in me own hand, don't ye know ?"

Shamus's expression turned to one of shock and hurt.

"Tis hurtin me pride ye be doin lass and after all I've done for you and himself.

She laughed quietly recognizing the impish glint in his eyes.

"I may be hurtin your pride Shamus but I'll be keepin me coin.

We arrived back at our B&B, bid our goodnights to Shamus and retired for the night.

Chapter   6

       The excitement of seeing the rainbow and pot of gold was still with us the next day as we continued our sojourn through the Iris countryside. My first wish was still in effect and we were able to view twice as much as planned. Jeanne was elated because of this. Her dream visit to Ireland was now far more than hoped for. Of course we could not have done this without Shamus O'Flaherty, but we could have done with far less of his antics. I think lunch stealing was his favorite pass time.   All in all I guess he was harmless.

       As with anything, all good things must come to an end. Our allotted time for Ireland was fast coming to a close. We arrived at Shannon airport, returned the car and checked in at security. We had just passed the metal detectors and were collecting our things when bells and buzzers started going off. We turned to see what was happening as did everyone else, but nothing was obvious. The red lights were blinking on the pass through stalls but no one was to be seen. The security people ultimately decided there had to be a power interruption or electrical failure some place. This sounded logical until Im heard a familiar snicker. Jeanne heard it also.

       "Shamus." she questioned quietly catching my eye.

       "It couldn't be." I answered, then we heard the all to familiar giggle.

       "Shamus." I said firmly, cut that out. Your shameless antics are affecting a lot of people. You could cause them to miss their flight."

"**S**orry." We heard in a non convincing voice while remaining invisible.

"**W**hat are you doing here anyway ?" I further inquired.

"**Y**e be hurtin me feelings now Ken and here I thought we was friends. I came to be wishin you and the lass a pleasant journey home."

"**I** thank you for that and I truly thank you for all that you helped us with. We are both extremely grateful."

"**T**is nothin lad, I enjoyed me time with you, especially the lunches ?" He snickered.

The PA system announced our flight boarding and we exchanged our farewells with Shamus.. In a way it was a little sad, the little man actually grew on you despite his annoyances. My final words to him were to try and stay out of trouble.

"**I** always do ?" was his laughing answer.

Halfway up the runway entrance to the aircraft I could hear distant buzzers and bells . I smiled to myself and entered the plane.

Comfortably settled in our seats, Jeanne and I were closely studying our treasured golden coin, not even considering it's worth. To us it was a memory we would keep forever.

"**W**hat a beautiful piece." Said the hostess interrupting our revery.

"**J**ust something we picked up as a souvenir of the trip. I smiled in answer - - - .

~The End ~

The Beavers

by
K.J.Goss

The Beavers

I live on a rural dirt road which is actually quite a nice thing. It's hard to keep a car clean, or in my case a truck, but life here seems so more quiet and relaxed. Well, on my way to town one day, as I passed a neighbors house I noticed he was at the street, picking up his mail. I stopped to say Hi.

"Hey Jack, how's the beaver problem going these day's.

"They're still driving me crazy, but I'm slowly gaining control again. I didn't really want to but I did shoot a few with my twenty two the other day.

~ ~ ~ ~ ~ ~ ~

You see, Jack has a rather large pond towards the back of his land. It's quite beautiful to see the way it is landscaped and flowered. And of course the pond is loaded with trout. Both rainbow and brook. They're sort of like his pets. He feeds them every day and that alone is quite a show.

Well the beavers moved in from the woods and streams above this spring and sort of took possession of everything. They muddied up the pond to the point you couldn't see the fish anymore. Then they worked on the water overflow by clogging it up with grass and twigs. This in turn raised the water level of the pond, which led to the fish being washed over the water fall and away down the stream. It was a chore to have to clean away the twig debris every day to protect the fish. So one can see how it could lead one to such drastic measures as shooting these cleaver engineers of nature.

Anyway back to Jack's sad story. I say sad because to have such a level headed guy end up the way he did is really a tragedy. His poor wife needs all the support she can get now. Luckily they have three wonderful children who can comfort her and hopefully ease her mind somewhat.

It all started a while back with Jack's daily struggle with the beavers. As I mentioned earlier he had to resort to shooting a few. Not too long after that Jack came across a bog just up stream from his pond. It was obviously always there but never noticed until the beavers started building a dam across it. While Jack was there breaking up the dam one day he could feel something under foot. With a lot of effort and help from another neighbor he salvaged an old, large wagon wheel, perfectly preserved. It was a beauty with about a four foot diameter and a large hub. I imagined it came from an old covered wagon or perhaps a stage coach. I understand they used to run nearby. Every one guessed it to be plus or minus one hundred and fifty years old. This wonderful thing was the start of all his troubles.

Revisiting the bog to see if other treasures could be salvaged, Jack stepped to the middle and without warning sank immediately. Down and down he went to an underground cavern. Or at least this is the story he told. The cavern was well lit without any signs of torches or electricity of any kind. It was well lighted so that all could be seen.

Curious as to where he was Jack also noticed that he was perfectly dry.

*"**H**ow could that be."* he thought. *"I just traveled through maybe twenty feet of mud and water."*

Contemplating these thoughts, he was startled by voices behind him. He quickly turned around only to see three very large beavers looking sternly at him. They were standing on their hind legs and walking as if they were human, except they dragged their tails which created a sound that could send shivers through your body.

"We have been waiting for you." said one.

"What took you so long." said a second.

"It's about time." added the third.

Poor Jack admitted he was frightened. He stepped back a few feet.

The first one continued,

"That's right, keep moving, we're all waiting for you."

Then the three laughed, hideously. Jack turned to run down this long corridor, the echo of the laughter following him. He turned a corner and went through a large door made of small logs. The tips gnawed to pencil point sharpness. Poor Jack's mind was working overtime.

"Once through these doors I'll be safe." He thought. As he closed the log door behind him the area filled with that same magic light. There was a chorus of voices.

"We are ready for you."

There before him were about thirty of these beaver humans. All standing upright. They ranged in size between two and a half to three and a half feet tall. Some looked as if they were smiling, the rest stared meanly. One of the larger ones approached Jack ,and directing him to a chair made of logs said,

"Welcome to beaver court, please sit down."

Jack, trembling with confusion, did as he was told.

"This can't be happening to me. This can't be real. Beavers can't talk. They don't walk on two feet. This has got to be a nightmare."

These thoughts raced through his mind only to be interrupted by a gavel banging.

"Court is now in session, the honorable King Beaver presiding."

In walked the largest of all beavers, and it was even wearing glasses.

"No ! No ! This is not real" screamed Jack and got up to run.

He almost made it to the door but was caught and carried back to the chair. King Beaver looked at him sternly and in a loud gravely voice said,

"Any more outbursts like that will have serious consequences Jack."

Startled at hearing his name, Jack shook with overwhelming fear. He felt like he was going to faint. In fact he did pass out.

He came out of his faint as he felt water being splashed on his face. Looking around he saw small beavers flapping the water of the pond with their tails splashing on him.
He jumped to his feet, shaking and screaming.

"Get away, get away." as he ran for the house.

"What's all the commotion about Jack ? Why are you yelling ?"

Jack pushed past his wife almost knocking her down. Once in the house he sat down, his head in his hands. Still trembling. His poor wife followed him into the house not knowing what to think.

"Are you alright Jack ?" she asked again.

Jack, his face extremely pale looked up at his wife,

"It was horrible, Jan. It was horrible."

"What was horrible ? Jan queried again.

"The beavers." Jack yelled. "They were going to try me in court like a common criminal."

"Nonsense." Jan soothed. "I was looking out the window and saw you fall. You must have hit your head. It was probably just a bad dream. I was on my way out when you jumped up and started screaming."

Jack, calming down slightly looked at his wife as she poured him some water. He sipped at the water reviewing things in his mind. Some where in a distance he heard Jan say,

"Lay down on the couch now and rest. You will feel better in a little while."

A half hour later Jack awoke from his nap feeling refreshed. He joined his wife in the garden and told her of his dream. He was somewhat embarrassed but better for having told her his story.

"See." said Jan, "It was just a silly dream."

I saw Jack the next day and laughing about it he relayed the same tale to me, which is how I came to know and write about it. I also assured him it was just a dream. Beavers are beavers, that's all there is to it.

Another day passed and Jack was again near the bog when he heard a voice behind him.

"Where have you been Jack. Why did you run away. You can't run away you know.."

Alarmed by the sound, he spun around only to see a large beaver standing there just like the other day. Starting to tremble again he stepped backwards into the bog and was sucked down as before. He was grabbed by other beavers and led to the chair in the court room. The entrance of King Beaver was repeated.

"You shouldn't have run like that Jack. This will go very hard on you. Won't it jury."

Jack's attention was directed to an area that was boxed in that held six large beavers. They all smiled at what the King Beaver said and nodded their heads affirmatively.

"Now it has been brought to my attention." continued the King, "That you may have shot and killed some of our beaver cousins. Is that true ?"

Jack was trembling again and started shouting.

"This isn't happening. You aren't real."

"Oh, but it is Jack, and we are." answered the King. "Answer the question Jack."

"NO !" Jack yelled again. "You're just a dream.

That's it . You're just a dream." he laughed.

Jack then continued to laugh uncontrollably.

"A dream, that's all, a dream." he kept repeating.

Finally becoming silent, Jack realized he was still in the beaver court being addressed by the King.

"Shame on you Jack. These outbursts will not be tolerated. Now as I was saying, did you or did you not shoot our cousin beavers."

Looking wild and terrified now Jack answered.

"Why not ? Why shouldn't I ? You are ruining my fish pond. I should kill all of you. Yes that's what I'll do. Kill all of you."

Jack was not in control of himself any more.

"This is not going well for you at all Jack. Is it ?" asked the King Beaver. "I'm going to call for a postponement of this trial until you can control yourself." the King struck the desk with the gavel and said,

"To resume at another time."

Jack awoke sitting on the grass by the pond. He heard his wife's voice.

"Oh there you are Jack, I'm going to town to do some shopping, is there anything you need ?"

Looking pale he turned to her saying,

"Please don't leave me alone, I was just with the beavers again. They still want to try me in court."

"Now don't start with that silliness again. Perhaps you're tired. Why don't you get some rest, I'll be back shortly." replied Jan.

Raising his voice, Jack was yelling at his wife.

"It's not silly. It's real. They're out to get me I tell you.."

Taken aback by these ranting's Jan went to the telephone and called me. I came over and sat with Jack while Jan went shopping. Jack relayed the whole story to me again.

"Tell you what Jack, let's both go over to the bog and

I'll show you that this is all not real."

It took some coaxing be he finally agreed and walked with me to the bog. I had old sneakers and jeans on so I didn't care about getting muddy as I stepped into the bog. Naturally I sank a few inches and that was it.

"See ! Didn't I tell you it was all nothing." as I proceeded to walk all over the bog area.."You're just having bad nightmares Jack"

I stepped out of the mud and with my arm around Jack's shoulder walked to the bench by the house. I took my shoes and socks off and sat talking with Jack until Jan returned. All seemed back to normal by the time I left. Jack thanked me and went in the house with his wife.

Jack stayed away from the yard for a few days to regain his composure. Agreeing that Jan and I were right about the nightmares, Jack went about his normal routine of yard work and feeding the fish. He still had to clean the overflow because of the beavers activity but this did not seem to bother him now,
until he heard that voice again.

"Why must you always destroy our work Jack."

Being startled like that he fell backwards and was sucked down the overflow pipe, to find himself back in the beaver court room, still bone dry.

"I'm glad to see you have recovered your senses, Jack." said the King Beaver. "Now, perhaps we can continue uninterrupted."

Jack sat in the chair feeling numb all over. He wanted to scream but could say nothing. He remained listless in the chair staring at the floor while the din of the King Beaver's questions flooded his ears. Tears started in his eyes and he was trembling again as he jumped to his feet.

"No ! This is not happening. You're only in my imagination. This is not real."

"Oh, but it is real." the King Beaver answered.

"Very real." chorused the jury.

"More real than you think." joined all the spectators.

"Now, settle down." said the King softly, "So we can continue."

Shaking all over, Jack sat down feeling nothing, seeing nothing and hearing only faint echoes in the background.

"Jack." called Jan. "Jack," she repeated after a pause. "Jack what are you doing sitting out here on the grass ? It's almost dark out and where have you been all afternoon ?"

Without looking at his wife he answered quietly, almost whispering,

"They're going to find me guilty, Jan. I just know they are. What am I going to do. I must get away. Help me run away and hide, Please." Jack begged.

In the house he sat on the couch repeating this again and again.

Jan called me again and I rushed right over. Both of us tried to calm him while he retold the story of the afternoons events. I sat with Jack while Jan called the doctor.
Arrangements were made for a visit to the doctors office the next day. I offered to stay the night with Jack and Jan which she immediately accepted. Jan made dinner for the three of us. Jack sat at the table but did not eat much.

"I wonder what beaver tastes like." he said. "I've had squirrel before but I never had beaver. Maybe we can have beaver tomorrow."

I interrupted Jack and changed the subject. Jan was obviously getting very upset. I called for my wife to also come over to comfort Jan. We finally put Jack to bed. The three of us then settled for a while not saying much.

I must have dozed off because the next thing I knew it was three in the morning and I was awakened by gun shots and wild laughter in the yard. I rushed out followed shortly after by the two women. I found Jack shooting wildly into the bog screaming,

"You will not take me. I am not going. I'll get you for this."

I grabbed Jack and managed to get the gun away from him safely. I threw it into the mud of the bog while leading Jack away.

"They found me guilty and they sentenced me to their beaver jail for life. But I got away again. They will never get me now. You'll help me, wont you Don ? Between the two of us we can wipe them out. We'll fix em, wont we Don.

I watched as the ambulance drove away. My wife and I followed with Jan in our car. At the hospital Jack only spoke of the beaver trial. How he thought it was unfair. They assigned him a beaver lawyer whom Jack said was totally biased. He asked me if I could help get him a retrial.

We don't know how long Jack is going to be away. Jan went to stay with her sister while I said I would take care of the fish

I hated to see such a nice level headed guy go off the deep end like that, but that's life I guess.

The next day at around five in the afternoon I was feeding the trout and enjoying their jumping show when I heard a noise behind me.

"Hello Don, We've been waiting for you."

~ ~ ~ ~ ~ ~

The End, Perhaps.

Detour

by
K.J.Goss

Detour

Hurrican Irene certainly took it's toll on Vermont. Although the wind did not reach the predicted velocities, the unusual amount of rain in such a short period of time produced unimaginable flash floods. Devastation was everywhere. Bridges down, houses washed away and roads undermined by rising flood waters. The states entire infrastructure was in jeopardy. Most interstate highways survived well, while lesser roads were severely compromised.

Two days after the event it was my job to document, photographically, some of the more severe damage spots. I was heading for the Hillcrest Road Bridge site. I was told by my editor that the bridge had washed away taking a good portion of the approaching road with it. Following my trucks GPS I knew I was zeroing in on my assignment.

I worked for a magazine monthly that liked to keep up with the more sensational disasters. In my short time driving around I realized that Vermont certainly fit the bill this time.

As I neared my destination I was suddenly confronted with road blocks. Even though I was a little annoyed with this, I certainly understood the necessity. Being naturally lazy, I did not want to park my truck and walk the few hundred yards to the bridge. Perhaps I can get closer by another road. I looked around and finally spotted a small hand written sign with a pointing arrow. I threw the truck in gear, hung a left and followed the arrow towards a dirt road. This particular road had not sustained much damage and except for a few minor culvert wash outs it was a good ride. Additional hand drawn arrows appeared and I happily followed. The road was mostly wooded but spotted with small clearings giving view to cornfields and an occasional old barn. The serpentine drive was now turning into a class four roadway with many and sudden left and right turns. It dawned on me that I really had no idea where I was, and at this point because of the tree cover and surrounding mountains my GPS unit was completely useless.

"Not to worry." I told myself, "I've been in tougher spots before and always found my way out."

I plodded blindly on. Another ten minutes of up hill, down hill and round and round I at last spotted a wooden sign, neatly lettered. It read HILLCREST ROAD BRIDGE, one half mile. Feeling somewhat pleased with myself for finding my way around again I followed the arrow. The road started twisting again and as I continued I got the feeling I was gradually traveling in a circle. There were more arrows which all read bridge, so I dismissed my thoughts about going in circles and slowly drove on. A few more minutes proved my original thoughts to be correct. I was staring at the same sigh I had seen earlier. HILLCREST ROAD BRIDGE, one half mile.

A bit confused now I figured I must have missed a turn somewhere. I started off again following the arrow, this time driving even slower. I laughed to myself when I considered the mileage that would show up on my expense sheet. Oh well that's life. I recognized the same trees, rocks and bumps in the road from my previous go around and I was getting that confused feeling again. Sure enough a short time later I was reading that same sign again, HILLCREST ROAD BRIDGE, one half mile.

In total frustration now I said the heck with this, I'll just go back to where I started from, park the truck and walk. Let's see, I made a left turn to get here so I'll just hang a right and return to where I was. I started to move my truck again, looking for the road I came in on. All I could see was woods. I stopped and looked around. All there seemed to be was the circle road that I was presently on. I got out of the truck thinking I had missed the road. I walked around searching, even walking into the woods a short distance. NOTHING !

I headed back to the truck and the wooded sign. I

remember the sign was straight ahead as I drove up to it. I walked to the sign and stood with my back to it, then looking straight ahead I saw nothing but trees and underbrush. No road.

"But how can that be." I thought. *"I just drove in here. Roads don't just up and disappear while you're driving on them."*

I closed my eyes trying to clear my head, but that didn't seem to help. When I opened them nothing had changed. There was still no road.

Resigning myself to the fact that nothing was going to change I climbed back into the truck and took the circle route one more time, following the arrows. Time wise I figured I was halfway round when I noticed that the road seemed to straighten itself. I thought this odd but continued on towards the clearing I could see ahead. A small rise in the road opened to the wonderful sight of the bridge.

A sign at the side read HILLCREST ROAD BRIDGE.

"That's funny." I thought, *"The report I got said this bridge was totally washed away. Well I'll get some shots of what damage there is and then move on to another site."* I moved the truck off to the side, grabbed my camera and stepped down to take a look around.

The river seemed extremely low considering we just suffered the flash floods of a hurricane. I saw no evidence of any damage what so ever. The river banks were intact, there were no fallen trees, no debris of any kind. There was absolutely nothing to take pictures of, other than pretty pictures for an art show. I guess somebody gave out the wrong information. Even the media said some parts of the state escaped relatively unscathed.

The small village across the bridge appeared to be carrying on business as usual. I might as well head over there, get their story and then move on. I drove across the bridge and found a parking spot on what I guessed was the main street. I looked around to get my bearings and sighted in on a local eatery..

"As good a place as any to start." I said aloud to myself.

Grabbing my camera, I walked to and entered the café'. Sitting down at the counter I ordered a cup of coffee. When the gal behind the counter brought my mug of coffee I asked her how she fared with Irene. She looked at me oddly and asked ,

"Who's Irene ? I don't know any Irene."

Smiling, I returned with "Very funny. You know hurricane Irene."

Still looking at me like I was a nut case she answered again seriously,

"What hurricane. You aren't from around here are you. We haven't had a hurricane in Vermont since I can't remember when.

She walked away to serve another customer. She whispered something to the man and they both looked in my direction and laughed quietly. I sat there sipping my coffee trying to digest what had just taken place. Either this was some elaborate practical joke or they were genuinely serious. If it was the latter maybe I really am losing it. I threw some money on the counter and made my way to the door feeling many eyes on my back. Once outside I relaxed a little collecting my thoughts.

"Someone in authority, that should be my next stop." I thought. Gazing around my eyes locked on a fire house at the end of the street.

"Good place." I mumbled quietly. "Since they are usually the first responders, they should be able to fill me in on how Irene affected their town.

Walking to the fire station I realized how routinely boring people were acting. As if nothing ever happened and that the disaster of Irene did not exist.

I reached the fire station only to find all was quiet and securely locked.

I asked an older gentlemen if he could direct me to the town hall which he did most willingly with a smile. I dared to ask what he thought of the hurricane. He smiled again and half laughed as he answered,

"I was just a youngster the last time we had anything like a hurricane here. It was too long ago to remember much about it. Good day young fella." He turned and walked away.

Confusion clouding my brain I followed the directions to the town hall. It also appeared to be business as usual as I approached the clerks desk. I showed my credentials and asked if I could get a rundown on the hurricane damage. I was answered with a blank stare and then the words,

"Excuse me ?"

I repeated my request to the blank stare. The middle aged women then said in a business like tone,

"Could you excuse me for a moment."

She left her desk and disappeared down a hallway. She returned moments later with a tall, graying at the temples gentleman.

"Can I help you sir ?" he asked as he approached.

I repeated the credential bit again and asked my question for the third time. After pausing for a moment, obviously reflecting on my question, the gentleman spoke politely but firmly.

"Look I don't know what game you people are up to, but it really isn't funny. There has been no hurricane, probably will be no hurricane and we don't need you or anyone else trying to create a false situation in our quiet little town."

I was somewhat taken aback by his statement. I replied by trying to give the facts as I knew them. He would have none of my pleas and politely asked me to leave or he would call the constable. Not knowing what else to say I slowly turned to leave. I only took a few steps then remembered something else. I asked if he could answer just one more question. He agreed but with obvious annoyance in his voice. Without giving him a chance to change his mind I inquired,

"A little while ago you mentioned *You People*. Was there someone else inquiring about this."

With an annoying partial laugh he answered,

"You people are really good at your game, aren't you. I figured you knew the young woman who was here yesterday with the same phony questions."

"Do you know where she went." I interrupted excitedly.

He gave me a raised eyebrow look and said he didn't

know, but I might want to check the local motel about a mile out of town. I thanked him and rushed out the door making a bee line for my truck.

"**If** someone else was inquiring about the hurricane that means I'm not crazy, or if I am I now have company." I said aloud, quietly.

Reaching the truck, I jumped in and spun the tires to get out of town as fast as I could. Traveling in the opposite direction of the bridge I left the tiny village looking for a motel. Sure enough, a little over a mile appeared the Hillcrest Mountain View Motel. It might have been nice in it's day, but it's day was obviously thirty or forty years ago. It sort of reminded me of the Psycho motel. I pulled in and parked by the office sign. There were only two cars parked there. One had Vermont plates and was probably the owner of the motel. The second piqued my interest. It was parked down in front of one of the small bungalow's. The plates were New York, most likely from the city area which I deduced from the letters on the plate. I went into the office, rang the desk bell and waited. It wasn't long before a middle aged man came from the attached house looking like I had just awakened him from his cat nap. A few pointed questions and ten bucks gave me the information I wanted. I thanked him and said I might see him later for a room. I exited the office, went to the truck to think.

This gal was a reporter or something like that, to use the motel guy's words. She must be the one. I didn't want to intrude but I felt this situation called for it. I started walking towards cottage number seven. About halfway there a not unattractive woman came out of the door. I reached her before she reached her car. I introduced myself, showed my credentials and asked about the hurricane. I guess I took her by surprise because she looked at me guardedly and answered my question with her own.

"**W**hat about the hurricane ?"

She obviously did not want to commit herself just yet. Accepting this, I took the lead and spilled my whole story gaging her reaction as I went along. I could see her becoming more at ease, eventually even smiling slightly.

"**N**o ! You're not crazy or if you are that makes two of us." she said echoing my own earlier thoughts. She then related her own similar story. She also got trapped on the circular road on the other side of the bridge.

We both agreed there were things to work out. She was just on her way to a local roadside bar and grill a few miles up the road and suggested I join her and continue the discussion. We used her car and within minutes we were eating cheeseburgers and washing them down with beer.

Our stomachs and curiosity about each other satisfied we began to talk in earnest about what to do next. Neither of our cell phones were receiving signals and the land lines could only dial local.

We decided to leave this place behind us and head west out of town away from the bridge. I picked up a few extra cool ones to take back to the motel where we said our polite good nights. The man running the motel seemed genuinely happy to be renting another room. I guess he needed the money. I was two cottages away from my new partner in crazy. The cottage was not the newest thing in the world but it was clean. I stretched out on the bed, set the alarm, killed the two brews and drifted off to sleep trying to figure out the day.

I was up just before the sun, showered, dressed, threw the key on the small table and went to my truck. Miss Crazy, or should I say Miss Dawes was already standing by her car. She smiled and suggested I take the lead.

We traveled west on a half gravel, half paved road bordered by nothing but woods. No houses, no barns, no open farm land. Just trees. We drove for almost twenty miles before I finally saw a sign. Something just didn't feel right about the sign so I pulled over and stopped. The lovely Miss Dawes joined me in walking to the sign.

"Look at that board." I said. "It's just like the bridge sign."

"And the lettering is just the same also." she added.

"This was freshly painted. There's not a trace of aging or weathering." I commented cautiously.

"The nails are new too." she pointed out.

Looking around I noticed an intersecting road up

ahead. More like a driveable trail really. There was an arrow nailed
to a tree, identical to the arrows on the circle road on the other side
of the bridge.

"**I**'m not liking the feel of this." I said. "Maybe we
should just keep moving on to the next town."

"**W**hy don't we split up, take the two different roads
and meet up again later." Miss Dawes suggested.

I considered that for a moment but decided it was not
a good idea.

"**N**o." I said. "We should stay together. At least then
we'll know there is someone who believes what we may see."

She laughed lightly but agreed.

Back in our respective vehicles we hit the road again
with me still in the lead. I chose to take the main road rather then the
intersecting trail. I checked the rear view mirror and was glad to see
my new found companion following. We drove for some ten or
twelve minutes when again I had this feeling of "Deja Vou." Upon
closer scrutiny my gut feel was correct. I was seeing the familiar
arrow signs again and then there it was. The Bridge ! I stopped,
exited my truck and walked back to Miss Dawes. She rolled down
her window and looked as confused as I was.

"**W**hat now Lone Ranger." she chided. I laughed half
heartedly and answered,

"**I** don't know."

We remained silent for a few minutes and then almost
as if by signal we both started to speak. We smiled and she said,

"**Y**ou first."

I took the invitation and replied that we should cross
the bridge again and maybe get some answers from the town folks.
Her idea was the same so off we went across the Hillcrest Road
Bridge.

To our surprise and confusion this was not the town
we had just left. The layout was similar, but the shop names were
different. We found two adjacent parking spots and pulled in. We
joined each other outside our vehicles. To follow up on her comment
I asked,

"**W**hat now Tonto."

"**V**ery funny." she replied. "There's a café' across the

street. Let's get some coffee and talk.

The coffee was hot and the waitress was friendly.

As the coffee was served I tried to play dumb and innocent by asking the waitress

"We're not from around here so I was curious, with all the trouble the east coast is having with hurricanes, have you ever had one hit here in Vermont ?"

Her reply I almost expected.

"I know, I saw that on the TV. Isn't that terrible. I feel so bad for those people but , no, we haven't had one since before I was a child."

She turned and left. Miss Dawes and I sat there not knowing what to think. Were we really crazy ? Were we the only two to have witnessed Irene's devastation. Again we sat in silence. Miss Dawes was first to break our mood.

"She just said she saw the coverage on Television. Perhaps our cell phones work now."

I reached for my phone.

"No, not here." she continued, "Outside in the car."

I nodded in agreement, paid for the coffee and we left the café'.

Outside we both grabbed our cell phones. Still no signal for either of us. We stopped a passerby and inquired about the lack of signal and asked how long service had been out. The man looked at us curiously and said,

"What's a cell phone ?" But if you want to make a call there was a pay phone across the street."

He nodded politely and walked on. Miss Dawes looked a bit uneasy.

"Let's get out of here." she said and walked to her car. She was already backing out of the parking spot before I even got my truck started. I then followed as she headed out of town away from the bridge.

The road was different this time. There were still many trees but the wooded areas were broken by open farm fields spotted here and there with barns. We traveled a while longer till we saw a sign. The same sign. We pulled over and this time she walked back to my truck.

"**I**'ll admit I'm becoming very uncomfortable with our situation but let's keep going. This time I think we should take the intersecting road."

I agreed. Moving on again we made the right turn to the trail. The road was narrow but relatively bump free and eventually melded into a paved road. I myself was beginning to feel better. The road began to curve and the forest became thicker and darker. There it was again. The familiar arrow signs. Miss Dawes kept going so I followed. Eventually we reached the bridge and my favorite sign. HILLCREST ROAD BRIDGE. My new lady friend did not stop but drove across the bridge to yet another different town. We pulled into a small parking lot and met between our two vehicles.

"**I**'m frightened." she said.

I wasn't exactly too comfortable myself.

"**I** want to keep going though. For some reason or other I feel safer locked in my car."

I did not disagree and told her so. As she headed back to her car she called back that she was returning over the
bridge. Before I could answer she was already on her way. I hurried to follow. Sure enough she re-crossed the bridge. She was in quite a hurry and was out distancing me. I increased my speed to catch up and noticed the road was not curved any more and was smoothly paved. The distance between Miss Dawes and I was becoming greater. It was like I just couldn't catch up. I finally gave up trying. I guess she really was frightened.

I continued driving not exactly paying attention to my surroundings. Suddenly, I realized things looked familiar. Yes very familiar. I was back in the town I started from the day before. Almost happy again I drove straight to my editor's office. *" He's never going to believe this story. "* I thought to myself. As I parked my truck I caught a glimpse of Miss Dawes car in the parking lot.

Walking to the office I could overhear people talking about Irene. As terrible as Irene was I felt glad to hear these stories again. Perhaps I wasn't crazy after all.

I reached the office and went in only to find Miss Dawes also there. I said,

"Hello again." only to be met with a polite smile but

no recognition.

"Come in Mike," said my editor, "I'm glad you finally got here. I want you to go out and get some photo coverage of the Hillcrest Road Bridge site. I was told it was washed away by Irene." Then indicating Miss Dawes he added, "And this is Miss Kiley, she's from our New York office. She'll go along with you to get some first person interviews.

Miss Dawes or Kiley if you will, nodded and smiled politely, again with no recognition.

Thinking back to the events of the last two days, I looked at the man behind the desk, gathered up my courage and quietly stated that I did not want this assignment.

His look of astonishment was priceless. I quickly made up an excuse about a cousin whose house was flooded and that I was committed to help him. You know family obligations and all that stuff. It took a while but he finally relented and said he understood and wished me luck.

I left the office but hung around the parking lot waiting for Miss whatever her name was. It took a while but she finally appeared and walked to the car I recognized. It was then I noticed the New York plates. It was the same number I had been seeing for the last two days.

I intercepted her before she opened her door and asked why the mystery and why didn't she admit we knew each other.

"I don't know what you're talking about sir. This is the first time I've ever been in Vermont. Now, if you will excuse me I have to meet someone for the assignment you chose to refuse."

I stepped back, she entered her car and drove away. I'll have to admit she looked extremely serious. I decided I would head for home, a drink and some rest. On my ride, I tried to make sense of the events of the last few days but came up without any answers. However I came upon a few detour signs which I totally ignored. That was a word I did not wish to read for a long time.

In a few minutes I was opening my front door. I poured my promised drink, sat on the couch and put my feet up on the coffee table wishing my mind to go blank. Instead all I could see was that confounded bridge.

"**I**'ve got to clear this up." I said aloud and headed out to my truck again.

I had no problem getting there. No curved roads, no sign and no arrows. Before I knew it I was looking at the washed away bridge. Gazing over to the other side I saw the polite gentleman from the town office.

He saw me, smiled a sly smile and waved.

The End

"Red Box"

by
K.J. Goss

"Red Box"

"**I** saw the greatest movie the other night that we got from Netflix." said Marge to her friend Jeanne. "You still get Netflix, don't you ?" Marge further asked.

"**N**o, I dropped Netflix. I now go to Red Box to get my movies." answered Jeanne strangely.

"**B**ut isn't Red Box only new movies ?" asked Marge.

"**I** dropped Netflix. I now go to Red Box to get my movies." Jeanne repeated with a faraway look in her eyes.

"**O**h, I see." answered Marge not knowing what else to say. Trying to change the subject she asked;

"**B**y the way Jeanne how did the recipe that I gave you the other day work out ? Did your husband like it."

"**Y**es, but now we get our recipe's from Red box." Returned Jeanne.

Feeling suddenly very uncomfortable Marge decided to leave. Jeanne's husband Ken just pulled into the driveway as Marge left the house.

"**I**s Jeanne alright ?" she inquired.

"**Y**eah, why do you ask ?" replied Ken.

"**I** asked about a recipe I gave her and she strangely answered that she now gets her recipe's from Red Box. It was such a strange answer I thought perhaps she was feeling ill or something." Marge replied sympathetically.

"**N**o, she's doing just fine." remarked Ken. "We get all our recipe's from Red Box now. You should try it, they have some great things there." He added excitedly then turned and walked to the house.

Marge, totally confused and now somewhat frightened, hurried to her car going straight home.

Ken entered the house thinking there was something wrong with Marge.

"**H**i sweetie, how was your day ? Say what's with Marge, she was acting very strange saying some stupid thing about Red Box."

"**I** know." Jeanne answered. "She was acting strange with me too. I hope she's not losing it. I'm becoming concerned."

"**W**hat's for supper. I'm starved." Ken inquired.

Jeanne answered excitedly, "You're going to love dinner tonight. I went to Red Box and got the most amazing recipe."

"**D**id you get a movie for tonight also ?" Ken asked matter of factly.

"**N**o." Was the reply, "Why should I do that, I already have dessert."

"**O**h right, It's left over from last night." Ken remembered.

Marge, still upset about Ken and Jeanne, decided to call another mutual friend. When Carol answered Marge asked,

"**H**ave you spoken to Jeanne recently ?"

"**Y**es, last night." She answered. "She sounded wonderful as always." We were exchanging recipe's we got from Red Box."

"You too." Marge thought to herself.

Carol continued, "Have you been there yet ? You should try it. They have the most wonderful things there."

Wanting to get away from this topic, Marge lied,

"**O**h sorry Carol, I think I hear my husband calling, I have to go now. I'll talk to you some other time." She hung up hone.

A feeling of shock shot through Marge.

"**I** wish Tom was home." Marge said out loud, "I need someone real that I can talk to."

She could feel herself getting tense and edgy so she prepared herself a cup of tea and sat gazing out the kitchen window at the garden. The flowers were doing their job with their calming effect and she was beginning to relax.

Marge heard Tom's truck pull up next to the garage and she could feel the additional calming it had on her nerves. Tom entered the kitchen and kissed his wife.

"I'm glad you're home." Marge started but was interrupted with Tom's excitement.

"You're going to love this Marge. I got the most terrific recipe from the Red Box today. I saw Carol's husband Sam there and he highly recommended it."

Marge was feeling frightened and even threatened now. Trying to remain calm she slowly asked;

"Isn't the Red Box for getting movie DVD's."

She asked this hoping that perhaps there was another Red Box store that was a cooking or kitchen store that she had not heard of before. Tom looking at her in a funny way answered,

"Why should I do that. We already have dessert."

A feeling of shock shot through Marge.

"What is happening ? Is everyone going crazy or is it just me ?" she wondered.

She was nervously holding tight to her shaking hands. "I must get out of here and go someplace where I can think.

Picking up her car keys, she directed herself to the door, hurriedly yelling back to her husband.

"I forgot something at the library today, I'm going down there now."

"Okay Hon." Was Tom's mumbled reply.

Backing out of the driveway she was thinking;

"I mentioned the library just because that was the first thing that came to mind, but it's not a bad idea at all. It's always quiet there, so I can get a chance to get a hold of myself and figure this thing out."

The library was quiet with only a few people there. Marge grabbed a magazine and seated herself in a corner out of the way of others. Or so she thought. Barely opening the magazine she felt a presence. It was Sally from down the road from her.

"**H**i Marge." was the friendly greeting. "It's been a while, how have you been ?"

"**J**ust fine." Marge answered cautiously thinking that Sally sounded perfectly normal. Marge relaxed and the two chatted about the every day occurrences for a while. Cynthia from the garden club joined the pair and they had some laughs. Then it began again. Sally started talking about recipe's and there it was the "Red Box."

"**B**ut what about getting movies ?" Asked Marge.

"**W**hy do we want to do that. We already have dessert at home." Sally and Cynthia answered together.

Marge instantly jumped up and ran from the building. Reaching her car on the run she jumped in and immediately locked all the doors. Shaking almost uncontrollably, Marge had trouble starting the car. She was beating on the steering wheel with one hand while continuing to turn the key with the other. The engin suddenly roared alive. Slamming it into gear she rushed from the parking lot to the street heading north away from the library. She maintained a high speed for some twenty minutes until noticing flashing red lights behind her. Marge slowed her car and finally pulled over. As the police officer approached the car she rolled down the window shaking noticeably and crying. The officer went through the usual routine with Marge giving garbled answers through heavy sobs.

"**Y**ou'll have to come with me Mam. Please step out of the car."

Marge, now more upset was screaming as the officer roughly pulled her from the drivers seat and forcibly put her in his patrol car, restraining her with hand cuffs.

At the police station she was cuffed hand and foot to a chair. Totally confused she kept asking,

"**W**hat am I here for ? What did I do ? What are you doing this for ? I didn't do anything. Please let me go. I want to go home. Please."

Her pleas fell on deaf ears. They all laughed at her. The door opened to many people, all familiar faces. Her hopes soared.

"**P**lease help me." Marge begged.

Instead of her prayers being answered the familiar friends laughed. And made fun of her.

Jeanne spoke up first, "You have to try the Red Box Marge. You're going to love it. We all like the Red Box."

"**Y**es," Tom chimed in, "You've got to go to the Red Box. The Red Box Is good for you, Isn't it Sally."

"**O**h yes Tom." she replied. "It really is good for you. Come with us to the Red Box Marge. We'll all be there with you."

They all chimed in as a chorus;

"**W**e'll go with you Marge. You will like it as we do. It's so good for you. Come with us now Marge."

The familiar faces all moved closer and held out their hands reaching for her. Marge tried to move away but was restrained by the cuffs. Screaming, now shaking all over she felt a hand touch her. It was like an electric shock. Her eyes followed where the hand came from. It was her husband Tom. He was saying something she could not quite understand. She concentrated on his words finally understanding.

"**W**ake up Marge. You were having a nightmare. Are you alright ?"

Slowly recognizing her surroundings, her heart still pounding she looked at Tom.

"**I**t was terrible. You were all against me."

"**I**t's over mow, relax, you're safe." Tom comforted her, his arms around her now.

"**T**ell you what as soon as you're fully awake and calm we'll take a ride and get a good movie from Red Box."

Her eyes widened and she ***<u>screamed.</u>***

The end.

<u>Bibliography</u>

<u>The Dream</u>

Full Duty
by Howard Coffin
pg. 274,275 & 278

<u>The Vacation</u>

George Washington's Schooners
by Chester G. Hearn
pg. 3

<u>Big Foot</u>

Wikipedia

<u>The Mysterious Wagon Wheel</u>

Life of Washington
by Washington Irving
Vol. 1, pg. 192
Vol. 3, pg. 73
Vol. 4, pg. 359 & 373-375
Ratification
by Pauline Maier
Pg. 255
Empire of the Summer Moon
by S.C. Gwynne
Pg. 274